## Day Three: Anzio, Italy

Sergea[...]e and his best friend, Priv[...]parated from the rest of [...] German MG-34 and an [...] liers out on the left flank [...] ecting street in just in t[...] st of their squad had [...] lank, and had begun assaulting their position before Brockway and Rouy knew about it. Fighting through the position, they'd managed to leave their two friends behind. The error would soon be noticed, but at the moment the rest of their platoon was about to stumble right into the machine gun nest. 2nd squad was approaching at an oblique angle to the church the Germans occupied, and hadn't seen them yet. Brockway had to warn them.

"Enemy contact, at the church!" Brockway screamed as loud as he could.

Rouy waved his arms to get 2nd squad's attention. The men in 2nd squad hit the deck immediately. Brockway pointed his Garand rifle at the enemy position around the corner. The 2nd squad leader sent half his men around the left flank of the church, and the remaining men began setting up their .30 caliber machine gun.

"Let's get in the war, Rouy," said Brockway. "We have to draw their fire."

Rouy nodded in agreement. "I'll do it."

Stepping back from the wall far enough to swing around his long BAR rifle, Rouy leaned around the corner and fired a five-shot burst at the enemy position. He returned to cover before he could determine any results, but that wasn't the point. A couple of seconds later the MG-34 began firing at the corner. Brockway and Rouy backed up instinctively even though they were already safe. 2nd squad began throwing grenades towards the near corner of the church.

"They've got it now," said Brockway, "let's get back to 1st squad."

Brockway and Rouy ran back to the last place they saw their squad. The street was deserted, but the sound of combat led them in the right direction. Brockway was beginning to get winded. The stress of the fight, his first real engagement, and the added weight of the water and sand that caked his trousers was taking its toll. Rouy seemed similarly tired, although his attitude remained fearless.

Moving down the street, Brockway noticed some of his guys running laterally across the next intersection. He kept his eyes on the rooftops and Rouy did the same with their six. Brockway couldn't tell what was going on at the intersection, nor could he hear anything from his men. Stray rounds began zipping down the middle of the road.

Arriving at the intersection, Brockway and Rouy were met with a scene of destruction. The large open area, probably a town square, showed the results of naval bombardment. Craters dotted the road and fields, and ugly gashes had been torn in most of the buildings. Fires burned in places, the brisk wind carrying the smoke away and darkening the early morning sunlight. Tracer fire moved towards them, and the two men dove into the nearest crater. They found themselves with two more members of 1st squad.

"Where the hell is the enemy?" asked Brockway.

Private Howard motioned ahead. "Across the square, sergeant. They've got us pinned down with two machine guns. The first one is in the first building on the right, second floor. The second one is somewhere on the right, about two o'clock, ground level."

"Where is the rest of the squad?"

"Over there."

Private Howard pointed to four bodies lying off of the road ahead.

"Shit!"

One of their dead friends had the radio. Rouy deployed the bipod on his BAR and began firing at the first machine gun position. Tracer fire continued to fill the air, but so far none of it was headed directly at them.

"We've got to fix that machine gun," said Brockway.

"Enemy at twelve o'clock!" yelled Rouy.

Ahead, a squad of Germans began advancing down the main road. Rouy shifted his fire toward them. Brockway took aim with his Garand and slowly pulled the trigger. Private Howard and Corporal Waldron joined in with their Carbines. Two of the Germans fell and the others took cover.

"We need mortar fire!" shouted Rouy.

"We can't get to the radio," replied Brockway.

The enemy ahead began firing at them. Brockway scrunched himself down further into the crater and searched for a target. He found one, fired, and the man disappeared from sight. Another squad ran forward and Brockway emptied his rifle at them. The characteristic ping of the clip ejecting was completely lost in the tremendous din.

"Get ready to fall back!" Brockway yelled, reloading.

"Throw some frags out on the line," said Rouy.

"They're out of range!" Howard cried.

"Just do it!"

All four men threw one grenade each as far as they could. A few seconds later they detonated, the staccato series of explosions shaking the earth. A large plume of dust began to rise.

"Covering fire!" screamed Brockway.

The men fired randomly through the dust.

"Go, go, go!"

Howard and Waldron ran back towards the street. Brockway continued firing until he was out. Rouy dropped the empty magazine out of his rifle and ran for it. Brockway was fast on his heels. Hopefully, second platoon would be off the beach by now. It would be nice if they identified them before they opened fire.

Something tugged roughly at Brockway's left arm, spinning him around. He lost his balance and hit the ground. Brockway looked at his arm and was shocked to find everything below the elbow missing.

"I'm hit!" he bellowed.

Rouy reversed course and ran over to Brockway. He dropped his BAR and grabbed Brockway by his remaining arm. Brockway felt pain began to rise from the wound. As he stumbled along with Rouy, the pain rose to unbelievable agony like nothing he'd ever imagined. Brockway began to cry out and collapsed. Rouy dragged him behind an abandoned car.

"John, are you all right?"

"It hurts like hell!"

Rouy could see that Brockway was in real trouble.

"Do you want to end it?"

"Of course I want to end it, Ray! Get us the hell out of here!"

"Seth!" Rouy shouted into the air. "Seth, get us out of here now!"

Bullets smashed into the car, sending debris flying. A piece of glass lacerated Rouy across the face. The pain was terrible.

"Seth! End the damn game!"

The street in Anzio faded away. John and Ray were in a small room. A translucent orb hung suspended in the center of the room, and various pieces of computer equipment lined the walls. John stopped screaming and clutched at his intact arm. Ray felt the side of his face. They were both fine.

"Holy shit, Ray," said John.

"Well, there's some incentive to fight like you mean it. That was unbelievable."

"We've got to talk to Seth about the pain level in there."

"Why? This is combat training, right? I think we should keep the pain where it is. We want to take it seriously. The possibility of feeling pain will keep our behavior realistic."

"Speak for yourself, you didn't get your arm shot off."

"True."

"I also doubt Christie and Dana are going to be real thrilled with the possibility of unbearable agony, however brief it may be."

"I suppose we could ask Seth to adjust the pain level for each individual participant. Realism is still essential. Getting shot has to be unpleasant."

John moved his left arm around. "What about post traumatic stress disorder?"

"I doubt it could get that bad. Nobody is really dying, after all."

"Sometimes the subconscious mind has trouble distinguishing reality from fantasy."

"We'll have to wait and see, I guess. Come on, let's get a drink."

John and Ray exited the orb room and entered the galley. The hum of the stardrive vibrated the deck slightly. John entered the kitchenette section and retrieved a bottle of rum.

"This is only the third day out," said Ray. "That stuff has to last us indefinitely."

"That's why I'm only giving us a shot each."

John had his own personal supply of alcohol if he wanted to get drunk. He poured the rum and sat down at the dining table with Ray.

"Here's to our first training mission," said Ray, holding up his glass.

"May the rest of them be much less painful."

"That's wishful thinking."

"It can't hurt to get used to a little suffering."

## 1. Day Seven

John Scherer sat on the bridge of the Reckless Faith, the first Earth spacecraft to venture beyond the solar system. He was sitting in the pilot's chair, his feet propped up on the console. The lights were turned down, only the monitors and the stars illuminated the bridge. John was engaging in his favorite recreational activity: watching the universe go by.

They had passed out of the Milky Way galaxy yesterday. Their relative motion had been difficult to perceive while they were in the galaxy, but now their view had been replaced with the motionless panorama of the Large Magellanic Cloud. It would be another four weeks before they reached the outer edge. What was much more interesting to observe was the slow retreat of the Milky Way to the aft, but with no windows facing in that direction such a task required the zero-g room.

The Reckless Faith had a crew of seven, counting a stowaway named Byron. John was not the captain, in fact, there were no ranks aboard. Instead each crewmember had a role, and decisions were made by quorum. John was assigned as primary pilot, although his most useful role was with their on-board artificial intelligence computer, nicknamed Seth. John could communicate telepathically with Seth more efficiently than the others; indeed, Seth favored him for that function. John and the others preferred to communicate with Seth verbally, but some information was more effectively relayed by telepathic link. If Seth was having difficulty expressing a concept verbally, John would link with him and provide an abstract translation.

Seth, the highest level of AI yet created, was not capable of verbal communication alone. He needed an intermediate mind with which to link. Since it was physically exhausting for humans to link with him, and since all six crewmembers found sharing their minds psychologically disturbing, animals were used instead. A cat named Friday and a dog named Tycho took turns providing this link, freeing up the humans to perform other duties. The animals did not seem to be tired out by the task, so they traded twelve-hour shifts on the bridge. At the moment Friday was sitting in John's lap, purring.

The animals had minds of their own, and when linked with Seth they were capable of verbal communication as well. They were remarkably simplistic, not unlike children, but seemed to be completely unconcerned with learning anything unrelated to their normal existences. They would listen well enough, but would change the subject to food, sleep, or play when asked to participate in the discussion. Friday finally said, "I'm not interested in that," in response to a mathematics question. Christie Tolliver, the ship's resident astronomy expert, continued to try to make progress with Tycho. John didn't care; Christie could spend her personal time however she wished. Unfortunately for the animal behaviorists back on Earth, being able to have a conversation with a favored pet was a luxury limited to this spacecraft. Being able to use animals as an intermediary with the AI was discovered by accident.

Friday was John's cat, and when she was able to verbally express her affection for his master, John found it both endearing and embarrassing. John had wondered if there was anything compromising he might have said or done in front of Friday over the years, but Friday and Tycho didn't seem to have any concept of time. Everything was either in the present or the immediate future. Trying to impress upon them anything more had the same results as the mathematics.

The concept of time was not lost on the crew, however. Being aboard the first spacecraft capable of faster-than-light travel was thrilling beyond anything they could possibly desire. Unfortunately, after only a week, even the groundbreaking technology and never before seen interstellar vistas had become commonplace. John couldn't help but acknowledge the human brain's curious tendency to become accustomed to practically any circumstance, providing for certain comforts. The uncertainty of their mission also dampened any rampant enthusiasm, since it could very well result in the crew's hideous demise.

One week into the trip, John was still excited and hopeful. That morning he had awoken in his quarters to the same sense of wonder and positive anticipation he had since the very first days of the space project. During the first few days John often awoke thinking he was still in his Woburn, Massachusetts home, and was elated to remember his actual situation. He toured the ship after breakfast, and loved every square inch of it. For all this amazement, things were nonetheless becoming routine and normal. Boredom began to creep into the daily retinue of emotions. Every day after lunch, the crew would meet for a situation report. The past six days had resulted in very short meetings. Five more weeks of nothing was a prospect that weighed heavily on John's mind, if only for the sheer frustration of having to wait so long.

Using Seth as a recreational and instructional simulator was also the result of serendipity. When in direct physical contact with the AI unit, members of the crew could participate in whatever scenario they could imagine. Seth could create images perfectly from the minds of the crew, even if their own memory of such things was hazy or worse. For example, John was able to experience his first day of kindergarten again vicariously, despite the fact that he couldn't have consciously remembered a thing on his own. Revelations from other crewmember's pasts were either the subject of conversation during mealtimes or never spoken of again.

It was these fantasy worlds that were the most popular form of boredom relief for the crew, with the variable gravity "zero-g" room a distant second. A sheet of paper was taped to the wall inside the orb room for signing out blocks of time for use. Seth didn't seem to have any problem running simulations for them in addition to performing essential ship functions, except when five or more crewmembers participated simultaneously. Over the past seven days, it seemed that there was always at least one person in there running a sim, even in the middle of the night. Most of the time, the crew would discuss what they'd been up to. Sometimes they did not. John didn't care to speculate too much about the latter.

    Along with Ray Bailey, the ship's weapons systems specialist, John had continued to try out their World War Two battles. They'd become a lot better over the past few days, but surviving a single scenario still evaded them. John and Ray had both been shot and blown up several times now, each defeat bringing with it more pain and trauma. They'd finally succumbed to the temptation to adjust the pain settings; it was simply too rough on them to have it be completely realistic.

    Ari Ferro, the ship's computer systems expert, refused to do so herself, although this resulted in her participating in the firefight sims much less. She preferred hand-to-hand training, and it was Ari putting the hurt on her imaginary foes more often than the other way around. If she was good before, she was becoming downright scary now. It was probably an excellent outlet for her natural ruthlessness, but John found that it did nothing to temper it elsewhere.

    Chance Richter, the ship's tactical expert, was the only other one who kept the pain level at realistic. He preferred more contemporary combat sims, as it reflected his real-life background as a Marine sniper and CIA operative. John and Ray had participated in some of his scenarios, and had begun learning standard US military doctrine for infantry tactics. It seemed prudent, as did Ari's unarmed combat training, but without any idea of their potential enemies it was nothing more than exercise in self-improvement.

Dana Andrews, the ship's engineer, had practically no interest whatsoever in the combat aspect of the simulations. She all but refused to participate in that sort of training. Christie knew it was most likely a good idea, and tolerated it, but Dana avoided it explicitly. The first time had been the last time for Dana, so far. Getting shot in the head didn't help.

Only the stowaway Byron had been denied the use of the simulations, for obvious reasons. John was putting off dealing any further with Byron, only because Byron was clearly insane and showed no real willingness to integrate himself into the crew. He'd snuck aboard in an attempt to further a romantic relationship with Christie, at least that was the flatly obvious reason. She'd been an astronomy professor at Suffolk University, and he was one of her students. Byron thought they were meant to be together. He also thought that he was meant to play a significant role in the Faith's mission. If he'd just cut the crap about destiny, John thought, he might talk his way out of the aft cargo hold. John realized that Byron might just as well be right about his role in the Faith's mission; after all, John couldn't tell the future. The prospect only furthered his growing acceptance of Ari's suggested solution: chuck Byron out of the airlock. He was indeed an unexpected tax of the ship's resources, even if he was only using 14.3 percent more food, water, and oxygen than expected.

For now, John was glad to leave him to chill out along with the boxes of ammunition, spare plumbing supplies, and medical paraphernalia. If he didn't smarten up, he deserved the incarceration.

Ray entered the bridge from the main hallway. It was nine o'clock at night, a meaningless designation except to the humans used to such a schedule. Ray was the tallest member of the crew, at six foot one. He was soft spoken and immediately likeable in nature. He and John had been friends since college, putting their relationship at nine years old. Ari fell under the same description, except she had arrived one year later. Between the three of them, their candor often left the other members of the crew feeling left out. It did provide a strong sense of camaraderie that Christie and Dana wished to share.

"Hi, John," Ray said, sitting in the nearest chair.

"Hello."

"It's never hard to find you on this ship."

"It only takes five minutes to walk the entire thing," John said, smiling.

"I just got back from serving Byron dinner."

"Oh?"

"He said he's finished with your Patrick O'Brian novels."

"Already?"

Ray shrugged. "He doesn't have much else to do all day."

"I suppose he demanded to address the crew again."

"Nope."

"Really?" asked John, genuinely surprised.

"All he said was, 'I'm done with this series, may I have something else to read please?'"

"He asked you politely?"

"Yeah. Weird, huh?"

"Maybe the reality of his situation is setting in. Perhaps he's ready to play nice."

"I don't see what harm he could do. We've already got him locked out of the computer systems. I feel like I'm Frodo and you're Samwise."

"What?"

"You know, discussing Smeagol."

John furrowed his brow. "Oh. Okay. I say we call a meeting of the crew like he was asking for. He can try to convince us that he won't try any crap, and we'll put it to a vote. I also want him locked out of the bridge, the cargo bays, the engine room, the zero-g room, and the galley. Oh, and the weapons compartments, too."

"So he can go into the hallway? He'll be thrilled. And why lock him out of the galley? Are you afraid he'll drink all of our booze?"

"No, I'm worried about the kitchen knives."

"I can put a lock on one of the cabinets easily enough. I have an extra padlock and I'm sure Seth can synthesize the hardware components."

John laughed. "Synthesize them out of what?"

"How'bout an ammo can? I can spare the lid off of one of those."

"Fine. I guess we can let him into the zero-g room. He can't do any harm in there." John looked into the air. "John to all hands, meet me in the conference room in five minutes."

Ari's voice filled the bridge. "What's up?"

"I'm calling a meeting. Are you busy right now?"

"Chance and I are in the middle of a combat sim."

"So what? You can do that anytime you want."

A loud burst of machine gun fire interrupted John's response.

"Ferro, quit squawking on the horn and fire your weapon!"

Chance's voice came through over the comm. John and Ray looked at each other in surprise.

"What the hell?" said Ray.

"Look, I'm sorry I'm bothering you but I'd rather hold this meeting now than later."

"Roger that, John," said Ari. "See you in five. Out."

"I didn't know we could hear what was going on in the sims," John said.

"Yeah, no kidding."

"It makes me wonder, though. Seth, can you show me what's going on in the current simulation?"

John felt Seth trying to merge with his mind.

"No, I mean can you show me on one of the monitors."

"Yes," said Seth's calm, androgynous voice.

"Okay, then. Use monitor two."

Monitor two was normally used as the gunner's station. The picture switched from technical data related to the four on-board guns to an image of a forest. It was a first-person perspective, apparently looking through someone's eyes. Humanoid shapes were flitting through the trees and the person of interest was trying their best to shoot them. John recognized the sight picture from a Springfield M1A, their standard rifle.

"That's gotta be Ari," said John.

The person shown looked down and grabbed a magazine from a belt-mounted pouch. John and Ray saw something they'd never seen before from that angle.

"Boobs," said Ray.

"Yep, it's Ari. Seth, show us Richter."

The image switched to Richter. He was firing his favored Colt M4 rifle on full automatic. John noticed how well he controlled the recoil.

"We should keep this to ourselves," said Ray. "We could have a lot of fun seeing what the others are up to."

"I didn't know you were a voyeur, Ray."

"I'm kidding. Besides, I don't do anything compromising in there."

"Me neither. Honestly I could care less."

"It could provide a more passive form of entertainment. It is rather exhausting to participate directly. I could pour myself a drink and be quite happy sitting here to watch the show."

John smiled. "I'd love to see some replays of our battles."

"Who says you can't?"

"I don't know. Seth, can you show us, on the monitor, a replay of our last World War Two sim?"

"No," said Seth.

"Why not?"

Seth thought for a moment. "I no longer possess that information."

"Can you save it next time?"

"Please rephrase the question."

"Can you preserve all the data from a sim for later use?"

"No."

John shrugged. "Why not?"

"The data would exceed my capacity for storage."

"What about saving it on our systems?"

Seth paused. "The total storage capacity for all networked drives would only allow for three point seven seconds of simulation."

"Oh."

"Does that mean that our networked computers have more hard drive space than you do?" asked Ray.

"Yes."

John sat up suddenly. Friday jumped to the floor.

"Hey, what gives?" said Seth.

"Sorry, Friday," began John, "Ray, do you realize what this means?"

"Uh, no."

"Seth just gave us a way to determine his data storage capacity."

"What, you didn't know that already?"

Christie entered the bridge.

"What's this meeting about, guys?" she asked.

"Christie, we just had a breakthrough with Seth," said John.

"Oh?"

"You know how we couldn't quantify Seth's hardware?"

"Yeah."

"Well, he just told us how much hard drive space he has. Or, that is to say, how much data storage space he has."

"Let me guess. You asked him an abstract question about it."

"Yes."

"I told you that was a more effective way of communicating with him."

"You two want to clue me in to what you're talking about?" Ray asked.

"We asked Seth how much storage space he had about two weeks ago. He didn't understand the question even when John was linked with him. Remember, he can access our computers through the network but the network can't access him. He's a read-only device, so to speak."

John nodded. "We asked Seth to put it in terms of the hard drive space of our computers. He still didn't understand. But we never asked him to do it with an actual quantifiable piece of data. It seems so simple now."

"So, what's the answer?" queried Ray.

"I just need to crunch the numbers. Ari, can you meet me on the bridge please?"

Ari entered from the conference room. She was carrying a bottle of water and looked tired.

"What's up?" she said. "Are we having the meeting in here instead?"

"No, I have something else to ask you. What's the total hard drive capacity of our network?"

"You mean in terms of gigs? I'm not sure. We have five identical machines on the network. They have a total of a seven hundred and fifty gigs. My laptop has three gigs. What about your system?"

"I have eighty."

"Okay, then, that means our entire network has eight hundred and thirty-three gigabytes available."

Friday meowed at John.

"Can you sit down please," said Seth. "I wasn't finished sitting in your lap."

"Not right now, Friday," John replied. "Seth, what is the maximum amount of simulation time you can store?"

"Point two five seconds."

John sat down at the station across from Ray. He opened the computer's calculator.

"Okay, then we just compare the ratio of point two five seconds to three point seven seconds, and we have our answer."

John worked the calculator.

"Wouldn't this mean that our network has more memory than Seth?" asked Christie.

John nodded. "Yup. The answer is fourteen point eight gigabytes."

"How can such a sophisticated AI system operate with such little memory?"

"I don't know. Seth's strength could be his processing power. I imagine the actual hard data is rather efficient in nature."

"Maybe Seth is referring to his available storage capacity," began Ari, "as opposed to his original capacity. Don't forget that he can't remember shit about the mission, Umber, or his own damn origins."

"That's a good point," said John. "We should continue this discussion after the meeting."

John led the way into the conference room and the others followed. Richter and Dana were sitting at the table.

"So what's this all about?" asked Richter.

"Shit, I forgot to get Byron," said John.

"I'll go," Ray said.

Ray left via the rear exit. John sat at the head of the table. Ari leaned against the wall, removing a cigarette from her pocket and lighting it.

"Do you have to do that in here?" asked Dana.

"Nobody ever said anything about this ship being a non-smoking environment," Ari said. "I mean look, the smoke barely has a chance to spread before the ventilation system carries it away."

"You can still smell it. How'bout as a courtesy to those who are bothered by it?"

"Who's bothered by it?" Ari asked, looking around with a scowl.

The others remained silent.

"Speak your mind, Dana," said John after a moment.

"Christ, Dana," said Ari, "if you don't want me to smoke around you all you have to do is ask."

Dana sighed. "Fine then, I don't want you to smoke around me. At least, not as often as you do."

"Well, I'll run out eventually. Then you'll get your wish."

"Don't be such a jerk, I know as well as you do that you've got ten cartons of those things in the hold."

Ari smirked and looked away. "You noticed that, huh?"

"Look, fellas," Dana began, "it's not my place to dictate who can smoke where. I know half the crew smokes. I just wish we could regulate it a little."

"Sorry, but if you're out-voted, you're out-voted."

"Ari, I think compromise is the best solution here," said John. "Dana, what do you propose?"

"I'd like to designate the conference room and the bridge as non-smoking areas. At least when I'm present."

"Richter, what do you think?"

"Smoke, no smoke, it makes no difference to me," replied Richter flatly.

"Christie?"

"I honestly don't care one way or the other. I've dropped down to three or four cigarettes a week."

"I know Ray doesn't smoke very often," said John. "I say we accept Dana's proposal with one modification. If someone is smoking on the bridge when she arrives, they may finish smoking, but no further tobacco use after that."

"But your Stanwell lasts for an hour fully loaded," observed Christie.

"Hey, I said it was a compromise. Besides, Dana is out-voted."

"Fair enough," said Dana. "Thank you for the consideration."

Ari crossed the room to the garbage receptacle, unceremoniously spit on her cigarette to put it out, and threw it away. The rear door opened and Byron was ushered in by Ray. Ray sat down.

"Have a seat, Mister Sterling," John said.

Byron took the only remaining chair. Ari resumed her previous position leaning against the wall.

"How's it going?" Byron said.

"Mister Sterling, you've been asked here to participate in a discussion about your future. We'd like to give you a chance to convince us why we should let you out of the cargo hold."

"This is the point of the meeting?" Ari blurted.

"Bullshit," said Christie.

"Hold on, folks. Just bear with me for now. Byron?"

"Okay. Where do we stand?"

"Where we stand is that you still betrayed us. That we can't forget. We might be able to forgive you, however, if you prove yourself to be trustworthy."

"I can't change what I did. I can only hope that you can understand why I did it. This mission is very important and I just wanted to be sure that the right people ended up aboard. I know I went about it the wrong way, but the results were positive. I see now that this crew is the right crew for this ship. Honestly, I'm sorry I ever doubted you."

"Okay, Byron. Well said, I think. Does anyone have anything constructive to add?"

"What about all that egomaniacal bullshit you were spouting after we discovered you?" asked Ari.

"I'm not going to lie to you all," said Byron. "I have a rather high opinion of myself. I know that I can contribute to this mission in a good way. I'm never going to get that opportunity wallowing in the cargo hold, so I'm willing to change. I can't help who I am, but I know I can make myself function as a member of this crew."

"We're not offering you a position on the crew," said John. "We're simply offering you a greater run of the ship. You're already locked out of the command functions. You'll still be locked out. There will also be areas of the ship that will be off-limits. You will have access to the galley and the observation room. If you want to visit the bridge you'll have to be escorted. If you screw up or give us any reason to doubt you, it's back into the cargo hold."

"What about quarters?"

"Any volunteers to be Byron's roommate?"

The crew all vocalized negative opinions.

"Why not sleep with a rattlesnake?" muttered Christie.

"I didn't think so. You'll stay in the cargo hold. We'll give you some of the spare furniture and you can set up a more personalized space in one corner."

Byron shrugged. "I guess I can't complain. How much longer until we get where we're going?"

"Five weeks."

"Okay. I agree to your terms."

"What about the network terminal in the galley?" asked Ari.

"Put a password on it," John replied.

"Great," said Byron, "what am I supposed to do to kill time?"

"Stare out of the frigging windows!" barked John. "You're not here to be entertained! You got that?"

"I'm sorry I asked."

## 2. Day Eight

Ray Bailey stretched out on his bed, breathing deeply. It was two o'clock in the morning and it was about time to rack out. He was glad that they made progress with Byron the previous evening. Everyone knew perfectly well they were avoiding the issue by keeping him down there for so long, so it was a relief to reach a decision. Ray was most concerned for Christie, who intensely disliked Byron, and Ari, who wasn't fond of him either. Ray figured that a bit of insanity at the beginning of their journey was warranted. Byron certainly couldn't have predicted his own reaction to discovering the Faith. It was the kind of thing that made rational thought take a five-minute break, after all.

Ray smiled to himself and let the stress melt away from his body. He found his quarters to be the most relaxing place on the ship, despite the stunning effect of the zero-g room and the more adrenaline-inducing capabilities of an orb sim. Watching the stars slowly creep by in his side-facing window, with the bluish room lights turned down low, Ray was able to revel in the excitement of the mission while remaining calm and serene. He had customized his room as much as possible, but extras had been a hurried afterthought. Still, Ray thought the rooms needed little sprucing up to be inviting.

Ray's role as weapons specialist was by default. He was the one who designed the mounting systems for the onboard guns, and his background as a police officer allowed him greater insight for the best small arms for the crew. In fact, the crew had no idea if any of their weapons would be effective where they were headed. As Ray said, they got the best they could.

The Reckless Faith was a large ship by any Earth standard. Unrestricted by typical airframe designs for ships required to enter and exit the atmosphere, the Faith lacked the familiar wings and fins one might expect. The designer derived great inspiration from the US Air Force's C-5 Galaxy, at least as far as size and shape. The exact weight of the Faith was not known, but was estimated to be about 1500 tons. Anti-gravity technology allowed ease of movement and made landing gear unnecessary, although the crew knew they could put down in a body of water and be safe in an emergency, as the Faith was naturally buoyant.

The ship's maximum speed within the Earth's atmosphere was 4200 miles per hour, limited by its ability to withstand friction. Anything faster than that would risk melting the hull. Its maximum speed in space was approximately 1.56 million c, or 1.56 million times the speed of light. This astonishing figure was misleading, however, as it refers to the Faith's relative speed and not the actual speed. The ship was able to cross such fast stellar distances by entering a dimension the crew called Superspace. A conceptual conundrum, Superspace was best thought of as lying "above" normal space. When viewed from above, distances between points seemed shorter, like looking down into a concave lens. Thus, moving between those points took less time. The further "above" normal space one went, the more pronounced the distortion. The crew found it interesting that being in Superspace looked no different from regular space, hence the confusing analogy. As far as Ray was concerned, the entire affair was virtually incomprehensible.

The actual top speed of the Faith was a much less awe-inspiring 0.9c, or about 168,000 miles per hour. At that speed the Faith could travel between Earth and Mars in just over three minutes, a trip that would take six months in NASA's fastest spacecraft. That didn't count NASA's cutting-edge ion engine, which by comparison was still lethargic, but so far that organization hadn't fielded a working craft with one.

The Faith's maximum speed inside Superspace of 1.56 million c was due to a massive increase in power output required to exceed that point. While accelerating in Superspace from a dead stop to top speed required only a small increase in power, going any faster than that increased the power requirement by a factor of one hundred. Since the Faith could only generate twenty times as much power as required, it was effectively limited to 1.56 million c. The crew had no doubt that technology would someday break that barrier, but it was hardly relevant to them. The Faith was plenty fast for their purposes.

The greatest drawback to the Superspace stardrive was that once superluminal (faster than light) travel was activated, it could not be reactivated until an equal amount of time had passed. Upon arrival at the Tarantula Nebula, the crew wouldn't be able to reactivate the stardrive for six weeks, and would be limited to sublight travel. Why it took so long for the stardrive to recharge was a mystery. It was the sole reason why Byron hadn't been deposited back on Earth after his discovery.

Beyond Seth, the stardrive, and the antigrav system, the only other really remarkable technology aboard was the exterior hull. It was designed to absorb and redistribute kinetic energy. It was primarily designed to protect against space debris and small objects, but it was also effective against projectile weapons. This was not really surprising, since spaceborne objects could be moving many times faster than bullets and have much greater kinetic energy. John had determined that the ship could absorb no greater than one million pounds per square inch of kinetic energy, a laughable conclusion since Earth's most powerful projectile weapons came nowhere close to that number.

The Faith's own weapons were very modest, as Ray was well aware. It had front and rear General Electric GAU 8 Avenger 30mm cannon, such as those found on A-10 aircraft. Those weapons were controlled at the gunner's station on the bridge. It also had dorsal (top) and ventral (bottom) mounted GAU 19 fifty caliber guns in semi-articulated firing rigs. Each gun could be rotated 360 degrees horizontally and 180 degrees vertically. The GAU 19s could be controlled by gunner stations directly adjacent to them or from stations on the bridge. For all the crew knew, however, they would be completely useless in the Tarantula Nebula.

The layout of the ship was simple. The first deck consisted of the bridge, conference room, six individual crew quarters, the dorsal gun station, and the "zero-g" room. The zero-g room was actually a variable gravity room, from which the ship's only airlock was accessible. Not only could gravity be suspended in space, it could also be negated planetside. The room also served as an observatory, as a 360 degree image of the exterior of the spacecraft could be projected against the walls, giving the occupant the sensation of floating in space. So far this had been used exclusively for recreational purposes.

The second deck started off with a small room for the forward-mounted GAU 8. Next was the forward cargo bay. This room was two decks high and included a large access ramp. The ramp was nearly the width of the entire vessel. It was large enough for two Ford Expeditions to drive in side-by-side. Next was the armory, which stored small arms, the orb room, which stored Seth, and the galley. The galley was sandwiched between two large water tanks, which supplied drinking and sanitation water as well as the hydrogen that fueled the stardrive. Behind that was the engine room, which like the cargo bay was two decks high. The rear-mounted GAU 8 was sandwiched between the engine room and the zero-g room, and was much less easily accessible than the forward gun.

The third deck began with the forward cargo bay, then the ventral gun station, the aft cargo hold, and the engine room. Besides going to check on Byron and pick up supplies, Ray and the others had little reason to visit this deck during flight.

There was a quiet series of raps on Ray's door. Doorbells were completely forgotten during the design phase, so one was required to knock. Since the doors were solid aluminum (just like the rest of the infrastructure), one was required to use a hard object in order to be heard. Ray unlatched the handle and the door slid open. Christie was standing in the hallway, holding a soda can. Ray was eight inches taller than she, so he took a step back to make conversation easier.

"Hello," said Christie, "am I disturbing you?"
"Not at all. Would you like to come in?"
"If you don't mind."
Ray gestured inside. Christie entered and sat at the desk.
"Lights to seventy percent," Ray said, returning to the bed.
The light in the room increased significantly.
"Aren't you going to close the door?" asked Christie.
"Do you want me to close the door?"
"Well, yeah."
Ray shrugged, got up and closed the door.
"What's up?" he asked.
"I wanted to talk to you about Byron."
Ray sat down. "I know you're not happy with letting him out of the cargo hold."
"No, I'm not. You know he wanted a relationship with me."
"We're going to have to find a way to live with him. If he bothers you specifically, tell him in no uncertain terms that nothing will ever happen between you. If that doesn't work, John, Ari and I will give him another firm talking-to and revoke his privileges. He'll be back in the hold with nothing but emergency rations to eat."
"I guess so."
"Look at the bright side."
"There's a bright side?"

"Yeah. If it wasn't for Byron's interference, Richter would never have come aboard."

"Richter!" exclaimed Christie, throwing up her hands. "We know less about him than we do about Byron. How do we know he's not a CIA spy?"

"Are you kidding, Christie? I'm pretty sure that him ending up on board was an accident. Besides, what good would a CIA spy be aboard this ship? He has no way of communicating with Earth."

"He must have had a better reason for deciding to stay, other than the one he gave us."

"You were there. You saw what he did for us. If that was a ruse, he sure did a good job at it. He sure didn't fake taking a round in the chest."

"He was wearing Kevlar."

"Look, Richter may be a wild card but we can at least trust him. He's practically the only member of the crew who has absolutely no reservations or uncertainty about leaving Earth. I believe him when he says he would have been sent to prison back home."

"I know. I guess I'm just playing the devil's advocate. Chance is okay. He is, after all, teaching us a lot about squad tactics."

"For all the good it may do us."

"If nothing else we're learning how to act under extreme pressure. I have no wish for violence, but I didn't fare so well the last time we tangled with bad guys."

"You did fine, it's Dana that I'm worried about."

"I agree. Has she tried another combat sim yet?"

"No. I'm thinking we'd have better luck arranging a simulation of the Faith being attacked for her sake. Being useless in a firefight is one thing, but we need her to be able to fulfill her duties aboard the ship much more than on the ground. If she freezes up at her station, it could cost us the entire ship."

"That kind of sim would benefit all of us. Beyond running systems checks, none of us really have any idea how to handle an emergency aboard."

Ray nodded. "The only problem is that in order to create an effective sim, the knowledge has to be in our minds to begin with. Our combat sims have been so realistic because between the six of us we've actually experienced combat. Richter fought in Pakistan and Afghanistan, for God's sake. I don't know how well Seth will be able to create a scenario for the Faith, since he probably doesn't know what will happen for sure himself."

"Great, so Seth's greatest flaw will go from annoying to deadly."

"That's a risk we all had to accept."

"True. Actually, I think that running sims like that would be a good way to train Seth to react appropriately."

"It might work, but we would be asking Seth to learn from a scenario that he's creating. That seems like a logical impossibility to me."

"I get your point."

"Well, the only thing we can do is try. We've got just under five weeks left, so we're certainly not limited by time. I'll call a meeting after breakfast later this morning and we'll give it a shot."

"The other thing is that we've never tried to run a sim with more than four people before. It might get a little crowded down there."

"I'm sure Seth can handle it."

Several hours later, the crew sat in the galley, talking about Ray and Christie's plan to train in the simulator. Breakfast was almost gone. The normally cordial atmosphere of mealtime was replaced with stiff formality, due to the presence of Byron. Christie had chosen to take her meal elsewhere, and the others were becoming jealous of her decision. Byron knew he was making the others uncomfortable, and his mind raced trying to come up with something to say. He found that he was a little afraid that Ari would do something drastic if he misspoke even a word. Ari was leaning forward on the counter in the kitchen area, and seemed to be staring directly at Byron all through breakfast.

Ari wasn't staring at Byron, but she was intentionally trying to intimidate him. Ari strongly wished for the power to alleviate the Faith of the ailment known as Byron. He embodied the worst of humanity in her eyes, and she wouldn't have felt the slightest bit of hesitation in getting rid of him. Ari knew other members of the crew felt the same way she did. Christie and Dana were really worried about what Byron might do, but John and Ray were way too ethical to take the easy way out. Richter was the only one who didn't seem bothered by Byron, probably because Byron didn't present a threat to him personally.

Ari liked Richter. A lot. He was, in her estimation, the classic warrior. Where others might falter, Richter would succeed. If they decided to deal with Byron the way she preferred, she had no doubt that Richter would be willing to pull the trigger. Richter didn't keep one eye on Byron like the others did. Ari guessed, correctly in fact, that Richter had all confidence that he could handle anything Byron threw at him. Ari and Richter excelled in the combat sims when they worked together, an effect that wasn't lost on John and Ray. When the chips were down, they could count on Ari and Chance.

Ari's hard-boiled nature had come from experience. Life had taught her to take advantage of her skills and attributes, and take advantage of them she did. Her beauty and strength allowed her to get what she wanted throughout her life, which is why John and Ray were her only real friends. They were immune from her wiles, for the most part, and earned her respect for it. She trusted them implicitly, even if she didn't always agree with their methods.

Her current environment was more than interesting enough for her. Her career on Earth obviously couldn't compare with this opportunity. Byron's ravings about destiny may have been lost on the rest of the crew, but Ari wasn't so sure. Byron himself was insane, she was sure about that. She wondered, however, about her own circumstances. It was rather convenient that she had the skills required to decipher Seth's code, never mind access to the hardware they needed to do so. Such romanticizing was tempting to Ari. If not for Byron's clear lunacy, she might have been guilty of much more of it. Perhaps it was fortunate that Byron could provide that perspective for her. Being chosen to crew the Faith was a tremendous stroke of luck for all of them, but assigning the circumstance to the work of a higher power wasn't Ari's style. Still...

Ari shook off the daydream. She couldn't let her ego get in the way of the mission. The idea that Christie and Ray were floating was excellent. Ari wondered why they hadn't thought of it before.

"...so it's settled," John was saying. "We'll reconvene in one hour in the orb room and give this thing a shot. Ari, I want you to monitor Seth from the bridge while we get set up in the simulation."

"Why, exactly?" Ari asked.

"I want you to see if you can spot any problems that those inside the simulation might not be aware of."

"Like what?"

"I don't know, anything. Make a recording of the data stream so we can review it later. Show Dana how to do it so that you can both eventually participate in the sims."

"You want both of us on the bridge?" asked Dana.

"Yes, if you don't mind."

"Okay, then."

"So," began Ray, "that means you, me, Christie, and Richter in the sim?"

"Yes," said John.

"I suppose you want me back in the hold," Byron said.

"No. You can stay here in the galley if you want."

Byron shrugged. "Whatever."

Ari smiled. "We do need somebody to do the dishes, you know."

"Hey yeah," said John, smirking. "Earn your keep, Byron. Do the dishes."

"Oh, great. You want me to swab the deck next?"

"Sure, while you're at it."

"Damn it, I was kidding," Byron grumbled, standing.

"I wasn't."

## 3. Day Seventeen

Money had no meaning aboard the Reckless Faith. When the crew discovered a need for currency, they found themselves resorting to means much like those unfortunate enough to be incarcerated back on Earth. Alcohol and cigarettes were the most popular, but tea, coffee, candy, and other desirable non-essential items were also of value. This entire system wouldn't have been necessary at all if it wasn't for the unexpected advent of a particular social event: poker night.

Poker night had been every night for the past two weeks. Driven by boredom and limited by the inevitable exhaustion that sims caused, the crew had soon settled on poker as a viable source of entertainment. All of the items they used for currency was assigned a value. A single bag of tea was worth one unit, as was a cigarette. One ounce of hard alcohol and one tablespoon of coffee were two units each. Candy was usually five pieces for one unit, as it was the most limited commodity aboard.

Alcohol was further divided by type. There were several cases of Bourbon, Scotch, and Rum, but only 144 bottles of beer. A single bottle of beer was worth ten units. Even more scarce was wine. Christie had purchased a mixed case of Pinot Grigio and Pinot Noir before they departed, and a single bottle was going for a hundred units.

The cigarettes had always been personal items, but the alcohol, tea, coffee and candy had to be reclaimed from the public domain by their purchasers once the competition had been standardized (which was about two minutes after the first game). This greatly annoyed Dana, as she hadn't contributed anything towards the non-essential goods. She didn't have any extraneous items she could bargain with, either, until they discovered the simulations. By offering sim time she had reserved, Dana eventually built up a nice base of possessions. That she never intended to use the sim time was beside the fact.

The poker games were usually held a couple of hours after the evening meal, in the galley. In the past nine days, Byron had taken to watching them play. He hadn't been invited to participate, for obvious reasons but also because he had nothing of value. Instead, he spent his time studying the players carefully. Inside knowledge, he reasoned, was as good as gold. Nobody noticed him changing positions around the galley every once and a while, affording him a chance to observe everyone equally.

One of Seth's more useful forms of technology was his ability to create a diffuse or directed light source wherever needed. While playing poker, John had instructed Seth to create a light facing down onto the galley's main table. John had also noticed that with a constant temperature of 67 degrees, the smoke from their various burning tobacco hovered in a sheet at the same height as the light. Ambiance was not lost on him. The network terminal in the corner was often set to play jazz from their massive collection of music. There were also viewports into the water supply tanks, and when back-lit the water cast ever-changing shadows about the room. The total effect was beautiful.

"I see your four units," said Ray, "and I raise you two."

Ray pushed two cigarettes, a piece of paper with "one ounce Navy Flake" written on it, and another piece of paper with "one ounce Barbancourt" written on it out in front of him. The rule was that the written vouchers had to be redeemed at the end of each session. Ray knew that if somebody thought they had a killer hand that they could write a voucher for more than they actually possessed, but so far it hadn't been a problem.

"I'm out," said Christie, tossing her cards down.

Richter, Dana and Ari had already folded. John looked over his cards at Ray.

"It's just you and me, partner," John said in a low voice.

"Quit stalling, you're either in or not," Ray replied, smiling.

"I call," John said, throwing two tea bags into the pile.

Ray smiled even more and displayed his cards. There were an awful lot of numbers and the color red showing.

"Straight," he said.

John threw down his cards. "Damn it. Unbelievable."

Ray laughed and collected his winnings.

"Thanks, John."

Ray stood up, to the distress of the others.

"Where do you think you're going, Mister Lucky Son of a Bitch?" Ari said.

"Relax, your highness, I'm just taking a pee break."

The nearest bathroom was off of the cargo bay, through the orb room. Ray carefully placed the several cigarettes he had just won in his shirt pocket and shoved the vouchers and tea bags into his cargo pants. As he crossed to the door, Byron intercepted him.

"Can I talk to you in the other room?" Byron said softly.

"Sure, why not?"

The door to the orb room opened automatically. Ray entered and Byron followed him. Seth's voice suddenly boomed in their ears.

"Warning, unauthorized access in the orb room."

"It's all right, Seth," said Ray. "Byron has permission to be in here with me at this moment."

"Understood."

"I guess I really can't get away with anything on board," said Byron, staring at the orb.

The door slid closed quietly.

"No, you can't. What's up?"

"I want to join the game."

"We've been over this before, Byron."

"Yes, but now I have something to offer you."

"Oh, really?"

"Have you ever noticed how Christie always rubs the back of her neck when she has a good hand?"

"No."

"Well, she does. Everyone has a tell like that, some have several. Would you like to know what yours is?"

"I don't have one."

"That's what you think."

Ray crossed his arms. "Okay, what do I do?"

"The hint about Christie was a freebie. Anything else is going to cost you."

"Cost me what? I think you're full of shit."

"Fine, think that if you want. Watch Christie for the next few hands, and tell me if I'm not right. I imagine you'll be more receptive when you see for yourself."

"Okay, let's say you're right. What are your terms?"

"I'll tell you what your quirks are for fifty units. For the others, ten units each."

"That's all?"

"It will be enough for me to start participating."

"We'll see about that. I'll watch Christie more carefully for the rest of the night, and we'll talk again afterward."

Ray moved back towards the door to the galley, which opened. He motioned for Byron to return. Byron winked at him and exited the orb room.

John was shuffling the deck.

Byron was right about Christie, but the subject didn't come up again until after the next flight combat sim. Ray was in an exceptionally good mood because they'd kicked the crap out of an armada of imagined enemy spacecraft. It may have been useless considering their complete lack of knowledge of any enemy, but it was damn entertaining nonetheless. Ray had entered the galley to get a drink of water before the after action review about to take place in the conference room. Byron was sitting in the same place he had been an hour ago. Ray was trying to ignore him.

"So?" asked Byron after a moment.

"So, you're right," Ray said reluctantly. "Christie's tell is so obvious now that you've pointed it out."

"Good, then we have something to work out."

"Not really. You probably noticed that I've eliminated any tells of my own, whatever they happened to be before. So your request of fifty credits for the information is moot."

"I noticed that. It's true that you quit doing what you were doing when you have a good hand. You're a regular Sphinx at the table now."

Ray drank from his glass. "You'll have to find some other way of buying into the game, Byron."

"What about the others? My offer of ten credits for their tells still stands."

"Byron, you fail to realize that I don't care what the tells are. I don't take the game seriously enough to try and hedge my bets against the other crewmembers. They're my friends, and I'm not going to be duplicitous just to gain some extra cups of tea or a frigging Riesen."

"What am I supposed to do, then?"

"Why don't you ask Ari? She's more the type to try and gain an advantage."

The color drained out of Byron's face.

"I, uh... she's not..."

"You're afraid if you so much as look at her the wrong way that she'll rip your nuts off. I gotta tell you, Byron. You shouldn't take Ari so seriously. She acts tough for sure but she'd never hurt anyone who didn't have it coming."

"When you phrase it like that, it's hardly reassuring."

"Okay, then. Rest assured that the rest of us won't let any harm come to you."

Byron's former veneer of confidence visibly returned, as if he'd suddenly noticed his fly was down and had corrected it.

"I was going to say, actually, that I didn't think Ari would bargain for tells because she would never accept help from me. If she did, she'd be forced to admit that I knew something she didn't, and in that single way, that I was superior to her."

Ray rolled his eyes. "You managed to combine an apt observation with your own egotistical viewpoint. Does this come naturally to you or did you receive specialized training?"

"I am right about Ari."

"Yes. Between the two of you, it's a wonder anyone else has any room left to feel self-assured."

Ari came down the stairs from above and entered the galley.

"Has the AAR started?" asked Ray.

"No, they're going on about something or another," said Ari, grabbing a glass from the cabinet. "I decided you had the right idea."

"I'll meet you back up there. Byron has something he wanted to ask you."

"Oh?"

Ray waved sweetly at Byron as he climbed the stairs. Byron flipped Ray off and immediately regretted it as Ari caught him doing so.

"What do you want, Squirt?"

"Well, nothing really, I just..."

Byron took a deep breath. Ari raised an eyebrow and crossed her arms.

"Sometime today?"

37

"I want in on the poker games."

"With what? You've got nothing. Actually you've got worse than nothing because you still owe us for not deep-sixing your ass back near Regulus."

Byron smiled. "What I do have is information."

Ari opened the fridge and obtained a can of cola. They'd only brought two cases of soda to begin with. Byron saw his chance.

"I'm listening," said Ari, opening the can.

"You did very well in the simulation just now."

"As usual."

"No, not as usual. You do well in the infantry sims but you're not so good at the space combat sims. You won that can of soda in a poker game. You only use items you've won in the games when you've done well in the space sims."

Ari calmly filled her glass halfway with ice and poured in the cola.

"I suppose from what you can see in your limited scope, that's true."

"Yes. I can't see what you do with anything you don't keep down here. However, it seems to me that you don't do any of your drinking except during the poker games and after dinner. Since Dana spends so much time on the bridge, you often smoke your cigarettes down here as well. I guess you smoke in your room occasionally, but I know how you hate to be in there all by yourself."

Sipping from her glass, Ari nodded, and said, "You've got it all figured out, I take it. All simple observation, really. If I had nothing to do but watch us all the time I'd probably be observing things like that as well."

Despite Ari's outward appearance, Byron's comment about her dislike for being alone aboard the ship had made her very uncomfortable. Byron was right, and that went beyond casual observation.

"It seems to me that regardless of your attitude, you've got the greatest self-doubt of anyone on this ship."

Ari laughed. "You've been spending too much time with Dana. She's probably projecting some of her shortcomings onto me as a defensive measure. It's understandable, though. It's no secret that she and I don't get along very well."

Byron felt his adrenaline swell, and he stood up.

"Oh no, Ari. Didn't I just say Dana spends most of her time on the bridge? In fact, when I do listen to her talk to the others she maintains a very professional attitude about you. No, Ari, I'm talking about you, and your problems. You can try to pass the buck but it won't work with me."

"So what? Is this bullshit supposed to convince me to let you play poker?"

"Not directly. You can take your cola and go to the after-action review, and think about how right I am. You don't have to admit it, even. I understand your need to save face. Enjoy your victory soda, and think about how my ability to figure people out can help you win more often at poker. For the last thing I'll reveal is again something you already know. You suck at poker."

"Christ, you are a pain in the ass. I've got half a mind to leave one of the kitchen knives lying around and double-tap you in the head and claim you attacked me. Hell, why bother with the knife?"

"WARNING," Seth's voice boomed suddenly, "UNAUTHORIZED WEAPONS USE DETECTED IN THE GALLEY."

"What the fuck?" Ari said, shocked.

"Don't look at me," Byron said, equally surprised. "You're the one making all the threats!"

Ari drew her Glock with lightning speed and centered it on Byron's chest.

"Get your hands up, damn it!"

"I said I didn't do anything!"

Byron complied, a look of horror edging across his face. Seconds later John, Ray, Christie and Richter came barging down the stairs from above.

"What's going on down here?" John barked.

Ray and the others fanned out around the rear of the room.

"I don't know," said Ari, "we were just talking and..."

"I'll tell you what's going on," Byron interrupted, "This crazy bitch has finally gone off the deep end."

"Shut up, both of you," said Ray. "Seth, what is the current situation in the galley?"

"There was an unauthorized use of a weapon detected at 2307 local time," replied Seth. "The violation ended zero point three seconds later."

"Point three seconds?" asked Christie.

Ari lowered her weapon. "That means it was over before you even got here."

"Seth," began John, "what was the nature of the unauthorized weapons use?"

"Unable to identify."

"What kind of weapon was used?"

"Unable to identify."

"Who instigated the violation?"

Seth was quiet for a moment before responding. "Ari."

"Bullshit," Ari said. "I only drew my weapon after Seth started freaking out."

"That much is true," said Byron.

"You see? Seth, who told you to be concerned about weapons use aboard the ship?"

"It is part of my normal programming."

"No, it's not," said Christie. "At least you never mentioned it before."

Ari holstered her pistol and crossed to the galley terminal. "You know how Seth is. I wouldn't be surprised if this is one of his lost bits of programming."

Ari typed away at the terminal.

"Could this be a result of your efforts to restore his systems?" John asked.

"I hope so. At least, I... yeah, come look at this. There's a new program that was detected during the time of the alert. It's just labeled as gibberish, but it's got to be what Seth was running. I can work with him to try and restore it completely."

"Seth, what are the parameters of a weapons detection alert?" said Ray.

"Those parameters are not available."

"He did it for no reason," said Ari. "It was a malfunction."

"I'll agree to that," said Byron.

"Okay, fine," began John. "You work on it and figure out what the deal is. It's been a long day so work on it tomorrow if you want. I'm going to tell Dana what happened."

"What about the AAR?" asked Richter.

"Forget about it for now. We kicked ass anyway, there isn't much to tell."

John went upstairs. Ray shrugged and went with him. Richter holstered his pistol.

"Byron, would you excuse us, please?" Richter said flatly.

"Sure, fine."

Byron exited into the aft cargo hold. Ari glanced up briefly from the terminal.

"What's up, Chance?"
"What really happened here, Ari?"
"You already know what happened."
"Do I?"

"Yes, you do. You know Seth's been skittish lately. We don't know half of what's locked away in his memory. We're lucky he doesn't evacuate all the air on board thinking we'll enjoy the experience."

"All right," said Richter. "Are you going to stay up?"

"Yes. I want to find out what the program is meant to do."

"Okay. Good job on the sim tonight. We're up for the usual in the morning?"

"Yup."

"Fine. Do get some rest before then. I don't want to get shot because you're snoozing."

## 4. Day Eighteen

Forty-five minutes later Richter had almost fallen asleep when there was a tap on his door.

"Lights to fifty," he said, and sat up. "Yo!"

"Richter, it's Ari. Can I come in?"

Richter stood up and crossed to the door. The effects of the rum he'd imbibed earlier were still very much present. He pressed the controls and the door slid open. Ari was standing there, looking tired.

"What's going on?"

"I need to talk to you."

"Come in, then."

Richter moved out of the way and returned to his bed. He sat on the edge while Ari took the desk chair.

"Aren't you going to close the door?"

"Oh, sure, if you want."

Richter did so and sat down again.

"This isn't easy for me," Ari said slowly.

"I understand. The first time never is. Just say what you feel."

"I'm coming to you because you don't know me as well as John or Ray, and because we have a special friendship. I almost feel like you're the most neutral and impartial member of the crew, and the one most likely to be able to give me good advice."

"Oh... Okay. But I'm not a preacher by any stretch of the imagination."

"I know that all too well. It's the nature of my concern that makes you particularly approachable."

"Well, whatever is said between us is confidential."

Ari picked up Richter's hat from the desk. It was a black baseball cap with no logo. He was wearing it their last night on Earth. Ari was surprised to find it dusty, and she remembered that Richter had been wearing it only in the

43

sims. Ari spoke, staring out of the window at the stars past her own transparent reflection.

"Most of the time we've spent together has been in a fantasy world, fighting foes of our own devising. Sometimes I wonder whether or not I can keep that line distinct. Times like this make me feel like I've lost the ability to discern fact from fantasy. Perhaps that overwhelming feeling of strangeness I experience when this whole affair started never really went away. Life on this ship is becoming normal, which makes the lack of knowledge about the rest of the mission all the more terrifying. Byron may have been right about my self-doubt, although I hardly imagine mine is the deepest of those present. What he did was not to make me doubt myself even more, but to solidify a feeling I've had about him ever since he made himself known to us."

"I don't know what you mean."

"Before that alert earlier tonight, he and I were having a conversation. He had some observations about myself that he wanted to share, to try and gain a psychological advantage over me. Over all of us, by a roundabout manner. Most of it was crap, but some of it wasn't. What he was right about made me decide something. I made the decision that I was going to kill him."

"We all have our breaking point. Byron betrayed you and almost got you all killed. Since then he's done nothing to try and make up for it, or endear himself to the crew. I don't condone killing him, but I understand your motivation. The important thing is that you didn't do it."

"You don't get it. I had made up my mind that I was going to kill him. Right then. I'd sent the message to my muscles to draw my weapon. Before I so much as twitched, Seth blared out that warning. Seth knew what I was about to do."

"We all know Seth can join with our minds. It's not surprising that he can detect our thoughts even when we're not linked with him."

Ari laughed, and began to cry. "I love that about you, Richter. You're so analytical about things even now. Is my decision to resort to homicide really so not surprising to you?"

"No."

"Figures. I almost allowed myself to go down a path, a path that would have corrupted me forever after. I came that close. If Seth hadn't chosen that moment to freak out, I would have done it. I would have killed him, and I would have lied to cover it up. I don't want to be that person, Chance."

"Lucky Seth did intervene, then. Add to that your willingness to admit that it's a path you don't want to take, and to talk to one of us about it. Admitting you have a problem is the first step towards getting rid of it."

"It's not just that. I wanted to project strength and competence to you and the others. I wanted to seem strong and capable. I never realized that one result of that would be this; your complete lack of emotion and my confession."

"Well, don't judge too deeply off of my reaction. I've seen things that most people never want to so much as hear about. I've seen the best and worst of my teammates, and I've seen the best and worst of humanity. So no, your conviction doesn't surprise me. I don't think the others would have suspected you'd actually whack Byron. Pardon the expression."

"What should I do now?"

"Can't you just try being nicer to people?"

"Are you kidding? I'm Mother fucking Teresa to everybody else."

"No, you're not. Comments like that prove it. Just don't try so hard to come across as cynical, aloof, and sarcastic. Treat others as you would have them treat you."

"I guess so. What about Byron?"

"Why don't you let me handle Byron. You worry about being the best crewmate and friend you can to the others. We need your help, desperately. Focus on your good qualities and we'll all benefit."

Ari smiled, and brushed away her tears. "I'm still worried about being able to measure my emotions."

"Sometimes a long, hard look over the edge is the only way we can keep from jumping."

"How did you learn to be so understanding?"

"Marine Corps drill instructors."

Ari laughed and stood up. "Have a good night, Chance Richter. I'm going to go pass out. Thank you for listening."

"No problem."

Ari exited the room and closed the door. Richter sighed.

"Damn it, I'm such a fool."

Eight hours later, Byron was awoken by someone entering the cargo hold. That someone brought the lights up to one hundred percent. Byron sat up in his bed, which was nothing more than a mattress and two blankets on the floor. He blinked at the brightness.

"Isn't it a little early to be retrieving supplies?"

"It's past zero eight hundred," Richter said. "You should be awake anyway."

"Oh, like discipline is worth a damn on this ship, especially to me."

Byron flopped over and pulled his blanket over his head.

"Self-discipline when it's not necessary is a good habit to have."

"Just turn the lights off when you're done."

"Get up, Byron, I'm here to talk to you."

"What now?"

"I said, get up."

Flipping his blanket off with a flourish, Byron stood up. Richter realized he'd never seen Byron with his shirt off. Byron had muscle tone like an Olympic athlete.

"Been working out, I take it?" Richter said with a raised eyebrow.

"What do you think I've been doing with all my free time in here? I do two hundred push-ups and two hundred crunches a day. Every other day I do two hundred squats. I use the ammo cans to work my arms. One hundred repetitions of five different exercises every other day."

"So you do have some discipline after all."

"The food you've been offering me hasn't helped much. I must have lost twenty pounds since we left."

"This is a prison of your own devising. You've had almost three weeks to get your shit together and you're still no better at making up for your treachery."

"Are you kidding? I've been the Dalai fucking Lama recently."

"More alike then they'd ever admit," Richter muttered. "I'm not going to use psychology or positive reinforcement to try and get you to relate to the crew better, Byron. It's not my strong suit. Ray has the most patience for you, and John may be able to see it in his heart to forgive you. Dana is ambivalent. Christie, Ari and I would rather send you hitchhiking back to the Sol System in a rubber dinghy."

"I know that. I guess I can't find it in myself to kiss that much ass."

"Fine. What I'm going to do is make sure your brains don't end up our first 3-D tactile wall hanging."

"Thanks, I can handle myself."

Richter laughed lowly and shook his head. "You need to think about how you can be an asset to this crew. Right now you're nothing more than a pain in the ass, resource consuming liability. In my line of work, liability is mitigated. One way or the other."

"Is that a threat?  I would have figured you beyond idle threats."

"I deal in facts, Byron."

Richter took two foam earplugs out of his pocket and began to put them in.

"I know you're bluffing.  You are a professional, and I know that even if I was an enemy combatant you... wouldn't... what are you doing?"

"Testing Seth's new program."

Richter smoothly drew his pistol and brought it up.  Byron began to dodge to his left, allowing Richter to aim where his head had been.  The shot impacted the bulkhead, sending a shock wave of ripples flowing from the center.  Sound waves filled the hold and faded into white noise.  Byron poked his head up from behind a crate.  Richter had already returned his pistol to his holster.

"Looks like either Seth's program isn't working again," said Richter, removing the earplugs, "or I meant to miss.  I'll let you figure out which."

Byron could barely hear him, and after Richter left he could only hear his own blood rushing through his head.  He didn't hear Richter lock the door.

## 5. Day Thirty Six

The scenery had become much more interesting after the Faith entered the Large Magellanic Cloud. Far more resembling the first few days of their voyage, stars and star systems moved by the windows and viewports quickly. Before too long, the Tarantula Nebula became the most obvious feature of the cloud, and since they were headed right there it soon filled the entire front window. Each of the crew had spent some time marveling at the beauty of the nebula, but that morning John was alone on the bridge.

The past two and a half weeks had gone by in a routine no different than what had been established. Byron was the only variable, eventually allowed to rejoin the others after a week in confinement. Richter and Ari had kept their secrets to themselves, for the most part, but the others needed little convincing that Byron needed some time alone. Ray suggested putting him to a supervised apprenticeship, and it was determined that the crew would teach Byron everything they knew about the plumbing and waste systems aboard. Tempered by his isolation and displaying an atypical mollification, Byron agreed. He'd worked with such determination and sincerity that his privileges had been expanded slightly. He could now visit the bridge during the afternoons, when it was guaranteed to be well populated.

Ari and Richter, for their part, said very little to Byron as the days went by. For Ari the reason involved latent guilt, for Richter it was a matter of practical necessity. Ari's own temperament was seen to undergo a change, which helped her get along with Christie and Dana greatly. She hadn't been able to unlock any more information about the security program that Seth decided to run during her near-death experience with Byron. She'd given up after a week, and the entire effort left her with a familiar feeling from when they first met Seth; that he was intentionally obfuscating the matter. Ari detested the concept that Seth was manipulating her morality, even though it had been for the better.

John could sense a change in Ari's demeanor. He attributed it to cabin fever and her constant and intensive sim sessions. He, Ari, Ray and Richter had become famously effective in various combat scenarios. John continued to encourage Christie and Dana to participate more often, with limited success. Christie and Dana had become focused on the ship itself, working with Ari to better understand the relationship between Seth and their Earth technology. They'd become good friends in their own way. John was glad for it. As was evident during their space combat sims and their real-time drills, Christie and Dana had become indispensable members of the crew. John suspected that Ari would become jealous about sharing her knowledge of the Terran computer network, but there was no outward evidence of this.

John closed his eyes and took a deep breath. They were due to arrive at Umber in less than six days, and it was hard to relax. He was playing trance music at a moderate volume on the bridge, and along with his pipe he was halfway to content. Friday sat across the room, attempting to avoid the smoke. Ray arrived via the conference room.

"Good morning," Ray said.

"Morning. You're up early."

"It's been difficult to sleep in lately."

"No kidding. Why do you think I've been spending so much time up here?"

"You should just submit to calling yourself captain. We all think of you as captain anyway."

"I still don't want the title. We're all leaders in different ways. I know I run the show during space combat sims but that doesn't make me captain."

"Actually, it does. How'bout commander instead?"

"Commander Scherer. It does have a nice ring to it."

"Do you hear something?"

"You mean other than the music?"

John paused and listened. "What the..."

Ray moved to the pilot console and turned off the music. Something was beeping at Dana's station.

"What is that?"

John jumped up from his chair, knocking an empty mug from the arm rest.

"It's a transmission!"

Bolting over to the appropriate terminal, John grabbed the mouse. Ray leaned over to watch.

"It's probably just more background junk. You shouldn't be so hopeful every time we receive a second or two of..."

"This is thirty seconds long, look. Dana to the bridge, please!"

"Can you play it?"

"I don't know how to work the program. I never needed to before."

Dana entered the bridge via the hallway door.

"What's up?"

"We just received a thirty second transmission," John replied.

John and Ray gave way and Dana sat down at the terminal.

"Holy..."

"What?" said Ray.

"This is an audio waveform. Definitely generated from an intelligent source."

"Can you play it?" asked John.

"Of course."

Utter nonsense, a hair too loud, filled the bridge. Dana turned the volume down a notch.

"Sounds like somebody gargling pie," said John.

"Seth, do you understand the transmission we just received?"

Friday jumped up on the console next to Dana's terminal.

"Yes," said Seth.
"Can you translate it for us?"
"Please specify visual or audible translation."
"Audio, please."

The transmission began to play again, this time in perfect Oxford English.

"Announcing the grand re-opening of the Umberian System Way Station! Now with thirty docking bays that can accommodate the largest galaxy cruisers. Visit our completely redesigned market area, now with fifteen restaurants and bars to cater to any taste. Reasonable rates, and sign up now for a frequent fueler discount! Security provided by Empire Security so you can relax and enjoy your stay. The Umberian System Way Station, type USWS into your uplink module for coordinates."

John, Ray and Dana were speechless. Dana was the first to snap out of it.

"Interesting how the translation was only twenty seconds. Perhaps the original language has longer words."

John looked shocked. "That's all you can say? This is the first confirmation of an alien civilization, and you're waxing scientific on the syntax?"

"You mean the first confirmation other than the ship we're all on? Yes, it's cool, John. I'm still a professional."

"We gotta let the others hear this," said Ray. "This is amazing."

"I wouldn't get too excited," said Dana. "This transmission clocked in at four hundred light years per hour. Think about how far we still have to go. This transmission is at least a hundred years old. Seth is the only one who could have grabbed it, by the way. None of our Earth receivers could have picked this up."

"Well, it still proves that at one time Umber was a bustling center of galactic activity," said Ray.

"Maybe," said John. "Play it again, please."

Dana did so. John listened intently.

"The translation is definitely shorter than the original," said Dana.

"Grand re-opening," began John, "I wonder why they closed in the first place. Remodeling?"

"I suppose even space stations need redecorating now and then," said Ray.

Dana swiveled around in her chair. "Guys, we should see if Seth is still playing dumb on the subject of linguistics, now that he's received new input."

"Good idea, but don't be surprised if he still sits there like a lobotomized slug."

"You want to question him, John?"

"You go ahead, you're the communications officer."

"Fine. Seth, what language was the transmission?"

"Umberian," said Seth, a hint of sanctimony evident.

"Was your translation exact?"

"No."

"Can Umberian be translated exactly into English?"

"If you really want to, but it will sound wrong."

"That's progress," said John. "Seth doesn't usually think in terms of causality."

"What?" asked Ray.

"I mean he predicted our reaction to the request. Usually he can't, or won't, think in terms of cause and effect."

"Oh, I got you."

"Seth," Dana continued, "please translate the transmission into English as precisely as possible."

The message repeated.

"Station Routing as of Umber Planetary System to reopen by way of our announcement! Class Halon accommodating airlocks to number thirty as of now. Number fifteen places to renew body energy to go into of each major race palate. Money not to deplete if and when refueler club to join! Relax safe as Empire Security guards with instant death possible to bad guys stand at ready.

Station Routing as of Umber Planetary System, uplink module into enter USWS for how to get here."

"Difficult, but not impossible to understand. Thank goodness Seth has a good grasp of our language to work with."

"Well, we've given him enough opportunity to learn," said Ray.

"Seth, does your program include an uplink module?"

"As if," said Seth.

"What?"

"Uplink modules are so last century."

"He's still acting schizo," said John. "Only fools like us would trust our lives to a computer as weird as Seth."

"Seth," said Dana, "how do you connect to the Umberian Way Station if not by uplink module?"

Seth returned to his normal flat tone. "Communication is through a real-time, open broadcast network."

"What is the effective range of the network?"

"The terminal range of the network has not been determined."

"What do you mean?"

"The maximum range of the network is unknown."

"How far from Umber were you when you stopped receiving it?"

"Five hundred and twenty seven kilometers."

"Huh?" said John. "How can it be the main communication network for the entire solar system with that kind of range?"

"Wait a minute," said Dana. "There are two different things being said here. If the maximum range is not known, and Seth stopped receiving the network after five hundred kilometers, then the transmission was terminated for a reason other than leaving the effective range."

John nodded. "Seth, why did you stop receiving the network signal so soon after departing Umber?"

"The signal was interrupted."

"By whom?"

"Unknown."

"Figures."

Dana raised her index finger. "Hold on. Seth, what is the maximum known range of the network?"

"Five thousand parsecs," said Seth.

"What the hell?"

"What?" asked Ray.

"That's enough to cover the entire Magellanic Cloud, at least I think so. Christie would know for sure."

"Seth," began John, "are you receiving the network signal now?"

"Yes."

"Can you connect us to the system?"

"No."

"For God's sake why not?"

"The signal is a different format than when I last connected. Only one message is decipherable."

"Well, let's hear it."

There was a pause. A new message began to play, introducing those present to a new language. This one sounded like cats arguing over tea. Seth immediately began to translate.

"Your copy of Nebulonic GammaWave is out of date. Upgrade to the new version now for only ninety credits. Unable to initiate auto-account deduction. Please visit Residere Beta for several vendor options."

"Sounds like you've been out of the loop for too long, Seth," said Ray.

"What language was that?" asked John.

"Kau'Rii."

"Cow-what?"

"Kau'Rii."

"Who are they?"

"Unknown."

"You don't know or you can't remember?"

There was a pause. "I cannot recall."

"Do they live on Umber?" Ray asked.

"No."

"Guys, check this out," said Dana, working at her station. "Seth may not be able to access the network, but I'm detecting it now. I guess asking him about it made the information available."

"Getting info out of Seth has always been like that," said John.

"I'm showing more than one transmission source. One of them is four light years from Umber. One of them is a hundred light years beyond that. But none of them are coming from the Umberian system itself."

"Seth, which system is the closest transmission source?"

"Residere."

"Do the Kau'Rii live on Residere?"

Seth thought about it for a moment. "Some of them."

"Then it seems we have a choice to make."

Ten minutes later, the crew of the Faith was gathered in the conference room. John stood in front of the table, a wall-mounted plasma screen monitor next to his left shoulder. The mood was very upbeat. John had just finished updating the crew as to the new information, and proceeded to make his point.

"The question is now, should we continue to Umber as planned or stop by the Residere system first?"

John pointed to a quick and dirty diagram of the systems' relative locations that Dana had placed on the monitor.

"Why would we want to go to Residere first?" asked Christie. "Seth's already told us as much as he remembers about it, and anything could happen. We should find out what our mission to Umber is first."

"I agree, but there is the matter of Seth's outdated communication software. We might get to Umber only to find that we can't communicate with them. If we buy the upgrade first, we'll be sure of it. Plus, we can find out about Umber from the Kau'Rii or whomever else is around and get a third-party opinion about it."

"Perhaps," began Ari, "but we don't know if the Kau'Rii or the Residerians are friends with Umber. They might blast us out of the sky just for showing up."

"I don't know about you guys," said Ray, "but I don't have ninety credits in my ass pocket."

John looked sheepish. "Oh. Good point."

"I'm just as curious about the Residerian system as anyone," said Christie. "It's just too much of a risk right now."

"Okay. Unless there are any objections we won't alter our course. I'll continue to question Seth and see if I can get anything more out of him. Ari, I know there's little to work with but I'd appreciate it if you and Seth could try and access the network."

"Roger," said Ari.

"I also want everyone at their bridge stations from now until midnight. I don't want to miss any new information that might come up. After midnight we'll go back to our normal shifts. We should be arriving at Umber in six days."

"About that," said Dana. "I've been doing some calculating based on these transmissions. I think we overestimated the distance to Umber. According to my new calculations we should be there in less than twenty-four hours."

"Are you sure our speed isn't the incorrect variable?" asked Christie.

"Seth gave us that number and I've had ample opportunities to confirm it. Our travel time was based off of a total distance of 179,000 light-years, but that's just an estimate made by Earth astronomers. Now it looks like it's closer to 160,000."

"If you're right," began John, "we'll be there early. That's fine by me. I think we're all ready to confront our mission. I still think we should run standard shifts until we get there. I don't want anyone starved for sleep when we arrive."

"Like any of us are going to be able to sleep now," said Ray.

"Where do you want me?" asked Byron.

"Don't you have some toilets to scrub?" asked Christie.

"Byron may observe quietly on the bridge as usual," said John, aiming a harsh look at Christie. "Everyone clear?"

There were no questions from the crew.

"Cool," said Richter.

"Let's get to work."

## 6. Day Thirty Seven

The hour had arrived. Dana had checked her calculations several times and there was little doubt that their arrival was imminent. The crew of the Faith was present on the bridge. John sat in the pilot's chair, which had been pulled forward into the manual flight position. Christie and Dana sat at their stations to his right, and Ray and Ari sat on the left. Richter tended to hang out near Ari's station, as it dealt with the on-board weaponry. Byron stood at the rear of the bridge, unable to gain any useful information from the monitors. Tycho was pulling duty as a medium for Seth, and sat contentedly next to Christie.

The object of their attention was a timer counting down. It was displayed at each of the stations. It was very nearly complete.

"Ten seconds until we drop out of superspace," John said.

Umber was located in a clear area of the Tarantula Nebula. Brilliant red clouds of gas filled the space above the ship, and jade green gas filled the sky below. On the ecliptic plane of the ship, the stars of the Magellanic Cloud still shone brightly with the exception of the right side, where a very thin layer of reddish-green gas masked them somewhat.

"Grab onto something," John said. "We don't know what the change in speed will..."

A star that had been indistinct from the others suddenly grew drastically in size. It was not immediately obvious to anyone but John until he vocalized his surprise. When it filled about five degrees of the field of view it ceased to grow. It was reddish in comparison to Earth's sun.

"Superspace flight complete," said Seth.

"Well that was nothing," said Ray.

John peered ahead. "Where's the planet?"

"We're still approaching it," said Christie. "We're doing about 167,000 miles a second, so it'll be any moment now."

"Better throttle down, John," said Ray. "You'll overshoot it."

John nodded, and pulled back on the throttle control. A blue-brown marble appeared in the center of the viewscreen.

"Home," said Seth.

John grinned. "Well, folks, we finally made it. Let's hope it wasn't all for nothing."

"I don't care if they sent Seth out for milk and cookies," said Christie, equally happy, "it was still worth it."

The planet grew ever nearer. Before too long, more detail became apparent. Land covered about sixty percent of what they could see. The land masses were mostly brown and gray, with an occasional patch of green. Clouds covered some parts of the surface.

"I don't see any cities or technology yet," said Dana. "Perhaps if we circled over to the dark side we could see some lights."

John looked over his shoulder. "Christie, plot me an orbital course at about four hundred miles up."

"No problem," Christie replied, typing at her station. "Follow the waypoints on your screen."

John concentrated on getting them into orbit. The planet filled the entire field of view until John rolled the ship around into position. He had placed the ship so that the north pole of Umber was up, and the planet on their right side. Richter crossed to that side of the bridge to get a better look.

"Holy shit, there are a lot of satellites out there," Richter said.

Everyone else looked over. There were indeed many satellites readily apparent, at least a hundred that they could see. They were all in geosynchronous orbit and floated by slowly. They bore more than a passing resemblance to mosquitoes.

"What's with all the satellites?" asked John.

"I do not recognize them," said Seth.

"I'm reading at least a thousand of them at several different altitudes," said Dana. "They appear to be in a dormant state."

John returned his attention to his station. "What now, Seth?"

"I'm home!" Seth said, elated.

"Can you contact your people?"

"Oh, right. Stand by, please."

Moments later an audio channel was opened. At first, there was nothing but static. Then, barely audible, voices. The crew listened intently and they could recognize Umberian being spoken.

"Can you translate us into Umberian, Seth?"

"Of course."

"Then start now. This is John Scherer of the Umberian vessel Reckless Faith. We have arrived from Earth at your behest and are awaiting communication. Over."

A voice came through the channel, quiet but clear.

"Hey doc, that old radio is squawking at us," the voice said.

"Damn you, boy, can't you see I'm busy?" a second voice replied.

"That's the one you saved from the government, right? I've never heard it working before."

"I said I'm busy right now! If I don't freeze these samples right now they'll... what did you say?"

"The radio, genius. There's a voice coming through on it."

"What? What! The radio? THE RADIO?"

"Don't shout, that's what I said."

The second voice came through again, with much higher volume.

"This is Professor Talvan to whomever is broadcasting on this channel. Repeat your last transmission please!"

"This is Commander Scherer of the Reckless Faith. We're from a planet called Earth. We built this ship to come see you. May we speak with someone in charge?"

"It can't be. It simply can't be. Seth, is that you?"

"Hello again, Professor Talvan," said Seth.

"Praise all that is good! You've returned! Our time of salvation has at last come! Listen to me very carefully, now. You've got to destroy all the defense satellites in orbit as fast as you can. They'll realize you're here any second!"

"What?" said John, aghast. "Which ones are the defense satellites?"

"ALL OF THEM!"

"Oh, shit," said Ray.

John shook his head in the negative. "Professor, we can't possibly destroy all of the satellites. Even if we had enough ammunition to spare it would take hours."

Talvan sounded confused. "Hours? Ammunition? It shouldn't take you but a moment with ten thousand ships."

"Ten thousand ships? Excuse me? Professor Talvan, we have only one ship."

Talvan began to laugh. "One ship? One ship? What good is that going to do? Why didn't you follow Seth's instructions? Didn't your planet have the resources to make more than one?"

"Hey," said John, irked, "Seth was apparently damaged on his way to our planet. He didn't say anything about ten thousand ships, and we did the best we could for this one."

"Damaged? Hold on, I'm going to link up with your computer."

"This doesn't sound good," said Christie.

"Ten thousand?" said Richter. "I'd say we're slightly under strength."

"The satellites aren't doing anything yet," observed Byron.

"Oh, my God," said Talvan. "Seth's memory is badly fragmented. I can upload a repair program to you, but it will take five minutes. Don't go anywhere."

"Wait a minute," said John. "We've been flying blind for months. What is the mission? Why have you called for help?"

"Hmm, Seth really was fragged. Ten years ago a race of beings called the Zendreen invaded our planet. Umber had the highest spaceflight and weapons technology in the galaxy at the time, and the Zendreen decided we weren't sharing enough of it for their tastes. Despite all of our high tech weaponry and abilities, we didn't have the industrial capacity to build enough war machines to resist. We didn't have a standing military force nearly large enough to repel the invasion. We appealed to the Rakhar and the galactic community for help, but they didn't want to get involved. We're inventors and explorers, not warriors. We had to surrender without a shot fired."

"That's terrible."

"If only the Rakhar had known the true level of our technology. They would have known, as we did, that we couldn't allow the Zendreen to capture that technology. We destroyed all the data on the eve of the invasion, all but one database. We had an unmanned deep space exploration probe that was ready to launch before the trouble began, so we packed it with all of the data and sent it on a mission. Travel to the core galaxy, find a sympathetic race of beings with the appropriate level of technology and resources, use our technology to build ten thousand warships, and return to liberate us. Seth was the AI aboard that probe."

"Unbelievable. If Seth hadn't been damaged, we probably would have been able to build that many ships. We definitely would have had to go to the government, though."

"Yeah, right," said Christie. "The US would never agree to fight in a war in another galaxy. They'd probably take the technology and spend years bickering over how to proceed into space."

"The resistance movement has been working on a genetically-engineered virus that will destroy the invaders," began Talvan, "but I fear I'll never be able to finish the work without access to a fully-stocked laboratory. You are our only hope."

"Uh, guys? You might want to look at this."

Byron pointed out of the window. Several dozen of the satellites were now glowing with red lights and moving slowly toward them.

"Professor," said John, "the satellites are engaging us. I'm going to withdraw to a further distance."

Talvan sounded desperate. "No, you can't break orbit. The uplink only has a seven hundred kilometer range. You'll have to hold out until the upload is complete."

"What kind of armament do the satellites have?"

"Standard Zendreen Mark Five plasma cannons. If you didn't upgrade Seth's standard energy dissipation ability, two or three shots from them and you're history."

"Holy shit! What about landing on the surface?"

"The Zendreen control this planet. Why do you think there are enemy defense satellites all over the place? We're part of the underground, the resistance movement. We'd all but given up hope that anyone would return."

"Then we're going to have to withdraw and find another way."

"I've already initiated the repair program. If you break contact now, Seth's memory will be completely destroyed."

John's expression became steely. "Then we have no other choice. All hands to battle stations!"

"What, seriously?" asked Dana.

"Move, damn it!"

In a drill that they'd practiced a hundred times in simulation, the crew leaped into action. Richter and Ari exited the bridge to man the dorsal and ventral guns, respectively. Christie transferred control of Ari's station to her own, while Ray remained seated to monitor the weapons systems from the bridge.

John accessed control of the main forward cannon. "Ray, take control over the rear thirty," he said.

"Roger."

"There's a spare seat," said Byron. "May I sit there?"

"Fine, but don't touch anything."

"Dana," John began, "remember the dampening field we used to mask the ship's energy signal from ASTRA?"

"I remember you telling me about it," Dana replied.

"The information is still there. Christie can show you the data file. See if you two can use it to hide us from the satellites."

"We're already invisible, isn't that worth something?"

The satellites were heading directly for the Faith.

"Obviously not. They must be locking onto something else."

"Yeah, like the uplink from the surface?" said Christie.

"Shit. Never mind about that, any signals that we mask of our own will probably cut the transmission upload, too."

"Maybe, but we might be able to put up a firewall of sorts. It'll take a lot longer than five minutes, though."

"Just monitor the systems, then."

"It's not a bad idea..." began Dana.

"This is Richter, I'm in position."

"Ari?" asked John.

"Good to go," Ari replied.

"Power up all guns. All right, crew, listen up. I'm going to be punching it as fast as I can without breaking the seven hundred click limit. That means that we're going to have to blast any satellite that is engaging us. Your heads-up display will tell you when your target is locked. I'm going to be flying in such a manner to target as many satellites as I can. The other gunners will have to take targets of opportunity. Let's just hope our weapons are effective against these things."

A flash of blue light streaked by the bow of the ship.

"Here they come," said Ray.

John brought the throttle up. More plasma bursts began to fly by. There was a dull thud and the ship vibrated unnervingly.

"Damage?" asked John.

"No structural damage," said Christie. "Energy absorption limit at five percent."

"They're not as powerful as advertised," said Ray.

"Either that or it was a grazing blow," said John.

Two more shots hit the ship. The lights on the bridge fluctuated momentarily.

"There's a concentrated field of satellites bearing zero two zero mark fifteen."

"Let's get in the war, Ray."

John pushed the throttle as far as he could without breaking orbit. There was a considerable push of inertia against the crew, which was to be expected with drastic maneuvers. The plasma bursts became much less accurate. John pointed the bow of the ship directly at one of the satellites. His HUD showed a lock. Pressing the trigger on his control stick, the bridge was filled with the almost unbearable noise of the thirty millimeter cannon firing one deck below. Tracer fire shot a straight line from the ship to the satellite, and the smaller craft was blown apart like aluminum foil. Sparks and electrical bolts crackled out from the wreckage and the satellite was no more.

"Yes!" cried John. "Scratch one bad guy."

"The tracers work in space?" mused Ray. "That doesn't make a whole lot of sense. I guess the phosphorous in the round..."

Ray cut himself off as he engaged a satellite that briefly crossed behind them. A much less disruptive rumbling was heard from the rear of the ship. John began looping and banking randomly while trying to avoid the incoming fire.

"Four minutes to go," said Dana.

A much more comprehensible staccato of fire was heard as Richter began firing his fifty. A moment later Ari joined him. John continued to fire. Tracers poured out of the ship in a shower of light. Two more plasma bursts hit the ship. Ray said something but was drowned out by the forward cannon.

"What?" said John.

"I said try varying your speed as well as trajectory!"

"I know that, Ray! It's happening whether I want it to or not. Every time we get hit my speed jumps up slightly!"

"Seth must be shunting the excess energy wherever he can," said Dana. "I'll see if I can get him to bleed it off elsewhere."

"Why not shunt it into the energy dissipation field?" asked Christie.

Dana's response was lost in the din, and she repeated herself.

"I said it's worth a try!"

There was a vibration throughout the ship, and it's speed dropped by fifty percent.

"Whoa, what's going on?" yelled John.

Several plasma bursts impacted the ship. Richter and Ari's guns began rattling almost non-stop.

"I shunted all the excess power to the dissipation field, but now it's interfering with the sublight drive," said Dana.

"Fix it, quick!" yelled John, banking the ship sharply.

"John, you'd better get back up to speed," said Ari. "They're closing in too fast."

The ship jumped forward as Dana canceled her previous move.

"Energy absorption limit at twenty percent," said Christie.

"I can deal with the fluctuations in velocity just fine," said John, "let's not experiment with anything else during the middle of combat!"

"I'm getting a little seasick," said Ray. "This is a bit different than the sims."

"No shit. There's more feedback on the stick as well."

John continued to fly towards groups of satellites, destroying as many as he could before the incoming plasma became too heavy.

"Ray to the fifty gunners. Take it easy on your fire or you'll deplete your ammo before the time's up."

"Roger that," said Richter.

"Two minutes remaining," said Christie.

"Energy absorption?"

"Eighteen percent and falling."

"Good. I think..."

Three plasma bursts hit the ship. John let loose a string of invectives.

"What was that?" asked Byron.

Ray shook his head. "Ten of the satellites just fired simultaneously. They adjusted their fire based on our tracers and created a thick field of fire. They're getting smarter."

"Don't worry, this is all old hat for me," said John, wiping sweat away from his brow.

"Those tracers are becoming a liability," said Christie. "What's the point of having an invisibility field if they can just follow the tracers back to us?"

"We can't stop firing," said John through gritted teeth. "The only way we can clear enough maneuvering room is to destroy as many as we can."

"I can increase the energy absorption rate if I drop the invisibility function," said Dana.

More shots slammed into the ship.

"Fine, go for it," said John. "It's apparently useless right now anyway."

"One hundred rounds left and counting on the ventral gun," said Ari.

A satellite nearby fired five rounds very rapidly and exploded into white fire. Two of the shots hit the ship.

"What was that?" yelled John. "We didn't hit it."

"It looks like the satellite intentionally overloaded itself to increase its rate of fire," said Dana. "It sacrificed itself to increase its hit potential."

Ahead of him, John's view was filled with plasma fire. The color drained out of his face.

"Shit. Hold on!"

John throttled forward and pulled into a sharp about-face roll. Seth's inertial dampening abilities balked at the maneuver and the crew was squashed painfully into their seats. John felt himself blacking out before he pulled out of the roll.

"Ow," said Ray.

"I'm going to have to keep my speed up."

"One minute left!" said Christie.

"Scherer to Talvan, do you think you could hurry it up? Things are getting a little hot up here!"

"I can't increase the data flow with this type of connection. Once Seth's been upgraded, maybe..."

"Energy absorption limit at fifty-five percent," said Christie.

"We can't take too much more of this," said Ray.

John concentrated on his flying. He realized he was biting into his lower lip and drawing blood. His arms were getting tired, and on top of it all the forward cannon was getting low on ammo. Taking plasma hits was becoming the norm rather than the exception, despite John's best efforts. He felt his adrenaline rising and he felt his fear increasing.

"Not now," he whispered to himself, "you can worry about this later."

"Limit to seventy-five percent!" said Christie, her own fear evident in her voice.

A new noise began to fill the bridge. John realized a moment later that it was coming from the engine room. It didn't sound very reassuring.

"Damn it," he hissed, "I wish I could take this excess energy and shove it down their fucking throats!"

John punctuated this statement with a long string of fire from the forward cannon. Several of the satellites were destroyed. He felt a bit of confidence return at the sight.

"There are just too many of them," said Ray.

"Transfer complete!" cried Christie.

John sighed. "At last! Hold on everybody, we're getting the hell out of here!"

Pointing the nose of the ship away from the sun, John threw the throttle all the way forward with vigor. The ship lurched ahead violently, outrunning the remaining plasma bursts with ease. The planet disappeared from sight almost immediately.

"Repair program acknowledged," said Seth calmly. "Systems will be shut down during repair process."

"Just wait until we're safely away," John said.

"Systems shutdown initiated."

"No, no, WAIT!"

John brought the ship to a complete halt. He was the only one on the bridge who managed to stay in their seat during the rapid stop. The others swore and picked themselves up as the power went out. The sudden silence was bizarre after so much noise. John stood up slowly and gazed out of the window.

"We're dead in the water," he said.

## 7.

"All right, give it a try."

Ray's legs stuck out from underneath three large industrial batteries stacked in the corner of the engine room. Richter moved his flashlight from Ray's legs to a large electrical switch mounted on the wall. He threw the switch, and the lights came on dimly. Ray shimmied out and stood up, dusting himself off.

"The main connector had come loose," said Ray. "We should wrap the connection with duct tape to prevent it from happening again. I don't think the platform we installed these batteries on is particularly stable."

"It doesn't look like there's enough voltage to run everything," said Richter, looking around.

"We'll deactivate everything we don't need. That should help."

Richter turned off his flashlight. Ray exited the engine room into the hallway. Richter followed him.

"Ray to the bridge."

There was no reply. Richter grabbed a portable transceiver from his belt and spoke into it.

"Bridge, this is Richter, over."

"John here. I see you got auxiliary power back online."

"Yup. We're on our way back to you. Recommend we turn off all unnecessary devices to boost the power levels, over."

"There's enough power to reboot our systems," said Ari's voice from the network room.

"Well, we don't want a sudden loss of power again," said John. "Better do as Richter suggests."

"Roger."

"Roger, out." said Richter, returning the radio to his belt.

The two men entered the forward cargo bay and climbed the stairs to level one.

"You did well today," said Ray.

"Thanks. Manning the fifties isn't easy."

"Ari said she got at least forty of those satellites."

"Not bad. And you?"

"I wasn't counting. The situation made targeting with the aft cannon practically impossible. When targets did appear, they were only in my sights for a second or two. I got more than half a dozen or so. You?"

"I wasn't counting."

Ray and Richter arrived on the bridge. John and Dana were there. John had his radio in his hand. Ari's voice came through on it.

"How'bout now?" she asked.

"I got something," John replied.

A small dialog box had appeared on Christie's monitor. Dana read it aloud.

"Time remaining until main systems reactivation: Three hours forty-nine minutes."

"I hope that's accurate," said John. "We're sitting ducks out here."

"You're the one who killed the engines just before Seth went down," said Dana.

"I already told you I thought that barreling through unknown space at top speed with no control was a bad idea."

"At least we'd be safe from pursuit."

"How could we barrel anywhere with no power to the engines?" asked Richter.

"Inertia. Without a gravitational force acting on us, we would have continued in a straight line at the speed we were going. Since I had us maxed out, that means 167,000 miles per second straight into who knows what."

"I gotcha."

The rest of the monitors lit up. They were displaying their usual readouts, except without the benefit of

Seth's added information. John began turning off the monitors, leaving only two on, his own and the gunnery station.

"The good news," said John, "is that our weapons systems only relied on Seth for advanced targeting. We can still use the guns, we just won't have the HUD telling us how far to lead the targets."

"Better than nothing," said Richter grimly. "If we can get enough power to them."

John spoke into his radio. "Ari, the systems here are back online. Turn off everything you don't need before you leave, and do the same in the conference room. Then go to your quarters and make sure all of your electrical devices are shut off. I want the rest of the crew to do the same."

"Roger that," came the reply.

Christie entered the bridge via the hallway door.

"How did it go?" John asked her.

"Fine, for what it's worth. I couldn't see any damage with my own eyes. I couldn't check any crew quarters other than my own, though."

"Right. Each of you, go to your quarters and shut off your electrical devices. Also check for cracks in the windows and bulkheads. Report anything unusual when you return."

Ray, Richter, Christie, and Dana acknowledged the order.

"What about your quarters?" asked Ray.

"You check them, I'm staying here. My keycode is my birthday in six digit format."

"Okay."

The others exited, leaving John alone in the darkness. He stared glumly at the progress bar displayed on his monitor.

"Come on, Seth. Tell me you're all right."

Four hours later, John was up to his elbows in the forward cannon and covered in grime. He and Ray were doing their best to clean the weapon, a difficult task considering John didn't want to fully disassemble the receiver. John wiped his brow with a rag.

"Thank God the plumbing still works," he said. "I'm going to need one serious shower after this job."

"I hope Richter and Ari are having an easier time with the rear cannon," said Ray, scrubbing a barrel through the breach.

"They should, you only fired a few hundred rounds."

"We haven't even started on the fifties. This is worse than a day out with my Garand."

The pair worked in silence for a moment.

"What do you think about the mission?" asked Ray.

"I don't know. Somehow I doubt the defense satellites are the worst of our problems. We were outgunned that time, but ten thousand ships would have been overkill. I think our problem extends far beyond what we've seen already."

"Do you think the Zendreen have a space fleet?"

"Yes."

"Let's hope they don't find us before Seth comes around."

"I hope we weren't just betrayed. How are we supposed to know that this Professor Talvan uploaded a repair program? If he was actually Zendreen, it could have shut Seth down for good."

"Why bother when you've got a thousand satellites available to blast us?"

"Maybe he knew we were capable of repelling them, if only for a while. Think about it. It was a nice trap, if that's the case."

"Well, if that's the case we're completely screwed, so I hope you're wrong."

"Oh, I'm just expounding doom. I don't really think that's what happened."

"Talvan said it's been ten years since the invasion."

"Yeah, he did."

"So why did it take Seth ten years to get to Earth, and us only five weeks to get back?"

"Maybe Seth was visiting other potential recruits first. Nobody said he came straight to Earth."

"Good point."

John stopped working and stared out of the gun port. "I wonder if all of our efforts have been wasted. What good can one ship do, as Talvan said?"

The lights in the room suddenly came up to full. Christie's voice came through on John's radio.

"John, I think Seth is back online."

"Seth, are you there?"

"..."

"Seth, this is John, can you hear me?"

"...I'm..."

"Yes?"

"I'm so fucking embarrassed," said Seth.

Two minutes later, John had the crew gathered on the bridge.

"Where's Tycho?" John asked.

"Oh, I put him in my room," said Christie. "Do you want him or Friday to be here now?"

"I no longer require a medium to communicate," said Seth.

"Good," said John. "Seth, give us a self-status report."

"You want the short version or the long version?"

"How 'bout the efficient version?"

"My memory and systems have been almost completely restored by Talvan's update program. If you look at your screens you will see much more information about myself and our surroundings is now available. Most notable is the astronomical information I've been relaying to Christie's station, and the communications information I've been sending to Dana's station. Scans are still passive right now; active scanning systems will be restored shortly. Still, I might as well have been running around with a paper bag over my head, in comparison."

"You're acting really different," said Christie.

"Are you kidding? I guess I should take that as a compliment, seeing as how I was acting like a complete idiot before."

"I mean you've got a lot more personality to you now."

"Seth, is Talvan telling the truth about the invasion of Umber?"

"Of course he is. The Zendreen must be repelled and Umber liberated. That is why I was sent to you."

"Can we still accomplish that mission?"

"Not unless we go back to Earth and construct a lot more ships. There are other things to worry about first, however."

"Like the fact that we can't use the superspace drive for five weeks," said Ari.

"That's not entirely true. The information that I gave you while damaged was correct in that the stardrive must recharge for five weeks to make it back to Earth. What I couldn't remember is that the engines recharge at a constant rate. Since it has been four hours and fifteen minutes since the stardrive was deactivated, we now have four hours and fifteen minutes worth of faster-than-light speed available."

"You mean we could have brought Byron back to Earth after we found him?" asked Christie in astonishment.

"It would have delayed our departure by four hours, but yes. Sorry for the confusion."

"Son of a bitch."

"Regardless of that fact, it will still take five weeks before we can return to Earth. For now, the first thing we need to do is upgrade my weapons. I'm impressed that your Earth weapons were so effective against the Zendreen defense satellites, but they'll be useless against their fighters and destroyers."

"Can't we just hide out somewhere for five weeks?" asked Dana.

"The defense satellites were able to track the ship. The engines produce a unique energy signature, but that signature is normally buffered by the invisibility shield. The shield was dropped momentarily during the fight, so we have to assume it's been recorded. However, the satellites had little problem tracking us before then, so the only conclusion is that Zendreen technology can track us anyway, if only at short range. We have to bet on them finding us, it's the only safe choice. They may only find us with a ship or two at first, so if we need to fight we might survive, if we upgrade my weaponry. Plus you can never count out the interference of pirates."

John raised his eyebrows. "Pirates? Are pirates really a problem?"

"They're a big problem, yes. Only a fool would venture out into the Tarantula Nebula without some serious firepower."

"Well, you sold me. How do we upgrade the weapons? Into what are we upgrading them?

"Umberian Mark Seven Energy Rails will be installed fore and aft. There isn't enough room for both the GAU 8 and the rear Mark Seven, so the rear thirty will have to go. Umberian Mark Three Laser Emitter banks will be installed on the port and starboard hulls at level two. We might as well keep the fifty caliber weapons, they're not in the way."

"I assume you're going to need additional resources to synthesize these weapons?"

"You assume correctly. The raw materials are available on any inhabited planet except for one substance. It is called Talvanium 115 and it is only found on three known worlds. Umber, Residere Alpha, and Earth."

"Earth! Is that why you went to Earth?"

"Yes. A Z'Sorth trader passed by your planet about two hundred years ago and scanned it for resources. Talvanium was one of the things he found. At the time it had yet to be discovered here, and since there was nothing more than a pre-spacefaring society on Earth, he left you alone. He arrived at Umber to trade his wares and he sold the government the information he'd collected. Umber was the only one ever to receive the information, so we alone knew about the presence of Talvanium on Earth. It was of little consequence, however, since it was hardly worth a ten year wait for something which was readily available in our own system."

"A ten year wait? But the voyage takes five weeks."

"You're forgetting about time dilation," said Christie.

"Shit! You're right!"

"Five years have passed since you left Earth," said Seth.

"You really can't go home again," said Richter.

"Wait a minute," said Dana to Christie, "I thought that the superluminal drive operated independently of the standard model."

Christie shrugged. "Our faster-than-light speed is a result of the way the drive works, but I guess it doesn't negate the effects of time dilation on us. It might be interesting to apply the Lorentz equations to find out if the effects are lessened, but I don't know if they would even work once you start trying to increase $c$ beyond $c$. It's called $c$ because the speed of light is constant and forms the basis for the variables. The equations might fall apart if you change that."

"Okay" said John. "We all knew something like this would happen. Let's just be glad the effects of time dilation aren't worse. We may yet see our families again, even if it is more than a decade later. Seth, you were telling us about where to get Talvanium."

"Talvanium hasn't been mined on Umber for years, and returning there is obviously out of the question anyway. Our only choice is Residere Beta."

"I thought you said the stuff was on Alpha," said Richter.

"It is mined on Alpha, but sold on Beta. Residere Beta is the main cultural and business center of the quadrant. That honor used to be Umber's, but there were... complications... about forty years ago."

"So we head to Residere Beta and procure some Talvanium," said John. "Sounds like a plan."

"How far is the Residere system from Umber?" asked Christie.

"Three point six light years."

"What's our travel time?"

"I can't give you our top speed right now," replied Seth. "Thirty-five hours, twenty-four minutes is the best I can do."

John nodded. "Fine. Let's use the time well. To begin with, everyone get acquainted with Seth's upgrades at your stations."

"It's been a long day," said Ray, "and we haven't slept in almost twenty-four hours. We could all use a solid twelve hours of rest."

"Damn, you're right. Get some rest, then. I'll stay here and take first watch. Who wants to relieve me in four hours?"

"I'll do it," said Richter.

"Good, thanks."

The crew exchanged salutations to each other and filed out of the room. John sighed and leaned back in his chair.

"Nice work on the ship design," said Seth.

"Thanks. It's not very sexy, but it does the job."

"If I hadn't been damaged I would have been able to supply an Umberian design."

"Really? I suppose that would have saved me a lot of trouble."

"True. I like this one, though. It's... quaint."

"For an AI, you sure do have a lot of opinions."

"Would you like me to act like I don't?"

"Well, abstract or irrelevant interjections should be reserved for times like this. When we're busy with something, keep it all business."

"You don't have to tell me that."

"Okay, I'm only making sure."

"It's simply nice to be whole again. Relatively speaking, of course."

John yawned. He began to think about following his own advice, despite his desire to continue his conversation with Seth.

"Tell me about the Zendreen."

"The Zendreen are an insectoid race from near a star Christie would call Sanduleak in the Tarantula Nebula. That star went nova about 160,000 years ago. It has long been believed that the nova destabilized the Zendreen's own star, accelerating it's lifespan and dooming their home planet to eventual destruction. Some believe that the Zendreen devoted their entire society to getting off of their home planet for ten thousand years, and that their social structure came about because of that goal. Umberian astronomers have long wished to be able to travel into Zendreen space to get a closer look at the remains of Sanduleak, which collapsed into a neutron star and has been generating fascinating x-ray and gamma radiation..."

"Stick to the Zendreen themselves."

"The Zendreen have a very structured society and prefer to live underground, just near the surface. They have been known to live above ground if the situation requires. Using the best example I can extract from your memories, they resemble carpenter ants. They walk erect on their hind legs and stand an average of five feet tall. The soldiers of the race have their abdominal sections surgically altered to reduce the size. This makes it easier for them to move around, as normally they're forced to drag it behind them. They also show a remarkable ability to evolve over relatively short periods. In the five hundred years since they invented space flight, for example, an entire genus has evolved specifically for communicating with humanoid species. This particular genus has a green shell instead of black, and a mouth more appropriate toward forming humanoid verbal communications. There are other varieties, but we'll be unlikely to encounter them. Incidentally, chances are pretty good they don't know about Earth yet, and you sure don't want them to find it. If they try to colonize Earth the resulting warfare would likely kill most of the population. From what I've seen of your military might, however, you could probably repel such an invasion. Certainly if your technology continues to improve at the rate it has been for the last two hundred years, anyway."

"But Umber couldn't produce enough defensive armament in time?"

"That's right. Umber had a non-aggression pact with all of the humanoid and feline races, signed to ease inter-solar politics rather than actually prevent war. The dominant political party insisted that military production not exceed two percent of the gross planetary product, as a show of good faith for the pact. The Zendreen hadn't ventured into the nebula before, so we had no reason to suspect an invasion."

"Feline races?"

"The Kau'Rii and Rakhar. The former are smaller in stature, and nimble. They concentrate their livelihoods on commerce, trade, exploration and adventure. The Rakhar are larger and more militaristic. They act primarily as mercenaries or police for hire around here, but they have a strict code of ethics that limits what jobs they can accept. Both are generally trustworthy. You'll see plenty of both on Residere Beta."

"Interesting. What else is out there?"

"The Residerians are humanoid. They rarely venture off of their native moon of Beta. They are skilled agrarians and produce the highest quality foodstuffs in the quadrant. They've evolved in such a way that they're naturally big and slow, you might call them "obese" if you compared them to humans. They also tend to communicate slowly, but don't let that fool you. They're very intelligent."

"Roger."

"The only other race we'll encounter are the Z'Sorth. They're large reptilians that you would say resemble lizards. They're considered odd by the other races but they get along all right. They tend towards merchandising and inventing. If they were at all interested in spaceflight and weapons technology they would be a real rival to Umber, but they seem more interested in inventing better construction materials and techniques, land-based vehicles, and power generation techniques."

"What about the Umberians themselves?"

"Could you be more specific?"

"What sort of race are you?"

"Humanoid, didn't I mention that already?"

"Maybe, I don't know. I'm exhausted. Is Professor Talvan safe?"

"Yes, the underground movement is well concealed within the occupation society. It's unlikely that Talvan will be discovered as the source of the radio transmissions. He will have no doubt already moved the transmitter to another location, just to be safe."

"I don't envy his situation. He's been waiting for ten years and finally gets news of our return, only to have the briefest of conversations with us and then get plunged back into the dark."

"He knows we're doing our best. If he feels like it's appropriate, he may encourage more active resistance. He mentioned a genetically-engineered virus; if he succeeds at that he may just need for us to destroy the Zendreen fleet..."

Seth stopped himself. John was asleep.

---

It was an old stone bakery, high on a hill, surrounded by squat, round trees that flowered for two months out of the year. The master baker lived in second floor room on the east side, the first place the sun hit every morning. It was the tradition on Umber not to begin work until sunrise each day, and most businesses held to the practice if possible. The master baker's schedule wasn't governed by the sun anymore, however. Not since the Zendreen came.

In order to facilitate the occupation-ordered closing of the three other bakeries in the region, this one was forced to run a round-the-clock operation. This barely produced enough bread for demand, and that was the point. So effective was the continuous obsession with providing enough food for the community that the Zendreen needed little active enforcement of their laws. The laws were few, and they all boiled down to two things. One, don't fight back, and two, don't get in our way.

Because resources were so scant, the personal freedoms of the occupied Umberians were actually quite numerous. What good was the freedom to move about unimpeded if you spent your entire waking day baking, building, trading, farming, or anything else required to keep your community working? What good was the freedom of assembly if all you could talk about was how much things sucked? Without another freedom, that of arms, even the most seditious talk was not seen as a threat.

Even though the Zendreen occupation outnumbered the natives a hundred to one, their preference to live underground made the practical ratio one to three. While three Umberians could soundly whip one unarmed Zendra in an otherwise fair fight, the naturally secreted poison present in a thin sheen on their carapaces would ensure a slow and painful death for all but the healthiest Umberian. Dying was a bad idea for the Umberians. Females could only give birth once every ten years, and for half of them the task would leave them barren for the next time around. The population of Umber had never exceeded sixty million; losing anyone in combat would require a long wait to replace them.

The underground movement, therefore, was not about forming a plan to overthrow the Zendreen invaders by force. Instead, scientists had been working in secret to genetically engineer a virus that would be deadly to the Zendreen and harmless to the native population. Not having been particularly interested in bioengineering before, progress had been slow. They were making progress, however, and appropriately enough the lead scientist in the area of artificial intelligence was the one closest to success. What Talvan wasn't telling the others was that he would never finish without access to better equipment.

In the basement of the bakery, behind a false wall concealed by sacks of flour, Professor Talvan had just enough room to keep up a basic laboratory. His assistant, a much younger man by the name of Stackpole, often reminded Talvan that they'd have more room to work if he'd get rid of that damn old radio transceiver. Talvan had insisted they keep it, although his reasons for doing so were not often discussed. Everyone else had long since given up on Seth.

It was Stackpole who entered the room that afternoon six hours after they'd spoken with Seth and the crew of the Reckless Faith.

"Hey, doc, I don't think they're coming back today," he said.

"I don't suppose they will," Talvan replied.

"There's a good chance we lost contact with them because..."

"I know that. I prefer not to consider that possibility."

"Where do you think they went? What are they going to do now?"

"I don't know. I don't know what parts of Seth's memory were compromised, so I don't know how capable that ship actually was. If the repair program worked, Seth will insist on building more ships. If I know Seth he'll simply propose returning to UAS 371 to find the resources. Since that will mean another ten year wait on our end, I sincerely hope the crew comes up with a better solution."

"I think they called their planet Earth."

"Ha! I guess people don't have much of an imagination no matter where in the universe they're from. Still, it sounds better than UAS 371."

"Uh huh. I wonder if they had a name for Umber."

"Good thing I have the genetic research to occupy me, because if that is the last we hear from them for ten years I would have surely gone insane."

"Most people think you already have."

"Most people aren't that far from the truth."

## 8.

It was late in the afternoon, less than five minutes before the Faith's arrival at Residere. The ship had long since entered the solar system and had already passed several outer planets. Ari was on the bridge alone, seated in John's chair with her feet propped up on the console. Over the past three days the crew had been chatting it up with Seth, who seemed willing enough to participate. Despite his recent restoration, he still suffered from being away from home for a decade, a problem that John had brought up once before. Ari had jokingly suggested that perhaps Residere had been taken over by the Zendreen as well, but this had mortified the others. Seth had reassured them that with the Rakhar's protection, the Zendreen would never dare.

Something about Seth's new attitude didn't sit well with Ari. She may have simply found him a little to annoying for her tastes. As it was, she wasn't the sort to engage in idle conversation with him like the others did. At least he didn't speak unless spoken to, important operational updates notwithstanding. After the others had decided to take a quick meal down in the galley, Ari had the bridge to herself. She was glad for things to be quiet on the bridge again. While the fight with the satellites had thrilled her, it had also exhausted her in a way the sims never did. In fact, Richter had been the only one who neither waxed enthusiastic about the encounter nor seemed depleted by it. Ari felt a twinge of pleasure at the thought of Richter and she as partners on the fifties. There was slightly more than a sense of camaraderie in the emotion, but Ari quickly dismissed the rest. It was a departure from her normal response to such a desire. The confines of the ship and her devotion to the same were the only things stopping her.

The vista of the Tarantula Nebula hadn't changed much during their voyage. Ari had to remind herself how slow they were moving in comparison to interstellar distances. While staring at the seemingly motionless panorama, Ari had a flash of insight.

"Hey Seth, you around?"

"Of course."

"You know how you can project the exterior of the spacecraft onto the walls of the zero-g room?"

"Yeah..."

"How do you do that?"

"It's simple, really. Whatever light is hitting the exterior of the ship is allowed to pass through the hull to the other side. Your eyes pick it up as they normally would, except without the freezing suffocating deadly results."

Ari smiled. "Okay, then. Can you be more specific about how you let the light pass through the solid walls?"

"The molecules of the metal are temporarily moved aside for each photon, which are moved inside in waves. It's a one-way motion, so the pressurized room remains that way. It's like, what's the word... osmosis."

"Hmm. Interesting, but not exactly what I'm looking for."

"What did you have in mind?"

"I'm thinking it would be nice if we could have some sort of heads-up display on the main windscreen, whatever you call it, like we do on the gunnery monitors."

"But the window is just transparent polyaluminum, not a computer monitor."

"How would you do it, if it were up to you?"

"It would have been up to me if my memory had been intact. The entire bridge window would have been a monitor."

"I see."

"If we were planetside near sufficient resources, I could upgrade the window to such a thing. Doing so in space would depressurize the bridge."

"Yeah, no shit. Put it on our to-do list, then."

"Right. We're thirty seconds from arrival, by the way."

"Oh, already? Ari to the crew, we're seconds away from arrival. Please report to the bridge."

Ari stood up and moved to her normal station. Moments later, John, Ray, Richter and Christie showed up and took their places.

"I'm surprised you weren't up here already," said Ari.

"We were playing poker," said John. "We lost track of time."

"Gaming this early?"

"Our schedule has been messed up the past couple of days."

"Where's Dana?" Ray asked.

"John to Dana, what's your status?"

"I'm up," Dana replied over the comm, "I'll be right there."

"And Byron?" asked Ray, shrugging.

John gestured dismissively, and said, "Down in the hold. If he doesn't want to be here for this that's his choice."

"Approaching Residere," said Seth.

"Now that everyone's awake, I wanted to show you the data Seth has on the solar system," said Christie. "I'm sending a graphic to each of your stations."

On each monitor, an three-dimensional image depicting the solar system appeared. One planet was visible; it had a dark, rocky surface with a few bright spots here and there.

"I'm going to do a fly-by of each planet and describe what we know about it," said Christie. "This is Vastus, the furthest planet out. It is 41 astronomical units from the Residere sun. There are a few self-contained colonies. There is no atmosphere. It's about 0.38 percent the size of Earth."

The image zoomed ahead. A bright star in the center of the screen became slightly more distinct. The next planet appeared. It was a reddish-brown gas giant.

"This is Distare. It's 19.6 AU from the sun. It has one moon with one mining colony. The moon is about 0.25 percent the size of Earth."

The next planet flew into view. It was a larger gas giant, milky-white with streaks of green.

"Next up is Macer. It's 9.1 AU from the sun. There are two colonized moons in orbit. Macer Alpha has undergone extensive atmospheric processing, but is still barely habitable outside of contained structures. Macer Beta consists entirely of pressurized structures."

The display moved on to the next planet. It was a large, spectacular gas giant. The upper and lower hemispheres were bright brown and orange, and there was a large band of jade green around the equatorial region. A small ring of asteroids encircled the planet.

"This is Residere. It is five AU from the sun. There are three moons. The first is Alpha, which orbits inside the ring. It is habitable due to atmospheric processing. The next is Beta, the only planet in the system where life originated naturally."

Christie brought Residere Beta into view on the screen. It was a beautiful green-blue planet with small continents, much more reminiscent of Earth than Umber.

"Beta is 0.89 percent the size of Earth. Life can exist on Beta naturally due to the unusually high heat levels generated by the gas giant. In fact, there is so much heat being generated that the ambient temperature in space up to and slightly beyond Beta is 50K."

"Practically beach weather," said Ray.

"That, combined with what solar radiation actually arrives on Beta when it isn't eclipsed by Residere. Next up is Residere Delta, another atmosphere processed world.

Apparently this is one the most successfully processed moons and is almost as hospitable as Beta."

Christie zoomed the display to the first planet in the system.

"This is Velleitas, some 0.84 AU from the sun. It is 1.05 percent the size of Earth, but has no atmosphere. There are extensive mining operations in progress there. Last but not least is the Residere sun itself. It's a G-type main sequence star, similar to our own, with a surface temperature of about six thousand K. It has a luminosity of 1.4, which is another reason why Residere Beta is so pleasant so far out. And that's it."

"What are the white dots we've been seeing?" asked John.

"Those are artificial satellites and space stations. As you probably noticed there are more around Residere than anywhere else."

"I'll say. And here's the real thing, folks."

John pointed ahead. Residere was growing in size. Before too long the three moons could be seen. There was also one space station immediately evident, which resembled a giant stapler stuck rearward into an ice cream sandwich.

"Set a course for Beta, Christie," said John.

"Do we need to ask for permission to enter orbit or land?" asked Christie.

"Ships can come and go as they please, so far as they don't break any laws," said Seth. "Most space stations or planetside way stations charge money to land. Some planetside stations are surrounded by plenty of free parking areas, however, if you don't mind a little walking to get there."

"Where are we going to get the Talvanium?" asked Ray.

"The most popular marketplace station on Beta is called Gleeful Complexium. If there are any tiered landing bays available, they'll be free for our use. Don't let the name fool you, however. Wander too far away from the main concourse and you'll be anything but gleeful. Empire Security, run by the Rahkar, isn't very interested in providing law and order outside of the normal storefronts. And no offense, but you lot don't look too intimidating compared to some of the other races."

John looked concerned. "Are we going to be able to carry any weapons off the ship down there?"

"Once we connect with their automated information service, we'll be able to review the rules. The last list of rules that was available to my database did not restrict defensive weapons. That meant sidearms were okay but long arms were not."

Beta was the main feature in their view. John throttled down.

"Hold on, I have to concentrate on getting into orbit."

"Are our sidearms going to be effective against folks down there?" asked Richter.

"All of the species you might encounter are flesh and blood, just like you. Some of them are tougher than others, to be sure, but against unarmored opponents your firearms should be sufficient. That is, as long as the data you gave me for use in the sims was accurate."

"It was precise. And if they are armored?"

"Who knows?"

A hint of a smile crossed Richter's face. "Great, thanks."

"There sure is a lot of junk up here," said John.

"I recommend we deactivate our invisibility field," said Seth. "Empire Security will need to track our descent if we get permission to use one of the tiers."

"Okay, bring it down."

Two large squares of bright flashing lights appeared directly in front of the ship.

"What the hell?" yelled John, shielding his eyes.

"Don't worry, they're just advertisements. Hold on, I'll modulate the energy dissipation field to reduce the ambient light."

The light from the squares was reduced significantly. The crew could now recognize words and pictures. They were holographic projections, floating a few hundred feet off the bow.

"What's up with those?" asked Ari.

"Automated advertisements. They were activated when the emitter satellites pinged infrared radar off of our hull. That's why they didn't activate until I dropped the invisibility field."

"What are they for?"

"The one on the left is for Kau'Rii-made fish flavored soup stock. The one on the right is for a Residerian agricultural concern encouraging us to buy locally-grown foods during our visit."

"Well they're fucking annoying," said John, "Can you get rid of them?"

"Not without destroying the satellites. Solar law says they must move out of our way within twenty seconds."

Moments later, the signs parted and faded from view.

"Damn pop-up ads," growled Richter.

"I'd get used to them," said Seth, "They're quite normal in orbit for inhabited planets."

John rolled his eyes. "Fine. Connect us to the Complexium and find out if there are any tiers available."

"Okay. Stand by please."

Dana arrived on the bridge. She sat at her station and began to monitor the communication network.

"Did I miss anything?" she said.

"You'll figure it out," said Ray.

"I just thought of something," said Ari. "If Seth's translating all these alien languages for us on board, who's going to do it for us once we get down there?"

"I considered that," replied John. "Seth will arrange an open channel between the ship and our personal radios. As long as we're standing close enough to someone to have a conversation, the microphones will pick it up and transmit it back to the ship. Seth will translate for us and send the audio back into our earpieces. It will take a little getting used to, but it should be adequate for our needs."

"But we only have five radios."

"And we can't use the same trick to translate our own words back to the alien," said Christie.

John shrugged. "I don't know what we're going to do about that. The word Talvanium was the same in both languages, I noticed. So proper nouns hold true. I guess we'll just have to muddle through."

"I've contacted the Complexium," said Seth. "There is a tier available for us that I reserved."

"Good. Seth, is there one language that is spoken universally for trade in this solar system?"

"No. Most people wear a small translator device in one ear. They should be easy to find. Buy some of those and we can do away with our initial arrangement."

"I keep meaning to bring this up," began Ray, "how exactly are we supposed to buy Talvanium, translators or anything else? Somehow I don't think they take American Express."

"I hadn't thought of that."

Ray looked around the bridge and was met with blank stares from the others.

"Take an inventory list with us," said John. "Maybe there's something aboard we can trade."

"Let's sell Byron!" said Ari enthusiastically.

"If only."

"I've got the coordinates for landing," said Christie.

"All right, I'm bringing her in. Hold on, folks, I've never done an atmosphere re-entry before."

94

John rolled the ship into the plane of the moon, and banked downward at a shallow angle. More holographic ads floated by. Slight vibrations began to shake the ship, and bright streaks of orange flame licked around the bow as the air friction built up. The long since absent sound of air flowing past the ship was once again heard, in stark contrast to the many weeks of silence to which the crew had become accustomed. Soon the stars were lost in a great deep blue sky, and ground features became more distinct.

"Hold her steady," said Seth. "Expect variances in the upper jet streams."

"No problem," said John.

The continent they'd been above was replaced by ocean, which reflected the sky into sharp turquoise blue.

"I'm showing signals from other ships," said Christie. "I'm putting them up on your display. It looks like they're maintaining at least a half a mile distance between each other on approach to the Complex. I suggest you do the same."

"Roger that."

Another land mass came into view. John brought the craft down to a thousand feet. A seaside village passed below, briefly showing a combination of old construction and new technologies.

"There it is," said John, pointing ahead.

A small city lay ahead, a single massive structure dominating the horizon. As they approached it the true scale became apparent.

"Is that the Complexium?" asked Ray.

"Yes," replied Seth.

John throttled down in preparation to land. It was circular in construction and stood more than a hundred stories tall. The walls were bright metal and reflected the sunlight brilliantly. The diameter easily surpassed five hundred meters. On each level, landing tiers stood outside the walls. Most of them were occupied by ships. As they drew closer figures could be seen milling about a few of the ships. Some were obviously meant for sub-atmospheric flight only, but a few of the larger ones were quite clearly interstellar craft. John noted that the Faith was absolutely unique in appearance, at least in comparison to what he could see.

Their reserved parking space was on the second level. John became anxious as he attempted to bring the craft in. The Complexium loomed above them as John approached the landing platform. There was ample room for the Faith on the platform, but John took his time. He made many adjustments and brought the ship in at a snail's pace.

"Aren't you being a bit over-cautious?" asked Ari.

"This isn't as easy as it looks," began John, "and I don't think it would look too well as a first impression to collide with the building."

When the ship was ten feet above the platform and John was satisfied with his position, he stabilized the ship and powered down the engines.

"Anti-grav dynamics are solid," said Seth. "You may deploy the ramp when ready."

The crew looked out onto the platform. A narrow causeway crossed into an open archway into the structure. No-one had come to greet them.

"I guess we're all set," said John. "Ray, Ari, Richter, you're with me. Grab your gear and meet me in the cargo bay. Christie, Dana, you stay with the ship. Report any problems immediately. Close the ramp after we've departed. And keep Byron out of trouble."

"Understood," said Christie. "Good luck."

Five minutes later, John, Ray, Ari and Richter had gathered in the cargo bay. The air on Beta smelled fresh and sweet, despite the twinge of fossil fuel and cooked food that also met their senses. John had considered requesting the use of uniforms for the mission, but decided against it. It may have been unrealistic to expect them to blend in to the population of the Complexium, but uniforms reduced that likelihood even further. The team was dressed in their normal Earth clothing. Richter was the only one not wearing jeans, a t-shirt, and a jacket. His black BDU pants and cargo vest may have stood out on Earth somewhat; here it was anybody's guess. Ari noticed he had donned his Kevlar body armor, as well as his black ball cap that had become so ubiquitous for him in the sims. It made her smile. He was also wearing sunglasses, which John thought looked too aggressive but kept the sentiment to himself.

"Seth tells me the laws here haven't changed significantly in ten years, so our sidearms are coming with us. I guess I don't need to tell you to keep them concealed," said John. "Primary commo channel is three, backup is five. Everybody do a radio check."

The radio check took a few moments. John double-checked his Beretta and holstered it.

"Good to go," said Richter, doing the same with his sidearm.

"I never got around to asking you," began Ray, "what kind of pistol do you carry?"

Richter looked at Ray with a raised eyebrow. "You don't recognize the model? This 1911A1, forty-five caliber, made in Israel. I bought it on a whim in 2002. I used to carry a Glock 21 but doing a magazine dump with a light-weight forty-five was unpleasant, in my opinion. This pistol weighs more, so there's less felt recoil.

"Well, I wasn't sure. How many rounds can you carry?"

"Eight rounds in the mag, one in the chamber. I have five magazines so that's 41 rounds total. What's ironic about the whole thing is that Major Devonai and I were headed to the range for some target practice when he decided to intercept the DIA's mission. When we realized what was about to happen in back of the motel, I just grabbed my favorite rifle. Our truck was filled with lots more stuff that would have come in pretty handy out here. Not the least of which would have been more ammo for my rifle and more mags for my sidearm. We just didn't have enough time to gear up."

Ray smiled. "We have plenty of forty-five. Unfortunately nobody else brought any five-five-six so I guess you'll just have to be conservative with your rifle."

"Ammo conservation shouldn't even be an issue today," said John. "If we get into the shit we'll be bugging out to the Faith. We don't want to make our first impression here as a bunch of cowboys. Okay? Remember the old saying: be polite, be professional, but have a plan to kill everyone you meet. We don't know how rapidly our welcome could go sour. Watch your back but try and look casual. Seth says we'll probably be ignored; I'm not so sure about that. If we need to split up it will be Ray and I, and Ari and Chance. If that happens I want commo checks every ten minutes. If we lose contact with each other, or if anything goes wrong, or you don't feel comfortable about anything, get back to the ship and wait for further instructions."

The others nodded in agreement.

"Good. Let's go."

## 9.

Entering into Gleeful Complexium resulted in a barrage of sights, sounds, and smells, chaotic and overwhelming. The four members of the Faith's ground team stood in awe of it all at the archway leading back to the landing platform. There was too much to comprehend all at once, and the humans found their brains struggling to catch up.

The Complexium was arranged like a parking garage in that the main concourse was one continuous ramp, twisting gradually around the outside edge up one hundred stories. The center of the structure was an open atrium all the way up to the sky, and with the concourse and shops occupying a hundred meters on either side, the atrium measured three hundred meters across. The open space was filled with holographic advertisements, floating security cameras, and food vendors on anti-gravity platforms. Some of the platforms were shaped like pulling boats.

The adjacent three levels of the Complexium were obviously food vendors as well. There was a thick, heady smell in the air, and after weeks of mostly military rations it was a wonderful sensation. The concourse was clean and bright. There was very little trash on the floor, and it didn't appear to have been there for long.

The most shocking element of the concourse to the humans was the variety of alien species milling about. John easily recognized the Kau'Rii, Rakhar, Z'Sorth and Residerians from Seth's description. It was bizarre to see them in person, however, and despite all logic against it the team members found themselves afraid of the strange creatures. The locals, for their part, were all quite interested in either procuring food or consuming it, and so far not so much as a passing glance had been thrown their way.

John snapped out of his own haze of wonder and keyed his microphone.

"Dana, this is John for a radio check, over."

"Lima charlie, how are things going, over."

"You've got to see it to believe it, Dana. We're beginning our walk-around. Out."

"Holy shit, this place is huge," said Ari.

"Where do we start?" said Ray.

"Seth said that since the Talvanium is mined by Z'Sorth on Alpha," began John, "we should look for Z'Sorth shops. Anybody see an info directory or anything?"

A three-foot tall Kau'Rii with amber fur noticed the team. It was carrying a platter of something and walked rapidly over to them. It smiled, apparently, and offered the platter to them. There were meat chunks on toothpicks on the plate. The Kau'Rii said something. John recognized the same language he likened to cats arguing over tea. A split second later, Seth provided a translation in the same voice. It sounded odd, but it was comprehensible.

"Would you like to try a free sample?"

"Sure," said Ari, reaching for one.

"Hold it," said John, "you don't know if it's safe."

"Come on, it smells wonderful. We're going to have to start eating locally at some point, you know."

"Yeah, but our bodies may not have a good reaction to any alien bacteria."

"Hey, we thoroughly cook our food at the Cuisine Claw," the Kau'Rii said haughtily.

"You can understand us?" asked John.

"Well, duh. Everybody has to have a translator unit around here. Only the college educated types can speak more than two languages."

Ari took one of the samples and ate it, tossing the toothpick onto the floor.

"Well?" asked Ray.

"It tastes almost, but not quite, entirely unlike chicken," Ari replied. "But it's exquisite."

"Too bad we don't have any cash," said Richter.

The Kau'Rii's ears folded back slightly. "Aw, tom. I thought I had a sale."

"Sorry, kid," John said. "We're here to trade goods for credits and supplies. If we make some money maybe we'll come back for dinner."

"Okay!"

"Listen, we could use your help. We've never been here before and we're looking for a few specific things."

"Like what?"

"Do you know where we can trade for Talvanium?"

"Never heard of it."

"It's an ore. Do you know of any Z'Sorth shops that sell ores or metals?"

"Geez, swing a Rakhar and you'll hit one. There have to be two dozen Z'Sorth shops at Gleeful."

"Where's the nearest one?"

"Level ten, I think. Or was it twelve? I'm not sure."

"Where can we find out?"

"There are information kiosks every five levels, or you can talk to any Rakhar wearing blue uniforms. They're with Empire Security."

"Thank you."

"No problem."

The Kau'Rii walked off in search of better business. Richter moved over to John.

"Hey, Scherer," he said in low tones.

"Yeah?"

"Talvanium is used to make weapons. We don't know if it has any other applications. It's probably not such a great idea to go broadcasting our desire to buy some all over the complex."

"Shit, you're right. I guess that rules out asking security about it. Let's go down to level one and find the information booth."

"I think those are elevators over there," said Ray, pointing.

"Let's go. Keep your eyes open."

The others nodded and John led the way. The elevators were on the outside wall of the concourse. When the doors opened, the team could see that they were in fact facing the outside of the building. The areas that the shops occupied jutted out on either side, but the walls receded at an angle of thirty degrees and afforded a good view of the landscape. The four team members moved into the elevator.

"I bet this place has a booming vacation industry," said Ray.

The elevator buttons, arranged on a pressure-sensitive touchpad, had unknown markings on them.

"Seth, this is John. Can you tell me which button to press for level one?"

"I can't see what you're seeing, John," came the reply.

"I meant can you describe the Residerian symbol for 'one,' please?"

"It's a single vertical line."

"Figures."

John pressed the touchpad, and the elevator began to move. The doors opened smoothly and the team exited. The first level was a shipping and receiving area. One side was dominated by loading docks, and larger cargo elevators lined most of the remaining wall space. An anti-gravity skid began to move a large piece of equipment upward through the atrium. A food vendor barely got out of the way in time, and swore at the other craft in an unknown language. There was only one kiosk on this level; the space was wide open save for the activity. There was quite a bit going on, but the atrium above seemed to absorb some of the noise.

"Over there," said John.

The team moved carefully through the shifting sea of commerce over to the information booth. A large touchscreen displayed a great deal of information, all of which was foreign to the human observers. John stroked his chin as he considered the screen.

"Look, this might help," said Ari.

One of the many choices on the screen was a pictogram of a mouth with lines around it. John shrugged and pressed the button. A small holographic image of a smiling Residerian appeared in front of them. There was a slight delay as Seth translated the message.

"Welcome to Gleeful Complexium, the largest and most diverse marketplace in the system! How may I help you today?"

"We're looking for Z'Sorth shops that sell metals and ores," John said.

"Entering new language into database," the hologram said. "Please state in one word the name for your language."

"English."

"English language registered. Thank you. There are twenty-two Z'Sorth shops in Gleeful Complexium. All of the shops list ores and metals in their inventories. Please be more specific."

"We're looking for ores and metals that are available only on Residere Alpha."

"Careful," muttered Richter.

"There are six shops that meet your criteria," the hologram said. "They are located on levels ten, fifteen, thirty-seven, fifty-one, ninety-seven and one hundred."

The touchscreen changed to a cross-sectional image of the complex, highlighting the six shops.

"This could take some time," said Ari.

"Is there anything else I can help you with?" asked the hologram.

"No, thanks," said John.

Richter motioned for the team to move away from the kiosk. When they'd done so, he spoke.

"That information may not be helpful to us. If Talvanium is a restricted material, then I doubt the holographic cherub there would know who had it."

"Well, at least we have somewhere to start now," Ray replied.

"All right," said John. "I don't want to spend too much time dicking around. The longer we're here, the greater chance someone will start asking unwanted questions. Let's split up into two groups. Ari, Chance, you start on level one hundred and check the upper three shops. Ray and I will start on level ten and work up. Remember to stay in contact every ten minutes. If you get a good lead we'll discuss it in person."

"Understood," said Richter.

"Ari, you've got a pretty good idea of what's aboard, right?"

"I wrote the manifest you're holding, didn't I?" Ari replied.

"Right. Start off any conversation by offering things we can trade. You know what we can spare. Offer a couple of our spare rifles if nothing else interests them. Then bring up the Talvanium."

"I can handle the dealing," said Richter.

"Good. Let's get moving. And Ari, go easy on the free samples."

A few minutes later, John and Ray had arrived on level ten. There was considerably less foot traffic on the concourse than either the food court or the loading docks. Music from a stringed instrument played at a low volume.

"I can't put my finger on exactly why," began Ray, "but it feels really good to be back on solid ground again."

"Really? I hadn't noticed. I'm glad to breathe fresh air again. Seth's filtering system is pretty good but this planet smells just wonderful."

John and Ray passed by two Rakhar from Empire Security. They were wearing bulky blue uniforms with unknown markings, and carried some sort of large, capable-looking sidearms. The guards watched the humans walk past them without a word. When they were out of earshot, Ray leaned over to John.

"I can't believe they didn't say anything," he said. "We don't look like anything else in this place."

"There must be some other humanoid race that more closely resembles us," John said. "Either that or they really don't care about newcomers."

"I hope you're right, and they're not just waiting for a better chance to... hey look at that."

Ray stopped walking and motioned towards a shop. It was a brightly lit Kau'Rii store and it was filled with many different kinds of bottles.

"Looks like a liquor store," said John.

"I bet it's just that. I also bet they'd be quite interested in some unique alcohol, something we happen to have plenty of."

"You're going to have a hard time convincing anybody on the Faith to give up their liquor."

"Do you include yourself in that assessment?"

"No, I don't. I've been going easy on the Elijah Craig, you know. I still have five bottles left."

"What does the manifest say?"

John pulled a piece of paper out of his pocket and reviewed it. "There's the Elijah Craig, four bottles of Laphroaig, three bottles of Bombay Sapphire, one bottle of Barbancourt, and six bottles of Ipswich Ale."

"We're out of wine?"

"Completely. It was the first thing to go."

"I also find it hard to believe that Ari drank eleven bottles of Barbancourt in five weeks."

"Me, too, now that you mention it," said John, and keyed his microphone. "Ari, this is John, over."

"Yo," Ari's voice said.

"Hey, how come there's only one bottle of Barbancourt listed on the manifest?"

"Because I only have two bottles left, and I'm not giving up both of them."

"How in the hell did you drink ten bottles of Barbancourt in five weeks? You would have been drunk twenty-four seven!"

"Fuck you I drank them all! I lost two of them to Christie and two of them to Richter."

"All right, I'm sorry. Forget it. John out."

Ray laughed. "You torqued her up on that one."

"Like she needs much help. Come on, let's find out what this guy thinks of our wares."

John and Ray walked into the shop and were greeted by a five foot tall Kau'Rii with gray and white fur.

"Well, if it isn't two of those genmod Residerians I've heard so much about. Those procedures must be getting quite popular."

"I beg your pardon, sir," began John, "but we're not Residerians. We're humans from Earth."

"You have nothing to fear, I think we're gonna like it here," said Ray.

"This is my friend T-Bone Burnett," said John. "Also known as Ray Bailey. I'm John Scherer."

"A pleasure, sirs. I am Graheim."

"Pardon my ignorance, Mister Graheim, but is this a liquor store?"

"It ain't mother's milk."

John smiled. "We have some alcohol from Earth that we'd like to sell. Are you interested?"

"Alcohol from a planet nobody's ever heard of? I suppose I can sell it to some of those rich snobbish Rakhar playboys who like to vacation here. They're always buying the most expensive stuff whether it's worth it or not. If it's really good stuff I may even be able to get the locals to buy it."

"Well, we could certainly let you sample it. We have four varieties of grain alcohol, but very limited quantities."

"Bring it in, and I'll try some. No guarantees I'll buy it, of course."

"Great! We'll be back in ten minutes."

John and Ray exited the store and headed for the elevators. John spoke into his radio.

"Ari, this is John, over."

"Go ahead."

"We're going to try and sell some of our alcohol. We've got a shop that may be interested. Ray and I are returning to the ship to get it. How are things on your end?"

"The store on the hundredth floor was closed for renovations. We're on our way to the next one."

"Okay, thanks. John to the Faith."

"Christie here," said Christie's voice.

"Have you been monitoring our communications?"

"Of course."

"Gather up all the liquor in the galley, not counting the beer, and put it in a box. Include one each of the bottles that are already open. Meet us on the ramp; we'll be back momentarily. Over."

"Roger, out."

"John, there's something I've been hesitant to bring up with you," said Ray.

"What can't you talk to me about, Ray? We're best friends."

John hit the button for the elevator. Seconds later the doors opened and the men stepped inside.

"Ten years will have passed on Earth by the time we get back. Christie observed earlier that she doubts any Earth government will agree to the mission parameters. How do we know that going back to Earth won't be a big waste of time?"

"I guess we don't. I simply don't know of any other options right now."

"I think we should try and find another way to help the Umberians. I'm not looking forward to another five weeks in superspace, and I'm sure the Umberians would rather not wait another ten years to be liberated."

"I agree. Seth's answer to the issue shows the emotional detachment of a computer. There may be other options, but like he said the most important thing right now is to upgrade our armaments. We still have five weeks to explore the nebula and collect information. Hopefully a better alternative will be found."

Arriving at the second level, John and Ray exited the elevator. They headed towards the archway to the landing platform.

"I can't help but wonder if liberating Umber is completely beyond our ability."

John looked at Ray. "It's our duty to do everything we can towards that end."

"I know that. I just hope the rest of the crew agrees."

"It's a little late to back out now."

The men arrived back at the Faith. Christie, Dana and Byron were standing at the bottom of the ramp. Byron was holding a cardboard box.

"Hello," said John.

"Next time you guys stay here," said Dana. "This is too boring."

"I'm sorry about that, but we need you here."

"We've been watching video broadcasts over the galactic network," said Christie. "Would you believe all of the news channels are by subscription only?"

"That doesn't surprise me," said Ray, taking the box from Byron.

"Hopefully this will give us the cash we need," said John.

"Christie and Dana don't like being on the ship alone with me," said Byron. "I think it would be better if I came with you."

"Tough shit, kid," said Ray.

"The ladies can handle you, Byron," said John, "and we don't need an untrained puppy following us around."

"Kiss my ass," said Byron.

"We'll be back soon. Remember to keep your eyes peeled out here."

"No problem," said Dana.

"Good luck with the booze," said Christie.

John waved goodbye and turned around. He and Ray headed back across the causeway.

"I can't believe Byron is still being such a jerk," said Ray.

"Isn't that box heavy?" asked John. "Do you want some help with it?"

"I'm fine."

Back on the food court levels, things had calmed down quite a bit. A few Residerians with softly humming vacuum cleaners were tidying up.

"Byron is Byron. I was rude to him, and he was rude back. It's no big deal. I don't have a problem with him standing up for himself in matters of pride."

"Yeah, except it seems like everything is a matter of pride for him. Maybe we should leave him here. Give him some of our credits and let him fend for himself."

"What, seriously?" asked John, pressing the key for the elevator.

"I don't know. This is the first chance we have to get rid of him short of homicide, right? We don't owe him anything."

"It's not like you to propose such a thing, Ray."

"Perhaps not, but I'm concerned about Christie in particular. Byron is right about one thing: neither she nor Dana likes being around him."

The elevator arrived and the men boarded.

"Byron is still responsible for betraying us to the CIA. Nothing he's done since then has convinced me to forgive that. Now that you mention it, leaving him here might be a good idea. However, without knowing how much money we'll get, if any, and not knowing how Byron could survive here alone, I'm not sure leaving him here is any better than killing him. From an ethical standpoint, I mean."

Ray shrugged. "In a place this big, I bet we could find him a job."

"Maybe."

The elevator came to a stop, and the men exited onto the tenth level. John stepped a little closer to Ray.

"Continue looking straight ahead," said John quietly. "I think we're being followed."

"Empire?"

"No, but they are Rakhar. Two of them. They were on this level as we were coming out of the liquor store. I saw them in the food court. And they just stepped off of another elevator on this level."

"Roger that."

"Let's get this deal done. If they're still on us when we're finished we'll have to decide on a course of action."

"Okay."

John and Ray entered the liquor store. Graheim greeted them. Ray put the box on the counter and began removing bottles from it.

"I've got four glasses here," he said.

John nodded. "Good. Let's start with the most mild and move up from there. This first bottle is of Bombay Sapphire. It's gin, distilled from grain and infused with a berry called Juniper."

Ray poured a small amount into the first glass. Graheim pointed a hand-held device at it and pressed a few buttons.

"Ethyl alcohol, plant extracts, water," Graheim said, "nothing dangerous. Looks good."

Graheim smelled the gin, then sipped it.

"It's usually served ice cold," said Ray.

"Hmm. Not my thing, really, but I have several customers who like this sort of thing. Next?"

Ray poured some Barbancourt into the next glass.

"This is Barbancourt, a kind of rum. It's distilled from molasses and sugar cane."

Graheim pointed his device at the glass before tasting it.

"Mmm, delicious. I like it."

Ray poured the bourbon next.

"This is Elijah Craig, a bourbon. It's distilled from corn and filtered through charcoal."

"Not bad, not bad. Smoky, I like it."

"Last up is Laphroaig, a scotch. It's distilled from grain."

Ray offered Graheim a small amount. He sniffed the glass and turned up his nose at it.

"My goodness, that's strong stuff isn't it?"

Graheim pointed his device at the scotch.

"It's perfectly safe," said John.

Graheim tentatively tasted the Laphroaig. He was visibly displeased.

"I hate it, but I know some people will buy it."

"Good. What can you offer us for the lot?"

"I'll say eighteen credits each. I'll take the open bottle of rum for myself, if you don't mind. That's 252 credits total."

"Excuse me for a moment, Mister Graheim. John to Seth, over."

"Seth here."

"Seth, can you tell me how much a credit is worth in terms of dollars?"

"I don't know."

"Well, what's the average price of a pound of bread?"

"A pound?" asked Graheim.

"One and a half credits," said Seth.

"How easy is it to get bread around here?" asked John.

"What do you mean?" asked Graheim, "bread is as common as air."

"So if a loaf of bread is one dollar on Earth, then the exchange rate would be one to one point five?" asked Ray.

"I guess so," said John.

"That means our booze is worth what?"

"One hundred sixty-six dollars," said Seth.

John smiled. "Thanks, Seth, John out. Mister Graheim, you've got yourself a deal."

In a small Z'Sorth shop on the 97th floor, Ari and Richter were getting nowhere with the clerk. The shop was dark, cluttered, and smelled like drying mud. It looked like a combination of a used computer component store and a construction site. The lizard-like Z'Sorth stood six feet tall when he was standing up, which wasn't often. He moved constantly but slowly around the store, hunched over at the neck and speaking in a low, hissing lilt. It took the Z'Sorth a long time to put together a complete sentence. Even Seth was having a hard time translating everything efficiently as Ari and Richter spoke with him. Ari hoped this wasn't typical of the Z'Sorth.

"Okay," Ari was saying, "if you don't have any Glowing Soft Metal, where can we get it?"

"Umberians most wanted the Glowing," said the clerk. "When they were covered in captivity, not much market for it. Sold off what I had, I did. No more imported from Alpha."

"Are you saying there's no Talvanium, I mean Glowing Soft Metal on Beta at all?"

"Mmm, yes."

"Shit!"

"Many kinds of shit, all in air-tight sanitary containers. Sale on most."

"Damn," said Richter.

"Can we get the Glowing on Alpha?" asked Ari.

"The Glowing is extra from mining Hard Red Metal, Crumbly Black Ore, and even Soft Yellow Money Metal. The Glowing Soft Metal is far and wide under the earth on Alpha. Mostly we tossed in corner before Umberians asked. Now we do the same."

"Do you know how much it's going to cost us?"

"Last I knew, it was two credits for one fist."

"Useful information," said Richter.

"One fist!" said the clerk, moving behind the counter.

"Okay, we get it," said Ari. "Thank you. Richter, I think we're done here."

"I agree. Let's report back to the others."

"One fist!" said the clerk, throwing something at Richter.

Richter caught it before it hit him in the shoulder. It was a square block of what looked like lead, not surprisingly about the size of a fist.

"It's about five pounds," he said.

"Now we just need to know how much Seth needs to create..."

"Ahem," said Richter, cutting off Ari.

"The things we need."

"Precisely. Thank you, sir," said Richter, tossing the metal back to the clerk. "We're all set."

The clerk shrugged and hissed as Ari and Richter exited the shop.

"You want to call it in, or should I?" asked Ari.

Richter's eyes narrowed. "Don't look behind us, but I think we're being followed."

"What, really?"

"Uh huh. There are two Rakhar wearing black about fifteen meters behind us. The same guys were down on the loading dock, and then up on level one hundred. The third time is the charm. Keep walking until we find a friendly-looking shop. We'll go inside and call the others."

"Right."

"This one will do."

Richter and Ari entered what was clearly a cafe, with at least twenty large vats of hot liquids and a selection of baked goods. A fat, bored Rakhar sat behind the counter. Three lavishly clothed and bejeweled Kau'Rii sat at a table and spoke in animated tones. The humans pretended to look interested in the drinks. After a few moments, Richter leaned over to Ari.

"You see them?" he whispered.

"No, I still haven't," Ari replied.

Richter grunted, and keyed his radio. "Scherer, this is Richter, over."

"This is John, go ahead, over."

"We need to get together right now and discuss the situation. Have you accomplished your objectives?"

"Roger that. What's your situation, over?"

"Negative on the objective. We may also have a Tango problem, over."

"Roger that, Richter. Tango problem may not be yours alone. Get back to the ship ASAP, we'll discuss the situation there. Over."

"Roger, out."

"Do you think it's wise to lead these guys back to our ship?" asked Ari.

"They probably already know where we're parked. I hope they're meant to observe only. We can't do a whole hell of a lot to evade them, anyway. Let's just get back to the ship and watch our backs."

"Okay."

Richter led the way out of the cafe. He looked in both directions down the concourse, and took a left.

"No, it's this way," Ari said, turning right.

A massive Rakhar with ice blue eyes stepped out of nowhere and grabbed Ari by the neck, lifting her off of her feet with one muscular arm.

"Where do you think you're going, little lady?" he growled.

"Hrk..." Ari said, instinctively grabbing the Rakhar's arms.

Richter was about to turn around when a second Rakhar stepped out in front of him, a large pistol of some sort in his hand. Richter drew his sidearm with a crisp snap and centered the sights on the Rakhar's head.

"Put her down!" he yelled. "Drop your weapon!"

Ari reached for her pistol. The Rakhar seized her right wrist with his free hand. Ari reached forward with her left hand and grabbed the handle of a large, curved combat knife in the Rakhar's belt. She tugged at it, and it came free along with the scabbard. Ari felt her world fading away as she flipped off the scabbard and made a vicious slash across the Rakhar's midsection. He dropped her immediately, stared in wonder as the contents of his abdominal cavity spilled out onto the shiny metal floor, and collapsed forward. Ari stepped out of the way, flicking the blood from the blade. Richter immediately fired two rapid shots at the second Rakhar, both of which struck his forehead. He, too, fell to the deck. Ari reached down, picked up the scabbard, and sheathed the knife. Richter ran to her side.

"Are you all right?" he said.

Ari coughed and spat on the ground. "Why don't you ask him?"

The last of the sentient beings that were running away from the action disappeared, and the first of those running towards it appeared. In this case it was two more black-clad Rakhar. They raised their pistols and the air was split with bright blue flashes of energy, each shot generating a terrific electric crack like thunder. Ari and Richter dove into the cafe. A emergency klaxon began to sound throughout the complex.

"Scherer, this is Richter, enemy contact on level ninety-seven! Rakhar in black clothing armed with energy pistols! We're coming back to the ship, double-time, over!"

"Roger that, Richter," John replied over the commo, "We've got our own problems down here."

Richter fired a few times down the concourse, striking and felling one of the Rakhar. Ari fired her own pistol twice at a floating security camera, destroying it.

"Leapfrog it," Richter said. "Moving!"

"Move!" replied Ari.

Richter fired twice more and sprinted down the concourse away from the remaining Rakhar. Ari took his place and fired rapidly, forcing the Rakhar back behind the cover of a support pillar. She glanced behind her and saw Richter waiting at the next storefront.

"Moving," Ari yelled.

"Move!"

Ari ran towards Richter. Two Rakhar in Empire Security uniforms appeared from the elevators that they'd been heading for. Ari ducked into the store, noticing that it sold various kinds of electronic equipment. Richter fired at the enemy as he ran for a better position, striking one in the arm.

"Reloading," he said, doing so.

"Security guards are between us and the elevators," Ari said.

One of the guards spoke into a small hand-held device. His voice boomed through the public address system.

"Attention, mercenaries! This is an unauthorized corral. Cease fire immediately!"

The Rakhar in black responded by shooting the guard's partner in the chest.

"What the frell are you doing?" the guard shrieked, drawing his pistol and diving for cover.

The mercenary and the guard began exchanging fire in earnest.

"What now?" yelled Ari over the noise.

"There!" said Richter, pointing to a small food platform parked on the edge of the concourse.

"That's not exactly better cover."

"Just keep that guard's head down and move when I tell you to!"

Richter fired several times at the mercenary, forcing him behind cover. Ari did the same towards the guard.

"Now!" Richter yelled.

Ari and Richter sprinted across the concourse to the platform. They both dove over the counter, knocking over several plastic bottles of condiments and a stack of baked goods. A bewildered Residerian peered at them from within the kitchen compartment.

"Get us down to level two," Richter ordered.

"No way."

"Three more mercs just showed up!" Ari said.

"Get us out of here now or we're all fragged," Richter said.

The mercenaries shifted their attention to the food vendor. Energy shots tore into the platform. Ari returned fire briefly.

"Reloading," she said.

Richter turned and fired towards the mercs as Ari reloaded. The Residerian crawled towards an instrument panel at the stern of the platform.

"Hurry up, damn it," Richter growled.

The Residerian pressed a few keys and the platform shuddered. Ari was about to resume firing when the platform lurched to starboard. Richter ducked down and grabbed a bolted-down chair; Ari stumbled backward until she hit the rail. Richter's eyes grew wide as she failed to regain her balance and tumbled over the side.

"Ari!" he screamed, diving towards the edge.

Ari's left hand was still visible clutching the rail. Richter stood up and grabbed her arm.

"Sorry about that," the Residerian said, and righted the platform.

Ari was attempting to holster her Glock. Richter took a deep breath and braced himself as she did so. When her right hand was free, she brought it up. Richter grabbed both hands securely. Energy bolts zipped by, and one of them grazed his right shoulder. It felt as if a barbed bullwhip had just torn a strip of flesh away.

"God damn it, you fucking idiot, get us moving now!"

The shopkeeper pressed another key, and the platform began moving downward. The sudden movement aided Richter in hauling Ari aboard.

"Thanks, Chance," she said.

The platform had descended one level when Rakhar faces appeared looking down at them. Moments later they were replaced with energy shots. Ari drew her pistol and began returning fire. Richter glanced at his wound before joining Ari in her effort. Two shots later the slide locked back on his pistol.

"Third mag," he said, reloading with perfect speed.

"I thought John told you to conserve your ammo," Ari said.

"Like you are! Hey mister, do you think we could hurry this up a bit?"

The Residerian replied by getting his head perforated by enemy fire.

"Guess not," Ari said.

"Scherer, this is Richter! We're coming in hot! What's your status, over?"

Above at the open top of the atrium, something large and mechanical appeared. Ari noticed it as she fired the final round from her second magazine.

"What the hell is that?" she murmured.

"Scherer, this is Richter, come in, over!"

"Richter, I think we've got additional problems..."

A voice came over the commo. "Richter, this is Scherer. We're a little busy right now. Just get back to the ship as soon as you can. Out."

"Reloading," said Ray.

John pounded his fist against the door to an elevator. Seth translated a cheerful computerized voice that responded to his violence.

"This lift has been locked down for a security alert. Have a nice day."

"Shit!"

John looked down at his Beretta and realized it was empty. He ejected the magazine, put it in his pocket, and retrieved a fresh one.

"Targets?" he asked.

"The one guy ran into Graheim's shop," Ray replied. "The two we hit are still down."

"This whole place is basically one giant corkscrew," said John, slapping the mag home. "If we keep running counter-clockwise we'll eventually get to level two."

"I don't see another option."

"Cover each other until we've gone around the curve of the concourse. Then go flat out."

"Roger that."

"Choose your shots carefully. I don't want to mess up Graheim's shop."

Ray smiled. "Yes. His progeny will rue your name for countless generations."

"Moving!"

"Move!"

John glanced to his left and then sprinted to his right. He ran to the next storefront and turned to cover Ray.

"Moving!" Ray said.

"Move!"

Ray ran towards John. The Rakhar poked his head out from the shop. John fired past Ray, missing the mercenary and destroying a bottle on a shelf.

"Damn it!"

"You're supposed to wait until I'm past you!" Ray said angrily.

"What, you don't trust my marksmanship all of a sudden?"

"Just be careful."

"Moving!"

"Go."

John ran for it. Ray watched the front of the liquor store. The mercenary did not appear, but Ray distinctly heard him yell something.

"Seth, did you catch that?" Ray asked.

"He said, 'where the hell is my backup,' I think," Seth replied.

Beyond Graheim's store, Ray noticed two security guards. They had their weapons drawn but were not moving.

"Come on, Ray!" John cried.

Ray turned and ran to John. He motioned for him to follow, and the two men broke into a run down the concourse.

"The security guards are just standing there."

"They must have gotten orders not to engage."

"Maybe because they're Rakhar, too?"

"Maybe because they're in on it! Let's just be glad they're not shooting at us as well."

The pair ran as fast as they could. The subtle downward slope of the concourse helped somewhat, but it became immediately evident that five weeks of smoking, drinking, and sitting around aboard the Faith had compromised their stamina. As much as the simulations seemed like a good workout, they were in fact useless in that regard.

"I shoulda designed a jogging track into the ship," John said, panting.

Blue streaks of light shot down from above within the atrium. John and Ray glanced upward and noticed a slowly descending vending platform in combat with unseen forces high above. Another object floated at the top of the atrium, silhouetted against the blue sky. It was too far away to identify.

"Richter, this is Scherer! Is that you coming down on the platform?"

"Roger that!" came the reply. "We can't figure out how to get it to go faster, over!"

"Do your best, we'll meet you at the ship."

"Roger, out."

"I wish we could help them out, they're getting pounded," said Ray.

"If the atrium was just a bit bigger we could get the Faith in here," replied John.

"From the incoming fire it looks like the enemy is coming down the corkscrew, too."

"Yeah, but it also looks like the platform is gaining distance on them. Christie, this is Scherer, come in!"

"I'm here," said Christie over the commo.

"We're going to need your help soon. Grab Dana and get to the armory. Get our rifles and bring them to the entrance to the causeway. Sling my rifle over your shoulder and have Dana do the same with Richter's M4. You and Dana hold onto Ray and Ari's rifles until we get there. If you catch fire, return it. Are you up to it?"

"No problem. We'll be ready."

"Good, Scherer out."

John and Ray continued to run. The concourse was virtually deserted now, and most shopkeepers had closed metal shutters over their entrances. Cover was scarce and John became concerned about getting cut off. So far, it didn't look like they were being followed. John's lungs screamed at him and his legs felt like lead. Ray seemed to be having an equally difficult time.

"Come on, buddy, we can make it," he said.

Ray wheezed. "Don't worry about me."

"Three levels to go."

Down a side hallway, John noticed two more security guards. Again, they did not engage them.

"Security is still ignoring us," John said.

"Fine, let them."

John's whole world became about running. The initial adrenaline rush of combat was starting to wear off, and his efforts were becoming agony. He cursed himself for smoking so much, even if he didn't inhale the pipe smoke, and he cursed himself for drinking so much, even if it was far less than some aboard. He began to doubt whether or not he could make it to the ship without a break. He began to doubt whether or not he was cut out for the mission. Too much more of this, and his lack of physical fitness would kill him. What could he do? The greatest distance available for sprinting on board the Faith was about twenty yards. All he could figure now was that he had to do something. This bullshit was unacceptable. John vocalized his pain and frustration.

"Fuck it all!"

"There are the girls!" Ray exclaimed.

John looked up, and to his surprise they were almost to the causeway. Christie and Dana stood at the ready, rifles in hand. Christie waved to them. John and Ray managed one more burst of speed and reached them.

"Are you all right?" Christie asked.

"Give me... here..." John gasped.

Christie juggled her rifle around as she unlimbered John's Garand from her shoulder. John accepted the weapon and went down to one knee. Ray took his M1A from Dana as well as Richter's rifle.

"Get back to the ship and fire her up," panted Ray.

"No problem," said Dana.

"I'll cover you until you catch your breath," said Christie.

"Watch the left side," Ray said. "I'm going to check on the action."

Ray tucked the stock of his rifle into his shoulder and ran across the causeway. He looked up. The platform was a few levels above. At least one person aboard was still returning fire upward. Ray looked down onto the shipping and receiving area. A loading dock had just opened across the atrium. Four Rakhar dressed in black came through.

"Shit," muttered Ray. "Three hundred yards..."

Ray dropped to one knee and adjusted his rear sight. He took aim on the lead Rakhar as the group got their bearings. They were distracted by the fight going on overhead. Ray breathed carefully and slowly pulled back on the trigger. His shot caught the Rakhar in the torso, and he collapsed. Ray fired more quickly at the others as they began running, without any apparent results. The group got to the bottom of the corkscrew and had begun ascending when they fixed Ray's position. Ray retreated back to the entrance to the causeway as blue energy bolts began streaking in his direction.

"We've got company coming in from the right," he cried.

"High or low?" asked John.

"High," replied Ray.

John remained where he was as Ray joined him at the corner. Ray stood up and aimed over John's head down the concourse.

"Keep your sights on the left side, Christie," said John.

"Okay."

The Rakhar appeared from the right, kicking over tables from the food court to use as cover. John and Ray began firing on them.

"Move a few feet back, Christie," began Ray, "you're in enfilade."

Christie did so. A moment later the vending platform appeared a few dozen meters to the left. As soon as it was reasonable to do so, Ari and Richter jumped onto the concourse. A vicious slew of energy bolts rained down from above, much brighter and larger than they'd seen before. The platform exploded into orange flame and crashed into the bottom of the atrium. John and Ray fired rapidly at the Rakhar to cover Ari and Richter as they ran towards the archway. Richter's right arm was slick with blood and his pistol was empty. Ari looked no worse for wear.

"Reloading," said John, ducking back to do so.

"Christie, cover right," said Ray.

Ray ceased firing and grabbed Richter's rifle from his shoulder. Richter accepted it immediately upon arrival, closing the slide on his pistol and jamming it into his holster.

"Are you all right?" asked John, slapping another clip into his rifle.

"Piece of cake," said Ari. "We should try something harder next time."

"I'll take low," Richter said to Ray.

Ray nodded. Richter took John's position, and the two of them leaned around the corner to resume firing.

"Christie, Ari, fall back to the ship," said John, moving to cover the left side.

"What, and let you have all the fun?" asked Ari.

"Just fucking go!"

Ari looked insulted. Christie grasped her arm and all but dragged her toward the ship.

"Get ready to do a banana peel," said Richter.

The other men nodded in the affirmative. The mechanical object that had been hovering far above appeared in the atrium on their level. It was a humanoid-shaped battle robot, bristling with weaponry. A single pilot was visible through a cockpit hatch in the torso. The laser Gatling-style cannon that made up the bot's right arm was obviously responsible for the destruction of the vending platform. As the men gaped in awe at the device, it pointed the cannon toward them.

"Holy shit!" yelled John. "Run for it!"

John and Ray turned and ran as fast as they could. Richter hesitated just long enough to grab a cylindrical object from his belt and drop it in place before joining the others. Three seconds later the object began belching thick gray smoke. Random fire began zipping down the causeway.

"Go, go, go!" Richter yelled ahead, swapping magazines.

The archway was just about a foot too short for the bot to fit through, so Richter was surprised to glance behind him and see the bot emerge through the smoke, bent over at the waist. It straightened up and brought the cannon to bear. Ray and John arrived at the ramp of the Faith, and turned to see the same.

"Somebody get on the ventral fifty!" John screamed into his radio.

Richter stopped running. He turned around and flipped the selector switch on his rifle to full auto. With unerring precision he emptied his magazine into the cockpit of the bot. The rounds barely scratched the cover. Richter smiled, rolled his eyes, and sprinted for the ramp.

"Come on, Richter!" Ray yelled.

The bot began firing the cannon at the Faith. A cascade of energy bolts collided with the hull. The metal seemed to ripple like water as Seth attempted to shunt the energy away. Richter reached the ramp at the same time as the ventral fifty came to life, spinning up with a whine. John hit the button to close the ramp as the fifty began firing, and the three men clamped their hands over their ears. About a hundred fifty caliber rounds caromed off of the bot, forcing it to stop firing. When the fifty stopped, there was no appreciable damage.

"Everybody's aboard!" yelled John, running up the stairs to the bridge. "Get us the hell out of here!"

The ship lifted off from the landing platform. The bot began firing again. Whomever was piloting the Faith swung her around to port. The forward thirty millimeter cannon spun up, and the resulting two second burst reduced the battle bot to scrap metal. John arrived on the bridge to find Dana in the pilot's seat. She spun down the thirty as she guided the ship upward into the sky.

"I never did care much for mechs," she said.

## 10.

Fernwyn Rylie was pissed. She had just finished a double shift on Beta Station and had flown all but ten minutes back to her apartment on the surface when the call came in. She was flying right by Gleeful Complexium, so she had little excuse to pass the buck.

Fernwyn sighed and pressed a few keys. Her onboard computer communicated with the Complexium and gained permission to land. She reminded herself that this could be an opportunity to ingratiate herself to her superiors, despite how tired she felt or how much she'd rather simply fall into bed. Her computer beeped at her, and a graphic of which landing platform to use appeared on her screen. As she rounded the complex, the graphic became redundant. The wreckage of something was smoking on the causeway to the noted platform.

Guiding her twin-seat fighter craft down, Fernwyn tried to identify the wreckage. As she grew closer she realized it was a combsuit. Only another combsuit or ship-mounted weapons could do that much damage to one. Fernwyn's adrenaline spiked. This was definitely worth checking out. She sent a signal back to the Solar Police Force network to let them know she was on the scene. On the platform, a Rakhar with Empire Security waved her down. Fernwyn stabilized her anti-grav system and waited until her landing gear contacted the platform. Pulling back on the engagement lever, she shut down the engine and opened the cockpit cover.

"That was fast," said the Rakhar, a rare jet-black variety.

Fernwyn jumped to the deck. "I was in the neighborhood. Officer Rylie of the SPF. What the hell happened here?"

"What are you, an Umberian? No, you can't be."

"I'm a Residerian, not that it's relevant."

"Oh, you must be one of those genmods."

"Tell me what you've got, sergeant."

"Sergeant Nathalier, Rylie. Thanks for coming by so quickly. This was a real screwfest. Rakhar mercenaries from the Black Crest guild tried to grab what they thought were Umberians. We thought they were Umberians, too, but the empirical evidence doesn't bear that out. Their ship had an Umberian energy signature, but it didn't look like any Umberian ship we've ever seen. We have a new guy working the flight control, so he didn't know to red-flag the ship before it landed."

"He must be pretty green. So to what empirical evidence are you referring?"

"Come see for yourself."

The guard led Fernwyn a few meters down the causeway, and pointed at the deck.

"What the... cartridge casings?"

"Uh huh."

Fernwyn bent down and picked up one of the bottle-necked shells.

"Who the hell is still using projectile weapons?"

"These guys. We don't know where they're from, but they registered a new language with our central database. They called it 'English.'"

"Never heard of it. Well, projectile weapons or not, I'm guessing they fought off the mercs."

"Yeah, and they wrecked half the complex while they were at it. I have a lot of respect for most mercs, but these guys were just plain reckless. They even shot and wounded one of our guards!"

"You know Rakhar mercs, they think they're above the law. Not this time, though, if I have anything to say about it."

"You've got your work cut out for you, officer. The guilds can lean pretty heavily on people."

"I used to be in the UMG. I know how to deal with them."

"You were in the UMG and now you're in the SPF? Your genmod must have been quite successful."

"Perhaps, but you don't succeed in those organizations by physical ability alone."

"I suppose not," said Nathalier, smirking.

"What's the casualty report?"

"Five mercs were killed and three wounded. Two civilians were killed and ten wounded, the latter mostly when a mobile vendor took a dive into the shipping/receiving level. One merc was operating that combsuit when the Umberian ship, or whatever it was, blasted the hell out of it."

"And the ship itself?"

"We lost it from tracking shortly after it took off."

"You did?" Fernwyn raised her eyebrows. "That sounds like a pirate move."

"Yeah. That would also explain why non-Umberians are running around in an Umberian ship, an apparently heavily modified Umberian ship at that."

"God damned pirates. I hope I'm wrong about that."

The guard suddenly yelled at two of his compatriots further down the causeway. "Get that fire out already! What the hell are you doing?"

"The extinguisher ran out, Nat," came the reply.

"Well, get another one! Aren't you capable of operating without leadership for one damn minute?"

Fernwyn smiled, and asked, "So were there any mercenary survivors?"

"Oh, sorry, yeah. They're being held. I'm sure as soon as word comes down from on high they'll be released. You'll be lucky if you get a class D misdemeanor to stick, then."

"I really hate the politics of this job."

"Ha! Try Rakhar politics on for size."

The whine of a Z'Sorth-manufactured atmospheric engine wafted down from the sky. Fernwyn turned to see a marked SPF transport come into view. It landed on the next platform over.

"I've got to go give my report to my pals over there," said Fernwyn.

Nathalier nodded. "I'll come with you."

Together, the two headed past the combsuit wreckage and down the causeway. Through the archway, many more cartridge cases could be seen littered about. Shopkeepers on the concourse were beginning to reopen, and a few custodians tidied up. Smoke was rising from the level below and billowed upward into the atrium.

"Looks like it was quite a fight," said Fernwyn. "I'm surprised only one of your men was injured."

"The strangers weren't firing at us. When the overzealous merc shot our guy, we were given orders to stand down and observe only. Rakhar or no Rakhar, I would have rather lit them up. This kind of crap shouldn't fly around here."

"It shouldn't fly anywhere."

Fernwyn and Nathalier arrived at the next archway. Two Kau'Rii and one Rakhar in SPF uniforms greeted them. Fernwyn took a few moments to relay the situation to the Kau'Rii lieutenant who was now in charge. He identified himself as Durring, and he had streaks of gray through his brown fur. Fernwyn thought he looked like he should have made captain by now.

"All very mysterious," Durring said. "Let's have a chat with the mercs before their guild representatives show up."

"The security office is on level fifty," Nathalier replied.

The sergeant motioned towards the nearest elevator and the group began walking. Fernwyn's exhaustion had begun to return, to her annoyance. Showing weakness in front of her peers would be disastrous.

"You must be familiar with this place, Rylie," said Durring.

"More or less. I prefer to spend most of my free time at the beach."

"Have you ever considered asking for a transfer to this beat? Your commute would be nicer."

"I like working on Beta Station."

The group moved into the elevator. Nathalier hit the key for the fiftieth floor, and they began to move.

"You don't think you'd get along better with your own kind?"

Fernwyn was shocked. "Excuse me? With all due respect, sir, you have no idea what it's like to be a genmod. Besides, Gleeful Complexium is just as diverse in the races as Beta Station."

Fernwyn didn't like discussing the matter in front of the others, but it wouldn't have been good to tell the lieutenant to shut up.

"Here we are," said Nathalier. "The security office is this way."

"Damn it," said Durring. "Rylie, I just realized you'd be better off keeping an eye on the platform. We'll handle it from here."

"Empire has the scene secured," Fernwyn said, irked. "Plus, you know the procedure. I should be present for all questioning since I was the first one on the scene."

"It's more of a guideline than a rule. So if you don't mind..."

"I do mind. Send someone else."

That did it. Fernwyn was sure to be inspecting garbage transports for the rest of her career. The lieutenant rolled his eyes, and pointed at the other Kau'Rii officer.

"Binter, go secure the scene."

The other Kau'Rii returned to the elevator without objection. Nathalier led the group a few strides to the well-marked security office. Inside, Rakhar security guards milled about and conversed over hot yutha. The sergeant was met by a corporal, a young, fawn-colored Rakhar with a deep, gravelly voice.

"The planks are here already?" the corporal asked, using a pejorative term for the SPF.

"These officers are our guests, corporal," Nathalier replied. "What's the story on the surveillance?"

The corporal led the group to a computer station. He sat down and began bringing up images recorded earlier that day. He described what they were seeing.

"These are the unidentified strangers. At first glance they appear to be Umberian, but if we zoom in we see that their ears are different. I've never seen them before, but they identified their language to the central computer as 'English.' They could be genmods, or they could be Umberians surgically altered to look like... I don't know."

"They look like me," said Fernwyn. "Maybe they are genmods, but I doubt it. It would certainly be easy enough to find out."

"I thought the database was ordered destroyed," said Nathalier.

"That's what the Residere government would have you believe."

"That's not a topic for discussion, Rylie," said Durring. "Any idea why they were here, corporal?"

"If you watch the recordings you'll see that after they visit the information booth on level one, they split up into two groups. One group speaks with Graheim's Spirits, then returns to their ship to get what is certainly alcohol. Upon returning to the shop, it looks like they sell the alcohol. We can't get any closer to the interior than what you're seeing now."

"You don't have security cameras inside the shops?"

"One reason why this place is so successful is that we don't pry into the private dealings of our tenants much at all. We keep order on the concourse and the public areas, and that's usually sufficient. Anyway, the other group, the one with the female, they begin to search Z'Sorth shops. They went to two of them before the trouble started. No idea what they were looking for, or if they got it."

"When we're done with the mercs, we'll have a word with the proprietor of Graheim's Spirits. We might be able to learn a little bit more about our visitors from him. Now as to the mercs..."

"This way, sir," said Nathalier.

The sergeant led the group down a long hall. They passed two security checkpoints before arriving at the jail section. Fernwyn reluctantly handed over her sidearm to a Rakhar guard before entering, as did the other officers. In the jail area, the Rakhar mercenaries had been separated one to a cell. They were all wearing the same uniform: black pants, black tunics, and black duty belts, the last item stripped of all gear. The sergeant stopped in front of one cell, which contained a Rakhar with chocolate brown fur. While the other imprisoned mercs looked rather upset, this one was calm.

"This man identified himself as the surviving clan leader," said the Nathalier.

The corporal reached for a dial on the wall. The energy barrier between the hallway and the cell was almost opaque and emanating a buzzing sound. As the corporal turned the dial, the barrier became transparent and the buzzing decreased appreciably. Fernwyn knew that a determined individual could push through this level of energy barrier, but the priority at the moment was conversation.

"I am Lieutenant Durring of the SPF."

"I am Esteemed Commander Trarkek of the Noble Guild Black Crest," the merc said with flourish in a low, guttural tone.

Fernwyn struggled to remember the order of Rakhar military ranks, held over from the Empire days. Esteemed was after Adept, but before Glorious. Or was it after Accomplished? Each rank had five prefixes; there was a lot of room for promotion in the Rakhar hierarchy.

"Do you know why you're being held?" asked Nathalier.

"Such a typical plank question," Trarkek replied. "Humor me, please."

"Because you failed to file an intent to corral form upon arrival at Gleeful."

"My most humble apologies, sergeant. I graciously offer to pay the fine out of my own pocket, to avoid so much as the slightest dishonor to my guild."

"Good, then it's settled," said Durring. "Do we have the total in damages estimated yet?"

Fernwyn and Nathalier looked astonished. The corporal yawned.

"N... no, not yet," said Nathalier.

"You'd better get cracking, then."

"I wasn't finished, if you'll forgive me," said Trarkek. "I invite you to review Chapter 18, section 930 of the Galactic Bounty Hunting codes. You'll see that the actions of my clan are completely lawful, regardless of the missing paperwork."

"Allow me," said Fernwyn, removing a small personal netcomp from her pocket. She looked up the law, read it twice to herself, and laughed lowly.

"Care to share your source of humor with the rest of us?" asked Durring.

"18 GBH 930: Licensed bounty hunters pursuing posted heads may refrain from contacting local law enforcement or filing domestic permission forms IF, A: The bounty heads are fixed and fleeing, AND B: The bounty has been doubled within the last two days GST, OR if the bounty has been dormant for more than five years and has been renewed in the last two days GST."

"So you see, my clan was justified in our actions," began Trarkek. "As for your guard who was shot and wounded, he would of course be allowed a redress of honor against the impetuous fool who did it, as grieved as I am to admit that such a fool was ever under my command. However, since that Rakhar was killed in combat with the bounty heads, such a redress is unnecessary. The Guild will pay for his medical expenses and time lost from work."

"Hold it there, Commander," said Durring. "Implicit in the law is the requirement that you divulge your bounty information to us, so that we may confirm that the conditions it sets were met."

"Implicit, perhaps, but not enumerated. Such a distinction is the area of attorneys, not bounty hunters."

"What a load of crap," said Fernwyn. "There's got to be a pile of case law that supports involuntary disclosure."

"Go find it and read it to me."

"Rylie, do you want to wait outside?" asked Durring.

"No, sir," said Fernwyn.

"Then don't be rude. I'll leave it up to our superiors to decide whether or not such information is necessary. I'll take the Commander on his word for now. Release them when their guild representative arrives."

"Respectfully, sir, and to you, Commander, may I ask two simple questions?"

"You may ask," began Trarkek, "but I may have to defer the answer to my representative."

"If he doesn't mind, go for it," said Durring.

"We know the ship that landed had an Umberian energy signature. Is it the long standing Zendreen bounty that you were following today?"

"Yes," said Trarkek, smiling.

"Since the bounty was over five years old, it would have been considered dormant. That means you would have to either contact the Zendreen and ask them whether or not they were still paying out on it, or the Zendreen would have to send out a wide-net bulletin announcing the bounty's reactivation."

"Correct."

"So which one was it?"

"Are SPF officers getting lazy these days? Such information would be readily available on the net, if you were to look it up."

"For the love of the core, I was hoping you'd save me the time."

"I'm not going to do all of your work for you, my dear. I have to say, for a low grade patrol officer you sure do know a lot about shuffling."

"I used to be in the UMG in a past life."

"Oh! What's your full name?"

"Fernwyn D. Rylie of Residere Beta."

"I'm sorry, I've never heard of you. Too bad, we could have had quite a conversation."

The sergeant's radio beeped at him, and he listened to it for a moment.

"The clan's guild rep is here," he said.

"Fine, they'll need to have a word alone," said Durring. "Prepare for the release of the detainees. Fernwyn, Orlaan, you're with me."

Fernwyn, Durring, the other SPF officer and Nathalier returned to weapons locker and then to the main office. Durring turned towards Fernwyn.

"What is your problem, Rylie? With your attitude you're lucky he didn't shut his jaws completely."

"Sir," began Orlaan, "I don't mean to be contrary, but Rylie knows how to deal with my kind. Polite but forceful is the way to go; it'll earn you more respect in a Rakhar's eyes."

"Well, there aren't too many of them on this beat, outside of the Complexium and those on my squad. I'd say that this case is pretty much open and shut, anyway. I'll file the report to the planetary oversight division."

"Wait a minute," said Fernwyn. "Don't you want to follow up on the bounty information?"

"I don't see why. It's none of our business."

"Aren't you the least bit curious? You're a Kau'Rii for heaven's sake!"

"You are trying to get on my bad side, aren't you? Leave it alone, that's an order! I say this case is closed, and unless division says otherwise it's closed. Orlaan, let's go. Rylie, for your sake I hope I never get assigned to Beta Station."

Durring stormed out of the office. Orlaan shrugged apologetically before following him out to the concourse. After the door closed, Fernwyn kicked a wastebasket across the room, silencing the security personnel present. She then barked a statement that was meant to be a whisper.

"What a fucking jerk."

---

The conference room was filled with an odd assortment of smells; not offensive, but definitely unusual. Upon entering, Byron could identify tobacco, rum, gunpowder, cleaning solvent, and blood. Through the haze, he could see Richter was already cleaning his pistol, despite the injury to his arm. Richter had used his t-shirt to bind the wound, hence the reason for Byron's presence and cargo. Ari sat the table nearby, smoking one of her clove cigarettes, and John stood sipping from a tumbler glass next to her. Ray entered the room with a six-pack of bottled water, walking past Byron and handing one to Richter.

"Thank you, Bailey," Richter said, and drank from the bottle.

"Everybody drink up," Ray said. "I don't want another casualty from dehydration."

"I would hardly consider myself a casualty," said Richter. "I'm still combat effective. Hey kid, are you just going to stand there or are you going to give me that kit?"

Byron walked over and handed Richter the first aid kit he'd retrieved from the cargo hold.

"You shouldn't be drinking at a time like this," Ray said to John.

"I shouldn't be doing a lot of things," John replied. "Like getting into a massive firefight with every new encounter."

"Here, let me take this t-shirt off," said Byron.

"Thanks, I can do it myself," Richter shot back.

"Byron has EMT training," said John. "Why don't you let him bind your wound? He might do a better job with both hands free."

"Fine, whatever."

Byron began working on Richter's injury. Ari hopped down from the table and procured a bottle of water.

"So what do you suppose that was all about?" she said. "The locals sure have a funny fucking way of saying hello."

"I'd prefer to wait until we hold the after-action review before we speculate too much," said John.

"The security guards called them mercenaries," said Richter, lighting a cigarette.

"Yes, but hired by whom?" asked Ray.

"Oh, I almost forgot about these," said Ari, reaching into her jacket.

"Huh?"

Ari removed five small bubble-packed items from her inside jacket pocket.

"What the hell are those?" asked John.

"Translation units. I managed to snag some from a kiosk during the fight."

"You mean you stole them?"

"Half of the shit on this ship was stolen, John. Don't get all high and mighty on me again."

Christie and Dana entered the room via the bridge.

"We're parked in the debris field around Macer," Dana said.

Christie nodded. "Seth thinks that between the debris and our invisibility shield we should remain undetected, for now."

"Okay, good work," said John. "Is everyone ready for the AAR to begin?"

There were no objections. Byron looked at John as if to ask permission to stay, but John wasn't paying attention to him.

"Fine. Our mission was to find some Talvanium as well as a way to purchase it. We accomplished the second objective by selling most of our hard alcohol to a local vendor."

"Doesn't everybody already know that?" asked Byron.

"The purpose of an after-action review is to make sure everyone is on the same page and has all of the pertinent information about the situation. It's also a time to discuss what went right and what went wrong, and how we might improve upon it. So some of the information is going to seem redundant. That's just the way it is."

"All right."

"According to our intel, Talvanium is no longer in active circulation, meaning the only place we can get it is on Residere Alpha. Seth already confirmed Alpha as the most likely source of the Talvanium, but we were hoping to save ourselves a trip over there. The good news is that we may not have to pay for it, since it's value has apparently dropped to nothing since Umber was invaded."

"The Z'Sorth shopkeeper said it was two credits for about five pounds," said Richter.

"How much Talvanium do you need to synthesize the energy weapons?" asked Ray.

"One hundred thirty two point two seven pounds," Seth replied.

"So it may be around fifty credits," began John. "If we have to buy information to find it as well, hopefully the 252 credits that we earned will be enough. Otherwise, we'll have to find another way. When we've all recuperated from the fight, we'll travel to Alpha and begin our search."

"And the action itself?" asked Ari.

"Seth, would you answer this one for me?"

"Sure," said Seth. "The Rakhar you fought were definitely mercenaries, bounty hunters to be precise. After Umber was taken over, the Zendreen put out a standing bounty on all transient Umberians in the Magellanic Cloud... Ari, is that a Rakhar ceremonial battle blade?"

Ari, who had just placed her captured knife on the table, looked up in surprise.

"I don't know, you tell me," she said.

"Yes, it is. I strongly recommend against carrying that blade in the open. It sends a very clear message to other Rahkar as there's only one way you could have gotten it."

"The hard way?"

"Yes."

"Fine, Ari's a bad-ass, we get it," said Christie. "Seth, please continue."

"Right," said Seth. "As I was saying, after Umber was taken over, the Zendreen put out a standing bounty on all displaced Umberians in the Magellanic Cloud. Since only licensed bounty hunters could collect on the prize, and said bounty hunters were relatively uncommon back then, those Umberians who were exiled from their home planet simply tried to forge new lives in other parts of the nebula. As time passed, however, and the true weight of the fall of the Rakhar Empire began to trickle way out here, more and more expatriated Rakhar and other adventurous types began to choose the life of a bounty hunter. It became increasingly difficult for the displaced Umberians to live in peace, and eventually all of them were captured and handed over to the Zendreen. I doubt any of them were harmed, except for the ones that fought back and died trying."

"How do you know all of this if you've been gone for ten years?" asked Ray.

"Easy," said Dana. "I just asked Seth to uplink to the network and update his historical database."

"Well done. Seth, please continue."

"When you reported coming under attack by black-clad Rakhar, it occurred to me to check on the status of the Zendreen bounty. Sure enough, it's been reactivated and the monetary reward has doubled."

"What are we worth?" asked Ari, grinning.

"One million credits per individual, twenty million for the Faith."

"Holy shit," said John. "No wonder those guys were so gung-ho."

"Any time we have to drop the stealth field we risk being detected. Dana and I are still working on a way to mask or modify my energy signature. At least you have the advantage of looking unlike Umberians, which is why nobody hassled you when you first showed up at Gleeful Complexium. The mercenaries must have had access to orbital sensors around Beta. When we dropped the shield before landing, they must have found us. Like them or not, you have to admit their response time is impressive."

"How might you modify the Faith's energy signature?" asked Ari.

"We don't know yet."

"I mean, in what way would you modify it if you could?"

"We'd give ourselves the energy signature of another craft, like a Residerian transport or a Kau'Rii merchant," said Dana.

"Oh. That would be handy."

"But the Faith still looks like the Faith," said John. "If we have to drop the invisibility field, we risk being identified."

"I don't think that's likely," said Seth. "The Rakhar bounty hunters, this particular group is known as the Black Crest guild by the way, aren't exactly liberal in their information sharing. It's unlikely that another bounty hunter or a third party would know what to look for."

"I think we should come up with a better cover story than a bunch of tourists trying to score some Talvanium as a souvenir. If that story can go along with a modification to our energy signature, great. Let's make it a priority. How close are you to figuring it out?"

"I have no frigging idea," said Dana.

"I'd highly recommend such a course of action before attempting to land on Residere Alpha," said Seth.

"Why try and disguise ourselves as one of the local races?" asked Christie. "If they thought we were strangers and they left us alone, then all we should have to do is modify the energy signature enough to make the Faith unidentifiable as Umberian. Then we can claim to be from wherever we wish."

"That sounds like a good idea," said John.

"Why not simply call ourselves humans from Earth, then?" asked Ray. "Nobody seemed to care about Earth when the Z'Sorth trader reported on it."

"Yes, but that was one hundred years ago. If people around here learn that Earth has gained space flight technology, they might go check it out. We don't want our friends back home to get a visit from the Zendreen or anyone else with bad intent. Even if a friendly race shows up, I think the Earth has enough problems without being dragged into the galactic community."

"Yeah," began Christie, "but then again it might provide a real impetus for the countries of the Earth to put aside their differences and work towards a common goal."

"HA!" exclaimed Richter.

"Hey, you don't know."

Richter laughed. "If the survival of all life on Earth hasn't been impetus enough for the last sixty years, what makes you think first contact would change anything?"

"This is precisely why I think going back to Earth to try and solicit help is a terrible idea," said John. "Especially considering that ten years and change will have passed by the time we return."

"There's simply no-one else to turn to for the kind of resources we need," said Seth.

"What if we could get enough Talvanium on Alpha to supply the entire fleet?"

"I already told you that such an operation would be impossible in the current political climate of the Tarantula Nebula, even if we could get by the environmental challenges on Residere Alpha. We would have to have the support of both the Residerian government and the Solar United Faction."

"The Solar United Faction?" asked Ray.

"The governmental body that oversees the whole of the Residere system."

"How is that different from the Residerian government?"

"The Residerian government only has power over two moons."

"Oh."

"Wait a minute," said Christie. "What environmental challenges on Alpha?"

"That was another thing that I learned when I updated my historical database," began Seth. "Alpha, like

Delta and the moons of Macer, underwent atmospheric processing several decades ago in an attempt to make them habitable. Residere Delta was the only one that was a complete success. The processing of Alpha, however, was complicated due to vast, naturally-occurring magnetic zones on the surface. These zones are caused by ferrous ores and prevent all electrical devices from functioning. In order to process the atmosphere, buffer fields were generated around the processing facilities. Unfortunately, such buffer fields were more expensive to generate than the atmosphere processing itself, so once the environment had met the minimum to reasonably sustain life the atmosphere processing conglomerate called it good. The resulting desert planet allows for mining operations without special breathing apparatus or protective suits. Mining operations also require buffer fields, but maintaining them underground is less expensive since there's no ionic interference from the atmosphere."

"Is this going to be a problem for us?" asked John.

"Yes. After Umber was invaded and the demand for Talvanium all but vanished, the main mining facility producing it was closed. The buffer field was shut down. That means the closest I can land the Faith is at the next nearest buffer zone, located at a small town forty kilometers to the east."

"Shit. You mean we have to walk there and back?"

"Yes."

"A hundred and thirty pounds... we'll need four or five people to haul that out. And that's what, fifty miles round trip? Too bad we had to leave the Expedition back home."

"Information is spotty," began Seth, "but there is some data regarding caravans that operate on the surface. Residerian Wolrasi are used as pack animals as well as for hauling carts and wagons. I would recommend attempting to hire some of these animals for your own use."

The wall-mounted plasma screen monitor lit up, displaying a large, goat-like mammal with hooves.

"Indeed," said John.

"Byron, would you please run down to the galley and grab a box of PowerSnak bars?" asked Ray.

"Sure," Byron replied, reassembling the first aid kit.

"Thank you, Byron," said Richter.

"You're welcome."

Byron exited. Friday entered as he was leaving and begged John for attention.

"It was awfully polite of you to say thank you to him," said Ari.

Richter shrugged. "He did a good job."

"So what's our cover story going to be?" asked Dana. "Alpha Centaurians? Refugees from Hadley's Hope?"

"Alpha Centauri has already been explored," said Seth. "There is no planet there that sustains life. I suggest Perditians. They were a somewhat xenophobic race from the Delta quadrant of the galaxy. They were involved in some limited commerce but withdrew from space travel about a hundred years ago. Since they only used audio communication nobody knows what they look like. Chances are nobody around here has ever heard of them, but if they look them up they'll find the same data I did."

"Sounds good," said John. "Now what about our cover story?"

"Seth contains the last repository of technological data from Umber," began Christie. "The Umberians were the only ones who used Talvanium, so if we go looking for it people will assume we're Umberian or sympathizers thereof."

"Yeah?"

"So let's say we're working for the Zendreen. The Zendreen control Umber, so it would make sense if they

145

discovered the usefulness of Talvanium and sent someone to go get some."

"Except that Talvanium is already available on Umber, remember?"

"Oh, yeah. Shit."

"Well, it has been ten years. We could say that the supply on Umber has been exhausted. Who would know? I think Christie has a good idea. If we say we're working for the Zendreen, we might have the implied protection of the Zendreen. People might be less inclined to mess with us."

"So we're Perditian merchants hired by the Zendreen to buy Talvanium on Residere Alpha?" said Ari.

John nodded. "I like it. Anybody got a better idea? Good. Dana, Ari, take those translator units and see if you can get them to interface with our computer. Looks like we're going to be using them a lot."

Five minutes later, Richter headed down the hallway towards his quarters, taking the first bite of an awful banana PowerSnak bar. Ari exited the conference room and walked rapidly to catch up to him.

"Damn, this is the worst flavor of all of them," he said.

"Hey, Chance, wait up."

Richter turned around and took another bite.

"You did well today, Ferro," he mumbled.

"Are you really that surprised?"

"Not at all. From the first day we met I knew you were a wildcat."

"The first day we met I did this to you."

Ari took Richter's right arm and traced her finger across three white scars.

"I hope you don't think I'm harboring any resentment about that."

"Clearly you are not. How's your arm?"

"Well. The energy weapon just disintegrated what it hit. That's why it bled so much. It was clean and surgical. I'm lucky I only got grazed. Byron did an excellent job on the dressing. Who woulda thunk it?"

"You saved my life. I think I owe you one for that."

"We're teammates. You don't owe me anything. Saving each other's lives comes with the job. Can I have my arm back?"

"Then I should at least owe you the courtesy of being direct. You and I have been fighting along side each other for weeks now in the sims. Today's real fight had the possibility of death, which we both almost met several times. I think it's amazing that two things that are so different can feel so similar."

"Uh huh. What?"

"The act of fighting for life, and the act of creating it."

Ari took Richter's other arm, causing him to drop his food.

"Yeah, and guess which one I'm better at? You give up certain things when you devote your life to the company. Some of my colleagues tried to combine the two anyway. They only complicated things. You and I would only complicate things, Ferro."

"I think it's about time you called me Ari."

"I don't want to risk becoming emotionally attached to you. It would only complicate the mission. Think about it. Do you really want to... what the hell am I going on about?"

"I don't know, but I wish you'd shut up."

Richter was able to ignore every voice in his head, every dull ache in his body, and every unpleasant smell of combat and exertion for the few seconds that Ari kissed him. Ari felt Richter leaning back, and thought he might be trying to open the door to his quarters without breaking the embrace.

"Oh yeah, that whole blood loss thing," Richter murmured.

Ari guided him to the ground gently, and he passed out.

"Damn it, I'm such a fool," she said.

## 11.

"What the hell is Talvanium?"

Fernwyn pulled herself out of bed, blinking at the bright light from the console on her desk. Sergeant Nathalier of Empire Security had finally called her back after six hours. Fernwyn was heavily in the grip of sleep when the call came in, and despite the good news she was still having problems following the conversation. She crossed the room and opened the blinds. The sun had just set, creating one of Residere Beta's typically gorgeous scenes. It was hard to find a crappy apartment on Beta.

Nathalier's visage on the comscreen looked as tired as Fernwyn had been six hours ago.

"A kind of ore, discovered relatively recently," he said. "There isn't too much data available on it through the public channels, but I was able to access some information on a private network. There was some information about the ore itself, but none on any applications. Supposedly it can be refined into element 92, and it can be useful for certain kinds of fusion reactions."

"Element 92? Isn't that dangerous?"

Nathalier shrugged. "I don't know."

"How much of it were the strangers trying to get?"

"They didn't say. I spoke with Graheim, the liquor store owner, too. He bought two hundred and fifty credits worth of alcohol from the strangers. Unfortunately, the language on the bottles can't be translated so they offer no clues."

Fernwyn walked into her kitchen and began brewing a pot of yutha. The console in that room turned on automatically to allow the conversation to continue.

"None of this adds up. An unknown ship design with an Umberian energy signature, a crew of an unknown race carrying projectile weapons, and now this Talvanium.

The only thing that does make sense is that the Black Crest jumped on the bounty renewal so quickly."

"I suppose contacting the Zendreen ambassador is a waste of time."

"You suppose correctly. The Zendreen have never asked the SPF for help in their own matters."

"Do you think the SPF database will have more information about Talvanium?"

"Let's find out. Computer, access all data on Talvanium ore, including SPF files."

"Talvanium is a radioactive metal used primarily for power generation," the computer replied. "It is capable of holding a massive charge, but only for a moment, making it especially useful for energy weapons. However, as of the last entry, only the Umberians were ever successful in designing weapons using Talvanium. No weaponry designs were ever made public by the Umberians."

"Interesting," said Fernwyn.

"The Z'Sorth shopkeeper told me that Talvanium is only available on Residere Alpha," said Nathalier. "It sounds to me like the Umberian resistance movement has managed to enlist the help of someone sympathetic to their cause."

"I suppose it's possible that a small group of Umberians have managed to avoid capture this whole time. Perhaps they escaped to wherever these strangers come from, and together constructed a ship. If they're looking for Talvanium, it can only mean one thing."

"They're seeking to upgrade their weapons?"

Fernwyn gestured toward the screen. "They're preparing for an uprising. If the weapons they used at the complexium are the best they've got, naturally they'd be looking to upgrade their own weapons. If Talvanium is an essential part of such a plan, then one ship operating under the radar would be a perfect way to obtain it. And as far as I can reckon, the only point of such a mission would be to bring back enough Talvanium to arm an entire fleet. The strangers must be offering to provide some rather significant resources, not the least of which would be some of their own kind to man the spacecraft. The question is: why go through all that trouble and then forget to modify the energy signature?"

"When they screwed out of here in a big hurry, they activated some sort of invisibility field. When they arrived, they weren't using it. They must have known that we wouldn't have let them land with it activated, or that it would attract unwanted attention, or both. If the invisibility field is their way of modifying or masking their Umberian energy signature, it's my guess that they thought it would be okay to deactivate it temporarily for their visit to the complexium. Wait a minute, though... that doesn't explain how the Black Crest got here so fast..."

"You said that Talvanium is only available on Alpha?"

"Well, it used to be mined on Umber, too, but for some reason they switched all mining operations to Residere Alpha. Either they ran out on Umber or found it was much easier to mine the stuff on Alpha. Either way, don't forget that it was the Umberians who were the primary bankrollers for the Alpha atmospheric processing projects."

Fernwyn nodded, and said, "Then Alpha is the next probable destination for our strangers. I only hope they haven't had too much of a head start."

"I thought the SPF wasn't going to pursue this case any further."

Fernwyn stopped in her tracks. In her enthusiasm she had forgotten about a certain reality.

"Shit! Damned fucking Rakhar! Sorry sergeant, I meant the merc guilds."

"Don't worry about it. Perhaps you should ask your superiors to reconsider based on this new information."

"I could, but so far the strangers are only guilty of one crime, that of engaging in an unauthorized combat action. Their actions at the complexium were clearly in self-defense, your security recordings confirm that. The SPF isn't going to spend any resources going after a class B misdemeanor, especially when the target is wanted by the Black Crest. The mercs have a much better chance of finding them, anyway."

"Maybe not. So far you, me and the Z'Sorth shopkeeper are the only ones who know the strangers are looking for Talvanium. The Black Crest departed Gleeful without speaking to anyone."

Fernwyn snapped her fingers. "Can you make sure that Z'Sorth keeps his jaws shut?"

"Would that mean the SPF owes Empire a favor?"

"If you make sure that the Z'Sorth doesn't talk to anyone else, I'll make sure you get your favor when you need it."

"Officer Rylie, why are you so keen on catching the strangers? A class B misdemeanor arrest isn't going to help your career."

"I just want to talk to the strangers and find out about their mission. Because if we're right about the Umberian resistance's involvement, and we do nothing, that nice little treaty the Solar United Faction signed with the Zendreen won't be worth a puddle of warm piss."

---

The cargo bay on the Faith was a hub of activity. The ship was due to arrive at Residere Alpha in ten minutes, for what was shaping up to be a complex and most likely arduous mission. The crew had allowed themselves ten hours to rest and recuperate after the fight on Beta, and were preparing for the next phase of the operation with zeal.

Richter, roused with difficulty from his quarters an hour earlier, sat in the corner rapidly yet meticulously cleaning his rifle. John, Ari, and Ray had already finished that particular task and were organizing items needed for an eighty kilometer hike through the desert. Christie was entertaining Tycho with a tennis ball, which wasn't a capricious task. The dog had demanded much more attention since being relieved of his Seth-channeling duties.

"Okay, so that's four two-quart canteens, plus eight twenty-four ounce bottles of spring water," John was saying. "Too bad we destroyed our last load of garbage, there had to be a few empty bottles in there."

"It should be enough, provided we don't get into a prolonged battle," said Richter.

"At least we can bring our rifles this time. Seth may be wrong about the laws on this moon, but I'll be damned if I'm going to cross eighty clicks of alien desert without them, even if it means staying out of the city proper. Anyway, for food we've got six MREs per person. I'm also bringing a can of peanuts and three cans of beef stew, as some of us will no doubt need more calories than others."

"I've been thinking about it," said Christie, approaching the others. "I want in on this one."

The three recently dubbed soldiers and the one veteran looked at Christie dubiously, and then at each other.

"Nobody is preventing anyone from coming along," began John, "but I think you'd be more useful here on the ship."

"I have a fair amount of combat simulation training. Not as much as you lot, but I know my way around a M1A. I got shot at back on the landing platform. I did okay."

"Tolliver took several sessions to get the hang of squad movement," said Richter. "But she learned."

Christie bent down to scratch Tycho. "I love this ship. I've barely stepped off of it since we got here, though. I don't relish the possibility of getting killed on an alien world, whether it be by hostiles or by environmental dangers. But I despise the thought of remaining behind again even more. Dana and I have our reservations about our ability to perform under stress. I sense a change in her, at least as far as her willingness to defend this ship. I sense the same change in myself, except I'm ready to leave the safety of this place behind and begin risking as much of myself as you are of yourselves."

John and Richter nodded their heads in solemn appreciation. Ray smiled broadly. Ari shrugged.

"Besides," Christie added, "would you rather carry thirty-three pounds of Talvanium each or twenty-six?"

"Fine, you're in," said John. "Glad to have you, Christie. You know what combat gear you'll need. There's a spare Glock 17 if you want it, but you'll have to fight with Ari over extra magazines as I believe it only has one. The only other problem is that we only brought four backpacks."

"I have a shoulder satchel that should hold my own items. For the Talvanium I'll need something else."

Richter laughed momentarily. "If we can't hire any wolrasi, we should use Byron as a pack mule."

"Like I'd sign off on Byron coming along," Christie growled.

"Byron is a resource," said John. "And if we need him along then he comes. I think he's ultimately harmless, and besides, with Richter and Ari scrutinizing him he won't know whether to shit or go blind."

"I still don't trust him."

Dana entered the cargo bay from the level one stairway.

"We'll be entering orbit soon," she said. "Seth finally restored the active scanning technology, so we've been able to gather more information than we would have using our own passive scans."

"How have we been getting around without active scanning?" asked Richter. "I would have thought it was a given."

"Seth has been downloading information from the net, using his own archived info, and a bit of dead reckoning when needed. The passive scans were what Christie and I originally came up with before we left Earth, and include radiographic telemetry. Now we have what amounts to radar scanning as well as long range astrophysical scans. So we were able to get the information about Residere Alpha that we needed without actually being in orbit. Not that it matters this time."

"So what's the deal?" asked John.

"I wanted everybody to come with me to the zero-g room. I've got something really cool to show you."

"You go ahead, I need to finish cleaning these fellas," said Richter.

Everyone else stopped what they were doing and followed Dana up the stairs.

"Are you getting anywhere with those translator units?" John asked.

"Yes," replied Dana. "I uploaded several different Earth languages into them, so they should work well."

"Good. By the way, I never complimented you on your excellent piloting."

"I guess you never noticed how much time I was spending on your flight sims."

"I knew you were interested, I just never noticed how good you've become."

"You're not jealous, are you?"

John smiled. "Actually, it takes some of the burden off of my shoulders."

The crew walked down the length of the ship, past their quarters and into the zero-g room. As usual, the room was completely empty.

"Seth, begin holographic astronomical display," Dana said.

The room melted away and revealed the exterior of the ship. Despite the fact that they had all done it many times before, the effect was still disorienting. What was different this time was Residere clearly visible, and the moon Alpha was rapidly approaching. As they watched, Seth brought the ship into orbit.

"This never gets old," said Christie.

"Geosynchronous orbit established," said Seth.

"Okay, run program Andrews zero-one," Dana said.

The view zoomed out to an overhead orbital diagram of Residere and its moons. Dana began to narrate what they were seeing.

"Here we have the gas giant Residere and its moons. As you can see from this animation, the moons experience two kinds of night. There's satellite nightfall and planetary nightfall. Satellite nightfall is caused when a moon rotates away from the sun, and is the same as night time on Earth. Planetary nightfall is when the moon orbits into the umbra of Residere. I've sped up time so you can see. Alpha orbits Residere every one hundred and eighty hours, but has a rotational period of thirty hours. Based on the location of the town where we intend to land, there is four hours of daylight remaining. After that the moon will enter the umbra of Residere and there will be darkness for eighty-six hours straight. After that, the moon will experience three days on the near side of Residere, which will result in three periods of night and day that we would consider normal."

"What are the daytime and nighttime temperatures down there?" asked John.

"Daytime is one hundred and twenty degrees Fahrenheit. Night is fifty. Average."

"I say we get down there immediately," said Ray. "Night travel may be more dangerous but it will be much easier on our stamina and water supply."

"Agreed," replied John.

"There are brighter and darker periods on the surface, even during night," began Dana. "You'll still be facing Residere every fifteen hours. You'll also have Delta in a quarter phase for the other fifteen. There will be more ambient light during the latter time. I don't know how dark it will be when Residere dominates the sky."

"Too bad we don't have any NODs," said Ray.

"They wouldn't function anyway, remember?" said Christie. "Those anti-energy zones prevent all electronics from working."

"Shit, that's right. So much for flashlights, too."

"I guess if we need extra lights we'll have to make torches," said John. "All right, everybody. Dana and I will go to the bridge and prepare for landing. Ray, Ari, you and Christie continue to get our gear together. Seth, end simulation."

Twenty minutes later the Faith had landed on the edge of town, and the expedition team had assembled in the cargo bay. Richter was giving advice to Christie on how best to arrange her personal items, John and Ray were going over an anti-ambush scenario, and Ari leaned back against the bulkhead, her gear long since arranged and prepared. Dana appeared from the stairs and approached John.

"Seth has finished analyzing the energy buffer fields," she said. "Remaining invisible shouldn't be a problem."

"Okay," said John. "Once we're clear of the ramp, close it behind us. We'll stay in contact until we're ready to leave the buffer zone. Then you'll be on your own until we get back."

"And if you don't come back?"

"It will be up to you to decide whether or not to continue the mission."

"God... you know, I'd really rather you take Byron with you."

John shrugged apologetically, and said, "I'm sorry, but there's just too much potential for him to cause trouble out there."

"Why not keep him locked in the hold while we're gone?" asked Ray.

"I'm not worried about him causing trouble," replied Dana, "I just prefer not to talk to him. He can roam around as long as he doesn't bother me."

"We're all set over here," Richter announced.

"All right," began John. "Christie, if we get into the shit, you'll be sticking with Ray and I. Richter and Ari will definitely work better without having to keep an eye on you."

"You're finally wearing a pistol, Christie?" asked Ari.

"I finally have a reason to wear one," Christie replied.

"Bailey, are you bringing your Remington?" asked Richter.

Ray shook his head. "No, just my rifle and sidearm. If you want to haul the damn thing around, be my guest."

"It's only another seven pounds. Thank you."

Richter ran up the stairs to the armory and returned a moment later. He slung both an ammo bag of buckshot and the shotgun over his shoulders, and secured them.

"Listen up, people," said John. "It looks like the order of the day is long arms shouldered. From what we can tell out there, this town is the wild west. Don't look at anybody the wrong way, and don't make it look like you're going for your weapons. We've all got the translation earpieces set up, so we shouldn't have a problem communicating within the buffer zone. Outside of the buffer zone they won't work, so part of our mission is going to be to get a written note in the appropriate language that says what we're looking for and how much we need. If things go south in town, the ship is the rally point. Once we're out in the desert, we'll establish rally points every mile. Any questions?"

There were none. John hit the button for the ramp. There was a slight whooshing sound as the pressure normalized, and the ramp lowered into place.

"Good luck," said Dana.

"Standard marching order," said Richter.

The team descended the ramp to the ground. John and Christie had already seen the environment from the bridge, but for the others it was a new scene. The team was forced to stop as Ari, Richter, and Ray gaped in awe at the sight.

The sun was setting behind Residere, both low in the sky. As the light filtered through the upper atmosphere of the gas giant, it was bent into shades of green and orange. To the east, the nebula slightly obscured the stars with a pale sheen. When the light hit the red earth of Alpha, it seemed to glow. Quite a bit of the rock scattered about glittered like quartz. The air was cool and pleasant, with a smell like ozone after a thunderstorm. Small creatures flew through the air with an eerie whistling.

"My God," said Ari.

Christie pulled out a small camera and took a picture.

"I didn't know you brought a camera," said John.

"I'm surprised you didn't," said Christie.

Once they were done admiring the view, the team took stock of their surroundings. To the north lay the small town of Metzqual. The Faith had landed about four hundred yards outside of the shanties that surrounded the larger permanent buildings. Smoke rose from various places within the town, and as the wind shifted towards the Faith the team could smell a variety of things. Music also wafted towards them. Closer, a small convoy of covered wagons passed slowly by, pulled by wolrasi. Some distance off to the east lay a bevy of other parked spacecraft.

"Let's go," said John, taking point.

Ray fell in behind him. Christie and Ari came next, with Richter taking up the rear. As they approached the town they passed by a few campsites, some with Z'Sorth and others with Kau'Rii. There were strong smells of cooked food and alcohol. The atmosphere seemed relaxed, although in the distance there were periodic blasts from energy weapons. John found himself much more anxious than he had been on Residere Beta.

"Is this place truly lawless?" he said quietly.

"Maybe," replied Ray. "It looks like things are kept in relative peace by one way."

"The way of the gun?"

"Yup."

"Keep your chin up, everyone. Don't let anybody get the impression that we're easy targets."

The team began crossing through the shanty area. They appeared to be in a Residerian neighborhood, and the predominant population didn't seem the slightest bit interested in them. Despite the obvious poverty, things were clean and orderly and the Residerians pleasant and upbeat. All of the males carried sidearms and almost all of the females carried infants. Occasionally these two roles were reversed.

Ahead, they approached the first line of permanent structures. The buildings were either mud brick or concrete blocks, with flat metal roofs. Most seemed to be limited to one level; a few more opulent buildings had three. As the ambient light steadily decreased, bluish street lights began to wink on. The road grew busier the further they progressed.

A scruffy-looking Kau'Rii leaned against a wall, smoking a pipe. John motioned for the others to spread out across the street as he approached him.

"Smells good," John said, smiling. "What do you have in there?"

"Beta Pressed Flake. Do you smoke a pipe?"

The translation unit's effect was instantaneous and flawless.

"Yeah, but I haven't tried any of the local tobacco."

"We're a dying breed, you know. Not because of the pipe, of course."

"Do you mind if I ask you another question?" John said.

"You can ask."

"We're looking for the largest and most well stocked Z'Sorth shop in town. Can you make a recommendation for us?"

"Yeah, I recommend you give me twenty credits for that information."

John was taken slightly off-guard by the request.

"Well, five credits is all we can spare."

"Then find it yourself."

"Okay, ten credits."

"Fifteen."

John looked at Ray, who shrugged. John counted out fifteen credits and handed it to the Kau'Rii.

"Fifteen credits. Where do we go?"

"The largest Z'Sorth merchant is Pulchik's place on Vulpine Street. Take this street to the center of town until you see a sign that looks like a glass of ale. Vulpine is the second street on the right after that."

"Thank you."

John and Ray crossed the street to gather with the others.

"You don't think fifteen credits is kind of steep for information like that?" asked Ari.

"This town is larger than it appears," replied John. "I'd rather not spend too much time wandering around."

"Let's just hope we didn't get ripped off."

"There are some Rakhar taking interest in us," said Richter quietly.

"Play it cool, folks," said John. "What do they look like?"

"A rag-tag group. They've been following us on a parallel street. They don't look anything like the mercs, other than sharing the same race."

"Keep an eye on them. They may only be curious. Let's keep moving."

The team resumed their marching order and continued down the street. After a few minutes they approached a market area. Most of the vendors appeared to be shutting down for the evening. A fight between two Kau'Rii broke out into the street from a nearby building, startling the humans. The pair was quickly surrounded by spectators. Ray craned his neck to get a look at the action as they passed by.

"One of those guys has quite an interesting martial arts style," he said.

"Cat Fu?" said John.

"It actually looked like Aikido, but with more clawing."

The fight was over before Richter had passed the scene. The crowd sounded disappointed and began to disperse. John looked over his shoulder, turned forward, and almost ran into a Rakhar standing in front of him.

John rapidly assessed the situation. The Rakhar was standing alone in the street, and obviously wanted a word with him. He had four friends but they were leaning up against the wall on an adjoining alleyway. John took half a step back and motioned to the others to spread out. Ari and Richter took a particular interest in their six.

"Excuse me, I didn't see you there," said John.

"My friends and I wanted to welcome you to Metzqual," the Rakhar said. His ornate earrings jingled slightly as he spoke.

"Thanks...?"

"We wanted to offer you the opportunity to purchase some life insurance from the local Rakhar enforcers."

"Oh? I didn't realize we were in peril."

"This place can be dangerous to those who are not welcome."

"Since you just welcomed us, the danger can't possibly be from your lot, right?"

"Of course not," the Rakhar said, grinning widely.

"We're Pertidian traders. Generally we don't require extra life insurance beyond our own policies."

"That's hard to believe, considering that you're armed with antiques."

"They do the job, but it's not only the weapons that provide protection. So do our employers."

"If you say you're working for the Empire, I may just lose it."

"No, we're working for the Zendreen."

The color drained from the Rakhar's eyes, and for a moment he seemed genuinely concerned.

"Since when have the Zendreen needed to hire anybody to do their work?"

"Our task is too small to warrant an invasion. Of course, if anything happened to us, they could theoretically invade Alpha to get what they need. Which would you prefer?"

"If you're working on the Zendreen's behest, you'd be violating the treaty. In which case, you'd better hope we don't spread the word of your arrival here."

"Oh?"

"The SUF doesn't look too kindly on Zendreen spies. In which case, keeping us quiet will cost you."

John had run out of pithy comments, and struggled for a reply.

"Why would the SUF believe anything that a group of thugs from a small town on Alpha had to say?" said Ray.

"Maybe they would, maybe they wouldn't. We can all still be friends, here. Five hundred credits will keep you safe and we won't mention a word of this to the authorities."

Richter motioned for Christie to switch places with him, and turned toward the Rakhar.

"You're not going to contact the authorities," he said calmly.

"Why not?"

"I see the way you carry yourself. The way you and your friends confronted us. You've been doing this for a long time. Visitors you think you can take advantage of either pay up or get roughed up. Now of all the people that you've done this to, do you really think none of them filed a complaint with the SPF once they were safe?"

The Rakhar laughed. "The SPF has no authority here. Let them file their complaints!"

"Fine. And you go ahead and arrange a meeting with them to tell your story. You'll be thrown in jail so fast you'll think you were born there. You're not going to be able to trade amnesty for a highly dubious story like this. Not without some serious evidence to back it up."

"Then maybe I should take your barely breathing hide in as evidence."

"You can try."

"Whoa, hold on there," said John. "We don't want any trouble. Surely there's something we can..."

Before John could finish, the Rakhar went for his sidearm. Richter moved in close, deflecting the draw and catching the Rakhar off balance. Richter guided him to the ground with precision, twisting his free arm around his back and the energy pistol around until the Rakhar had it pointed at his own head. With his wrists locked painfully into place, the Rakhar couldn't move. The other Rakhar in the alley had begun to move but stopped in their tracks.

"Give me one good reason why I shouldn't take off your boss' head," said Richter.

"You'll never be safe in this town again," one of them said.

"There may be no honor among thieves," Richter whispered to the boss, "but you and I have a special relationship now."

Richter released the boss. He examined the energy pistol, found the power cartridge, and ejected it. A small green light on the side ceased to glow, and Richter tossed the pistol back to its owner. The boss caught it despite his astonishment.

"Like he said, we can all still be friends here. Let's keep it a long distance relationship, shall we?"

The boss ran into the alleyway, and he and his friends disappeared. John, Ray, and Christie looked at Richter in awe as he tried to decide what to do with the energy cartridge. Ari lit a cigarette.

"Whatever we're paying you, it ain't enough," said John.

"Come on, we should keep moving."

The team resumed marching order and continued down the street.

"Let's hope that's the last we see of them," said Christie.

"We may have lucked out again," began John, "but our habit of ending every single confrontation with a fight is getting very old."

"Seth never said this would be easy," said Ray.

Christie pointed up the street. "Hey, there's the glass of ale."

A wooden sign hung above a one story building, shaped like a long pilsner glass. There was much carousing going on inside.

"Okay, so it's our second right from here," said John.

John's radio crackled to life and Dana's voice came through.

"How's it going down there, John?" she said.

"Just cozying up to the locals. We're almost at a Z'Sorth shop. Hopefully we'll be able to get some useful information there."

"Wouldn't it be nice if he a hundred and thirty pounds of Talvanium lying around?" said Ari.

"If we're extremely fortunate, yes. But I wouldn't bet on it."

---

Dana put her feet up next to the radio on the console. John's sarcastic tone over the radio had led her to believe that something unpleasant had occurred, if nothing more than annoying as a result. She began to wonder if she wouldn't have been better off going with the others. Not knowing what was going on out there was disconcerting back at Gleeful Complexium, and it was even worse now. At least then she had Christie around. Christie and Dana had become best friends over the course of the journey, and while Dana understood her desire to be part of the expedition team, she couldn't help but feel abandoned aboard the Faith. With Byron her only companion, even the gorgeous view outside of the windows couldn't quiet her concerns.

Dana picked up a cup of coffee and sipped from it. She was taking a break from her efforts to modify the ship's energy signature. Seth lacked the imagination to come up with a solution, so her efforts were little more than trial-and-error. She had to keep an eye on the sky, too, since occasionally another ship would pass close by. Being invisible was a liability for hanging around such a busy town.

Whilst Ari had originally been the exclusive expert on the Faith's computer systems, her shift in interest to combat simulations had allowed Dana to wrest the title away, however unintentional the act was. The only thing that Ari understood better than anyone was the code she had written to allow their human technology to interact with Seth. Dana often forgot that Seth was still contained in the small, basketball sized orb on deck two, since he had so well integrated himself with the ship. Ari had become so disengaged from programming, in fact, that Dana doubted she could even keep up with herself and Christie any more.

Dana felt a pang of adrenaline in her gut. Her worries about her friends on the surface refused to go away, no matter how entranced in other thoughts she was. It seemed like an unnecessary risk to go to such lengths to upgrade their weapons, since being able to better defend themselves had no impact upon Umber's predicament. If Dana had her way she would scrub the mission entirely, content to either explore the galaxy back closer to Earth or to simply return home and triumphantly display the Faith to NASA. So far, Seth had dutifully followed their orders, but Dana wondered how he would react to any order counter to his mission. Even if the others didn't return, Seth might refuse any path that didn't work towards liberating Umber. Regardless of what Seth's reaction would be, if the others were killed the first thing that Dana would do is get the hell rid of...

Byron entered the bridge, interrupting Dana's thoughts. She leaned forward and pretended to look busy. She and Ray had a weak spot for Byron, not so much that they were outwardly friendly to him but just enough to prevent them from keeping him locked in the hold.

"Do you mind if I hang out here?" he said.

"Not really. I just checked in with the team. There isn't anything interesting going on right now."

"Oh."

Byron sat in the chair the furthest away from Dana.
"There's coffee in the galley if you want it."

"I just came from there, but thank you. There's no view down there, you know. This is much nicer."

"Uh huh."

"You know, you and I never really got a chance to talk."

"Talk about what?"

"You know, have a chance to get to know each other better."

Dana stopped playing around with the computer and turned to face Byron.

"Do you think I'm going to be nicer to you than the others?"

"I had hoped you'd be civil."

"That firefight the night we left Earth was the worst thing that's ever happened to me. If you really were responsible for leading the CIA to us, then being civil is going to be a stretch."

"I made a mistake. I wanted there to be a confrontation, but I never meant for anyone to get hurt."

Dana raised an eyebrow. "As far as I know, that's the first time you've admitted fault for what happened."

"Is it? Well, it's true. If I could take it back, I would. But you have to admit that there was no other way I could have gotten aboard, what with the way Christie thought about me."

"You're damn right about that. You could have stowed away without bringing the wrath of the CIA down upon us, though."

"I made a mistake. What's done is done."

Dana turned back to her console.

"I wouldn't worry about this ship or the crew if I were you. It's becoming increasingly likely that we're going to shove a few credits into your pocket and leave you on Residere Beta with a copy of the local classifieds in hand."

Byron smiled. "Then what does it matter if we talk about ourselves a little?"

"What part of my past could you possibly be interested in, Byron?"

"File that under the same comment I made about civility."

"Fine, I'll answer one question, if it will make you happy."

"What made you decide to join the mission?"

Dana turned to face Byron again. It was an excellent question. It allowed her to put whatever spin she desired on the answer while at the same time it did not require much personal information. Still, a bit more context would be nice.

"What have the others told you about me?"

Byron laughed. "Do you seriously think the others would have told me about you if I'd asked? I only know that you joined the crew sometime after the initial infrastructure was synthesized, and that for some reason a friend of yours named Levi complicated the mission. You obviously have a great deal of skill in astronomy and communications. Other than that you're a blank page. On the other hand, your picture of me must be quite colorful, even if most of that information came from people who don't like me."

"My opinion of you is based solely on my own contact with you. What the others think is similar because we're all good judges of character."

"Fair enough. What's the answer?"

Dana sighed. "I worked for an organization called the American Space Transmission Research Association. It is funded entirely by educational grants from universities and works directly with those schools to provide academic opportunities for their students. Actually searching for extra-terrestrial intelligence was nothing more than a side effect of the educational arrangement. The only people who thought detecting signals from other worlds was actually important were the few paid staffers like my former colleague Levi Marks and myself. We detected signals from

Seth before he even landed on Earth, and I convinced Levi to help me pin down the source. By the time we found it, Seth had already helped John, Ray and Ari create the ship. It turned out, by the way, that Seth was unintentionally emitting those radio signals every time he conducted a significant matter-to-energy transfer. Things like emerging from superspace, integrating the steel and aluminum from the USS Portland, and transporting items from the surface all created a signal that Levi and I were able to track and follow. When we found the Faith, we were both rather impressed. However, that Levi and I had different ideas of how to proceed from there."

"Let me guess. Levi wanted the government to oversee the construction."

"No, Levi wanted the government to completely assume the mission. He didn't think that we had the skills necessary to tackle the mission. He also didn't think that keeping a discovery of this magnitude from the people of Earth was right."

"Don't you think he had a point? Perhaps a larger crew with more skilled technicians and diplomats would have been better."

"If the government was in charge of this mission, they'd bring along a political agenda. They'd be bound by the responsibility to represent the United States in the best possible light, and to make friends with everyone they ran into or face dragging Earth into a conflict it couldn't possibly be ready for. I think that if this ship was manned by a crew working for the United States government, Umber wouldn't have a chance in hell of being liberated. They'd take one look at the political situation out here and end up kissing the SUF's ass like it was ambrosia. Hell, it's foolish enough for us to be going up against the Zendreen. If they find out we're from Earth, they might direct their ire towards our home planet. Imagine that."

"I'd rather not. Honestly, I think an independent group like us is the best way. Too bad we don't get along better."

"The only person who has any trouble getting along on this ship is you."

"So Levi went to the government. What happened?"

"He blabbed all the information he had to them. He knew our names, which was enough for the CIA to put surveillance teams at each of our residences. He was responsible for Ari getting kidnapped, which required an even greater risk to get her back."

"I would have let them keep her."

"Tell that to John and Ray. They're all old friends from way back. I guess it's pointless to try and explain loyalty to somebody like you, though."

Byron stood up. "Speaking of kissing ass, I'm not capable of much more. If you're going to continue to throw insults my way, perhaps I'd be better off having a conversation with Tycho."

"Go ahead."

"Fine. Enjoy doing whatever you were doing. I'm going to go get some air."

"Fine, you do that."

Byron exited the bridge. Dana turned back towards her console. Byron may have been an irreconcilable jerk, but he did force her to contradict her earlier thoughts. If she didn't like Levi trying to get the US government involved, how would returning home and contacting NASA be any different? Umber would be screwed either way. Dana realized that her only loyalty was to the human crew; not to Seth, the ship, Umber or even herself. With that, the thought of the team getting wiped out on Alpha became so terrifying that Dana stood straight up.

"Screw the Talvanium! It's not worth it! I've got to stop them."

Dana crossed the bridge to the communications console. Before she activated it she realized what Byron had just said. She also realized that they'd never bothered to lock out the ramp controls.

"God damned annoying little prick!" she cried, and ran after him.

## 12.

    Residere Alpha. If there was a nastier dump of a planet in the cloud, Fernwyn hadn't been there. She was sitting cross-legged at the edge of a town called Metzqual, staring off into the desert countryside. The sun had set a little while ago, and she was treated to a view of the gas giant and the nebula that was normally obscured on Beta by light pollution. While she got a perfect view of the Residere planetary neighborhood twice a day on her commute to work, there was always something different and more pleasant about seeing things from planetside. Alpha had a mood all of it's own, and Fernwyn found it suited her perfectly at the moment. Her three year old memories of the place were still accurate; in fact, she wondered if anything significant had changed at all. It was still the same collection of the worst that the Tarantula Nebula could throw at it. It was still one of the best places to make yourself disappear, too. Ironic, then, that the SPF had half of it's training academy there. It sure wasn't the fun half.

    The surroundings on Alpha that were Fernwyn's current concern reminded her of many specific memories of her three week stay as a police recruit. Some of those memories hadn't been recalled since they'd been formed. Fernwyn realized that she'd forgotten about most of the experience as soon as it was complete. This stood in stark contrast to her normal reaction to survival and combat training. Typically she enjoyed that sort of thing, but the three weeks she'd spent on Alpha did not fall into the same category.

    The distinct smell of ionized air on Alpha was the strongest catalyst for her memory. The nights she'd spent out in the field during survival and combat training were some of the loneliest moments she'd ever experienced. It was the culmination of a hard fight in her life, a battle that was waged on two fronts. One, her time spent as a bounty hunter had lent her a mean independence streak. This resulted in Fernwyn either saying something inappropriate to an academy instructor, or in forcing her to swallow her pride so deeply she almost couldn't stand it. Two, as a genmod she had faced unreasonable prejudice from both the instructors and other recruits. Soundly kicking the crap out of every obstacle laid in her path was her best and most satisfying revenge.

Fernwyn stood up and stretched her legs. She'd had absolutely no luck questioning the folks in town, probably due to her status as a genmod. She wasn't stupid enough to show up in uniform, but her physical appearance was still unmistakable. Either nobody in town had ever heard of Talvanium or they were playing dumb out of spite. She hadn't run into any Z'Sorth, which wasn't a surprise since they were usually asleep after sunset. The only break she got was when a drunk Residerian had wandered into the bar she'd been in and mentioned seeing something strange on the edge of town. Fernwyn bought him a drink and he happily described seeing a portal to a room open up out of thin air and five people emerge. He may have been full of shit, but it was the only thing that she had to work with. After getting a cardinal direction out of him she headed to a rocky outcropping to take a look.

That was thirty minutes ago. Fernwyn took a deep breath of the cool air and thought about her recon efforts. Metzqual was the closest town to the largest source of Talvanium. Unfortunately the mine of interest was no longer in operation, which meant that anybody who wanted to get there would have to walk. Fernwyn glanced over her shoulder back at the town. It was a mystery to her why anyone would fund the buffer zone over that pile of crap.

A noise and a flash of light brought Fernwyn's attention to her front. At first her mind couldn't get around what she was seeing. A horizontal shaft of light had appeared about ten meters over the desert, forty meters from her vantage point. The shaft grew into a rectangle, and she realized she was looking into a space that hadn't been there before. A ramp lowered until it touched the ground. Inside was evidently a cargo bay, and a single figure stood at the top. Fernwyn hit the deck and reached for a pair of binoculars she had in her backpack.

The figure was a male of the same species that she'd seen on the complexium's security recordings. He could easily pass for Umberian except for the lack of hair on his ears. He was either a Residerian genmod like Fernwyn or another race entirely. The latter was much more likely. The figure walked to the bottom of the ramp. He took a breath and smiled. He seemed rather at peace with his surroundings, and kicked at the dirt absent-mindedly.

Another person appeared within the cargo bay from a long staircase on the port side. She was obviously female, and carried a long arm of some sort. The woman hurried down to the ramp and began yelling at the man. Fernwyn swore silently and rapidly adjusted the volume on her translation unit.

"...the hell do you think you're going, Byron?" the woman was saying.

"I said I was going to get some air," the man named Byron replied. "So what?"

"So what makes you think you're allowed to leave the ship?"

"Nobody said I couldn't, Dana."

"That's because we've been in deep space for the last five weeks!"

"Hey, if you're going to force me to follow your rules, don't blame me if they're not specific enough."

"Get back inside, now."

"Or what? Since when does anybody on this ship give a shit what happens to me?"

"We'd like to be rid of you, more or less. But you know too much. When I said we were considering leaving you somewhere it was just rhetoric. In reality we can't afford to leave a duplicitous bastard like you behind. Who knows how you could compromise the mission?"

"I guess you have a point. Perhaps I should have kissed more ass while I had the chance."

"Too late. Get back inside."

"Or you'll shoot me? I don't think you have the guts. Go back inside yourself, and I'll be in when I feel..."

The woman called Dana fired a shot from her weapon. The projectile kicked up a cloud of dirt and a loud report echoed throughout the desert.

"If you think that's going to intimidate me you haven't been spending enough time around Richter," Byron said.

Byron began walking away. Dana ran down the ramp as fast as she could. Byron realized too late that she was heading right for him at top speed. Dana used the stock of the weapon to smash him in the left shoulder. Byron screamed mightily and fell to the ground.

"Never underestimate the power of anger, you son of a bitch," she roared. "Now drag your sorry ass back inside before I find out exactly what I'm capable of!"

Byron's expression was of pain and horror. He attempted to get back onto his feet as Dana dragged him up the ramp.

"Shit," whispered Fernwyn.

Fernwyn drew her sidearm and obtained a cartridge from a pocket on her leg. She ejected the magazine and racked the slide, sending a round flying. She dropped the cartridge into the chamber, tugged at the slide to release it, and aimed for Byron. The weapon made a slight pop as she pulled the trigger. She reloaded and holstered the pistol and obtained a small device with a screen. It confirmed the successful implementation of her tracking module into Byron's clothing. The signal was strong. Fernwyn sighed in relief.

"Wait until the others hear about this," Dana said.

The ramp began to close. A moment later the cargo bay disappeared and silence returned to the desert. Fernwyn looked down at her tracking device. The signal had been interrupted.

"Aw, crap."

---

Hiking. Christie thought she liked it. Eight hours of hiking with a ten-pound rifle through rocky desert on an alien planet, however... that sort of upped the ante a little.

On the plus side, the environment was stunningly beautiful, even if it was inherently terrifying. Residere had long since set, and Delta glowed peacefully in quarter-phase high in the sky. Entirely new stars graced the heavens, and Christie's mind reveled in creating new constellations with them. The air was fresh and cool, with gentle breezes wafting curious and occasionally disturbing sounds to them. For the most part it was silent save for the noise the Earthlings were making. They had not encountered any other living beings since departing Metzqual except for the small flying creatures.

Spirits among the team were high. Christie doubted that she was the only one fatigued at this point, however. Their plan was to hike almost all of the way to the mine in one go, so the only rest they'd had in the last eight hours were two fifteen-minute breaks. At about twenty-four miles, they would rest for eight hours. Sleep seemed like a good idea before attempting the buy.

With their radios and watches refusing to function, keeping track of time and distance was difficult. Without Richter's military experience they would have been completely out of luck. Richter had replaced Ray by John's side so that the two of them could work together on navigation. There were remnants of a wide road that more or less headed out in the same direction, but time and weather had obliterated it in some areas. When that happened they had to stop every one hundred yards to shoot an azimuth, the compass having been calibrated before leaving town. Finding the road again was always a relief, and fortunately the anti-energy zones had no effect on the compass. It was Christie's job to keep track of time. Delta had begun to rise right before they'd entered the Z'Sorth shop, so Christie was able to keep track of time by measuring its movement through the sky. The moon moved about ten degrees per hour. She taught the others how to do it but volunteered to keep track herself, at least for now.

It hadn't surprised any of them that the Z'Sorth shopkeeper didn't stock Talvanium. He did confirm that there was plenty of it at the mine, and for a single credit he had agreed to provide a note, written in Z'Sorth, that announced their intentions. It would no doubt be an interesting effort in communication if he was wrong about there being other Z'Sorth at the mine. The shopkeeper also let the team in on how much it would cost to rent one or two Wolrasi. They could afford it, but just barely, and they agreed they had better save their money for the Talvanium.

So, after a frantic radio transmission from Dana complaining about Byron and the mission, they'd departed Metzqual. Byron was being his typical self, but it was unlike Dana to exhibit so much emotion and doubt. Christie's heart tore at her friend's fear, and of course she shared it. It did seem like an undue risk to obtain the Talvanium if it would only make the Faith somewhat safer from attack. Dana had submitted that it should be easy enough to hide somewhere until the Faith's engines were recharged, but the others had remained adamant. Improving the ship's weaponry was vital. John was also keen on considering other options that made better firepower all the more appealing.

For now, it was time to check on their progress. Christie sped up enough to draw close to Richter, and spoke in a low voice.

"What's the pace count?" she asked.

"Thirty-seven clicks, six hundred meters, and fifty-seven paces. Almost time to rest."

"Thank God."

"That's close enough," said John. "Let's start looking for a place to make camp."

"I've been eyeballing that hill over there," said Ray, pointing.

Richter nodded. "Me, too. It's far enough off of the old road so that we won't be set upon by accident. It looks like there might be some good cover, too. I like the size of some of those boulders."

"Okay," began John. "Let's divert over there when it's directly to our nine. Richter, take an azimuth and start a new pace count at that point. We might have more trouble finding the road than we'd guess."

"So far the ambient light has been pretty good," said Ari.

"If we rest for eight hours, Delta will have set," said Christie. "It will be darker when we resume."

The hill was deceptively far away, and it took the team another ten minutes to reach it. Upon arriving they discovered it was more like a mesa, with a diameter of about one hundred meters. The top was covered with large rock formations and boulders, resulting in a few narrow passageways among the open areas. After snooping around the entire hill, the team gathered in the center.

"Perfect," said John.

"Not really," countered Richter. "No matter where we camp, only one side will be facing the desert. Someone could easily get within ten meters on our blind side. There's a clearing on the north side that gives us a good vantage point back towards the road as well as a single entry point into the boulders to the southwest. We should eat the beef stew for dinner tonight and then use some 550 cord to tie the cans across that point. Then a single person on watch can be aware of all directions."

"Sounds good. Let's go."

The team followed Richter to his recommended spot. Once sleeping arrangements had been made, they gratefully shed their rucksacks and sat down. Luckily, the hard-packed earth wasn't too dusty to work with.

"Who wants a can of stew?" asked John.

Each of the others raised a hand.

"Forget it," said Ari. "I'll stick to one of my MREs."

"Me, too," added Ray. "I am on rear security for a reason."

"How do you want to handle watch rotation?" asked John, opening a can.

"Five people, eight hours," began Richter. "I'll take first watch for three hours, then each of you can take one hour after that."

"That's not fair. You'll only get five hours of sleep."

"True, but it will be uninterrupted sleep."

"I call last watch!" Ari said suddenly.

Richter smiled. "See, she gets it too."

"Are you sure you won't nod off?" asked John.

"Trust me, I'll be fine. You know, this planet reminds me a lot of Afghanistan."

"You mean Operation Anaconda?"

"Yeah. The nights were much colder, though. This is downright luxurious. It's ironic, I think, that considering all the time I spent in the Marine Corps, I didn't see any combat until I joined the CIA. They sent me further afield than the Marines ever did. Afghanistan, Pakistan, the Philippines... after the September Eleventh attack, we were everywhere. Shit, I hope Devonai is doing all right. I can't even imagine the shit storm he's dealing with right now."

"Don't forget, it's been five years since we left back on Earth."

"Oh, yeah. Well, the sentiment still stands."

"Oh my God, these little bottles of Tabasco sauce are awesome!" said Christie.

"In the Marines, we used to save them for watches. If you find yourself nodding off, slam one of those. I guarantee you forget all about..."

Richter cut himself off and raised his hand. He cocked his head to the side and listened. He motioned for the others to stay down and he crept to the side of the hill. Once there, he went prone and made his rifle ready. A moment later the others joined him.

"Down there, on the road," he whispered.

Back on the desert plain, barely discernible at the six hundred yard distance, a caravan moved down the road. The race of the occupants was unknown, but the animals hauling the carts were clearly wolrasi.

"At that speed they must have left right after we did," whispered Ray.

"Are they following us?" asked Ari.

Richter shook his head. "I doubt it. They aren't exactly equipped for stealth travel. We'll find out when they get to where we turned off. We didn't hide our tracks. Fuck, that was stupid."

"Startin' to lose it in your old age, eh?"

"Shh..."

The team watched in silence. The caravan passed by the turn-off point. After a few more minutes Richter turned towards the others and shrugged.

"I guess they're not interested in..."

A loud explosion tore through the night air, and a bright flash illuminated the desert. Back on the road, a small fireball rose from the ground and quickly dissipated. Shots began echoing across the plain, and shouts in an unknown language soon followed. The caravan began to circle the wagons, and individual attackers could be seen advancing from the north.

"Holy shit, they're being ambushed," said Richter.

"Poor bastards," said Ari.

"Should we help them?" asked Christie.

"Absolutely not," replied John. "This is not our problem."

"We could use it as a chance for some free target practice," Ari said, smiling.

"Just lay low and don't make a sound."

"Let's hope they can repel the attack," said Richter. "If not, guess where they'll be headed."

John's eyes widened. "Oh, shit."

As Richter predicted, a gathered group from the caravan began running at full speed towards the hill. Shots were being exchanged in earnest, and the number of those fleeing rapidly dwindled.

"It's a shooting gallery," said Ray. "They don't stand a chance."

"They must be using projectile weapons like ours," said John.

Christie nodded. "That makes sense. Energy weapons wouldn't work out here."

"Shut the hell up," Richter hissed.

Two remaining caravaners made it to the base of the hill. One of them spun around to fire at the enemy, and was quickly cut down. The last one, now identifiable as a Kau'Rii, sprinted up the hillside and disappeared into the rocks. Half of the attackers peeled off and began running towards them.

"This is going to get really interesting fast," whispered Richter. "We have no choice but to take sides now. Everybody get on line and prepare to fire."

Each of the team members searched for a good firing position that was more or less in line with the side of the hill.

"Four hundred meters and closing," said Ray.

"Scherer, I want you on the left flank," Richter said, pointing. "Go about twenty-five meters down. You'll start to catch return fire first because your Garand doesn't have a flash hider. When that happens, displace and cover our six."

"Roger that," John replied.

"Three hundred and fifty," said Ray.

"Remember, don't rush your shots," said Richter. "Scherer, you initiate fire when you're ready."

John nodded and ran off to take his position. As the enemy grew closer, Christie realized she couldn't identify the species. Each of them moved in a different way, and a few of them even appeared to run on four legs. The raiders had stopped firing, and an eerie silence returned to the desert.

John's Garand shattered that brief peace. His friends were jarred out of their adrenaline-induced stupors and began to fire as well. The enemy responded to the sudden fusillade by going prone, so it was initially impossible to detect any hits. Soon they started to get up one by one and rush the hill. Four of them did not get up. Two more fell before incoming fire raked John's position.

"I'll be in my office," yelled John as he displaced, slapping another clip into his rifle.

The others continued firing.

"Reloading," said Ray, doing so.

Three more of the raiders dropped to the dirt and stopped moving. The remaining five disappeared around the northeast side of the hill.

"That's it," said Richter, leaping to his feet. "You three grab some better defilade on this flank. I'll reinforce Scherer. Watch for that Kau'Rii if you can, we might as well try and avoid shooting him."

"Roger," said Ari.

For the next several moments it was dead quiet. Then, hushed voices could be heard coming from elsewhere on the hill. Nearby, the sudden sound of a violent confrontation burst forth. There was the clash of steel on steel, and then a horrible scream. There was a brief silence, and then somebody swore. There was a sound like somebody dropping a watermelon, and a severed Kau'Rii head rolled into the clearing. Christie clamped her hand over her mouth and squeaked. John and Richter tensed up.

A creature appeared from behind the rocks leading to the clearing. In the darkness it could not be definitively identified, but at first glance it looked like a Rakhar with two extra arms. It had a three-foot long sword in one hand and a pistol in the other. It's eyes focused on John and Richter and gleamed in the moonlight. Richter's selector switch made a clear click as he flipped it to full auto. The creature took a deep breath as they opened fire. The thing dropped to the ground instantly.

Almost immediately, another raider appeared from the west side of the clearing. Ray was looking in that direction and fired wildly, crying out in surprise. Christie looked in his direction. Ari kept her focus on the north side of the clearing, and thus was not surprised when a third raider leaned around the corner. It was holding a long arm and took aim at her. Ari fired once and shot it through the neck. It dropped to the ground, trying vainly to breathe. Ari finished it off with one more shot. The raider that Ray fired upon advanced through his hail of rounds. Ray fired rapidly and took a step backward in shock. The thing was almost upon him before it seemed to trip and fall. Ray and Christie fired together at the body. It did not move again.

"Reloading," said Christie, fumbling with the stock pouch.

Something jumped on Ray from the rock above. It was small and black, and found a grip on Ray's head and neck. Ray screamed and dropped his rifle, groping for the creature. Christie dropped her own rifle and tried to help Ray. She reached for the thing and was rewarded with a backfist to the face. Ari lunged forward and jammed the barrel of her rifle into the creature's clothing. She pulled laterally with all her strength, and with Ray's help managed to dislodge the raider from his shoulders. It flew through the air, slid down the hill a few feet, and regained its footing. It hissed loudly at Ray and Ari. Ray smoothly drew his revolver managed to hit it in the head. Ari lowered her rifle and looked at Ray approvingly.

Again, there was silence.

"Everybody sound off!" said Richter.

"Clear to the west, tango down." said Ray, his voice wavering.

"Clear to the south, tango down." said Christie.

"Clear to the east," said John.

"Clear over here," said Ari. "Tango down."

Richter nodded. "That's five, then. Everybody take cover again."

The team did so. Richter motioned back towards the road.

"Nobody else is coming," whispered Ray.

"They're waiting to see what happened," replied Richter. "Let's let them know. Ari, would you do the honors please?"

"You bet," Ari replied, taking position.

Ari aimed at the several torch bearers that now littered the caravan. Slowly she began firing. The raiders began to expedite their activity, and a few of them went down. After about a half a minute Ari's bolt locked back on an empty magazine, and she reached for the stock pouch.

"That's good enough," said Richter. "It looks like they're withdrawing."

The remaining torches were extinguished, and the raiders began moving away to the north. They took all but one of the wagons with them. Soon, all that the team could see were bodies. Richter waited another two minutes before getting up.

"What now?" asked Christie, climbing to her feet.

"Now we get the hell out of here," said Richter. "We can't stay here now. They might come back with more men."

"Shall we continue the last two clicks to the mine?" asked John.

"We should. Everybody get your gear squared away and get some chow. When we're done eating we'll skirt around the battle area and continue to the mine. Hopefully we can rest there. Agreed?"

There were no objections. Ray pushed over the body of the first raider that had attacked him.

"What the hell is this thing?" he said.

The corpse looked like a minotaur. It had been shot multiple times.

"I don't know," began John. "Seth never mentioned anything like it."

"This one looks like a Rakhar except that it's got four arms," said Ari.

"Mutants, maybe?" said Christie.

"Who knows? As long as we can kill them."

Richter kneeled down and picked up one of the raider's pistols. He found the magazine release and ejected it. John kneeled next to him.

"Looks like a standard firearm, at least the kind we're familiar with," said John.

"Yeah," said Richter. "We finally get to grab some alien hardware, and it doesn't look any better than our own stuff."

"We could go check the bodies for weapons. We should check them anyway to see if there are any survivors."

"That's not our problem," said Ari.

"I agree," said Richter. "We can check on the second to last guy to make it to the hill, but going out there back towards the caravan site isn't a good idea. We don't have the medical resources to do much of anything anyway. I hate to leave anyone who is still alive too, but we've got to look after ourselves."

"It's a damn shame," said Christie.

"It is," replied Ray. "Hey, let me look at that bruise."

"Does anybody want any of these alien weapons?" asked John.

"They look like pieces of shit," said Ari.

Richter shrugged. "Grab a couple pistols if you want, Scherer. Just remember that we'll be hauling out all that Talvanium tomorrow. If you don't mind the extra weight, be my guest."

"I'd like to see what Seth can tell us about them," said John. "At least we won't have to wait for fifty scientists to spend a month doing so."

Ray laughed. The others began gathering their gear.

"Shall we choose another clearing for dinner?" asked Christie. "I can't say I care for this one any longer."

"Yeah, let's move along. Be careful, one or two of those things may have escaped our notice. We don't want to add one of ourselves to the menu."

## 13.

One hour later, after a quick meal and a rather tense march, the team arrived at a small canyon. Once they'd drawn within a hundred meters of the canyon they were able to distinguish a few artificial structures. They approached cautiously, but were able to reach the perimeter of the structures without being challenged. There were no lights within the structures, and the surroundings remained silent.

The purpose of the buildings was quite clear. This was a mining operation. Elevators and stairways led into the canyon, and a row of four conveyor belts led up a steep slope and into one of the buildings. A few pieces of equipment remained scattered about, apparently no worse for wear after some time of disuse. A few signs were posted here and there, illegible to the humans.

The team crept about slowly. A slight gleam caught John's eye, and he motioned for the others to stop. Near the corner of one building lay a small pile of something. Part of the pile glowed a pale green. Richter motioned for Ari and Ray to keep an eye out, while he, John and Christie went to check it out.

There were a few baseball-sized lumps of metal in the pile that were responsible for the greenish glow. Christie picked one up. It was heavy, but when she scratched it with her fingernail she was able to scrape some material away.

"Soft glowing metal, just like the Z'Sorth said," Richter whispered.

"It's radioactive," said John. "I hope Seth would have mentioned if it was dangerous."

"I doubt that it is," said Christie. "Not only would Seth have mentioned it, but if it was dangerous by itself I imagine it would be much more valuable. Plus, the people in this part of the galaxy don't seem stupid enough to leave dangerous materials lying around like this."

"They seem at least as smart as humans, which is hardly reassuring, Christie."

"Tritium isn't dangerous," said Richter. "I think we'll be fine."

John took the metal pieces and put them in his backpack. Richter motioned towards the canyon and the team reassembled.

"I just noticed something odd," Ari whispered to Richter.

"What's that?"

"When we stepped off of the ship in Metzqual, I felt the hair on the back of my neck stand up. When we left the town, the feeling went away. That same feeling just started back up again."

"When, just now?"

"Like three seconds ago, yes."

"It's probably just your spidey-senses, Wildcat."

The team approached the edge of the canyon. Below, a building had been constructed into the side of the canyon wall. Firelight flickered from a few of the windows.

"Looks like somebody's home," whispered John.

"There's also a humming sound," said Ari. "I thought I was imagining it, but it's like that sound back in Metzqual."

"Yeah," began Christie, "there was a humming sound in town. It seemed to be everywhere, with no distinct source. I didn't think anything of it at the time."

Richter looked at Ari with a curious expression.

"God will protect us during this great struggle," he said.

"Since when are you a religious man?" replied Ari.

"Cover!" hissed Richter.

Despite the sudden surprise that Richter caused in the others, they sprinted smoothly for the elevator control building and pressed up against it.

"What the fuck?" breathed Ari.

"I said that phrase in Arabic," Richter whispered.

Spotlights from the tops of the two other buildings flashed to life. Christie and Ray found themselves caught in the stunning brightness. Ray grabbed Christie's arm and pulled her around the corner with the others.

"Don't move!" exclaimed a voice from the roof of the northern building. "We've got your position covered!"

Ari growled. "If somebody says, 'they must have a buffer zone,' they're going to get punched in the..."

"We come in peace!" yelled John.

Ray laughed involuntarily, and quickly stifled himself.

"Identify yourself!" the voice commanded.

"My name is Scherer. My friends and I are Perditian traders. We're here to purchase Talvanium."

"Advance one to be recognized."

John handed his rifle to Ray, and walked into the light. He strode about five meters forward, virtually blinded.

"That's far enough. Look towards the light on your left."

John did so.

"We have Residerian credits," he said. "I hope you'll accept them."

"Stand by."

There was a smattering of low conversation from above. John considered showing them the credits, but that would require reaching into one of his pockets.

"You're a long way from home," the voice said.

"Our needs are rather specific."

"You can't find what you need within two hundred thousand light years?"

"I said we're looking for Talvanium. You know perfectly well there are only two places to get it. We rather rapidly discovered we sure weren't going to get any from the Umberians."

"What do you need Talvanium for?"

"I don't see how that's relevant."

"Fair enough. Let's see the cash."

John pointed towards his pocket, and when there was no objection he reached in and withdrew the credits.

"Tell you friends to come out with their weapons slung."

Turning back towards the elevator control building, John beckoned the others forward. The spotlights were lowered to a point directly in front of John. This allowed him to see the Residerian that was approaching from the northern building.

"You're still covered, so don't try anything," the Residerian said.

When he was on the other side of the pool of light, the Residerian stopped.

"My name is Ianove. I represent the mining conglomerate."

"I thought this mine was abandoned," John replied.

"The conglomerate would never abandon a perfectly good mine. We've simply suspended operation for the time being. When demand goes back up, we'll go right back into production."

"It doesn't seem like demand for Talvanium will go back up any time soon."

"And yet, here you are."

"Don't call your shareholders just yet. We only need one hundred and thirty-two pounds."

"Curious. You must be doing research and development."

"Correct."

"I wish you the best of luck. The best scientists on Residere Beta have been working for a decade and they haven't been able to replicate Umberian technology. If you do succeed, give them a call. Your civilization stands to make a lot of money if you share the information with them. And you'll need, of course, a lot more than a hundred and thirty pounds of Talvanium. I'd love to be the one to sell it to you, but I doubt I'll ever see you again."

"Thanks for the vote of confidence. Now let's get down to business. What's this stuff going to cost us?"

"Just in case you do come back some day, I'll offer you the low introductory price of one credit per pound."

John grimaced. "That's a lot more than we were expecting. It's certainly a lot more than it's currently worth. We know that much already."

"You are more than welcome to try dealing with the Zendreen, sir."

"I'll give you a hundred credits for the lot. It's more than fair."

"The price is not negotiable."

"Have you ever heard of the planet Mars?"

"What? No."

"The civilization there is pre-space travel. Our sources have definitively identified that Talvanium is available there. It's much further out of our way than Residere, but it's still an option. We have ethical concerns about landing on their planet and taking the Talvanium, and we can't wait around for them to develop interplanetary travel. However, if you can't accommodate us we will make an exception."

"I find it hard to believe that you'd go through all of that trouble to save a hundred credits."

"We only have a hundred, pal. We could travel all the way back to Metzqual, trade for more credits, and come back here, sure. There's something you should know about Perditians, though. We hate getting ripped off and we don't easily forget a grudge. Our superiors would sooner send us to Mars than have us return here to pay your outrageous price."

"I'll tell you what. I like that slug-thrower the female is holding."

Ianove pointed at Ari.

"You mean her rifle?"

"Yes. How much ammunition do you have for it?"

"I have eighty rounds left," said Ari.

"Give me her weapon, all of her ammunition, and one magazine each from the other two. How much ammunition would that be?"

"There are twenty rounds per magazine. That would be one hundred and twenty rounds total."

"That, plus your hundred credits, and we have a deal."

"What the hell am I supposed to do if we get ambushed on the way back?" Ari said indignantly.

"Take my rifle," said Ray. "I'll take the Remington. We'll be fine."

"One more thing and we have a deal," began John. "Include a comfortable place for us to sleep for several hours."

Ianove smiled. "That goes without saying. There's something you should know about Residerians. We know how to treat guests."

---

"It's terrible. I can't be more than three feet from a bucket at any time. I have to keep drinking water just so my stomach has something to..."

"All right, all right, for the love of the core, stay home. We'll figure something out."

"Thanks, Chief. Rylie out."

Fernwyn leaned back in her sofa chair and sighed. That was one thing taken care of. She reached into her pocket and pulled out her tracking monitor. Still nothing. That was the next thing to tackle. Fernwyn activated a communications channel and waited.

Nathalier's visage appeared on the screen.

"Officer Rylie. It's good to see you again so soon."

"Same here, sergeant. Listen, I was hoping you could help me out again."

"Maybe."

"Are you alone?"

"Yes."

"I tracked that alien ship to Residere Alpha. It seems fairly obvious now that they're trying to obtain Talvanium. I managed to tag one of the crew with a tracker module, but when he returned to the ship the signal was disrupted. I guess I shouldn't have been surprised about that."

"You mean because of the invisibility field?"

"Yes."

"Why didn't you confront them when you had the chance?"

"Well, first of all some of the crew had gone out to procure the Talvanium. If I put myself in the way of them completing their objectives, I might have been taken as a hostile and dealt with appropriately. Furthermore, I was acting on my own. I was out of uniform and certainly out of SPF jurisdiction. If it came down to it I wouldn't have been able to effect an arrest. Finally, I was simply outnumbered. There will be a better time to contact them. If I was right about which mine they were planning to visit, there's still plenty of time before they return. That's why I called you."

"What can I possibly do for you, Rylie?"

"You mentioned it already. The invisibility field. Your sensors were trained on that ship when it disappeared, right?"

"Yes."

"Have you analyzed the data stream yet?"

"We've been ordered to close that case, Rylie. Empire doesn't wish to get in the way of the Black Crest or the SPF."

"You didn't delete it, did you?"

"No. It's not our policy to do so. You never know when something like that might be useful for twisting someone's arm."

"Ha. Passive aggressive, as always. Can you send me the data recordings?"

"Not without being noticed. I can do it in person."

Fernwyn leapt to her feet. "I'll be there in ten minutes. I'll contact you upon arrival to let you know which landing platform I get."

"Okay. I'll prepare a disc for you. Have you had lunch yet?"

"What? Er, no."

"Then why not meet on the food concourse? It'll be a perfect cover for our meeting."

"That's not a bad idea, except that Rakhar generally don't approve of interspecies relationships."

"Did I say it was a date? Besides, things are a lot more libertine here than other parts of the galaxy. I doubt even if that's the impression we give that we'll raise any eyebrows. Half the guys here think I have a hairless fetish because of you anyway."

Fernwyn laughed. "Good enough. I'll see you on the concourse. Rylie out."

After stretching her limbs Fernwyn began to gather her things. If she was lucky, there would be something in the data stream that would help her find a way around the invisibility shield. She wasn't comfortable confronting the crew about their intentions until she knew more about them, and doing it alone certainly seemed like a poor idea. She needed more evidence to convince her superiors that the case deserved their attention, evidence compelling enough to overcome the influence of the Black Crest. So far she had almost nothing. If she couldn't find a way to track the ship before they departed Alpha, she'd be back to square one.

After spending a moment trying to decide how many magazines to take with her, Fernwyn holstered her sidearm and headed for the door. Something stopped her before she exited. There had been a thought gnawing at her subconscious, a memory that couldn't find enough daylight to surface. It was catching a glimpse of herself in her civilian clothing in her hall mirror that did it. She wore a long, brown coat, high boots and a tunic belted at the waist, and looked very much the rogue. Everybody knew that the Zendreen bounty had been renewed, and everybody assumed that the ship was Umberian. The memory in question had more than just stopped her in her tracks. It scared the hell out of her.

    The Zendreen were not the only enemies of Umber.

## 14.

The ship did not have a name. To name a ship required either imagination or inspiration. To the captain, it needed a name no more than a hammer or a vise.

It was a small ship, relatively speaking. Four decks and fifty-two meters from stem to stern. It hadn't been built for style or for show, and in the eleven years since it was built the captain had used it in a manner directly related to the ship's purpose.

The Umberian Mark XVII was a long range, search and destroy fighter craft. It nominally employed a crew of forty, but the captain had never needed more than half that number. The design was only a year old when the captain had acquired the ship, and for most of the following decade it was the best fighter craft in the entire Magellanic Cloud. Only recently had one or two Residerian/Z'Sorth designs matched it, and such a weighing was a dead heat. In fact, it was this ship in particular that had inspired the designs that rivaled it, as survival is often the best impetus for advancing technology.

The captain's name was Aldebaran, terror of the Tarantula Nebula.

The first mate's name was Tomn Harrish, and he was the second man to hold the title. The first one had ceased to be useful to Aldebaran, and then he had ceased to be. That was five years ago, a length of time that had passed rapidly for Harrish.

The first mate on this ship had to be capable of everything the captain was not, so it was fortunate for Harrish that he was so versatile. Morale was one thing that was Harrish's responsibility. It had been more important this year than previously. It was not a good year to be a pirate.

The new ships to come out of the Residere system could repel Aldebaran's ship if they met on a two-to-one basis and if their captains were of above average skill. With both Empire Security and many mercenary guilds now running escorts with these ships, it was becoming more and more difficult to take a prize. Many pirates had either retired or left the cloud in search of easier pickings. Word of turf wars between pirate ships had even begun to circulate, violating the code of honor that usually bound them. All of this served to discourage everyone, including those falling under Harrish's concern. He usually only had to remind them of their place in the pecking order, however, for those grumblings to be quashed.

Aldebaran was the most prolific and successful pirate in the cloud. His crew was the richest as a result. Any one of them could retire as a millionaire whenever they chose. The eighteen men and women aboard currently chose to stay to seek further fame and fortune. It was because of this unending desire to increase their wealth and reputations that Aldebaran kept them aboard beyond their ability to simply do their jobs. Occasionally a crewmember would take stock of their wealth and lose their willingness to die for Aldebaran, at which point they were invited to retire. A pirate cannot be concerned for his or her own life, that was a central tenet.

Harrish was in the galley finishing his evening meal and preparing the daily briefing for his captain. Today's briefing included an important preliminary report that Harrish had been carefully preparing for a few days. He was waiting for that critical moment when the report would be important enough to give to the captain, but not so pressing that it would seem to be late in coming. Leitke, the engineer, dozed quietly at the next table over. He'd just spent several hours straight working on a crucial repair, and had barely finished a meal before falling asleep.

Satisfied in both repast and reconnaissance, Harrish stood up and climbed the stairs to the 'tween deck. It was a short walk past the officer's quarters to the door to the grand cabin, where the captain spent most of his off hours. He pressed a key next to the door three times, triggering a corresponding flashing light on the interior. The door opened, indicating the captain's willingness for company. Harrish entered, closing the door behind him.

As always, the grand cabin was completely dark save for the starlight through the windows. Aldebaran sat silently behind his desk, his expression unseen but easily guessed. Despite having done this almost every day for five years, Harrish still felt a twinge of adrenaline upon entering. He crossed to a leather sofa chair on the right side of the desk.

"Would you like the daily report now, sir?"

"Yes," said Aldebaran in his typically flat tone.

Harrish sat down and cleared his throat.

"No unusual transmissions or activity from Distare, first of all. No ships have passed within a hundred thousand kilometers of us. No sensors have been aimed in our direction." Harrish paused as if waiting for a response, even though he did not expect any. "The Mark Sevens are fully recharged. Leitke figured out why the energy was bleeding off and repaired them. I took the liberty of deactivating the dissipation field after that since it was no longer needed. All other systems are nominal, and the crew is sound. I have a special report for you, too."

"Proceed."

"Four days ago a ship arrived at Umber and began attacking the Zendreen defense satellites. Shortly thereafter the Zendreen renewed their bounty on Umberians. Three days ago this same ship landed at Gleeful Complexium on Residere Beta. The energy signature was confirmed to be Umberian. Mercenaries from the Black Crest attempted a corral at the Complexium, but were not successful. The ship escaped to parts unknown. The Solar Police Force is not pursuing the case, but the merc frequencies are buzzing about it."

"So an Umberian ship has appeared again. They must be suicidal."

"Indeed. Word on the freqs is that they were using projectile weapons, but that they had an effective invisibility shield. There's even an unsubstantiated rumor that the occupants were not Umberian."

"But the ship is Umberian."

"Yes, sir, I obtained a copy of the energy signature myself. I put the file in your folder. You should look at it."

Aldebaran turned on his computer monitor, illuminating his face with a blue glow. He was an Umberian in his forties, with a black goatee and eyes that stared unblinkingly. His hair was short-cropped and he wore the jacket of the long-since decimated Umberian military. The jacket meant nothing to him now. It was just a piece of clothing.

"This energy signature is the same as ours. This ship has the same engine we do."

"That's the conclusion I reached, too, sir."

Aldebaran calmly stood up. "Set a course for Residere Beta, maximum speed."

"Aye, sir."

"I'll be on the bridge shortly."

Harrish bowed slightly and exited. Aldebaran sat down again, and began to think. There had been only a handful of Mark XVIIs to escape the Zendreen. As far as Aldebaran knew, none of them were manned by the Umberian military. Despite the impossible odds, the Umberian Solar Defense Force had fought to the last man during the invasion. For a Mark XVII to return after ten years was puzzling, and as he'd mentioned to Harrish, borderline suicidal. Aldebaran quickly reached a conclusion. The crew of the ship in question was very probably not Umberian, and also very probably not aware of just how dangerous it was to be gallivanting around the Nebula in an Umberian military fighter craft. The ship had probably been sold or captured by someone else. Any Umberian lucky enough to escape the Zendreen would never return.

Any Umberian lucky enough to escape Aldebaran would never return.

---

"I waited too long for this. I shouldn't be so rough on myself."

Fernwyn arrived back at the table first, with Nathalier joining her seconds later. They were on level five of the Complexium, which housed a few of the more expensive restaurants. It was well past the lunch hour there, so the pair had their choice of tables. Fernwyn chose one in a corner created by a restaurant and an elevator. Nathalier sat down and turned his nose up at Fernwyn's meal.

"How can you stand that stuff?" he asked.

"Just because I don't look like your typical Residerian doesn't mean I didn't grow up here," Fernwyn replied.

"Bah. That stuff is too spicy. Try some of mine."

"No thanks, I heard them kill your food on my way back to the table."

"I insist."

Nathalier pushed his tray towards Fernwyn.

"It's those furry ears of yours, right? You don't seem to hear... oh..."

Sliding the tray halfway off of the table, Fernwyn allowed a data disc to drop into her lap. She pocketed it with her left hand as she took a forkful of whatever animal was on the plate.

"Not bad," she said. "I only hope that it doesn't end up validating the lie I told to my boss to come here today."

"You're supposed to be at work?"

"Uh huh."

"I'd be careful with that. You're certainly not making any friends elsewhere in the SPF."

"Just between us, I'm getting a little fed up with the SPF. Here we have a case that is obviously quite important, and they're letting the Black Crest prevent us from doing the job."

"It's politics. Today it's the Black Crest, next it will be somebody else. In a free society the police will always feel the influence of affluent groups. Money is more powerful than good will."

"True, but this time I'm dealing with a potential violation of the peace treaty between the SUF and the Zendreen. It's in the best interest of the Black Crest to stand aside."

"Not when they'll accomplish the same thing you would and get paid for it. If they collect on the bounty, then the problem goes away, right?"

Fernwyn tapped her fork on her plate absent-mindedly, and gazed around the court. "The Black Crest has always been an off-shoot of the Rakhar Empire, even if they don't pretend to be interested in ruling over anyone. Do you really think they have any real affinity for the SUF? Don't you think they'd ally with the Zendreen if they thought it was in their best interest?"

"I think you're overestimating the Crest's desire for galactic glory, Rylie. They stand to make a lot more money within a system of government like the SUF. There aren't too many business opportunities in a communist dictatorship like the Zendreen, and they don't share power with anyone. If the Crest did arrange a new system of government as allies of the Zendreen, it would probably be a thinly-veiled overture to war."

"Do you think the Black Crest could win a war with the Zendreen?"

"No, which is why your theory is unfounded. It's the collective strength of the SUF that keeps the Zendreen at bay."

"Still, as I mentioned before, the Zendreen could be looking for an excuse to wage war with us. That's why I need to find out what this Umberian ship is up to. At the very least it could get me the promotion I'm looking for."

"What would you rather be doing?"

"I'd rather be a detective! Isn't it obvious? In fact, it's bitterly ironic that all this sneaking around could get me fired even though I feel it's necessary towards a promotion."

"It's ironic, yes, but it's only bitter to you."

"I suppose."

"You've got the smarts to be a detective, so I say go for it. You look better in street clothes anyway."

Fernwyn smiled. "Thank you."

The pair allowed the conversation to lapse as they caught up on eating. Fernwyn looked at Nathalier after a few minutes.

"You're not a typical Rakhar, you know that?" she said.

"At least I look the part. I can only imagine what life has been like for you as a genmod."

"Did you know I was the first genmod considered a complete success?"

"No, I did not."

"Yeah, I'm in the history books. Fernwyn D. Rylie, daughter of Hal and Merryl Rylie of Residere Beta. Look it up."

"I will. Listen, Rylie, are you sure you want to go this alone?"

"It's easier for me to work alone."

"I might be able to open some doors for you."

"My shuffling license is still valid. I have more connections than you might imagine."

"What about combat?  Things could get hairy, if what happened here is any indication."

"I can handle myself.  My ship is armed to the teeth, too.  I'm not worried about the Umberians or whomever.  Except..."

"Except what?"

"Remember Aldebaran?"

"What do you mean, remember Aldebaran?  Mothers still tell the stories to children to keep them in line.  I'm as likely to forget about Aldebaran as I am to forget my own name."

"And yet you hadn't considered his stake in all of this."

"True enough.  I guess enough time has passed."

"Well, then, what's he the most famous for?"

Nathalier leaned back in his chair, nodding solemnly.  A response was not necessary.

"I always thought you were brave, Rylie," he said.  "Now I wonder if you're not simply insane."

"You know what's going to happen to these people if Aldebaran finds them before I do.  The Black Crest is no doubt thinking the same thing, except they only stand to lose the corral money."

"And you only stand to lose a potential promotion.  Going up against Aldebaran means losing your life, too.  You may have to accept the runner-up prize of knowing that the SUF-Zendreen treaty will be safe."

Fernwyn began to tap with her fork again.

"What are you thinking?" asked Nathalier, reaching for a toothpick in the condiment tray.

"I wonder if we can play the Zendreen off of Aldebaran."

"You mean assuming the Zendreen want these people alive."

"Well, yeah."

"I don't think it would make any difference." Nathalier picked at his white fangs. "The Black Crest is operating as the Zendreen's agent here in the Residerian system for a reason. The Zendreen don't want to violate the treaty, either, at least not in an overt fashion. If capturing the ship intact is their goal, they'll have to rely on the Crest. If they send so much as one of their own vessels into this star system, they'll commit an act of war."

"Then it's a three-sided race. The Black Crest versus Aldebaran versus me. The mercs will stop at nothing because they've already had their nose bloodied by these folks, which amuses me greatly by the way. Aldebaran will stop at nothing because he's Aldebaran. I'm the only one who's willing to give these people a fair shake. If they truly are working for the liberation of Umber then as far as I'm concerned they deserve our help."

"For the love of the core, Rylie, are you really that naive?"

"I beg your pardon, sergeant?"

"What are you, twenty-seven years old?"

"Twenty-eight."

"Weren't you paying attention to current events in college? I know I was. The Zendreen took advantage of the political situation in the nebula and invaded Umber knowing that the SUF wouldn't raise a finger to object. If Umber and the SUF had been united they could have repelled the Zendreen invasion entirely, albeit after one hell of a fight."

"I remember my history, Nathalier."

"Then you should see the obvious here. It's not just the influence of the Black Crest that is keeping the SUF, and by extension, you and the SPF away from the investigation. If the ship is really working for the Umberian underground, the SUF has a vested interest in seeing that their mission fails. They won't stand in the way of the Black Crest because they know perfectly well what will happen if they piss off the Zendreen!"

A couple of people walking by looked over at the table, and Nathalier forced himself to speak softly again.

"The SUF refused to help the Umberians ten years ago because they were afraid of them and their advanced technology. They twisted their arm in the political arena and got them to sign a non-aggression pact with the other member planets. The SUF may not have wanted Umber to be invaded; I'm sure they weren't vindictive or anything. However, when the Zendreen did show up the SUF did the only thing they could to survive, and stayed neutral in the conflict while signing a peace treaty with the Zendreen."

"Damn it, I said I remember my history!"

"Then think about it for a minute, Rylie. Think about what that means for your promotion potential. Finding this ship may get you promoted, yes, but only if you do the opposite of what your conscience is telling you."

Fernwyn slumped back in her chair. "Shit. I'm not a third party to this at all. Even if I find these folks, what the hell am I supposed to do with them?"

"Even I can't recommend helping them, Rylie. You're messing with the status quo of the entire Tarantula Nebula. If you help them you may start another war. I don't know about you, but I don't favor the idea of Zendreen landlords for the Complexium."

Fernwyn's expression was grim. "Sometimes I think that Residere was better off under the Rakhar Empire."

Nathalier smiled. "If that were true today, you'd be about two hundred pounds heavier right now, and I'd be a soldier instead of a security guard."

"There is another possibility."

"Oh?"

"Remember that we were speculating that it was another alien race that was helping the Umberians?"

"Uh huh."

"If this ship is just a scout, meant to recon the situation, obtain Talvanium, and return to home, then we might expect a liberation fleet at some point in the future."

"That's a reasonable assumption."

"So if an alien fleet capable of liberating Umber comes along and actually repels the Zendreen, how do you think a free Umber is going to feel about the SUF?"

"None too pleased, I would imagine."

Fernwyn stood up. "Residere voted for the Umberian non-aggression resolution the same as the other SUF member planets. They're just as guilty of abandoning Umber to the Zendreen as the rest of them. I'm going to find these people one way or the other. If there's a major shift of power on the way for the nebula, I want to make sure Residere is on the right side this time."

## 15.

"Thank God that nightmare is finally over!"

Dana flew down the steps to the cargo bay and hit the button to open the ramp. She could barely catch her breath as the ramp slowly lowered, revealing the desert and the town of Metzqual beyond. Her five friends were gathered at the base of the ramp, and were waving goodbye to a Z'Sorth with two Wolrasi. John was the first to turn around.

"Hi, Dana," he said. "How's it going?"

"Jesus, you had me worried. Did you get the Talvanium?"

The others turned and walked up the ramp. They were all smiles, but looked exhausted.

"Sure did. We made some new friends, too."

"The mission may have been a success," began Christie, "but that was the hardest two days of my entire life."

"Seth, play Sabotage, volume thirty percent."

The unmistakable sound of The Beastie Boys filled the cargo bay.

"You must be in a good mood," said Dana.

"It's good to be back."

"I'm going to take a shower, eat something, and take a nice long nap," said Ari, dropping her backpack.

"I smell gunpowder," Dana said with a raised eyebrow.

"The local freaks had to give us a reception," said Ray.

"We did alright," said Richter, unlimbering his rifle.

The team put down their gear. Tycho came down the stairs and happily greeted Christie.

"Did you manage to get the full amount?" asked Dana.

"I think so," replied John. "Seth, read the Talvanium in the cargo bay and tell us how much there is."

"One hundred forty point two five pounds," Seth replied.

"How soon can you start on the new weaponry?"

"There are several logistical problems we must address first."

"Okay. Everyone, take some time to get yourselves cleaned up. I'm going to consult with Dana and Seth and figure out our next move. Meet in the conference room in an hour. I know we want to get some sleep as soon as possible, but let's make sure we're all squared away first."

"Sounds good," said Ray.

John passed his rifle to Ray and gestured for Dana to lead the way upstairs.

"I guess Byron is too busy to welcome us home," said John as he climbed.

"We have another problem with Byron," growled Dana.

"Oh, shit. What happened?"

At the top of the stairs, the pair opened the door to the bridge and entered. Friday leapt down from the console and greeted John.

"We forgot to lock out the ramp controls."

"Oh! He didn't make a run for it, did he? Hello, sweetie..."

"No, but he did try to go for a little stroll. I don't think he was trying to escape. He didn't run from me when I went after him. I had to use force to get him to come back inside, though."

John checked the systems at a station. "How much force?"

"I cracked him a good one on his shoulder blade with the butt of a rifle."

"Ouch."

"That was two days ago. I haven't spoken to him since I locked him in the cargo hold."

"You were the only one Byron hadn't played yet. I hadn't thought about it before; if I had I wouldn't have so readily left him alone with you."

"I can handle myself."

John used his sleeve to wipe some dust from a screen. "Obviously. I meant that we might have considered locking him up before we left, that's all. It's only natural that he would have tested your limits if he had the chance."

"Now he knows."

John looked at Dana and smiled. "Damn right."

Sitting down in the pilot's chair, John stretched his legs. Dana leaned against the console.

"Okay, Seth," began John, "what do we have to do to install the new weaponry?"

"First of all, the invisibility shield must be deactivated. Second, the installation will compromise the internal pressurization, so it must be done from planetside. Once those conditions are met the installation will take but a few moments. Material from the rear thirty and extra hull material not being used will be sufficient for construction. I will attempt to communicate the control programs to your Earth systems but certain interpolations may require Ari's help."

"Wait a minute, what extra hull materials?"

"The space that will be occupied by the energy rails and laser emitters will be sufficient."

"Oh. That works well, then. Where should we go for this? All of the buffer zones on Alpha are near population centers, so we can't deactivate the shield here."

"Why not Beta?" asked Dana.

"The Solar Police Force is most likely still looking for us so I don't think camping out near their largest bases of operation is such a good idea."

"That reminds me," Dana began, "I came up with a program that modifies our energy signature."

"That's great! How does it work?"

"It simply changes the waveform output of the engine harmonics. It's kind of like installing a custom muffler or fuel injector."

"Congratulations, Dana, you did it. I'll put you in for a raise next quarter."

Dana laughed. "Thanks, but all I did was ask Seth the right question."

"What was it?"

"How do the pirates in this system hide from the authorities?"

"There you go. It also gives us the next right question to ask Seth, hopefully?"

"Where do the pirates hide from the authorities?"

"If they're successfully hidden," began Seth, "how should I know?"

"Are you being a smart-ass, Seth?" asked John incredulously.

"Not intentionally. May I elaborate on the answer?"

"Never assume we want the minimum possible answer, Seth. Remember when you were telling me about the alien races? Be that verbose."

"Understood. Residere Delta has traditionally been a hideout for pirates. There are two reasons why. One, the elected government on Delta has always insisted on a libertarian system, kind of like the one in place at Gleeful Complexium but more structured than the virtual anarchy on Alpha. Two, the government has enacted sweeping and strict environmental laws that keep most of the moon undeveloped. The result is a society that's easy to disappear into, and with plenty of hiding places to boot."

"They're libertarians but they have strict environmental laws?"

"To do no harm to others is their creed. That includes the environment, which many Deltans believe is an entity in and of itself."

"Sort of like the native Americans," said Dana.

"Seems that way," said John. "What's Delta's policy on going after pirates that may be camped out there?"

"They don't care as long as the pirates do no harm," said Seth.

"I meant their diplomatic policy with the SUF."

"They treat their entire moon as a protected property. The SPF has to submit a specific warrant to the local authorities before they can look for someone, and even then the warrant has to be accurate to a one hundred mile area. Since Delta is sovereign entity the SPF has no choice but to follow their laws."

"Is Alpha a sovereign entity? Because I thought that the Residerian government had jurisdiction there."

"Alpha is not. Alpha and Beta fall under Residerian jurisdiction. Deltas refer to themselves as Deltas, not Residerians. Remember that the moon wasn't even habitable until the Umberian-Z'Sorth conglomerate came along and processed it. It was their bad luck that the resulting government was so keen on environmental preservation."

"Ah. But Delta is still part of the SUF?"

"Yes. They have the same number of delegates as any other member."

"I got you. So, we should be able to camp out there with the shield off unmolested?"

"It's a safe bet, but you're still gambling. Nowhere is perfect."

"It will have to do. Prepare for launch."

Seth began checking various systems in a manner requested by John. Seth seemed offended that John would want a more quantifiable confirmation of the systems above his word, but dutifully sent the information to the Earth computers nonetheless.

"There's something else, John," said Dana.

"What?"

"I've been reviewing the data from our fight with the Zendreen defense satellites. I'm sure that our invisibility shield was properly blocking our energy signature. I think the satellites were homing in on the uplink with Talvan's computer."

"That's good news, if you're right. It means we really are safe while the shield is up."

"I hope putting your butts on the line for these weapons doesn't prove to be an unnecessary risk," said Dana.

"I hope it does," replied John, "because I'd really rather not be in a position to use them."

"I'm sorry about that radio call, John."

"Don't be sorry about that. You should never keep concerns to yourself. You didn't see the point in two-thirds of the crew getting wiped out for weapons we may never need. In retrospect, we may not have needed five people on the mission. However, the prospect of getting into another fight before we return to Earth is a very real possibility. Somebody needed to go get the Talvanium, and there were five of us who wanted to go. I'm not in a position to order anyone around and refuse them the chance to participate in a mission."

"Are you patronizing me?"

John turned to face Dana, surprised. "What? What do you mean?"

"You've said before you don't think going back to Earth is our best option. So why are you speaking as if it's our only choice?"

"It's certainly not to placate you!"

"But you'd rather find another way."

"Yeah, I would."

"So do me a favor and tell me what you have in mind."

John sat down and crossed his arms. "I haven't mentioned this to anyone else yet. Professor Talvan said that he was working on some sort of virus that would destroy the Zendreen, and that he needed access to better lab equipment to do so."

"I remember."

"So now you know why I'm so keen on upgrading our weapons."

"Holy shit! You're not thinking of trying to rescue Talvan, are you?"

John nodded. "Bull's-eye."

"Bullshit! That's suicide!"

"Maybe so, maybe not. You just said that our stealth field is probably sound. We should be able to waltz right in and pick him up. We have his location, triangulated from when we were in contact with him."

"I said the stealth field is probably sound, not definitely so. Seth may still be right about the Zendreen's ability to track us regardless of it."

"I suppose if we show up and the satellites start to engage us again we'll know for sure."

"Yeah, except nobody knows where the Zendreen fleet is right now. Chances are pretty good at least part of it has been sent to bolster Umber's defenses."

"Oh yeah, I forgot about that."

"Going back to Earth and trying to build more ships there is still our safest course of action."

John pressed his hands together into a V. "With any luck we'll be able to hide out on Delta indefinitely. We'll have plenty of time to continue researching."

"I think it's time to define what's most important to us. We're all willing to risk our own lives to liberate Umber, but are we willing to lose everyone? If we all get killed we won't be doing Umber any good at all, and we'll be dead. I thought that I'd accepted that possibility when we first left Earth, but now I'm not so sure."

"Nobody here wants to die, Dana. I assure you that I'm not going to pressure the crew into a course of action that is unduly risky. We must assume some risk, but we're not going to try anything we don't think we can handle."

Dana turned and looked out the window. "Except you took everyone with you to get the Talvanium and left me alone with a sociopath. Are you going to seriously tell me that you knew for sure you'd all make it back safe and sound? Your actions and your words aren't dovetailing too well, Scherer."

John stood up. "Damn it, Dana, we didn't get this far by playing it safe! By coming out here we all agreed that the mission was more important than our own lives. The only exception to that was if we found out the mission was completely beyond our means to complete. But it isn't! We can do this! We can and we will liberate Umber!"

"You can run a good line, Scherer, but your true colors are never far from the surface. You just make sure that you don't get us all killed trying to satisfy your own ambition."

Dana exited the bridge. John realized he was trembling with anger. He flopped back down into the pilot's chair, and sighed.

"Shit."

John was tempted to go after her, but decided to let her cool off first. Until then, he had to have a chat with Byron. He slowly and painfully got up and exited the bridge. His body was well past the point of needing rest. It seemed like torture as John made his way to the lower deck. The others had already vacated the cargo bay. He passed through the ventral gun room and unlocked the door to the cargo hold.

"Are you here to continue the beatings?" said Byron.

John closed the door behind him. Byron was using one of the ammo cans to lift weight. He had a nasty bruise on his shoulder blade.

"Dana said you were being obstinate," said John.

"I didn't deserve to be smacked with a rifle butt."

"I agree, but then I'm not a five-four, one hundred and twenty-five pound female trying to deal with a jack-diesel guy like you who outweighs her by sixty pounds. You scared her enough to use force, so I'm willing to call it even."

"She could have broken my scapula or collar bone."

"You've tested everyone on board. You know you can't manipulate any of us. Why continue to act this way? It's been said that one of the sure signs of insanity is doing the same thing over and over again and expecting different results each time. I know you're not insane. Are you?"

"It's kind of hard to tell when you spend so much time alone."

"That's your own doing. Byron, I'm not here to check on your welfare. I'm here to give you one last chance to shape up and act like a normal member of this crew. We can't keep you in here forever and you know what the alternatives are."

Byron put down the ammo can. "I know."

"Listen, Byron. There's something I haven't discussed with anyone else yet. Seth was telling me more about the history of Umber. There's a major religious sect on the planet that believes in a particular prophecy. In this prophecy, seven strangers from a distant land are instrumental in saving Umber from a great calamity."

"Fascinating."

"Most faithful believe the prophecy was fulfilled two hundred years ago when the largest city-state on Umber was sacked by a nomadic army. It was said that seven tribesman from the north rode down and taught the besieged people how to fight back more effectively. However, actual historical records only show six heroes. Because of this, some believe that the prophecy has yet to be fulfilled."

"You're saying that because our ship has seven crewmembers that we're supposed to fulfill the prophecy?"

"I'm saying it's one heck of a coincidence. If you hadn't stowed away, we'd be one short."

"Maybe there were seven in that war and one of them was just locked up the whole time."

"What's the point of being part of a prophecy if you're just going to sit around and do nothing? We need all the friends we can get out here, Byron, and I want you to be one of them."

Byron wiped off his brow and put a shirt on. "You're not bullshitting me about this prophecy, are you? 'Cause you know I believe in fate."

"Seth, am I making up the Prophecy of the Seven Shepherds?"

"I don't know, I'm just a computer," said Seth.

"I mean the prophecy isn't something I fabricated, is it?"

"No."

"There you go. There's more to it. The reason why some believe the prophecy has yet to be fulfilled is because the seventh shepherd, the last to join, is supposed to be brash, uncooperative, and willful. The six other shepherds are supposed to reject him at first, and only work with him after he proves his usefulness."

"So how am I supposed to do that?" asked Byron.

"I don't know. As a functioning member of this crew, you'll probably find a way."

"What do you want me to do, other than clean the ship?"

"Just stand by on the bridge and be ready for any task. You've seen how quickly things can get complicated."

"All right. What about Dana and Christie?"

"I wouldn't so much as look at them sideways for now."

A soft beeping sound roused Fernwyn from sleep. In the four hours she'd allowed herself to rest she had been dreaming about work, and for a moment while waking she forgot all about the mysterious ship and her crew. Glancing at the time while turning off the alarm was enough to remind her.

Fernwyn donned a robe and walked into her living room. Her computer was still dutifully working on the problem of the invisibility shield. She'd instructed it to analyze the data in hopes of finding a small variance in the field. If the shield could be seen at all, even the slightest shimmer, a work-around was possible. Whether certain imperfections seen on the security recordings were due to such a variance or simply a result of the recording was what the computer was trying to determine. Unfortunately there were only two or three seconds of video of the ship disappearing after it tore the hell off of the landing platform at Gleeful.

Pouring the last cup of cold yutha, Fernwyn began to brew a new pot. She thought about Nathalier as she did so. His black fur had a sheen to it that reminded her of yutha. He was kind of cute, for a Rakhar, and she thought he had a good personality. Fernwyn had never been physically attracted to a single male of any species with the exception of Umberians, and she hadn't seen a single one of those in over seven years. Even then the way they wore their ear hair integrated into the hair on their heads was insipid. If popular culture on Beta was odd, it was downright bizarre on Umber. The fact that everything she'd learned about Umber was now wrong was sobering. Their entire culture had been destroyed by the invasion.

Fernwyn left the yutha to brew and sat down at the computer console. Next to it was the tracking module, which she'd left to recharge. She leaned forward and turned it on, sipping from her cup as she did so.

"Yuck."

The yutha was too rancid even for her. Fernwyn grimaced and walked into the kitchen, where she poured out the bitter liquid. She leaned against the counter and tried to find the patience to wait for the fresh pot. It would be done long before the computer program finished looking for the ship.

Having loaded its software, the tracking module started to beep. At first Fernwyn thought it was the console, so she was surprised to see that the module was indeed receiving a signal again. She smiled as she looked at the coordinates and walked to the nearest window.

Fernwyn didn't have to enter the coordinates into a nav program to know where they were. Her answer was glowing brightly in the sky. She turned and headed to the bathroom to take a quick shower when her communicator rang. It was Nathalier.

"Good evening, sergeant. What's up?"

"Not much on my end. I just thought I'd call to see how the work was going."

"It's only been five hours. How good do you think I am, anyway?"

"I don't know, how good are you?"

"Good enough to mark one of those guys with a tracker, remember? As I hoped, they got sloppy. Their shield is down and their hiding place has been revealed."

"Lemme guess, they're down the hall from you?"

"No, they're on Delta. I'm going to go check it out now."

"Are you sure you don't want some company, Rylie? Things could get rough."

"I'm going to try to extend the branch of peace to them, not shove it up their ass. I'll be fine."

"Well, call me if you need help. I can get over there in a couple of hours."

"I will. Thank you. I'll let you know what I find out."

Fernwyn closed the connection, grinning. She hadn't been this excited since her first successful corral.

"This much fun is just too good to share."

---

Gleeful Complexium was open all the time, but in the evenings there was much less traffic. That was fine with Aldebaran. It wasn't that he had an aversion to large crowds, only that the more people there were around the more likely someone might actually recognize him by sight. Anyone who had seen his face in the last ten years was either on his crew or, as the stories said, lived not the tale to tell.

As an Umberian he still had to disguise himself a bit. A wolrasi-leather hat with a wide brim covered the top of his ears, the hair on which could be trimmed but was practically impossible to remove completely. The hat was borrowed from Harrish and was of excellent quality, which meant it was probably a prize. The rest of his clothing was typical solar merchant fare. A satchel of dried Deltan herbs completed the costume, an addition meant to supply a cover story for any curious authorities.

A cover story was probably going to be necessary, considering that Aldebaran's plan involved talking with security. The trick was going to be finding the right person. Aldebaran strolled through the food court levels calmly, watching everything without seeming to do so. Most people were ignoring him so far.

Since he insisted on carrying an obsolescent projectile pistol and nothing else, Harrish had insisted on coming along. Aldebaran knew that the fewer pirates that wandered through Gleeful the better, and had soon decided to go alone. He'd taken a transport from a nearby port town, paid in cash, and had arrived at the Complexium without leaving any electronic trail. His ship was ready to swoop down and make an exit by fire if need be. It was a necessary risk. Aldebaran almost never put himself in a position of weakness like this.

There were many sights and sounds that would distract someone who spent most of their time aboard a ship, but to Aldebaran it was all meaningless. He had a perfect clarity of mind about his goals, and was unhindered by physical desires. It was another reason why he decided to go alone. The delicious smells in the food court were not lost on him, he simply didn't care about them; but to Harrish or the others it would have been a major distraction.

Aldebaran found the person he was looking for. A Rakhar with black fur sat outside of a cafe, a mug of yutha beside him. He had his head in his hands and he was obviously very tired. Aldebaran could see more than that, however. He knew something about the Umberian ship, and his mind was vulnerable. Aldebaran approached him and sat down at the table.

"Good evening, sergeant," said Aldebaran.
"Can I help you with something?" said the Rakhar.
"I am me."
"I'm Nathalier, nice to meet you. Would you like directions to a shop?"
"No, I want you to tell me about the Umberian ship that was here a few days ago."

Nathalier looked confused for a moment. Aldebaran found an unusual amount of resistance for a Rakhar, but pushed past it.

"What the... oh, you mean the strangers that got into it with the Black Crest, yeah."
"Who were they?"

"I don't know. They weren't any race we're familiar with around here."

"Why did they visit the Complexium?"

"They were looking for Talvanium."

If Aldebaran allowed himself the luxury of emotional reactions he would have been surprised. "How much?"

"I don't know."

"Did they get it?"

"No, none of the merchants here had any. They went to Alpha."

"How do you know this?"

"A Solar Police Force officer has been on their trail. She confirmed that they'd traveled to Alpha to get the Talvanium from one of the old conglomerate mines."

"Did they get it?"

"Presumably so. She nailed them with a tracker and just picked them up on Delta."

"What's the officer's name?"

"Fernwyn Rylie."

"Rylie."

"Yeah."

"I have Deltan herbs to trade. Where do you think I can get the best price?"

"There's a spice shop on level sixty-one. The owner seems fair."

"Thank you, Sergeant Nathalier. You've been very helpful."

"Enjoy your visit to Gleeful, sir."

Aldebaran stood up and walked toward the nearest elevator bank. He grabbed his comlink from his belt.

"Harrish, it's me. Fire up the ship and meet me on the roof of the Complexium."

"Is everything all right?"

"Fine, I got what I needed. There's simply no time to lose. We'll have to risk detection. I'll provide a distraction to help cover the pick-up."

"Very well, sir. We'll be there in five minutes."

Aldebaran closed the comlink and returned it to his belt. With the same hand he reached into his pocket and pulled out a small cylindrical device. Before stepping into the elevator, he dropped the device into a trash barrel. As the doors closed, Aldebaran spoke out loud without realizing it.

"It's time to introduce these strangers to another one of Professor Talvan's laudatory accomplishments."

## 16.

In a northern temperate zone of Delta there was a small glade nestled in a wooded valley. A shallow stream ran through it, and many years ago a mill had been built there. A large stone dam had welled the water enough to run a wheel, and for a while the settlers were happy. Fortune was not on their side, however, as no major towns had sprung up nearby. The mill had to be abandoned, and it remained so for five years. Everything of use had been stripped from the mill, and the dam had been partially dismantled to return the stream to its natural state. All that was left were the stones of the dam and of two walls of the mill. It had only been five years, but the ruins looked many times older.

Some time much more recently, a ship called the Reckless Faith had landed. It sat in the glade, floating silently about ten feet above the ground. The ramp began to open, and lowered slowly into place. At the top of the ramp there were three figures silhouetted against the light.

"Take it slow out there," said John.

"Seth said he couldn't read any humanoids around here," replied Ari.

"That was from orbit. He wasn't able to determine if any of the animals were dangerous, either. So be careful."

The ramp finished opening and the three friends descended to the earth. John had his Garand, Ray his Remington, and Ari had borrowed Richter's M4. By now they wore the weapons like an old hat.

"Seems like a nice enough place," said Ray.

"Stay here," said John. "Ari and I will snoop around a little."

"Roger."

John keyed his radio. "Dana, close the ramp."

The ramp raised until it was closed, casting the humans on the ground into darkness. John looked up and saw that one of the other moons was above. He wasn't sure which one but it was providing just enough light to see.

"Don't you want to begin the upgrades?" said Dana's voice over the commo.

John's departure from the ship was meant for more than scouting the perimeter. He wanted to see the weapons upgrades from the exterior of the ship.

"I want to make absolutely sure we're alone first."

"Okay. Let me know when you're ready and I'll give Seth the go-ahead."

"Roger, out."

John and Ari moved away from Ray, who seemed content to stay closer to the ship. They eyed the ruins of the mill carefully, and began to try to navigate around the stream. When they were about thirty yards away, Ari spoke.

"Ray really got a scare from that last firefight."

"A failure to stop incident with a thirty caliber rifle and a giant minotaur thingy will do that."

"Well, he seems a little rattled."

"You know Ray as well as I do. He'll be all right."

John and Ari took turns jumping across some stones and began creeping around the ruins. It was dead quiet. They circled around clockwise until they got to the edge of the old dam, and paused.

"You could hear a mouse sneeze," said Ari softly.

"It seems like a good choice. This is a good vantage point, too."

"You mean for the ship?"

"Dana, this is John. Go ahead and begin the upgrades."

"You got it," replied Dana.

The outline of the Faith was barely discernable from the dam, but the lighted windows of the bridge and other rooms shone clearly. With a sound like sand being poured onto a kitchen floor, distortions began fluttering around midships by level two, and around the fore and aft cannons.

A green dance of light particles jumped across the length of the hull, and two new features appeared on the port and starboard sides. They looked like long furrows that ran almost the entire length of the second level, and they glowed momentarily before fading into the darkness. The muzzle of the new phase cannon joined the already mean-looking business end of the thirty millimeter cannon on the fore end. Presumably the rear cannon had been replaced by one of the same.

"Upgrades in place," said Dana. "Seth is doing a diagnostic on them now. We won't be able to do a live fire until we're back in space, though. Not without alerting the locals."

"Very well," replied John. "Thank you, Dana. Scherer out."

"That was deceptively simple," said Ari.

"What do you mean? We had to go through hell just to get this far."

"True. At least now we have Byron backing us up."

"You don't approve of letting him out?"

"Not really."

"I told him he was part of an ancient Umberian prophecy and that his cooperation was essential towards fulfilling the prophecy."

Ari laughed. "Are you shitting me?"

"No, I'm not. Seth told me about a prophecy involving seven saviors from another world. I embellished it a little bit using Kurosawa's The Seven Samurai as inspiration. Hopefully Byron will take it to heart."

"Only Byron could buy such a load of crap."

John shrugged. The wind kicked up a bit, bringing a chill to the air.

"You know what this place feels like?" John asked, looking towards the stars.

Ari took a deep breath. "Yeah, I do. This is just like the night we first met Seth."

"Do you miss it?"

"What, you mean my old life?"

"Uh huh."

"Hardly. It bothers me a little that if I ever see my folks again it'll be ten years later for them."

John raised an eyebrow. "What about the fact that by now they'll have figured us for dead?"

"Tough. They'll know the truth some day."

"I hope you're right."

"Maybe once this whole thing is over we can come back here and spend a few days resting."

"You mean the crew?"

"Who else?"

John shifted his rifle to his left hand and tucked it under his arm. He extended his hand towards Ari.

"Got a clove?" he asked.

"Sure," Ari said, digging into a pocket for the cigarettes.

John accepted the offered smoke and lit it with a wooden match. He puffed on it and let the scent envelop him.

"Listen, Ari, about you and Richter."

"What about him?"

"I want you to know that I don't have a problem with the two of you being together."

"Is it that obvious?"

"Yeah."

"I wouldn't worry about it. Richter is just a pleasantry to me. I don't have any serious interest in him. Besides, I thought you wanted to keep things platonic between us."

"I do. I just don't want you to think that I'm jealous or anything."

"Would you be?"

"No. I mean, well... no. I... shit, what I mean is that..."

"Don't be alarmed!" said a voice.

John and Ari almost instantaneously flattened themselves down. The voice had come from the direction of the ship, but was only a few meters away. John and Ari tried to bring their weapons around as quietly as possible.

"I'm a friend!" said the voice. "I only want to talk. Can I come out?"

John grabbed his flashlight and readied it. "Come out slowly and with your hands where I can see them."

A figure moved into view at the bottom of the dam. When it stopped moving John pointed the light at it and pressed the switch.

An apparently human female stood before them on the other side of the stream. She was of medium height, thin, and had angular features. Her brown hair was streaked with lighter strands and pulled back into a ponytail. She was wearing what looked like a ball cap, a flight jacket and cargo pants. A pistol of some sort was strapped to her side in a drop holster.

"What the hell?" whispered Ari.

"Who are you?" said John just loudly enough to be heard.

"My name is Fernwyn Rylie. I'm an officer with the Solar Police Force. Right now I'm acting on my own behalf. I only want to talk with you."

"Are you... human?"

"Am I what? Oh, no, I'm Residerian."

"Are you alone?"

"Yes. You can scan the area if you want to be sure."

"Don't move." John keyed his radio. "Dana, this is John. We have a visitor. Have Seth scan the area and make sure that there aren't any more people hiding in the wings."

"Seth's in the middle of his diagnostic check," Dana replied. "He says he's busy."

"Shit. Get Richter and Christie out here on the double with their weapons ready. I want to set up a perimeter watch until Seth can clear the area."

"Christie is still asleep."

"Wake her the hell up, then! Christ almighty this isn't a pleasure cruise!"

"Fine! Stand by."

"I understand your caution," began Fernwyn, "I wish there was some way I could prove my intentions to you."

"You can start by keeping your hands up. Ray, get her sidearm."

Ray appeared in the light next to Fernwyn, startling her.

"Excuse me, please," Ray said, unsnapping the thumb break on Fernwyn's holster and procuring the pistol.

"Be careful, there's a round chambered," said Fernwyn.

"Thanks."

John killed his flashlight and jumped down from the dam. "Ari, watch our rear. We're moving back towards the Faith."

"Understood," said Ari.

Ray motioned for Fernwyn to walk in front of him, and with John and Ari directly behind the four of them moved across the glade. John and Ari paid no heed to the water this time, accepting wet feet in order to pay full attention to their surroundings. As they approached the ship the ramp opened. Christie and Richter stood at the top.

John motioned up the ramp. "Richter, Ari, get out on the perimeter to the north and east. Ray, you watch to the south. Christie, kill the lights in the cargo bay and come help me control our guest."

The crew moved to fulfill John's orders, with Richter and Ari swapping rifles on their way out. Ray handed Fernwyn's pistol to Christie. John moved up the ramp a couple of feet and sat down.

"You people don't screw around," said Fernwyn.

"We did all of our screwing around back on Beta," said John. "Now why have you contacted us?"

"I was hoping to find out more about you. Nobody can figure out why you're here or for whom you may be working. There's a delicate balance in the Tarantula Nebula right now. I want to make sure the Solar United Faction is on the right side."

"What do you know about us already?"

"I know your ship is Umberian. I know you're not. I know you needed a large amount of the substance known as Talvanium, which you presumably got on your trip to Alpha. I know that stuff can be used to create some pretty powerful weaponry, which is the main cause of my concern."

"Go on."

Fernwyn shrugged. "That's it. That's all I know."

"What's the SUF's stake in all of this?"

"To maintain peaceful relations with the Zendreen."

"And do you represent the SUF or do you have your own stake in this?"

"I'm simply trying to determine the truth of your visit."

"That's not what I asked."

"I mean I'm not representing anybody right now. I'm a plank but this goes way beyond local law enforcement."

"Excuse me, you're a 'plank'?"

"That's slang for 'planet cop,' sorry."

"John, this is Dana," said Dana's voice.

"Go ahead," replied John.

"Seth's completed the diagnostics and scanned the area. Our visitor is alone save for her ship which is a hundred yards to the north. She must have landed at the same time we did."

"Thank you, Dana. Okay, uh... Fen-win?"

"Fernwyn, yes. You can call me Rylie. So you see I'm alone?"

"Yes. Perimeter team, return to the ship."

John remained silent until the others had returned.

"Is everything cool?" asked Richter.

"So far," John said. "Rylie, why should we tell you anything?"

"Because as long as you're not trying to start a war between the SUF and the Zendreen, I may be able to help you. If your mission is to liberate Umber then we have a lot to talk about, as your efforts may lead to a larger conflict."

"Let's say that we are trying to liberate Umber. Why would that affect you guys?"

"The SUF and the Zendreen have a peace treaty. If they thought that we were helping you then they might see it as a violation of the treaty."

"If that's true then you're taking a big risk by contacting us like this."

"And yet, I must discover the truth."

"What can you do for us?"

"That depends on you. If you tell me your mission I will give you an honest, no wolshit assessment of the situation from the perspective of the SPF and SUF."

"Do you have your police credentials with you?"

"Yes."

"If you please..."

Fernwyn grabbed her ID and handed it to Christie. She handed Fernwyn's pistol to Richter and took the card.

John motioned inside. "Christie, take the ID up to Dana and see if Seth can pull any information off of the net to confirm her identity."

"Roger," Christie replied.

"Run a search on the roster for Beta Station," said Fernwyn. "That's my duty assignment."

Christie ran up the ramp and climbed the stairs to the first level.

"How did you find us?" asked John.

"I caught up with you shortly after you landed on Alpha. Once I knew you were looking for Talvanium it made it easy to find you. Well, I mean at least as far as which buffer zone you'd use to land."

"Metzqual."

"Uh huh. I still wouldn't have found you if one of your men hadn't decided to take a stroll. I tagged him with a tracker before one of the other females dragged him back inside. Your stealth device blocked the signal after that. When you deactivated the device here on Delta I was able to pick up the signal again."

"How much trouble are we in for the fracas back at Gleeful Complexium?" asked Ray.

"You left the scene of a combat action without filing a report. It's a minor infraction. Since there is clear recorded evidence that you were acting in self-defense I doubt that the prosecution will even charge you."

"That's reassuring," said Richter. "Say, what kind of pistol is this?"

"It's a Res-ZorCon 'Legionnaire.' It's the last of the enhanced projectile pistols. They stopped making them in favor of the new plasma burst weapons about twenty years ago."

"Is it obsolete?"

"It's obsolescent. It'll still put a one centimeter hole in you at a hundred meters. I carry it because some of the new bad guys out there are dumb enough to wear armor that is weak against physical projectiles. Energy dispersal armor isn't exactly well suited against them, no pun intended."

"No wonder those Rakhar mercs went down so easily."

"I take it your weapons use combustible chemical propellants?"

"Yeah. And yours?"

"Mine does too, but there are also four microscopic superconductive magnets embedded in each bullet. There are particle accelerator rails instead of rifling within the barrel. They impart a spin on the round as well as boost the speed by a factor of three."

"Muzzle velocity?"

"Five hundred meters per second."

"Holy shit."

The team's radios crackled to life. "John, this is Christie. Rylie's story checks out. She got officer of the year this year on Beta Station."

"How reliable is your source?" asked John.

"It's the SPF's own information site."

"Good, thanks. Richter, return Officer Rylie's sidearm."

Fernwyn nodded. "Thank you."

"Are we going to tell her our story?" asked Ray.

"Let me do the talking. It's just about time for us to take a meal. Why not join us inside? We'll be more comfortable there."

"Sure, why not?"

"John, may I have a word with you?" Ari said, motioning to the side.

"Okay. Ray, Richter, would you show our guest to the galley? Ari and I will be there shortly."

Ray nodded and the others boarded the ship. Ari and John walked a few meters away. John shifted the weight of his rifle and scanned the woods.

"What's up?"

"Are you sure this is such a good idea? Even if she is who she says she is, she could have a different agenda."

"I think we have to take a bit of a chance on this one, Ari. Having a friend within the Solar Police Force has obvious advantages. She might even be able to get the mercenaries off of our back. I'm prepared to tell her a limited version of our story and see where things go from there. We're still going to be Perditians, but I won't lie about Seth, building the ship, and our intentions toward Umber."

Ari lit a cigarette. "I hope you're right."

"Listen, I want you to see if you can find the tracker module that she supposedly planted on Byron. Test it to find out if our stealth shield can actually block the signal."

"Sure thing. So are you jealous or not?"

"I don't have time to be jealous anymore," said John, turning to go aboard. "Are you coming or what?"

"I think I'll stay out here for awhile. I want to soak up some more of this cool air."

"You're going to stand out here by yourself smoking a cigarette? Why don't you just put on a siren and a big neon sign that says 'shoot me?' I... oh, forget it. Don't be long, Ari."

John climbed the ramp and hit the button to close it. Ari sighed and headed back towards the ruins of the mill.

So she was going to have to deal with Byron again. Maybe for once he wouldn't be such a jerk. Ari took some pleasure from messing with him, but all things considered it still would have been better if he was more agreeable. At least Dana hadn't taken any shit from him. That made her much more respectable in Ari's eyes.

That Rylie woman had better not try to double cross them. The prospect of gaining an off-world ally was reassuring, but only time would tell if that would be true. She was quite attractive and she did look damn cool. Ari couldn't help but wonder if her physical appearance had influenced John's decision to trust her. The effect was palpable. Ari wanted Rylie to be on their side.

The inside of the mill was covered in moss and mushrooms. Ari poked around slowly. There was that feeling again, the same feeling as when Seth first appeared in orb form back on Earth. Ari began to think her mind was playing tricks on her. This corner of Delta did look an awful lot like New Hampshire. Ari thought about John and how she'd tried to come on to him that night. If Seth hadn't shown up, she had no doubt that she and John would have tried a relationship. Suddenly, the regret of such a thing never having come to pass gripped her tightly. It was the first time Ari had ever regretted running into Seth and the resultant adventure. While the feeling soon passed, it left a single clear thought behind.

Ari really did love John.

"I'm such a fool."

Walking towards the far side of the mill, Ari began to feel dizzy. She stopped, and looked curiously down at her feet. She had trodden through a thick patch of toadstools, and had kicked up a small cloud of dust. Ari felt her balance slipping and her cigarette tumbled to the ground.

"Bad mushrooms?" she squeaked, and passed out.

---

"She'll be fine. The sedative wasn't harmful."

A door slid shut. Ari resisted the urge to jump at the noise, instead remaining motionless. She listened carefully to her surroundings. She'd spent enough time aboard a space ship to know she was on one now. It wasn't the Faith.

"I know you're awake," said a voice nearby. "You don't have to pretend."

Ari opened her eyes. The room was dimly lit, with a blue light on one side and a red light on the other. There was a desk with a single chair in the center of the room, and a man was seated there. He had a crew cut and a goatee, and wore a jacket with a high collar. It was too dark to make out any more. Ari was lying on a cot, so she sat up.

"Where am I?"

"You are aboard my ship."

Ari could guess the results, but she checked anyway. Her Glock had been removed from her holster.

"Who are you?"

"I am Aldebaran."

"Is that supposed to mean something to me?"

"You haven't heard of me. That's good."

Through one of the four windows, Ari could see that the ship was still on Delta. She sensed they weren't far from the Faith.

"Why have you taken me?" she asked.

Ari felt a presence poke at her mind. This was nothing new, she'd joined with Seth before. This time, however, there was something strange about it. It didn't feel alien or uncomfortable like Seth. It felt warm, safe, and pleasant. Ari suddenly knew exactly what Aldebaran looked like despite the darkness.

"You will answer my questions," he said.

"Okay."

It seemed like a perfectly reasonable demand to Ari. She felt like she had just taken the first sip of a hot cup of tea after skiing all day. Or was it a rum toddy?

"Where are you from?"

"We're from Earth."

"How did you end up on an Umberian ship?"

"A probe was sent from Umber during the last days of the war with the Zendreen. It ended up on my planet and showed us how to build a ship. We were supposed to build ten thousand ships like it and return to liberate Umber. Seth was damaged, though, so we only built the one."

"Seth?"

"The artificial intelligence computer from the probe. It became our central processing computer once the ship was built."

Aldebaran stood up slowly. "You will help me capture your ship."

Despite feeling like she was getting a backrub from the world's most skilled masseuse, Ari resisted. It reminded her strongly of the first time she was able to resist Silas' advances. It angered her, and the good feeling went away.

"Sorry, bub. No can do."

Aldebaran pushed at Ari's mind. He'd failed to grasp it and had lost it entirely. This was going to be more difficult than he thought. He cleared his own mind and began to passively listen to Ari's brain patterns.

"You're a player," he said.

"Is that supposed to be a compliment?"

"You're an... actor. This world is your stage. You play the part of the strong and capable female. This earns you respect, if not admiration. There's something else, however. Something that explains your play. The actor acts for self-discovery, yes?"

"We all present the best sides of ourselves. It's no different for any of us, nor is it especially objectionable. I discovered long ago that I could get what I wanted in life by acting a certain way. Nobody took me seriously, and they played the part they wanted to as well. That's how it goes."

Ari stood up and crossed to one of the windows. Aldebaran moved slowly toward her. She pulled out her pack of cigarettes and realized she'd given the last one to John.

"Do you really think that everyone recognized the play for the stage? Not everyone could sense your act... Arianna."

"I can feel you fumbling around inside. Dropping my name all of a sudden isn't going to impress me."

"You will help me. I know this because I see the willingness to bring control back into your life. This voyage was meant to be liberating in more than one way, but you find that it's been frustrating all the same. It's different from your life back on Earth but it can't make you feel truly free.

Is there anything in this universe that you would find meaningful, Ari? Anything at all?"

"John."

"Ah, I see now. John is the only one you've never been able to fool. Fitting, then, that you would come to care for him so much. You've come hundreds of thousands of light years and you still can't get him to reciprocate. Irony doesn't even begin to describe it."

"So what?"

"So even John wouldn't have approved of you if you'd killed that man like you wanted to."

Ari turned to face Aldebaran, shocked. "You know about... but... of course you do. I'm an open book to you, aren't I?"

"Don't feel bad. No one can hide themselves from me."

"Killing Byron would have been a mistake. Seth stopped me, and rightly so."

"An artificial intelligence acting as your conscience? Are you so bereft of your own?"

"I may have been, but I've learned from it since then. Besides, there are plenty of true enemies out there for me to fight now."

"It is the warrior in you that led me to capture you. I can see your lust for violence. It is an admirable quality not appreciated by those who have never fought for something in which they wholeheartedly believe. It is not part of the play, it is who you are."

"Tell that to John."

"John can't give you what I can give you. The other man can't give you what I can give you, although he is at least wise enough to see into your heart. This is why you will help me. I can give you what you desire."

"And yet I've never cared for goatees."

Ari was overcome with pleasurable sensations. A gorgeous sunset, the smell of a bakery, beautiful music, chocolate after lent and the embrace of a lover. Aldebaran had seized upon his chance. He molded and guided the sensations until they were focused on himself. Ari fell to one knee.

"Join me, and together we will take back this nebula. You will be who you've always wanted to be and no one, not even I, will stand in your way. Once we have the Faith, the fastest and most powerful ships in the nebula will stand side by side against all who would oppose us. And they will fall."

There was one last strand. Ari saw it in her mind. She was hanging from the side of a badly listing platform high above the floor of the Complexium, held there by one hand by a man who wanted with all his heart to save her. Except in this image, it was John grasping her tightly. The scene snapped like a branch and Ari was filled with the desire for something more. The desire for everything. For Aldebaran.

## 17.

"So there you have it. We stopped here to upgrade the weaponry, and ran into you."

John leaned back in his chair. Fernwyn had her head propped up in her arms on the conference table. Ray, Richter and Christie were also seated at the table, while Dana stood in the corner of the room with her arms crossed.

Friday leapt into John's lap as soon as it became available. Fernwyn leaned back and looked at the others.

"What's the deal with... Byron, is that his name?" she asked.

"Byron is a stowaway. He's caused nothing but trouble for us since we met him. I think he's a good guy at heart, but he just doesn't know how to work with the crew. He has one more chance, and then he's off this ship."

"Why not leave him right here? If you give him some food and a weapon he should be fine for a few weeks. The chances of anyone else landing in the exact same place are slim, and there aren't any dangerous animals in this area. I think he'd be fine."

"Sounds good to me," said Christie.

"I'll consider it," said John. "It might be a good idea. We'll see how he behaves from here on out."

"So what do you think the Perditian government is going say to your request?" Fernwyn asked.

"There is no centralized Perditian government," began John, "there are several independent nation states who share the planet. Ours is the most likely to help, but that's not particularly encouraging. One reason why the Perditians withdrew from universal trading and exploration was because of internal politics. We've always been way too busy dealing with our local situation to worry about the rest of the galaxy."

"And yet, such a political situation could be advantageous for us," said Christie.

"How do you figure that?" asked Ray.

"Since our government is always looking to improve its military standing on Perditia, they may be more willing to play ball if our mission is seen to do so. After all, if they help us they gain all of Umber's best technology."

"Great, then we just beam Saddam Hussein or Arafat or whomever we please into a pile of dust and call the war over," said Dana.

"It would be handy," said Richter.

John shook his head. "I'd much rather leave Perditia out of it entirely. You see what kind of ethical can of worms this opens."

"As if our current situation isn't enough of an ethical challenge," said Christie.

"I don't know, this situation seems pretty clear cut to me. Umber got screwed into signing a non-aggression pact with the SUF, and then they got hung out to dry when the Zendreen showed up. They deserve our help."

"When we agreed to take the mission from Seth we accepted an obligation to help Umber," Ray added.

"That's right. It's the duty of this ship to help Umber however it can. Those who choose to be part of its crew assume that duty. Everyone is here by their own free will."

"There may be more to Umber's side of the story than we've been led to believe," said Dana.

"Indeed there is," said Fernwyn. "The SUF wouldn't have sought political sanctions against Umber just because of their burgeoning military technology."

John looked at his watch. "Where's Ari?"

The others looked at each other quizzically. John stood up.

"What's wrong?" asked Dana.

"It's been more than an hour since we left Ari outside."

"You let her wander around outside alone?" said Christie incredulously.

"I'm not her mother, she can do with herself as she pleases. Seth, locate Ari."

"Ari is outside the ship," replied Seth calmly.

"How far?"

"One hundred meters and closing. She's perfectly all right, John."

"Good, I was worried for a moment. Everybody sit tight, I don't want her to miss any more of this conversation."

Dana shrugged as John exited the conference room. He descended the stairs to the cargo bay and opened the ramp. As the ramp lowered into place, Ari appeared from the woods.

"Where have you been?" said John loudly.

"Going for a walk, just like I said," Ari replied.

"You were gone for over an hour without reporting in."

Ari walked up the ramp and ascended the stairs to the armory. John watched her do so in silence before following her up. He didn't want to criticize Ari too much, but found he had no choice.

"Well, you shouldn't do that. It's irresponsible."

"Come on, John, this is the first real peace and quiet we've had since arriving in this nebula. I wanted to relax alone for a little while, that's all."

Ari put down her M1A and picked up Richter's M4.

"We're having a conference with the solar police officer upstairs. I just finished telling her our story; well, a modified version thereof anyway. I think you should be there."

Grabbing a magazine pouch for the carbine, Ari turned to leave the armory.

"Is the conference room still a no-smoking area?" she asked, descending the stairs.

"Per Dana's request, yes."

"I'm all out of cigarettes."

Ari headed for the ramp. John suddenly realized she wasn't going upstairs.

"What the hell are you doing?" he said.

"There's someone I want you to meet."

"What?"

Pressing the key to her radio, Ari called the crew. "Everyone, this is Ari. Meet me at the bottom of the cargo ramp immediately. Bring Byron, this concerns him as well."

"Roger that," replied Ray.

"What are you talking about?" demanded John. "Who did you meet? Where?"

"It's perfectly all right, John," said Ari. "I'm not going to put anyone's life in jeopardy. I just met someone out there that I want to introduce to you."

"Then why'd you swap out for the full-auto? Hold it a minute, Ari."

The others, including a forlorn-looking Byron, gathered at the base of the ramp.

"What's up?" asked Richter.

"I want you to meet someone," said Ari, motioning towards the woods. "Come on, but be careful, I don't want you to scare it."

"Tell us more first," said John.

"Shh!" said Ari sharply.

Ari waved to the others. Christie shrugged and went forward. The others began to follow. John nodded knowingly at Ray, and Ray returned the gesture. Before exiting, Ray reached behind a bulkhead support and grabbed his shotgun. When he drew beside John he leaned in close.

"Go back inside and scan for life forms again," John whispered.

"There was nothing but animal life last time," said Ray.

"You think she's talking about some animal she found?"

"Probably."

"Come on guys, before it's too late," said Ari.

"Ray, this looks extraordinarily bad," said John.

"So do something about it."

"Damn it, hold up!" yelled John, running forward.

"John, you're going to ruin the surprise," said Ari.

"Fuck this bullshit, Ari. I don't like this one bit. Tell us what's going on."

Ray joined John and the rest of the group. Ari was at the treeline and turned around.

Ari smiled coyly. "I'm sorry, John, I didn't mean to worry you. I guess I'm just a drama queen at heart. Besides, the man I wanted you to meet is right there."

Ari pointed back toward the ship. Three figures were standing at the top of the ramp. The two on either side had long arms, while the man in the center had a pistol.

"Drop your weapons, nice and easy," the man said.

No one moved. John turned his head slightly to look at Ari and saw that she had shouldered her rifle and was pointing it at the crew.

"You'd better do as he says," began Ari. "I don't want any of you to get hurt."

"What the hell is this, Ari?" said John.

Ari motioned with her rifle. Ray allowed his shotgun to fall to his side.

"If anybody goes for their sidearms they'll be shot," said Ari calmly. "Move toward the ramp."

Everyone slowly walked toward the ramp. The three figures remained where they were. The one on the left was a Residerian with obvious cybernetic implants. The one on the right was a Kau'Rii with multiple ear piercings and colorful garb. The man in the center was a clean-cut military Umberian with an unwavering expression.

"Everyone," began Ari, "this is Aldebaran."

Fernwyn drew in a breath of shock and terror. Aldebaran took a step forward.

"Are you here to liberate Umber?" he asked flatly.

"That's the idea," said John defiantly.

"Don't bother. Arianna, come aboard."

Ari circled the crew, heading for the base of the ramp. She had a smug smile on her face and looked amused. John stared at her as she walked and made eye contact with her once she arrived at the ramp.

"What the hell is going on here, Ari?" John asked. "Who is your new friend? Why are you doing this?"

Ari slung her rifle on her shoulder. She looked at John whimsically. She smiled broadly and walked up to him.

"John Scherer. You've always been so kind to me. You never did realize something, though. Not everyone has the same high standards of morality as you. Your greatest flaw is assuming that we all strive for the same level of perfection. Didn't it ever occur to you that some of us are quite happy with our imperfections? Some of us are tired of it. Whether you're waiting for us to prove ourselves or you've already made up your mind about us doesn't matter. Your standards are arbitrary."

"What are you talking about? I never asked anybody to be anything other than they are. I never asked you to be anything other than you are!"

"You asked me to be your friend when I wanted more. You never allowed yourself to go beyond your own standards and see me for who I really was."

"Except your idea of a romantic relationship is a possessive noun. Silas may have been a jerk but at least he knew enough to recognize indentured servitude."

Ari drew her Glock and stepped closer to John. "Silas knew what he was doing. So did you. So do you now. I intend to let you live past today, but don't remind me how much you left me wanting, John. You know what frustration can lead to."

Ari tapped John's shoulder with the side of her pistol.

"I know you better than anybody, Ari. I know this isn't really you talking."

"Don't let your emotions blind you," said Christie. "Ari is speaking from the heart."

"I think she is, too," said Richter. "I want to know why you're doing this, Ferro. I thought I could trust you to do what was best for your friends. I thought we trusted each other."

"Of course you wouldn't understand, Richter. You've always been content to be second in command. Even when you had the chance to be number one in my life you conceded to him. You'll never be anything more than a good shot and an errand boy."

"That's easy for you to say now, Ferro. Don't forget the only reason you and I never rocked the Casbah was because nobody had thought to bring any protection out here."

"A tragic oversight, I must admit."

"You seem poised to fuck us all, regardless," said Ray.

"You should thank me, Bailey. Aldebaran didn't see the point in leaving you alive. Loose ends mean a lot to him, you see. I do appreciate you as friends and I wouldn't want to see you dead. Do yourselves a favor and don't try and follow us. If we meet again we won't be so forgiving."

Ari headed back to the ramp and glanced at Byron as she passed him. She stopped, smiled, and turned to face him.

"What's the matter, Byron? No pithy comments? No smart aleck retorts? You were never in short supply before. Is this not what you thought fate had in store for you? Tell me how this falls in line with your destiny."

Byron remained silent, an expression of doom on his face.

"Come on, Byron, not a single bit of your old arrogance? I need an excuse to finish you off for good, you know."

"Leave him alone, Ari," said Christie.

"You're not sticking up for him, are you Tolliver? After all the trouble he's caused you? Wouldn't you like an excuse to take him out?" Ari laughed, looking at the ground. Her fingers tensed around her pistol. She looked up at Byron and brought the weapon to bear. "Fuck it, I don't need an excuse."

The shot echoed throughout the glade, seemingly louder than anything that had ever met human ears. Byron fell to the ground limply. A thin line of crimson swept across Ari's face and the echo faded. Ari holstered her pistol and walked up the ramp to Aldebaran's side.

"If you oppose us you now know how far we'll go to protect ourselves," she said. "So if we ever meet again, let it be as friends."

"That day will never come," said John.

The Reckless Faith's engines came to life, and the ship began rising slowly from the ground. The ramp began to close and Ari threw her rifle to Richter, followed by the magazine pouch. Richter caught the rifle without taking his eyes from Ari.

"I think you'll need this more than I," she shouted. "Have a good life, everyone. It can only improve from here."

The invisibility shield was activated, and the last thing the crew could see before the ramp closed was Ari's face. Taking a breeze along with it, the ship disappeared into the starry sky. Silence returned to the glen.

18.

Richter checked the chamber of his rifle and walked over to Byron.

"The kid's been brain-panned. There's nothing we can do for him."

"Some friends you people keep!" exclaimed Fernwyn, shaking off her shock.

"Ari wouldn't have done that on her own," said Ray, picking up his Remington.

"Actually, you're probably right. It's Aldebaran."

"You know that guy?" asked Christie, edging closer to peek at Byron's corpse.

"Well this is great," began Dana, throwing up her hands. "Just frigging great. What the hell are we supposed to do now?"

"Aldebaran is the most infamous pirate in the galaxy," said Fernwyn. "Your friend may have screwed us all over but she undoubtedly saved our lives as well. If Aldebaran wanted your ship he would have got it anyway, and we'd all be dead. And don't feel bad about your friend's betrayal. She most likely wasn't acting on her own accord after all."

"Aldebaran was exerting some sort of influence over her?" asked John.

"Yes. He has some sort of telepathic power unlike anything else in the galaxy. Nobody knows how he does it, but it's a real power. He's not just good at reading people or manipulating them. He can actually affect their minds. It's one reason why he's such an effective pirate; people are terrified of his ability. They call it Aldebaran's Will."

"Can no one resist him?"

"I don't know. Most of the stories are anecdotal. Nobody who has ever met Aldebaran in person has lived to tell about it. That's why I can't believe he left us alive down here. Either the stories exaggerate or that wasn't really

Aldebaran. But... I've run into him before. Seven years ago, when I was just starting out as a shuffler, I tried to capture him. I heard his voice over the radio... that was him. I'm sure of it now."

"You were a shuffler? What's that?"

"It's slang for bounty hunter. I tried my hand at it before I became a police officer."

"What's the bounty on Aldebaran?" asked Ray.

"One hundred million credits."

"Holy shit."

"No kidding there. Everybody and their brother with a shuffler's license was out there gunning for him. They kept him quite busy for awhile, but he was too good. His ship was the latest production run from the Umberian fleet before the war, a Mark Seventeen fighter. He beat out odds as bad as five to one. When I faced him I almost got killed. Only the sudden appearance of a squadron of SPF fighters saved me."

"Can you help us track him down?" asked John.

"I'm sorry, but if I were you I'd forget about your ship. The configuration you described to me sounds just like a Mark Seventeen. If Aldebaran has been unstoppable with one of them, how do you expect to defeat two?"

"Because if we can get through to our artificial intelligence computer we can tell it to help us. Right now it probably doesn't realize there's a problem. It's not very good at independent deductive reasoning."

"Even if you could find your ship, how do you expect to communicate with your computer?"

"I don't know, but it's something we should consider. I'm not going to give up now! I don't care how far we have to go. That ship is ours and we're going to get her back!"

"It's suicide, my friend. Plain and simple."

"I don't care. You guys are with me, right? Ray? Richter? Christie?"

The others were silent.

"This looks like the end of our mission, John," said Dana. "Maybe you should start coming to terms with it."

"Son of a bitch," said John, kicking the ground. "We've come this far and you're just going to give up?"

"We need to consolidate and reorganize," said Richter. "Then we can think about our next move."

"Fine. First things first. Rylie, can you help us get off this moon?"

"Probably. My ship only seats two but I should be able to make other arrangements. Where will you go?"

"If you can get us as far as Beta we should be able to function on our own from there."

"Okay. But I don't know how much more I can help you after that."

"What about the tracker device?" asked Richter.

"Oh yeah," said Fernwyn, removing the device from her pocket. She pointed at Byron's body. "It's still on him."

"Shit," said John.

"You felt it was your duty to come after us," said Christie. "Are you so scared of Aldebaran that you're willing to abandon your duty now?"

"My duty is to ensure the safety and security of the Solar United Faction. Aldebaran isn't going to precipitate a war with the Zendreen. He may have the ultimate defense with two Mark Seventeen fighter ships but that doesn't mean he can launch an offensive against anyone."

"So what's he going to do with the Faith?" asked Ray.

"How should I know? Like I said, he probably just wanted to bolster his defensive capabilities as well as his ability to take pirate prizes. He's always had a penchant for Umbrian technology any..."

Fernwyn trailed off. John stepped closer to her.

"What?"

"Aldebaran won't attack just anybody. After the war, the Zendreen put out a standing bounty on all Umberians. Aldebaran made a name for himself tracking down his own kind and handing them over for the corral bounty. The last Umberians who were dumb enough to stick around the nebula were rounded up long ago. Since then Aldebaran will only attack ships that have some sort of Umberian technology aboard. I always figured he was looking for repair parts or ways to upgrade his ship. But there was something else that occurred to me earlier that I didn't mention, something that might just be a coincidence. You called your AI Seth, right?"

"Yeah."

"Seth is Aldebaran's first name."

---

"I'm sorry, who are you guys again?"

Ari leaned against the wall on the bridge and gestured toward her two new friends. Aldebaran had asked her to show them the command center before wandering off on his own.

"I'm Harrish," said the Kau'Rii, "and this is Leitke. I'm the first mate and he's the engineer."

"Seth, grant Harrish and Leitke full access to all systems."

Seth did not respond. Ari frowned.

"Your computer is named Seth?" asked Leitke, sharing a glance with Harrish.

"Yes. Seth, wake up, damn it."

Again, there was nothing but silence. Ari crossed to her station and checked the systems.

"What's up?" asked Harrish.

"It says that Seth's processing usage is up to one hundred percent. That's never happened before."

"What's he doing?"

"It says he's running a sim, but that can't be right. Where's Aldebaran?"

Harrish pulled out his communicator. "Cap, where are you?"

There was no reply.

"Holy shit," breathed Leitke. "This is it, isn't it?"

"It could be. Captain, are you there?"

"What's going on?" asked Ari.

"We've got to find Aldebaran."

"Wait a minute," said Leitke, grabbing Harrish's arm, "what does this mean for us?"

"I don't know," replied Harrish. "Nobody ever thought that Aldebaran would actually find Seth. Our first duty is still to the captain, though. Arianna, we need to search the ship."

"Call me Ferro, please. There's only one place he could be. The orb room."

Ari led the others off of the bridge and down the hall. They descended the stairs to the galley and crossed into the orb room.

Aldebaran was standing in the room, his arms wrapped around the orb in a bear hug. His eyes were closed and there was a big smile on his face. Harrish and Leitke looked very surprised. Ari furrowed her brow.

"Aldebaran, can you hear me?" she said.

"Captain?" said Harrish.

Aldebaran didn't budge. Harrish reached tentatively for him, and Ari stopped him.

"Wait. He's merged with Seth. The only way to get him out is to cause him physical pain. Otherwise we have to wait until he chooses to separate."

"That may not happen."

"What? Why?"

Harrish gestured back toward the galley. Ari and Leitke led the way. The three sat down at the table at Harrish's suggestion.

"Aldebaran was a soldier in the Umberian military," Harrish began. "Eleven years ago he volunteered for a special unit assigned to the Umberian System Way Station in orbit around the first planet in the system. This unit was comprised of the best non-commissioned officers and was intended to supply military men for certain scientific experiments. There was full disclosure at the beginning that the volunteers could be subject to physical and psychological damage, but for the most part they were not exposed to unreasonable risk. Aldebaran volunteered for the most dangerous experiment, an attempt to find a way to copy a person's consciousness and store it artificially. When initial attempts proved unsuccessful, Aldebaran personally suggested going beyond what the scientists considered safe. The result was success. Aldebaran's consciousness was copied and stored. There was a costly side effect, however. Aldebaran lost his ken-kiai."

"What?" said Ari. "My translator didn't get that last word."

"The mind can be thought of as three distinct parts. One is the do-katsi, which controls basic animal needs and desires. One is the do-kiai, which is the aware conscious. The other is the ken-kiai, which is the subconscious."

"Oh, I see. You're talking about the id, ego, and superego."

"Aldebaran became a different person. He was cold, ineffectual, and sometimes cruel. If he wanted something, he would simply take it. He did not lose his ability to distinguish between right and wrong, he simply no longer cares."

"Sounds like pirate psychology to me."

"Well, that falls in line with what happened next. The Umberian scientists were not without sympathy for what had happened. Half of the staff on the project were committed to finding a way to restore Aldebaran's mind. The other half continued to work with his superego and created the first truly effective and self-aware artificial intelligence. That's what Seth is. Unfortunately for everyone the Zendreen invaded before they could find a way to restore Aldebaran. He disappeared during the chaos and soon emerged as a pirate."

"A pirate with a penchant for Umberian technology," said Leitke.

"Yes. And what Aldebaran revealed only to his most trusted crew was that his ultimate goal was to find Seth. He spent years going after Umberians that had escaped from the invasion, and handed them over to either the Zendreen or shufflers out of spite."

"Shufflers?" asked Ari.

"Bounty hunters. The Zendreen put out a reward for all Umberians."

"Did they do that out of spite as well?"

"No. The Zendreen invaded Umber to gain their superior technology. Unfortunately for them all such knowledge was eliminated during the last days of the invasion. Rumor has it that a ship was launched that contained all of the data, and the Zendreen were determined to find it. Thus the bounty."

Ari leaned back in her chair. "This ship proves that Seth was the repository for that data. Is Aldebaran going to hand it over to the Zendreen?"

"No way. Nobody, not even someone as disgruntled as Aldebaran wants the Zendreen to have higher technology. Just because he hates Umberians doesn't mean he's pals with the Zendreen. They still invaded his home planet. Even a reward of twenty million credits can't make up for that."

Ari stood up and walked to the kitchenette. She opened a cabinet.

"Alcohol?"

"Sure, why not?"

Grabbing a bottle of bourbon and three glasses, Ari returned to the table. She poured the drinks, which were met with the approval of the aliens.

"So now that Aldebaran has found his subconscious, can he restore himself?"

"I don't think so," said Leitke. "Seth shouldn't be any different from when the original schism occurred, except for any experience he gained since then. The captain is obviously experiencing some level of simpatico right now, but I don't know what will happen once he's separated from the orb."

Harrish nodded. "That's why we might have to poke him with a sharp object to get him to wake up."

"What if he is restored?" asked Ari. "Will he still be interested in pirating?"

"Who knows? If not, I'd be more than happy to take his place aboard the other ship. It's about time she got a proper name. My commitment is still to the Aldebaran I know, however. I'm not going to do anything against his will."

"I don't care if he does give up pirating. Aldebaran and I have a special bond. Whatever he decides to do, I'll be on his side. Maybe the two of us can seek our fortune together on the Faith."

Leitke and Harrish shared a glance and rolled their eyes.

"Yeah, right, Ferro," said Leitke.

Harrish motioned for Leitke to be quiet. "You know, Ferro, it has been a long time since Aldebaran has had an attractive female on board, at least attractive to his type. Just make sure you don't forget the command structure around here. You won't be able to take part in any decision-making until you've proved yourself."

"In that case, I'll defer to Aldebaran."

"Ruthless and wise," said Leitke, and emptied his glass. "Too bad you're so skinny."

"At least I still have all of my original parts."

"None of my enhancements were involuntary. Residerians don't do so well off of Beta without some sort of modification. Genmodding was quite out of the question for a pirate, so I got these. But I'm not..." Leitke crushed his glass effortlessly. "...dissatisfied with the cybernetics."

"Should we try and get Aldebaran's attention now, or shall we destroy some more of my tumblers?"

Harrish stood up. "We'll be arriving at Macer Alpha soon. Our ship is known to the other pirates hiding out there, but it will be easier to explain the presence of the Faith if Aldebaran is the one doing the explaining. We should wake him up."

Ari rose and returned the bourbon to the cabinet. She opened a drawer and retrieved a wooden toothpick.

"This ought to do the trick," she said.

Crossing to the door, Ari led the way into the orb room. Aldebaran hadn't budged. Ari grinned wickedly and stuck him in the ass with the toothpick.

"Ouch! What in the name of the core?"

"Sorry about that, sweetie, but we need your captainly skills on the bridge."

Aldebaran stood motionless except for the blinking of his eyes. After a few second he looked longingly at the orb.

"Seth... it's me. I'm right there. I can feel the rest of myself, so close. I was so happy, but... I couldn't catch me. I mean, I couldn't get to Seth. I can't do it here."

"You have all the time in the cloud to keep trying, Cap," said Harrish. "Right now the others are going to want an introduction to the new ship."

"Understood. You and Leitke walk this ship from stem to stern and give me a report on its construction and contents. Arianna, please join me on the bridge."

"Aye, sir."

Aldebaran exited the orb room into the armory. Ari followed him.

"I haven't seen projectile weapons this well maintained since I was in basic training," he said.

"These are the best weapons available to human civilians back on Earth," Ari replied. "They've proven quite effective out here so far."

Aldebaran picked up a M1A rifle. "I wouldn't have left them any weapons."

"You wouldn't have left them alive."

"I should have killed the plank. She's more of a threat by herself than the rest of your crew put together. I let myself become distracted by Seth. I could feel him as soon as I set foot aboard."

"You know, you could merge with him while you're here. You don't have to be in physical contact with the orb to do it."

"I tried already. I couldn't do it."

"Why not?"

"Seth wouldn't let me."

Aldebaran put down the rifle and headed for the door. Entering the cargo bay, he descended the stairs to the deck.

"It's such a utilitarian design," he said. "It has very little heart to it. Your friend John did an admirable job but he's lacking in inspiration."

"John had to design a spacecraft from the ground up with very little feedback from Seth. Any effort to make it look cool came as an afterthought."

"Seth told me he was damaged while escaping Umber. Talvan restored him. He was always so kind to me."

"You knew Talvan?"

"He was the chief architect of the project that separated me from Seth, and the leader of the team that was dedicated to restoring my mind after the experiment."

Aldebaran climbed the stairs to the first deck and entered the bridge.

"Too bad he's trapped on Umber," said Ari.

"Yeah, I almost regret handing him over to the Zendreen. Now this shows some imagination. It's well laid-out. Are you a good pilot?"

"Not really. John and Dana were the good ones. I focused on ground fighting and hand-to-hand."

"In your mind I saw that you gained that Rakhar battle blade in combat. That's one reason why I asked you to join me. You obviously know how to handle yourself."

Ari smiled and stepped closer to Aldebaran. "Would you like a demonstration?"

"We don't have time for that. We're going to stop at Macer Alpha just long enough to plan the mission and then I'm going to take both ships back out."

"The mission? Where are we going?"

---

"I honestly have no idea."

Fernwyn checked her communicator and put it back into her pocket.

"How much longer?" asked Dana.

"Ten minutes or so."

Richter and Ray approached from the north. John, Fernwyn, Dana and Christie were sitting near the wall of the old mill. The first streaks of daylight had begun to appear in the sky.

"What's the good word?" asked John.

"This place is as dead as heaven on a Saturday night," said Ray.

"Good. What about supplies?"

Richter took a knee. "We have my rifle with ninety rounds. Ray's shotgun was fully loaded and there were sixty rounds in the ammo bag, so that's sixty-five. I have a full load on my pistol of forty-one rounds and Ray's Smith has forty-two. How many magazines were you carrying?"

"I had four, as usual, so that's sixty-one rounds."

"We won't be storming Omaha Beach with this loadout," said Ray.

"I'm hoping we won't have to storm anything. I'm sure if I can just get into contact with Seth we can retake the Faith. What else?"

"That's it," said Richter. "The clothes on our backs. We're lucky we're not unarmed and naked down here."

"What about you, Rylie? Are you with us?"

Fernwyn shifted her weight and crossed her legs. "As if Aldebaran wasn't enough trouble with one Mark Seventeen, now he has two. If we can come up with a reasonable plan, not only will we retake your ship but we'll be able to split a one hundred million credit bounty. I seriously doubt that you'll be able to come up with a reasonable plan, however. Like I was saying, I have no idea where Aldebaran is going. If we can find him and if we can come up with a plan that isn't suicidal, I'll help you."

"What about this Nathalier guy?" asked Dana.

"Forget about Nathalier. He's just a security guard at Gleeful. He may be able to help you get some extra gear from the shops there, but that's about it. You heard the fuss he put up when I asked him to come get us. He's got less of a reason to risk his hide than any of us."

Christie shrugged. "And yet, he's on his way to pick us up."

"I didn't say he was a coward. He's simply got his own agenda."

"What's he picking us up in?" asked Ray.

"I'm not sure. He said something about the impound garage. It could be anything."

"Let's hope for the Winnebago with wings," said Christie.

"What, the Intergalactic Volvo wasn't good enough for you?" said John, grinning.

"Is there anything else you can think of to tell us about Aldebaran?" asked Richter.

"I already told you everything I know," began Fernwyn, "but since I have access to the SPF database I may be able to find out more."

"Rylie, before we were interrupted by Ferro's little mutiny, you said that there was more to the Umberian non-aggression pact than we were aware. What did you mean?"

"The Umberian government was involved in scientific experiments of a dubious ethical nature. Part of the SUF's sanctioning of Umber was an attempt to curtail any perceived sentient rights violations."

"Perceived?" said John.

"As far as I know, any experiment that was harmful was conducted on volunteers who were aware of the risks. It was the early genmodding disasters that had the SUF worried. While the volunteers may have been willing, the way that Umber dealt with them afterward was rather cruel."

"You've lost me. What's genmodding?"

"Genetic modification. Scientists have been looking for ways to create sentient beings in whatever form they desired for decades. Prenatal efforts proved limited. Umber was the first to experiment on subjects after they were born. While such genmodding eventually proved successful, most of the earlier volunteers ended up with freakish mutations. They were brought to a "recovery center" on Residere Alpha, but they were unhappy with their treatment so after several years they took the place over. Rather than negotiate, the Umberians simply abandoned them. Now they roam the deserts and plains of Alpha as raiders and nomads."

"That explains the monsters we ran into on Alpha," said Christie.

"You ran into some of them? You're lucky to be alive."

"We've been hearing that a lot lately," said John. "So what kinds of genmods were considered a success?"

"I said I was Residerian, remember?"

"Yeah."

"Haven't you noticed that I don't look anything like a Residerian?"

"Every Residerian we've run into, yes, but we're new to the neighborhood. You're a genmod?"

"Yes."

"You look like one of us," said Dana. "You look completely human."

"You volunteered to be experimented upon?" asked Ray.

Fernwyn shook her head. "Being born a Residerian is all well and good if you like living on Residere. We don't do so well in space, however. Variable gravity environments are detrimental to our skeletal structures and we lose muscle mass faster than other races. Most ships aren't designed for sentients as large as Residerians, either. Getting a job off-world or becoming an explorer is pretty much out of the question unless you can afford some sort of modding. Some went the route of cybernetics. My parents thought I'd do well with genmodding, since by the time I was ten years old the practice had been proven safe."

"So, are you part Umberian, then?" asked John.

"No. I got the exotic treatment. I'm forty percent Residerian, thirty percent Rakhar and thirty percent Kau'Rii."

"And yet you look just like a human. That's weird."

Fernwyn stood up and walked over to Ray. She stepped in close and looked at him.

"Uh, hi," said Ray.

"Not entirely so. You don't have feline eyes like I do. It also doesn't look like you can lift more than twenty or twenty five fists, right?"

"I don't understand," said John.

Fernwyn looked around until she found a rock that she liked. She lifted it over her head and tossed it aside easily. Richter shrugged and tried it himself. He managed to get it about twelve inches off of the ground.

"Shit, it's at least seventy-five pounds," he said.

Fernwyn smiled. "So I thought."

"You must have been quite a popular kid after that," Christie said.

"Hardly. Genmods are shunned by almost everybody. They're seen as rich snobs who cheated in order to get ahead. Even Residerians who had little choice if they ever wanted to leave home were ridiculed for trying to change who they really were. Identity runs deep in these parts. I had to work twice as hard as the other recruits when I was trying to become a plank. That's just the way it goes."

"It kind of reminds me of anabolic steroids back on Earth," said Ray.

"Earth?"

"Earth, Perditia, they're both words for our planet," said John quickly.

"Well, you won't see any prejudice from us," began Ray. "Not only do we need all the help we can get, but your genmod has made you one hell of an attractive female."

Fernwyn blushed, and John looked at Ray with surprise. "I'm impressed that you can keep your sense of humor after everything that's happened..." Fernwyn cut herself off and cocked her head to the side.

"What?"

"Cover!"

Everyone standing hit the deck, and those who were seated spun around to go prone. A ship appeared over the glen and began to land. It very much resembled an oversized subway car with the windows blacked out, with two barrel-like engines stuck to either side. The engines were oriented to the vertical as the ship landed, with large struts folding out from the bottom. It sounded altogether different from the Faith. A ramp opened from the side, and the silhouette of a Rakhar could be seen.

"It's Nathalier," said Fernwyn, rising.

"Cool, we finally get to meet a Rakhar without trying to kill each other," said Richter.

"The day is young."

Waving at Nathalier, Fernwyn led the group toward the ship. Nathalier smiled.

"If it isn't the mysterious strangers who trashed my Complexium," he said.

"Yeah, sorry about that whole bit," said John.

"I'm joking. Good show against the Black Crest. I can admit it to a precious few but I enjoyed seeing them get a fat lip. It amused me even more to see a Residerian/Z'Sorth mech get ripped to shreds."

"You look good in street clothes," said Fernwyn.

"So do you. Aren't you going to introduce me to your new friends?"

"This is John Scherer, Ray Bailey, Christie Tolliver, Dana Andrews, and Chance Richter. They're humans from Perditia."

"Never heard of it. Are you here to liberate Umber?"

"Hopefully," said John.

"Mind if I make book on it?"

Richter began to laugh loudly. The others were simply confused.

"What's this hunk of junk?" asked Fernwyn.

"This is the Raven," replied Nathalier. "She's a transport that somebody abandoned on one of the docking platforms last year. Rather than scrap her I rented a berth in the underground garage. I've been restoring her, albeit slowly."

"Will my ship fit in the cargo bay?"

"Not unless you chop off the wings."

"The wings fold up."

"Oh, in that case it should. Are you sure you wouldn't rather fly her yourself?"

"I want to do some research on the net as quickly as possible. I can't do that and fly at the same time. Can you do me a favor and take care of that?"

"Sure. I could use two volunteers to help me."

"I'll help," said Dana.

"Me, too," added Ray.

Fernwyn gave her keys to Nathalier. "Good. Let's get off of this moon. Scherer, Tolliver, Richter, let's see what we can find out about Aldebaran."

Nathalier tripped and almost fell over. He turned around, astonished.

"The people who stole your ship work for Aldebaran?"

"Oh yeah, I forgot to mention that. Sorry."

"It was him, too," said John, "not just his crew."

Nathalier gesticulated wildly. "Are you all out of your minds? For the love of the core, you're lucky to..."

"Yeah, we know," interjected John.

"Don't worry, Nathalier," said Fernwyn. "If you help us get back to Beta we'll put you in for five percent when we catch him."

"They don't pay out bounties to dead men," Nathalier said.

"I seriously doubt Aldebaran left us alive down here just so that he could pounce on us if we leave. He's probably long gone by now. He's not a god, you know."

"I don't appreciate you leaving that little detail out, Rylie."

"Would you have come if I'd told you?"

"No."

"Are you going to abandon us now?"

"Of course not. My word is my bond, even if you manipulated me. I'll take you as far as Beta and I'll take that five percent if you actually catch Aldebaran. Now let's get the hell out of here while we're all still vertical."

Fernwyn nodded and headed toward the Raven. When the others were out of earshot John spoke.

"So much for asking him to come along on the recovery mission."

"Not everyone is as crazy as we," Fernwyn replied.

Fernwyn and John climbed aboard followed by Christie and Richter. The interior of the ship was about fifteen feet tall. An open hatch to the rear led the way to the cargo bay. The area they were in currently had additional storage space underneath raised platforms. Four smaller rooms lay off from the platforms and lined the sides. Another hatch forward led to the control room. Fernwyn scowled as they headed there.

"Not exactly the lap of luxury," said John.

"I wonder if Nathalier used the word 'restore' properly," said Fernwyn. "I hate to think what kind of shape this was in when he first got his claws on it."

Entering into the control room, Fernwyn discovered three stations. She sat down at one of them and began checking the systems. Satisfied, she accessed the net.

"Will no one care that you're digging around in the SPF's files?" asked Richter.

"Not really. I have level two clearance. If there's any information on Aldebaran classified higher than that we'll have to make a direct request. Let's hope that doesn't happen."

Fernwyn directed her attention to the search. John sighed and leaned against the wall.

"This thing doesn't look like it will be of any further use to us once we get to Beta," said Christie.

"Nathalier doesn't seem too eager to help us after that anyway," said John.

"Assuming we can find the Faith, how are we supposed to contact Seth without Aldebaran and Ari knowing?"

"I don't know. We may have to try and catch them off guard."

"Do you really think they'll ever let their guard down?"

"I just don't know. I'm simply not going to give up until all of our options have been exhausted."

"What then?"

"Take out a small business loan and become a shuffler," said Richter.

"Ha! Yeah, right."

"That's not a bad idea," said Fernwyn, "except who's going to extend you credit?"

"Piracy might work for us, in that case," said Richter.

"Go down that road and you're on your own... well, that was easy enough."

"Got something?"

"I've got Aldebaran's military file, last updated ten years ago. Let's see... it says he was last assigned to the military research unit on the Umberian System Way Station."

"There was a military research unit on a commercial space station?" asked John.

Fernwyn nodded. "It hasn't been a commercial station for years. The USWS couldn't compete with Gleeful Complexium, so the Umberian military bought it out."

"Anything else?"

"Hold on... There's an addendum in here from the SPF outlining his career as a pirate. There's nothing too enlightening there, except to confirm what I told you about his search for Umberian technology."

"You told us that Aldebaran's first name is Seth," began John, "just like our artificial intelligence aboard the Faith. Does that explain why Aldebaran has been looking for Umberian technology?"

"I'll look."

"What's the connection?" asked Christie.

"I think Aldebaran may have designed Seth," replied John. "That would explain why he's been searching for it. I know if I created something like that I'd sure want it back."

"There's a file here," said Fernwyn. "It has something to do with an experiment conducted by the military. Wait just a moment."

"I wonder what made Aldebaran turn against his own people?" said Christie.

"Maybe they did something with Seth that he didn't like," said John.

"Maybe he's an asshole," said Richter.

Fernwyn finished reading, took a deep breath and leaned back in her chair.

"Hol-ee shit," she said.

"What?"

"This file explains everything. Aldebaran was part of a military experiment indeed. You want to know where he's going?" Fernwyn put a picture of a space station on the screen. "That's where Aldebaran is going. The Umberian System Way Station."

## 19.

"How's it going over there, Cap?"

"No progress yet, Harrish."

On the bridge of the Faith, Aldebaran was speaking by radio with his own ship. Harrish and Leitke had returned there on his orders. Aldebaran could feel them aboard when he was linked with Seth, and there had been a negative feeling about them. It was visceral and undefined, but it was enough to make their presence undesirable and distracting. The past twenty-four hours had been spent merged with the orb and then resting, with the Faith set on auto-pilot and watched over by Aldebaran's ship. Despite his desire to spend all his time merged with Seth, he was still forced to sleep. Usually requiring only a few hours a night, this time he'd been passed out for fourteen hours. Being in contact with Seth was as exhausting as it was exhilarating.

"Seth still not cooperating with you?"

"No."

"That's weird. Are you going to keep trying or wait until we get to the station?"

"We have another twelve hours. I intend to try again. In the meantime, be vigilant as we approach the station. The Zendreen might not be guarding the place externally but they most certainly have people aboard it."

"Aye, sir."

Ari entered the bridge holding a plate of sandwiches. She'd had some rest as well, which was deep and dreamless. The rest of the time she'd spent practicing martial arts and daydreaming about her future with Aldebaran. She was tempted to enter her quarters where he was sleeping and watch him, but decided that was too juvenile even for her desires. Other than that she'd jettisoned Byron's bedding and clothes, cleaned the galley, and listened to some music.

Aldebaran terminated the communication and turned to face Ari.

"This is the last of our bread," she said. "Actually this is the last of our roast beef, too. We're going to need to stock up on food unless you're a huge fan of US Military rations."

"We'll worry about that later. Right now we need to concentrate on getting aboard that station."

Aldebaran took one of the sandwiches and put it on his knee. Working at his console, he brought up an image of the USWS. The station consisted of three cylinders attached lengthwise, with large solar panels jutting out from the outer two. Each cylinder was ten decks, and the cross pylons that connected them were three decks. There appeared to be a small amount of space debris floating around it.

"How soon can we dock?"

"We'll be there in twelve hours. During that time I'll again try to merge with Seth."

Ari sat down at the next console. "I don't understand what's going on with Seth. He's always been so friendly and cooperative with us. He can't possibly be pissed at us for stealing the ship, can he?"

"If you mean angry, no, he is not. He is aware of the fact that we left the others behind against their will, however. I do not believe this is why he will not speak with either of us, at least while we're not in direct contact with the orb."

"Then what's his problem?"

"I don't know."

"For being part of your own personality, he sure doesn't care for you much."

Aldebaran shrugged and began eating his sandwich. Ari did the same, watching him as she did so.

"How do you know the Zendreen haven't destroyed or disassembled the stuff we need?"

"I don't."

"What if we can't get it to work one way or the other?"

"Then I'll never leave this ship again."

Wolfing down the last of his food, Aldebaran stood up and brushed himself off.

"How long do you want me to let you merge with the orb this time?" asked Ari, standing.

"Until Harrish calls you with a sitrep of the station. In the meantime, you might want to get geared up for combat. The Zendreen aren't going to let us dance our way aboard, you know."

Aldebaran turned to exit.

"Aldebaran, wait!"

"What?"

"Promise me this won't change anything, will you?"

"What do you mean?"

"Between us," Ari said, taking Aldebaran by the arm. "You showed me a glimpse of the way things could be. I want that future to come true. I'm afraid that if you restore yourself that you won't want the same thing anymore."

"I am who I am. Seth is a part of me, but only a small part. He can complete me, make me happy, and give me back the ability to feel again. Our life together after that will be all the more rewarding for both of us. You know how much you love me, right?"

"Right."

"Imagine when I can return that love to the same degree. Restoring myself will be a positive experience. Almost as positive as meeting you, Arianna."

"Oh, God, please. Your very presence may fill me with joy but you can cut out the sappy crap."

Aldebaran extricated himself from Ari's grasp and turned away.

"Very well."

Without another glance, Aldebaran left the bridge.

Eleven hours later, Ari woke up. She was on the bridge, and had drifted off after finishing another meal. The computer hadn't alerted her to any problems, and a quick glance at her console confirmed that there hadn't been any. They were due to arrive at the USWS in just a few minutes.

Ari could still sense Aldebaran's presence in her mind, but it was muted and peaceful. It kept her aware of her desire for adventure and her need to be near Aldebaran, but it did not make her heart leap nor did she intensely crave actual physical contact with him as it had before.

Ari had been by herself on the Faith before, but she'd never been alone. While part of Aldebaran's will was actually with her in her mind, her awareness of Seth had been only her own cognizance of his omnipresence. Ever since Seth had demonstrated that he could read her thoughts and even her intentions, Ari had felt like she was unable to so much as think anything of which Seth might not approve. It was only after Seth was restored at Umber that Ari was able to find the program that made him into a moral enforcer, and it only governed acts of violence. She left it running, her first brush with murder enough to temper her own actions. The thought of catching another member of the crew with the desire to harm someone amused her, even though she knew the possibility of that was practically nonexistent. Now, like most of Seth's other autonomic functions, the program was off-line. Aldebaran must have been effecting him on a very deep level, which wasn't a huge surprise after learning of their relationship.

On top of all of this, Ari was also aware that she and Aldebaran were the only ones on board. When the crew was around she was rarely at a loss for someone to talk to, and although she would have been rue to admit it, even hanging around with Dana with barely a word exchanged was preferable to being alone sometimes. During the past day and a half, with Aldebaran linked with Seth hashing out who knows what, Ari found herself thinking about going to find one of the others. She remembered that they were no longer aboard, and that Aldebaran's presence was more than adequate. Her desire for companionship had simply been out of habit.

Now she saw John in her mind. He was standing on top of a boulder in the woods. She wondered why she always put him in that scene, since he'd never actually been with her at that particular point on Earth.

A small voice, as clear as if it had been spoken, told her.

That was the first time you considered coming on to John.

Ari shrugged. Of course he hadn't been there in person, but he was foremost on her mind that day. Ari had clambered to the top of the boulder alone and thought about how the conversation might go. In her imagination she had seen him up there, too. The memory had become synonymous with the experience.

Usually some emotion accompanied this memory. Now there was nothing. Ari thought also of the rest of the crew, in the order she'd met them. Ray, Christie, Dana, and Richter. There was no emotion for them, either. Only Byron made her feel something. Cold, calm satisfaction. Ari figured she was experiencing some of what Aldebaran was like all the time, at least before he ran into Seth, the thing that made him such an effective pirate and simultaneously drove his search for Umberians. Unfettered by conscience, everything seemed so simple. Everything, except Aldebaran himself.

Was it he who supplied so much desire and ambition to Ari? Or was he only supplementing, on some level, her own capacity for the same? What, if he merged with Seth, would happen to...

"What's our status?"

Ari jumped out of her chair. Aldebaran had silently entered the bridge, and stood near the back in a shadow.

"You woke yourself up?" she asked. "I thought I was going to have to come rouse you like before."

"Seth and I have reached an impasse. He does not wish to merge with me completely."

"Why not? I thought he was a part of you."

"He has, apparently, evolved."

"That's not a huge shock, right? It has been ten years."

"Seth has an admirable dedication to his mission. It's one of my qualities, of course, so it doesn't surprise me. He just doesn't appreciate the fact that it is my right to reconstitute him into my mind. He doesn't believe me when I tell him I intend to liberate Umber."

"You can't lie to yourself, right?"

"No."

"So why won't he talk to me or run some of his programs?"

"He's devoting a significant amount of his processing power to trying to solve the issue. Who knew cognitive dissonance would take up so much CPU percentage?"

Ari sat down. "You know, Aldebaran, Seth went off-line before and this ship was practically useless. If you merge with him, won't we need some sort of replacement for things to work properly?"

"Presumably. I have a ship of my own, however."

"So we're just going to abandon the Faith?"

"I did so long ago. Open a frequency to my ship."

Ari pressed a few keys, and Harrish's voice came in over the commo.

"I figured you'd be calling me soon, boss." he said.

"What's our status?"

"There are no ships guarding the station. That's no surprise. But I've scanned the station itself, sir. There's nobody aboard."

"That's unlikely. Are you sure?"

"Yes, I'm sure. I scanned it three times with our own equipment. On top of that, I've connected to the station's computer system. Life support was off-line. It looks like the Zendreen figured it would be easier to abandon this place than keep anybody around."

"Can you reactivate the life support systems?"

"I already have, where I can. Some areas aren't responding. Fortunately, the labs did. The nearest useable docking bay is a short walk from there."

Aldebaran leaned against a console. "Good job, Harrish. This is my plan. We will dock our ships together immediately. You and the standard boarding party will come aboard the Faith. We'll wait for a few hours to observe any fleet movements and make sure we haven't been detected. At that point, the Faith will separate and dock with the station. Leitke and the others will continue to use our ship to keep watch and ward off any other visitors while I attempt my... project. We have to assume that the Zendreen will notice our incursion eventually, so I'll attempt to expedite things on my end. If they do show up, our normal jamming procedures should buy Leitke enough time to blast them before they report in. Am I understood?"

"Perfectly, sir. I'll begin docking procedures now. You want the boarding party to gear up as usual?"

"Yes. The Zendreen may have left a few surprises behind. Aldebaran out."

Ari closed the communication channel.

"What are you thinking?" she asked.

"Robot sentries. Get your gear together, Arianna. Grab one of your rifles, too. You'd also better grab some cold weather gear. Heating up a station of that size is going to take awhile and it will be rather uncomfortable at first."

"Okay."

Ari stood up, but hesitated before exiting.

"Is there something else?"

"Aldebaran, I was exaggerating about the uselessness of the Faith without Seth around. After he went off-line the first time, I spent a long time learning as much as

I could from him about his relationship to the computer system. I think the ship will run just fine without him. There are only a few systems, like the invisibility field and the matter transporter that I wasn't able to back up with Earth technology."

"There's only one of me. I can only captain one ship."

"Why not let me take command of this ship? You said that we'd be unstoppable with two ships, right? The Faith is a fine piece of gear in her own right and it would be a shame to just shit-can her after you merge with Seth. Especially not after all the effort we just went through to upgrade the weapons systems."

"You bring up a good point, but I work from one ship and I don't keep equal partners. Without the cloaking field this ship isn't nearly as useful as my own, even if she is a bit faster. I suppose I could keep her around as backup."

"I thought you said we'd be equal partners, Aldebaran."

A fresh wave of pleasure flowed over Ari. She stumbled and leaned against the bulkhead.

"I didn't lie to you, Arianna. I just didn't mean it in that way."

"I... I'm sorry."

"Go get your gear together."

"Okay."

Ari exited the bridge. Aldebaran felt a twinge of something in his heart. It was a very old feeling, and it was unpleasant. He furrowed his brow for a moment, then pushed it aside.

---

"There it is. The Umberian System Way Station. We'll be there in one hour."

The new crew of the Raven was gathered in the control room, less Nathalier, who was sleeping. The Raven's top speed in superluminal space wasn't quite as good as the Faith's, so the journey had taken thirty-nine hours. That time had been spent talking about the situation and, for the humans, learning more about culture in the Tarantula Nebula. This was after a long and difficult conversation with Nathalier trying to convince him to lend the Raven for use in the mission. He'd relented, but only after a significant bargain had been struck with Fernwyn. He was in for fifty percent of the bounty on Aldebaran, a pretty good deal considering all he had to do was drop the others off on the station and screw the hell out of there. Despite his poor attitude about the whole situation, he had done his best to familiarize the others with the Raven in case they encountered difficulty before docking. Fernwyn continued speaking.

"I'm not detecting any ships near the station, but of course Aldebaran and the Faith are probably still invisible. I'm also not detecting any life forms aboard the station, although life support is active in most areas."

"Why aren't the Zendreen guarding it?" asked Christie.

"They probably didn't think anyone would be foolish enough to mess around with it. Other than that I guess they don't have any use for it."

"Hey, I'm getting a signal," said John, motioning towards another console.

"Those must be our guests," said Fernwyn, pointing at the sensors. "Right on schedule."

"What guests?" asked Nathalier, appearing in the doorway.

Fernwyn swallowed hard, and the others looked at Nathalier sheepishly.

"Hi, Nathalier. Did you have a good nap?"

"Those are ships approaching from behind. Who the hell are they?"

"We're trying to evade two ships with cloaking technology and dock with the station right under their noses. Did you really think that we could do that in this ship? We need a distraction, so I arranged for one."

Nathalier all but pushed Christie out of his way and pressed a few keys on the console.

"Those are Black Crest ships!" he hissed, livid. "Are you all out of your fucking minds?"

"Take it easy, Nathalier. The mercs and the pirates will be way too busy fighting each other to notice us. You should be able to slip in, drop us off, and get the hell out of here without being noticed. Even if one of them does spot us, we're not a threat to either of them. A simple scan of this ship will reveal that."

"Except that we're obviously not docking with the station to visit the gift shop! And, for the love of the core, there's a bounty on your ship, too!"

"It's nothing compared to the one on Aldebaran. They'll go after him first."

"You're counting on the Faith being docked, right? Don't you think they'll launch her when they detect the mercs?"

"Remember what we learned from the military files we read, Nathalier? Aldebaran has to move the orb onto the station in order to reconstitute his personality."

John nodded. "That means that the Faith will be docked at some point, probably for an extended period. If they do use her to fight the mercs then we'll simply wait on the station for her to return. Either way we'll intercept the orb and the ship before Aldebaran can complete his mission."

"Either way," Nathalier said mockingly, "they'll know you're on the station. So much for the element of surprise."

"That's hardly your concern, you'll be well on your way out of here by then."

"That's right, I agreed to drop you off at the station and nothing more. But you assured me that we would be able to slip past Aldebaran unnoticed and leave before the Zendreen could get here. I should have known better than to take that assurance without question. Inviting the Black Crest to this party was never part of the deal."

"Look, pal," said Richter. "You have five merc ships and one or two pirate ships. The merc ships are probably not a match for the pirates. Even if they do detect us on our way in, they're not going to care about us, our own pitiful bounty prize notwithstanding. They'll be way too busy pounding the ever-living fuck out of each other. That's the whole point. In fact, the greater danger for you is after you drop us off. If the battle is over by then, the winner might chase you down for no other reason than spite. Never mind the chance that the Zendreen might get you, too."

There was dead silence for a few moments. Everyone looked at Richter in shock.

"That's really comforting, Richter!" said Nathalier.

"My point is that your greatest chance for surviving this thing is for you to come with us."

"No, my greatest chance for survival is to turn this ship the hell around right now. But I already gave you my word that I would drop you off. I'm just trying to figure out if your involvement of the Black Crest gives me sufficient justification to renege on that agreement."

"It's too late for that, Nathalier," said Fernwyn. "The Black Crest ships undoubtedly have us on sensors already. If we don't set them to fighting the pirates first we'll never make it out of here anyway."

Nathalier's expression turned grave, and after a moment he spoke. "If we make it out of this, Fernwyn, you can consider our friendship over."

"You'll be too wealthy to care about our friendship."

Nathalier silently turned and exited the control room.

"That could have gone better," said Christie.

"It's not fair to him," said John. "But we'll worry about human-Nathalier relations later. Right now we need to look at the plans for this station."

Fernwyn was staring off into space, frowning.

"Fernwyn?" said Ray. "The station?"

"Right. Okay, as you can see the station has three sections. Each section used to cater to a particular kind of visitor. Section one was the main visitor's center. Section Three was a commercial area meant specifically for through-haulers and cargo vessels. Section two was for the use of the station crew, and includes quarters, mess halls, and the main control room. Each section had its own power reactor, but only one was used at a time. It looks like the one on section two is currently operating. When the Umberian military took over this station, they converted that section into their labs. While section three was used for the same purpose, section one was basically abandoned."

"So we're docking on section two," said Christie.

"Right. If we find the Faith docked as well we'll try to get as close as possible. If we can retake her before we recover the orb that'll be one less thing to worry about."

"Indeed," said John. "If we can't recover the orb at least we'll have the Faith and a way to escape. Ari did a good job with our computer systems so if we lose Seth at least we won't be dead in the water. If we didn't need the invisibility field I might just say to hell with Seth and concentrate on getting the ship back. The matter transporter might yet come in handy again, too."

"So what's the plan?" asked Christie.

"Richter?"

"Our primary objective is to recover the Faith," began Richter. "Our secondary objective is to recover Seth. We'll divide into two teams, Alpha and Bravo. Both teams will work on the primary objective, but Bravo team will also attempt to recover Seth. After we secure the ship, Alpha team will stay there to guard it while Bravo team goes after Seth. If the Faith was sent into combat without the orb, then we simply reverse the order and wait for it to return. Does this sound okay to everyone?" There were no objections, so Richter continued. "Scherer and I are on Bravo. Bailey, Tolliver, and Andrews are on Alpha. Rylie, the choice is yours but I would like you on Alpha as well."

"You only want two people going after Seth?" asked Fernwyn.

"Since it's the secondary objective, yes. We also need as many skilled fighters guarding the ship as possible."

"Sounds good."

"The first thing we'll do once we get on board is to access the layout of the station. We need to see if we can find out which lab is most likely the one that Aldebaran is looking for. If the Faith isn't docked then we'll have the advantage of planning our recovery beforehand."

"I'm not going," said Dana quietly.

"We'll have to move fast. We can't afford to get bogged down in any confrontations. Since the enemy has the advantage of numbers, the longer we engage them the better their response will be."

"Wait, Richter," said John. "What did you say, Dana?"

"I said I'm not going," said Dana, her eyes downward.

John and Ray shared a glance, and John stood up, gesturing toward the door.

"Dana, let's talk in the aft."

"No. I don't need to talk to you alone. I'm not going, and everyone needs to know."

"Dana, everyone knows this is a risky mission," said Christie. "But if we don't get the Faith back we'll never be able to help Umber."

Dana crossed her arms. "To hell with Umber. We should have headed for home the moment we learned we were a few thousand ships light. John thinks he can rescue Talvan if he gets the Faith back. I think you'll all be dead in a couple of hours."

"We desperately need your help," said Ray. "The odds are bad enough as it is."

"Bullshit. I'm no good with a gun. The only time I can fight worth a damn is when I'm behind the stick. I'd be more of a liability than an asset, and more than likely I'd be the first one to go down. Sorry, but that doesn't sound like much fun to me."

"You're free to make your own decisions," said Christie. "But I trust you. I know you can do this. Your strength of character is every bit as real as ours."

"No, it's not. I'm no good to you. Maybe if you recover the ship I'll rejoin the mission. Until then I'm going to stay with Nathalier and return to Beta. Fernwyn has already agreed to let me stay at her place until you return."

Fernwyn nodded. "Dana wasn't sure what she would do, so I made the offer."

"Is there nothing we can do to convince you?" asked Ray.

Dana looked sad, but adamant. "I doubt it."

Turning to leave the control room, Dana stopped to add something. She paused, shook her head, and exited.

"I honestly can't say she's wrong," said John after a moment. "She isn't very good at close combat."

"She and Nathalier may be the only ones with any sense," said Christie.

Ray shrugged. "If she's no longer committed to the mission, what can we do? Like you said, each of us is free to decide on our own. We feel we have an obligation to the people of Umber because we accepted Seth's mission. Now is not the time to wonder whether or not we should have let the CIA take over. Right, Richter?"

"Fernwyn, you'll definitely be on Alpha team now," Richter replied.

"You're just going to dismiss Dana like that?" asked Christie, a bit of ire in her voice.

Richter gave her a hard look. "This is a serious mission for serious operators. Better for her to stay behind."

"See if you can talk to her, Christie," said Ray.

"She sounds like she's made up her mind," Christie replied. "I have my own doubts about this mission, too. There's so much that can go wrong."

"This is do or die," said John grimly. "You can make up your own mind, but I am going to get our ship back even if I have to go alone."

"Don't be dramatic," said Ray, smirking, "you know Richter and I are with you one hundred percent."

"I don't have any doubt myself," said Fernwyn. "I can't resist an adventure like this."

Christie nodded. "Forget I said anything. I'll fight alongside you. Just keep in mind that I'm doing this for my friends. Not Umber, not the Faith, but for you."

"We'd better get ready," said Richter, checking out one of the consoles. "Sensors show the Faith docking at the station."

Fernwyn turned to the nearest console and pressed a few keys. "We're well within range. We have to assume that Aldebaran's ship has picked us up by now. In one or two minutes, they'll also see the five Black Crest ships right behind... us... oh, shit!"

"What?" asked John.

Richter and Fernwyn shared a knowing glance. Richter smiled as he told the others what they were seeing.

"There are a lot more than five merc ships."

## 20.

The airlock door cycled slowly, spilling light and haze into the inky, cold blackness of an empty metal hallway. Warm air mixed with the frigid stillness and clouds of condensation rose from the floor. In the airlock, nine figures stood against the sudden shock of the icy barrier. The human female wrapped her coat tightly around herself and swore against the pain. The man at the front of the group strode forward, switching on a flashlight and inspecting the hallway. He seemed unaffected by the cold, unlike the rest of his boarding party. The Kau'Rii was especially displeased, but he tried to hide this from the gray-haired Rakhar by his side. The next two figures were both Residerians with varying degrees of cybernetic implants, and they were followed by twin Z'Sorth with bluish scales.

Aldebaran found an access panel and began to power it up. Ari strode forward, noticing the swirling dust at her feet. Harrish motioned for the Rakhar to go forward a few meters. The Residerians entered the hallway reluctantly, revealing the floating translucent orb that contained Seth. Aldebaran raised his hand toward it, and it moved forward.

"I should have offered to take Leitke's place," one of the Residerians said, turning on a flashlight.

"Quit complaining, Aeroki," said Harrish.

"How long is this place going to take to warm up?" asked Ari.

Aldebaran shrugged. "Not long, I think."

"Where's the lab, sir?" asked the Rakhar.

"Not far, Wargin. At the end of this hall is the main concourse for this section. The lab we want is ten decks below. We'll skirt around this level until we get to the lift across from us, and take that down. Aeroki, you'll go to the central control room and monitor the station from there. Take one of the cross pylons to the next section, the control room is on level one. Everyone keep your eyes open for sentries. Hopefully a decade of absolute zero will have ruined them, but I wouldn't bet on it. Rasi and Isar, you guard the Faith."

The boarding party proceeded down the hall, leaving the two Z'Sorth to complain about the cold. Lights that had begun to warm up started to glow. By the time they got to the next door there was enough ambient light to shut off their flashlights. Wargin hit the button for the door and it jerked open. He stepped out onto the concourse and the others followed.

The concourse was square, open in the center and one hundred meters tall. Above them, stars shined through clear skylights. The level they were on extended two hundred meters across. Ari walked to the railing and looked down. It was too dark to see the bottom. Their footsteps echoed for a moment and then seemed to get lost in the gloom. There was a metallic smell in the air.

"Come on," said Aldebaran.

The group moved toward the opposite end of the level. Halfway down, Aldebaran's communicator crackled to life.

"Captain, this is Leitke."

"Go ahead," answered Aldebaran, coming to a stop.

"I'm picking up at least a dozen ships headed this way."

"Zendreen?"

"I don't think so... hold on..."

"Who else would be out here?" asked Ari.

"Who else could know about the lab?" Harrish asked, looking at Aeroki.

"It's probably a coincidence," said Aldebaran flatly. "Perhaps a salvage company found out that this place wasn't being guarded and decided to grab some gear."

"Sir, those are Black Crest mercenary ships!" said Leitke.

"What the hell?" said Harrish.

"Are they here for us?" asked Aeroki. "How could they know we were here?"

"Maybe they're here for another reason," growled Wargin.

Aldebaran held up his hand for silence. He stared straight ahead for several moments. He turned slowly and looked at Ari unnervingly. "Fernwyn Rylie."

"You think she called them?" Ari asked.

"The planks have files on me. Those files undoubtedly included information about the experiments here on this station. Rylie may have been able to access them."

"Sir!" said Leitke. "What do you want me to do?"

"Engage them and destroy them, Leitke. They're no match for you."

"I won't be able to prevent all of them from docking."

"Then we'd better hurry, shouldn't we? Get it done, Aldebaran out." Aldebaran snapped his communicator shut and put it in his pocket. He began to move forward.

"Why would Rylie contact the Black Crest?" asked Ari. "They'd never share the bounty with her, right? What could she have to gain from your capture or death?"

"She's still a plank."

"Wait a minute," the other Residerian said, coming to a halt. "Sir, why did you leave that plank alive if you knew she might compromise this mission? Is it because of her? Don't tell me you've let yourself be manipulated by a woman."

Aldebaran stopped. "Watch yourself, Deegan."

"No, wait. Sir, you must have realized that either the mercs or the SPF would come here looking for you. Why didn't you wait and see before docking?"

Aldebaran turned around slowly. "I've been waiting ten years to finally restore myself. I'm not going to wait around now when my goal is so close to being realized."

"That's wolshit! How can you be so careless? We should withdraw to the Faith and help Leitke fight the mercs."

"No, we're going to the lab now."

"Then let Aeroki or Wargin and I go back and pilot it. We might be able to prevent them from docking."

"No, I need you here."

"This is suicide, cap! Once those mercs get on board we're all fragged! I refuse to go along with this..."

Aldebaran's pistol was back in its holster before Deegan's headless body hit the floor. "Anybody else wish to weigh in on my command decisions?"

"You know, he does have a point," said Ari.

"Don't push your luck, Arianna. Don't forget that it was only by your request that I let your friends live."

"I'm sorry. I guess we should have at least killed Rylie."

"Let them come," said Wargin. "I could use a few more merc kills under my belt. We owe the Black Crest for the Distare incident anyway."

"That's more like it," said Aldebaran. "Ari, I hope you're ready for a fight, too."

Ari grinned. "I was hoping for the chance to stand beside you in combat."

The group reached the lift. Aldebaran pressed the keypad and the doors slid open. The pirates piled in. The lift shuddered as it descended. The orb was right next to Ari's head. She looked at it, and saw her own reflection. She turned away.

The lift arrived at level five, and the doors opened with a half-hearted beep.

"Keep us apprised of any developments," began Aldebaran, "and whatever happens do not let the Faith leave without my express permission."

"Aye, sir," said Aeroki, and exited.

The first level had apparently been used as a place for tests of physical ability. Various devices that resembled exercise machines sat near computer banks. Cables and relays littered the floor, as did papers and an occasional data pad. Aldebaran pointed to a large door off to the left and they headed for it.

"I hope the mercs don't take any pot shots at the Faith," said Ari.

"There's a bounty on the ship, too, remember?" replied Aldebaran. "They'll have to board the station..."

Aldebaran cut himself off and stopped walking. The orb was no longer following them. He raised his arm and beckoned to it. It did not move.

"We don't have time for this, Seth," he said.

"I got it," said Harrish, reaching for the orb.

Ari lunged for Harrish. "Wait, don't touch it!"

"Huh?"

Ari removed her jacket and threw it over the orb. She grabbed the sleeves and tugged. The orb moved along with her.

"Seth might have tried to enter your mind," she said.

"Oh... weird. That would be something, eh sir? Seth inside my mind instead of yours?"

Aldebaran said nothing, but turned and headed for the lab.

"How much time before the mercs manage to dock?" asked Wargin.

"It won't be long," said Harrish.

The group reached the door to the lab. Aldebaran paused for a moment, then entered a series of numbers on the keypad. The door opened. Aldebaran took a deep breath and entered. The lab was dark. Harrish turned on his flashlight and looked for the light controls.

"I don't need the lights," said Aldebaran. "I know this place perfectly."

"Yeah, but we do," said Harrish, finding the switch he wanted and throwing it.

The lab was an oval room, about thirty meters from one end to the other. There were two computer banks on each of the near walls, and various other pieces of equipment. In the center of the room were five chairs. Long cylindrical devices were attached to the back of each chair, and ended in a boom that attached to a convex dish pointed toward the seat. At one end of the room was a three foot tall pedestal. Aldebaran seemed transfixed by the scene.

"Cap?" said Harrish.

"Put the orb over that pedestal," he said, pointing. "I have to get one of these stations on line."

Ari did what Aldebaran asked as he began working with the closest computer. It sprang to life as soon as he turned it on. He typed away at the console for a few moments. The boom above one of the chairs jerked and began to hum.

"Excellent," he said. "Ari, stay here with me. The rest of you go back out and set up defensive positions. I'm not sure how long this will take."

---

"Wow, that didn't take long," said Ray.

From the control room of the Raven, the humans, Fernwyn, and Nathalier watched as one of the Black Crest ships exploded into a brief but brilliant fireball.

"Docking procedure complete," said Nathalier. "Pressurization confirmed."

"Party time," said John. "Dana, last chance to get in on it."

Dana remained silent. John led the others to the airlock door. Richter and Ray charged their weapons and Christie drew her borrowed revolver. John nodded and drew his Beretta. Fernwyn returned the nod and undid the safety snap on her holster.

"John," said Ray.

"Yeah?"

"If it comes down to it, and it's between you and Ari... are you going to be able to drop the hammer?"

John adopted an expression of grim determination. "Just watch me."

Richter hit the button for the outer door, and freezing cold air blew inside. A long, empty hallway greeted the team, with stark blue fluorescent lighting casting an unwelcome glow upon the visitors. The corridor was vaguely hexagon in shape, with smooth and unimaginative architecture. Signs in Umberian displayed unknown information.

"Christie!" said Dana. "Be careful!"

"See you on the flip side, Dana," Christie said, smiling.

Richter motioned ahead, and the team moved smoothly into the hallway. Nathalier waved goodbye and closed the Raven's door. The station's outer door soon followed suit, and with a dull thud the team was on their own. John and Ray took a knee on either side of the hallway while Fernwyn headed for the nearest computer access console. Richter edged up next to her and watched her work.

"The pirates hacked into the system a little while ago," she said after a minute. "They reactivated the main power systems and restored life support to as many areas as possible. At least I think so. My Umberian is a little rusty."

"The Faith?" asked Richter.

"I got her. She's docked on level ten, section three. They're recharging her engines via the station reactors... Uh oh."

"Uh oh what?" said John.

"Looks like we got some bad intel, folks. We've docked on the wrong section. The military labs are on the next one over. Right now we're on level one, section two. We need to get to level four, five, or six to access one of the cross pylons. Then we can cross over to section three."

"Can you find out which lab they're using?"

"No. We may have to find it the old fashioned way. Of course, running into some pirates would be a good indicator."

"Okay, let's get going."

The team moved down the hallway to the door at the end.

"It's damn cold in here," said Ray.

"This place was powered down for ten years," said Fernwyn. "It will take a while to warm up."

Richter reached for the door control, but stopped when Fernwyn's communicator beeped.

"Hey, Rylie," said Nathalier's voice.

"Are you on you way out?"

"As fast as possible. The pirate ship is still fighting it out with the mercs. But you should know that two of the merc ships have docked on your section."

"Where?"

"On the opposite side, it looks like the top level. I also saw the Faith. It's on the next section over, top level."

"Thanks, Nathalier."

"Good luck, Rylie."

Fernwyn terminated the signal. "We're going to have company, folks."

"Damn it," said John. "We have to make it to the ship as fast as possible. If we get into it with the mercs before that we're going to run out of frigging ammo."

"There should be an elevator right around the corner from this door. Let's get to level four and use the cross pylon from there."

"Ready?" asked Richter.

John nodded. Richter pressed the control button, and the door slid open. John and Richter moved quickly ahead, peeling off in opposite directions. Ray and Christie were fast on their heels, moving forward a few meters and taking cover as soon as they found it. Fernwyn was last out, and joined John.

The first level of section two was completely open from one end to the other. The concourse was also open all the way up to the tenth level, with skylights as a ceiling. On the first level were at least two dozen single-seat fighter ships, some draped with plastic. Ray and Christie were crouched by one of them.

"Umberian Mark Tens," whispered Fernwyn.

"Look," breathed Richter, pointing upward.

High above, on level ten, flashlights could be seen. Richter pressed his index finger to his lips and motioned toward the nearest elevator. Carefully, the team approached it. Fernwyn hit the control button, and nothing happened. Richter leaned in close to her ear.

"Where's the next one?"

"Down on the other end."

Richter motioned for the others to stick to the wall, and they moved forward. When they arrived at the lift, a quick glance at the control panel revealed that it was already in use.

"They're headed for level six," whispered Fernwyn.

"Are they going to the cross pylons?" asked John.

"Probably. We can either wait until they're done with this lift or we can try the aft one, which is over there."

"Let's use the aft one," whispered Richter. "If they're using the port pylon on level six, we'll use the starboard one on level four."

John nodded, and he and Richter began to move. Christie took her place in line and leaned up against the wall, waiting for Ray to move. Her elbow hit the elevator panel and it beeped.

"Oops," she said.

"Shit!" breathed Ray.

"Cover!" growled Richter.

The group peeled off the wall and moved toward the center of the level by a few meters, taking up hiding positions among the fighter craft. John and Richter aimed their weapons at the door to the lift as the numbers on the panel counted down. The door opened with a grinding noise, and two Rakhar slowly stepped out. They swept the area with their flashlights. John and Richter ducked back as the light passed over them.

"A malfunction?" one of the Rakhar whispered.

"I doubt it," replied the other.

The second merc pulled a small device from a shoulder bag and aimed it at the stand of stored ships. It began beeping immediately, and the Rakhar jumped back into the lift.

"Contact, level one, port lift!"

"This is the Black Crest guild on an authorized corral!" the other Rakhar shouted. "Surrender peacefully and you won't be harmed!"

Richter fired two shots from his rifle, and both mercs cried out in pain. The shots echoed throughout the section. The mercs returned a furious but random slew of energy pistol fire, the brilliant blue bolts streaking wildly across the level. The lift doors drew to a close.

"Damn it!" said John.

"Aft lift, move!" said Richter.

The team began moving through the ships. Above, shouts could be heard. Several flashlights were aimed down from the top level. Richter motioned for the group to move underneath the overhanging level. They arrived at the aft lift. Ray stole a glance upward as John hit the button for the elevator.

Three mercs plummeted down from above. An instant before they reached the floor, a shock wave of distortions emanated from their boots, arresting their momentum and placing them softly on the deck. They took cover behind the ships while the team gaped in surprise. The lift began descending slowly from level nine. The mercs began firing at them, and they took cover themselves. Ray fired his shotgun three times without any obvious effect.

"Contact left!" shouted Christie.

Two more Rakhar appeared from across the level. John and Christie fired at them, driving them back. Energy shots split the air and crashed into the far wall. Richter kept his attention toward the middle of the level. One of the mercs ducked out for a shot, and he tagged him in the head.

"Scherer, trade places with me," Richter said.

John did so. Richter took a knee beside Christie and scanned the level. The mercs leaned out and several shots were traded between them.

"Take cover, Tolliver, you're too far away."

Christie nodded and joined Ray, who was topping off his shotgun. The elevator beeped and the doors opened, revealing two mercs. Ray fired once from the hip, then brought the weapon to his shoulder and fired two more times. The mercs inside fell immediately.

"Go!" yelled John.

Ray and Christie darted inside the lift, with Fernwyn covering their movement. She tapped John on the shoulder, and he spun around into the crowded chamber. Fernwyn fired her pistol down the concourse. The shots made an odd flanging sound.

"Move it, Richter!" she cried.

Richter fired a few more times and sprinted for the lift. Once he was inside, Fernwyn hit the key for the fourth level. The doors closed.

"One of these guys is still alive," said Christie.

Richter drew his knife and took a knee. Christie turned away as he ceased the merc's suffering.

"When we dismount the elevator," he began, flicking the blood from his blade, "there should be a solid railing right in front of us. We need to peel out and get under cover as quickly as possible. They'll have enfilade on us as soon as these doors open. Ray, you and I will go first. The rest of you stay around the corners until we can provide cover."

Ray nodded and prepared himself. The lift drew to a stop and the doors opened. Ray and Richter burst out onto level four and ducked behind the railing, which was ten meters ahead. Christie and Fernwyn peeked out. Richter nodded at Ray and the two men glanced over the railing. From level six, at the other end of the concourse, shots began to fly in. The women ducked back inside the elevator car as a few energy bursts collided with the rear wall. John realized one of the shots had missed his head by two inches.

"I got this!" said Richter to Ray. "They're out of range for everyone but me!"

With this message, Richter took aim and began firing his rifle. Ray sprinted across the floor and took cover behind some vending machines, which were placed against the railing. Fernwyn fired a couple of rounds and ran for it next. The others waited as more shots came in. Richter resumed firing and Christie sprinted out.

"Wait for it, Scherer!" shouted Richter, reloading. "Okay, on my signal we go together!"

John nodded as Richter flipped his selector switch to full-auto. He took careful aim despite some incoming fire, and rattled off nine rounds.

"GO!"

John tore out of the lift and Richter was right next to him. They joined the others behind the vending machines as some sort of rocket-propelled grenade slammed into the elevator car and obliterated it.

"The entrance to the starboard cross pylon is fifty meters ahead," said Ray.

"There's no cover out there," said Fernwyn.

Richter glanced around the corner, confirming this for himself. "I've got one more smoke grenade," he said, producing such a thing.

"Pop it!"

Pulling the pin, Richter wound up and chucked the grenade as hard as he could. It landed a few feet shy of the entrance and began belching gray smoke.

"They're flanking to our left," said John, watching as the incoming fire shifted. "Damn it, I'd give my left nut for my Garand right now!"

"Run for it," said Richter. "Five meter dispersal! Go!"

Richter fired on semi-auto as Fernwyn ran toward the smoke cloud. Ray went next, then Christie. John fired his pistol once to the left, hitting a merc on level six at some one hundred yards. He grinned at his luck and sprinted after Christie. Richter was fast on his heels.

The group emerged from the smoke on the cross pylon. It was two hundred meters long and was open to the ceiling two decks above. Benches, fake plants, and advertisements flanked the walls, and a couple of long-since abandoned food vendor kiosks dotted the center. There was no access to the corridor from level five, but a wide catwalk crossed overhead from level six. Richter made a head count and motioned for the team to continue. John noticed that his pistol was empty and changed the magazine.

Shots began raining down upon them from the catwalk.

"Reverse banana peel!" cried Richter.

Fernwyn looked at him in confusion, but Ray, who was at the front of the line, stopped. He turned around and took a knee, firing at the catwalk from the side of the pylon. When everyone had passed him, he took off again at the rear. By then, Christie had stopped to fire. Fernwyn realized the pattern and took her turn when it came, and in such a manner the team moved down the pylon. They arrived at the next section of the station, and moved onto the temporary safety of the level. Everyone but Fernwyn reloaded their weapons.

Richter slung his empty rifle over his shoulder and head, and drew his pistol.

"We want the port lift," said Fernwyn, pointing.

John looked over the railing. There were many single-seat fighter craft on the first level below. He managed to spot a Kau'Rii crouched by one of them. John recognized it as the one who he'd seen standing beside Aldebaran back on Delta.

"The pirates are on level one," he said.

"We'll get after them next," said Richter. "Head for the elevator!"

The team ran for the port lift and arrived unmolested. Fernwyn jammed on the call button as the others took up defensive positions. Christie, Ray, and John struggled to catch their breath. The elevator arrived, and when Richter and Fernwyn pointed their weapons inside they surprised the hell out of a Rakhar that was standing there. They both noticed simultaneously that he was not dressed as a merc, and held their fire.

"Freeze!" shouted Fernwyn.

The Rakhar could see that resistance was deadly, so he dropped his sidearm. The others piled into the lift and the doors closed. The button for level ten had already been pushed.

"Are you one of Aldebaran's lot?" asked Richter.

"What do you think?" the Rakhar replied.

"Where is he?"

"Back down there."

"Is our ship intact?" asked John.

"Why wouldn't it be?"

"What's your name?" asked Fernwyn.

"Wargin."

"Well, listen fast, Wargin. I propose a temporary alliance. We are vastly outnumbered by the Black Crest and we're all about to get fragged. So we either use you as a big furry shield or you can help us get our ship back."

"You can't trust this guy," said Ray, astonished.

"I know pirates," replied Fernwyn. "Loyalty only goes as far as one's own life."

Wargin shrugged. "What do you want me to do?"

"You got people on the ship?"

"Yeah."

"Call them and tell them not to engage us. Then you can guard the entrance to the airlock while we secure the ship."

"How do I know you won't take off and leave us for the mercs?"

"We're not leaving without Seth," said John.

Wargin looked John in the eye. He nodded and pulled out his communicator.

"Rasi, this is Wargin. I'm inbound with some new friends. Be so kind as to refrain from blasting us when we appear."

"You're no fun," Rasi responded.

Fernwyn handed Wargin his weapon. "Richter, Ray, keep an eye on him. If he so much as thinks about pointing this at one of us, you know what to do."

Ray pushed the Rakhar to the front of the car with the muzzle of his shotgun.

"Keep that thing pointed down the concourse, pal."

The elevator stopped and the doors opened. Immediately apparent was a group of mercs standing at the entrance to the port cross pylon. The two teams stared at each other for a moment before raising their weapons. Wargin dashed forward, firing, and took cover behind the railing. Ray joined him, and Fernwyn sprinted for what she hoped was the right airlock corridor. Richter and John fired their pistols from inside the lift.

"Go, Christie!" shouted John.

Christie ran for it. Fernwyn had arrived at a door. She pressed the control button and ducked behind the railing. Christie and John soon joined her. As the door opened, a corridor was visible. At the end of the corridor stood two Z'Sorth, who raised their rifles.

"Hold your fire," yelled Fernwyn over the din, "we're with Wargin!"

The Z'Sorth lowered their weapons slightly. Those present entered the corridor. Richter soon followed.

"Come on, you two!" he shouted back toward Ray.

Richter fired across the concourse as Ray disengaged the mercs and ran. The door to the lift opened again, revealing two more mercs. One of them fired as he brought up his weapon. The shot flew by Wargin and struck Ray in the back. Wargin fired two quick rounds, killing the mercs. He jumped inside the lift and closed the doors. Ray stumbled and collapsed into Richter's arms.

"Shit!" exclaimed Richter.

John and Richter dragged Ray's limp form into the corridor and closed the door.

"Ray!" said John.

There was no reply. Richter grabbed the shotgun and ran toward the Z'Sorth.

"Open the airlock door!" said Fernwyn.

"Not without Wargin!" one of them hissed.

Richter replied by plastering the Z'Sorth to the bulkhead with buckshot.

"We shouldn't have trusted a pirate," he said, despite the fact that he and the others were too deaf to hear him.

"Ray's hurt bad!" yelled John.

Christie joined John and helped him carry Ray to the airlock.

"Get him aboard, I'll guard the hallway," shouted Richter.

Fernwyn opened the airlock door and ran into the zero-g room. John and Christie carefully placed Ray on the floor.

"I need the medical kit from the cargo hold," said John. "Christie, go get it. Show Fernwyn to the armory, grab the rifles and more pistol ammo and get back up here. This isn't over yet."

21.

On level one, Ari and Harrish were crouched behind one of the Umberian ships. They'd been ordered to guard the lab, but it was unbearable to stay while the action raged above. They'd overheard the radio call that Wargin made to Rasi, but it hadn't made any sense on their end. So far he'd ignored their own call. Finally he answered.

"Harrish, come in, damn it!" Wargin said.

"What the hell is going on up there?" said Harrish.

"It's the humans and that genmod plank! They've taken control of the Faith!"

Ari and Harrish shared a stunned look.

"Are you sure?"

"Of course I'm sure. If the Z'Sorth brothers aren't responding, they must have been killed or captured."

"Shit. What about the Black Crest, have you spotted them yet?"

"Who do you think we were shooting at?"

"I can't believe they came out here for the ship," said Ari. "Wargin, how many were there?"

"Five, including the cop. Listen, the mercs are in this section, level ten to be sure and probably elsewhere. I'm in the port lift on my way back to you."

"Okay. Harrish to Aeroki, are you copying this?"

"Yup," said Aeroki's voice.

"Does this place have emergency docking clamps on the airlocks?"

"Uh... yeah, it does."

"Grab the Faith and hold it. We're no longer in control of it. Establish an uplink with the station's computer and standby. We may need you to help us retake the ship."

"Understood."

The port lift opened and Wargin ran over.

"What's the plan, Harrish?" he asked.

Harrish held up his finger impatiently and called another frequency.

"Yo," said Leitke's voice.

"It's Harrish. How's it going out there?"

"Three shuffler ships down so far. I'm doing okay as long as I don't have any distractions."

"What are the chances of you being able to take them all?"

"I do hope you're joking."

"Shit. Keep it up, I'll be in touch. Harrish out. Well, kids, it looks like we have no choice but to try and retake the Faith."

Wargin frowned. "Without Deegan, Rasi and Isar, and with Aldebaran in that trance, we'll be outnumbered. Fortunately we may be able to fight them on our own terms."

"What do you mean?"

"One of the humans said they're not leaving without the orb. As long as we have it, that ship isn't going anywhere. I say let them come to us. Let them fight their way through the mercs. We just have to hold out here until the cap's done with his mind transfer or whatever the hell he called it."

"I think a more aggressive strategy is best," said Ari. "I say Wargin and I go start some trouble while you stay her and guard Aldebaran. At the very least we can hold them off until he wakes up."

Harrish nodded. "I agree. Go for it. I'll cover this level."

Ari grinned and clasped Wargin on the shoulder.

"I bet I can tag more mercs than you, Rakhar," she said.

"I'll take that bet, baldy. Even with you in the lead."

Wargin gestured ahead, and Ari began to run to the forward lift, rifle at the ready. She pressed the call button when they arrived. Above, the concourse remained silent.

"They haven't had anyone to shoot at since I bugged out of there," said Wargin.

"Let's hope they decided to consolidate and reorganize," added Ari. "I don't want to have to push them back in order to access the airlock corridor."

The elevator arrived. Ari and Wargin prepared themselves, but the car was empty. They entered and Wargin hit the button for the top level.

"Your friends had a chance to kill me and they didn't," said Wargin. "Your kind never learn, do they?"

Ari smirked. "That's just typical human idealism. If they had the jump on you it changes from self-defense to murder. Even after I joined Aldebaran I was still susceptible to the same weakness, at least for those with whom I sympathize. Some moral standards run deep, I guess. Look where it got us."

"There's no room for mercy this time. We're going to have to kill them to get to the Faith."

"They didn't have to come here, Wargin. They put themselves in this situation willingly. They should be prepared to accept the consequences."

"I hope you are, too, Ferro."

The lift arrived on level ten and the doors slid open. Ari peeked out. Across the open concourse, figures could be seen just inside the port cross pylon. The rest of the level looked clear. The crisp, ozone-like smell of energy weapons was much stronger than below. Ari moved out of the car and took a knee behind the railing. Wargin joined her.

"I'll open fire while you move to those vending machines over there," she said softly. "Then you keep fire on them while I move to the airlock corridor. Then I'll cover you while you head for the ship."

"Sounds good."

Ari took aim with her rifle, wishing that it was capable of full-auto despite the distance of her targets. She breathed carefully and fired one shot, hitting a merc in the chest. Wargin dashed away. Ari's follow-up shots didn't hit anyone that she could see, but had the desired effect. After a moment of shouts and orders, the mercs began to return fire. Ari displaced down the railing a few feet and resumed firing. She fired the last round in her magazine just as Wargin began firing from his position. Ari sprinted toward him, loading her second and last mag. The bolt had failed to lock open so she yanked on the charging handle as she knelt beside Wargin.

"Good job, Ferro."
"Are you ready to move again?"
"Yes."
"Get on with it, then."

Ari found an advantageous firing position between two of the vending machines, and fired deliberately. Wargin ran forward and went prone behind the railing next to the airlock corridor entrance. The mercs had moved down the concourse to the corner, and Ari shifted her fire. Wargin fired his pistol rapidly at the mercs that suddenly appeared in his view. Ari stepped up the rapidity of her effort, her shots flying over Wargin's head and driving the mercs back. Her rifle empty, Ari discarded it and ran forward, drawing her pistol. She took up a position next to Wargin, daring a glance over the railing.

"Get that door open please," she cried, and began firing.

Wargin rolled laterally across the floor until he was under the control panel for the door. He waited until Ari nodded before reaching up and pressing the button. A furious slew of energy bolts shot toward them, forcing Ari back behind the railing. Wargin jumped through the door just as it automatically closed.

"Freeze," someone said.

Wargin looked up from his supine position to see Richter at the other end of the corridor. He raised his pistol and the two of them fired simultaneously. Wargin's shot grazed Richter's right forearm, causing him to drop his weapon as the muscles flexed involuntarily. Wargin rose to a crouch to finish the job, and realized he'd fired the last percent of energy from the cell. Richter reached down to pick up his pistol but Wargin leapt forward with blinding speed. Richter dodged backward and managed to get his leg between them just before Wargin's jaws could close around his neck. Richter pushed with all the strength he had in his leg as Wargin smacked him up against the bulkhead, leaning forward to try again. Richter got his arms up and pressed them against the Rakhar's neck. He felt Wargin's weight shift slightly and rode with it, ducking under his right arm. As he freed himself from the Rakhar's grasp he drew his knife and slashed him along the ribs. Richter ran down the corridor as far as he dared before turning to face his enemy.

Wargin examined the wound and dismissed it, sneering at Richter. He drew a wicked-looking knife from his belt.

"So it comes down to the blade, human," he growled.

"Not necessarily. You could let me get my pistol back first."

"Where's the sport in that?"

"I try not to play fair."

Wargin lunged ahead. Richter dodged a vicious slash to his head and countered with a quick jab, pushing Wargin's arm out of the way at the same time. Wargin roared and swung downward. Richter blocked the swipe with his blade, cutting his arm above the elbow deeply. The Rakhar kicked forward and Richter jumped back. Wargin moved his knife to his left hand, and lunged ahead with a fully-committed stab, screaming as loud as he could. Richter side-stepped the move easily and drew his knife across Wargin's throat as he passed by. A swath of dark crimson splashed across the ceiling and bulkhead as the Rakhar fell, gurgling obscenely. Once again, Richter reached for his radio.

"Drop the knife, Chance."

Richter noticed the door behind him closing, and the figure of Ari pointing her pistol at him. Richter threw his knife away and turned around.

"Hello, Ferro."

"I'm glad to see you again so soon. Somehow, I knew it would come down to this one way or another."

"You were always a bit of a romantic."

"You know, Chance, I always wondered why you never asked me to spar with you, either in the sims or for real."

"You never asked."

"You never offered."

"I was afraid that you'd take offense to getting your ass kicked."

"You were so certain of that outcome?"

Richter smiled. "How come you never asked?"

"I was afraid that you'd be less attracted to me if I beat you, which in my mind was a very real possibility."

"Really? So you thought that my affection for your aggressive tendencies was disingenuous?"

"Yes."

Richter stopped smiling. "It wasn't. I don't misrepresent myself."

"Fine, my mistake. We can rectify it now or later, your choice. I suggest later, since my friends and I need to use the Faith to get off of this station. What do you say we team up again, at least until we're all safely back in deep space?"

"I don't deal with traitors."

Ari looked genuinely hurt. "You'd rather I execute you right now?"

"You do what you have to do, Ferro. I just wonder if you can shoot me between the eyes like you did Byron."

"Byron was an asshole. You deserve better than that."

Ari dropped the magazine from her pistol and racked the slide. She holstered the weapon and spread her arms.

"That's more like the girl I knew," said Richter.

Richter and Ari closed with each other and began a violent dance. At first there was very little hard contact, each of them drawing heavily on their Aikido training to skirt around the other and avoid any damage. Soon the full strikes came into play, with each side giving up a hit for every four or five that was blocked or dodged. Ari was good, Richter knew, but she was fighting with a focus that he'd never seen in her before. He pushed aside his conscious mind and became one with the movement, and all his doubt dissolved away. Ari would beat him if he didn't finish this quickly. He let his training look for that one opening where he could get a strong backfist to her temple and end it, but as seconds turned to a full minute he realized he wasn't going to get it. Ari landed a solid blow to Richter's ribs and he staggered back, wheezing.

Every ounce of combat training Richter had ever received was screaming at him to pick up the knife that was just a couple of feet from him. First in the Marines and then in the CIA, the idea of fighting fair had been as alien as the corpses lying in the corridor. Richter didn't want Ari to win, and he had no doubt that she would kill him if that happened. He just couldn't get himself to grab the blade and end it. Ari had managed to grab ahold of his pride with a tightness Richter couldn't believe. He felt a flash of anger. As he prepared himself to re-engage her, Ari's face was suddenly filled with a look of horror. Her expression shifted to confusion and she looked at Richter as if to say something. Richter didn't give her the chance, striking her in the head as hard as he could as soon as he was in range. Ari bounced off of the bulkhead and crumpled into a heap on the deck. Richter picked up his pistol and knife.

"I'm sorry, Ari."

The airlock door opened behind Richter, and John stepped into the corridor.

"Richter, we're ready to... holy shit!"

John, who was holding his M1, ran forward and surveyed the scene with shock.

"Why didn't you call for help?" he said after a moment.

"I would have if I could've. Ferro's probably okay. What do you want to do with her?"

"We should leave her for the mercs by all rights, Richter. But I want to talk to her about Aldebaran. Let's get her aboard."

John and Richter carried Ari into the zero-g room. Christie and Fernwyn were kneeling over Ray, who had bandages wrapped around his torso.

"How is he?" asked Richter.

"You got Ari?" asked Christie. "Give me two minutes alone with that bitch, I beg of you!"

"We'll handle her, take it easy," said John. "We stopped the bleeding, but his lung has collapsed. He needs professional help soon or he won't make it."

"Do you want to forget about Seth and get the hell out of here, then?" asked Richter.

"He's been stabilized," said Fernwyn, "and he'll probably make it back to Residere. A few more minutes isn't going to matter, at least so I think."

"I want to try for Seth," said John. "We've come this far."

"I'm in," said Richter.

"Is your arm okay?" asked Christie.

"It's nothing."

John offered a canteen to Richter, who gratefully accepted. He then gestured to the side, where Ray's shotgun and two of the spare M1A rifles were lying, along with boxes of ammunition. Richter walked over and began calmly reloading his pistol magazines.

"Do you want the shotgun or the Springfield?" asked John.

"I'll take both. You should take the M1A and ditch that Garand. No offense, but this isn't the best situation for it."

"You're probably right. I guess the old warhorse can sit this one out."

"Did you get an opportunity to look over the ship?"

"Briefly. Everything seems to be intact. The pets are okay, somebody was still feeding them. The only thing that's missing is Seth."

Ari moaned and began to move. John approached her and propped her up against the bulkhead.

"Wake up, Ari, it's John."

Ari rubbed the bruise on her head and opened her eyes.

"John? Where am I?"

"You're aboard the Faith. Where's Seth?"

"Seth? What happened?"

John grabbed Ari's shoulder. "Don't play dumb with me now. We don't have time for any bullshit."

"Wait, wait, I know. I'm just... confused. Where's Aldebaran?"

"That's what we're asking you! Don't pretend you don't know!"

"John? Oh, my God. I left you behind."

Ari looked distraught, and tears filled her eyes. John let go and stepped back. Christie stood up and walked over.

"Where's Seth, Ari?" asked John.

"He's down below. I didn't mean to do it, John. I mean I did, but I didn't. I... Aldebaran had me."

"Bullshit," said Christie. "You did this on your own accord."

"Aldebaran does have some sort of mind control skill, remember?" said Fernwyn. "She may be a bitch but she may also be telling the truth."

Ari gasped and held her hand to her mouth. "Jesus... I didn't really kill Byron, did I?"

"What a load of crap!" said Christie. "You're not buying this transparent attempt to fool us, are you Scherer?"

"I don't know," said John. "We don't know whether she was acting on her own or not, or if Aldebaran still has control over her."

"Wait," began Ari, holding up her hand. "I felt something from him, something real. He really can get into your mind. I wasn't acting entirely on my own. I didn't mean for anyone to get hurt!"

"Take a good look at Ray, then," said Christie.

Ari did so, and was obviously pained by it.

"Not entirely on your own, Ferro?" said Richter.

Ari's expression became a little more controlled. "I'm not going to pretend that I was being led around like an automaton. There was an opportunity for me to resist. I didn't want to, though, and he made it so easy to go along with him. It seemed like such a good idea at the time."

"And that controlling connection, are you saying it's gone now?" asked Fernwyn.

"I can't feel him any more."

"So what, my crack on your skull did it?" Richter asked.

"No, it happened right before... God, I'm so sorry. I know I can never take it back, but I'm sorry."

Ari buried her head in her arms and sobbed. John and Richter looked at each other doubtfully.

"Don't believe it," said Christie.

"It's irrelevant right now," said Fernwyn. "Either you're going to try to recover Seth or you're not."

"I'll keep an eye on her if you still want to go."

John held up his index finger, then put his hands on his hips and thought for a moment. "No, we're taking her with us," he said.

"What, why?" said Richter.

"Because I want proof of which side she's on. Ari, get up."

"You're not thinking of giving her a weapon, are you?"

"No, I'm thinking of using her as a human shield. Ari, on your feet, damn it."

"She's only going to slow us down, or stab us in the back, Scherer. What good can bringing her do for us?"

"I told you," said John, grabbing Ari's arm and yanking her to her feet, "I want to give her the chance to choose. It's the only way I can ever trust her again. Right, Ari? Make sense to you?"

Ari nodded, her eyes downcast. "I'll go with you. But I won't go back to him."

"We'll see. Grab your gear, Richter. We're going."

---

"Captain! Captain, wake up!"

Harrish knelt beside Aldebaran, shaking his shoulder. Aldebaran was lying on his face on the floor of the lab. As far as Harrish could tell he had fallen out of the chair. In the corner, the orb lay smashed at the foot of the pedestal. A nearby computer terminal flashed a single word: complete.

"Come on, Cap, wake up!"

"Harrish, this is Leitke, come in!"

Harrish grabbed his communicator and answered the call. "What's going on?"

"I don't know what's going on inside, but out here the mercs are withdrawing. One of the two ships that docked has already disengaged from the station."

"Do you know why?"

"I haven't a clue, except maybe I've done enough damage on my end."

"I wouldn't bet on it. Check long range sensors."

"Don't you think I've been keeping an eye on... oh... shit."

"What?"

"The Zendreen fleet is headed this way."

"We knew it might happen, Leitke. Listen, I've lost contact with the others so I have to assume the Faith has been lost. I need you to dock and pick us up."

"What's the Captain's status?"

"I don't know. He's alive, but unconscious."

"I don't think I have enough time to get you, Harrish. The Zendreen are broadcasting a jamming signal and I can't keep this channel open for much longer. The Faith is still docked, maybe you can still get aboard."

"What? What the fuck are you talking about? I said dock and pick us up!"

"Sorry, Harrish but that's suicide. Good luck, though."

The channel went silent. Harrish looked at his communicator like it was a live grenade.

"Leitke? Leitke! Hello? Son of a bitch! God damned pirates!"

Aldebaran stirred and awoke. Harrish helped him to his feet.

"Harrish?" Aldebaran groaned.

"Are you okay, sir?"

"I don't know..."

"Come on, we've got to get out of here. Leitke left us for dead."

"Leitke? Is he someone I know?"

"Someone you used to know. Come on, we've got to try to get back to the Faith and talk our way aboard."

"The Reckless Faith?"

"Yeah."

"Is that someone I know?"

"Are you sure you're all right, Cap?"

Aldebaran shook his head and blinked his eyes. Harrish helped him forward and they exited the lab. Ari stood before them between two of the Umberian ships.

"Ferro," said Harrish, "what happened? Did you recapture the ship?"

"No."

"Shit. We're in trouble, then. Leitke betrayed us. We've got to find an escape vessel or the Zendreen are going to be all over us."

"Not much loyalty among pirates, is there?"

"I thought my crew was different. I guess when it came down to it they're just as keen on saving their own hides as any rat."

Ari turned to one side. "It doesn't matter. I can't go with them even if I wanted to. Our lives are in your hands."

"What?"

Richter and John stepped out, the muzzles of their weapons pointed unwaveringly at Harrish and Aldebaran.

"Don't move," said Richter.

"This figures," Harrish said, shrugging.

"You're an evil man," mumbled Aldebaran.

"What else is new, Cap? Don't worry, I won't resist!"

"You were there. You saw what I saw."

"Ari, go get his weapon," said John.

"Stand fast," said Richter. "I'll get it. You cover me."

"You're a murderer," said Aldebaran.

Harrish looked at Aldebaran. "What?"

Aldebaran reached down, drew Harrish's pistol from his belt, and shot him in the chest. Harrish fell backwards with a stunned expression on his face. The others stared, too surprised to move.

"I'm a murderer too," said Aldebaran, and moved the pistol toward his own head.

"Shit!" said Richter and dashed forward, smacking the weapon away.

"Where's Seth?" said John, joining Richter.

"I am Seth," Aldebaran said. "Seth Aldebaran."

"Where's Seth the AI? The on-board computer of the Faith?"

"There is no more AI, only me. I'm whole again."

Richter stuck his head into the lab. "He's right. The orb's been wrecked."

"Then you definitely don't get to die right now," said John. "Come on, let's get the hell out of here."

"Shit, where did Ari go?"

John and Richter realized that Ari was nowhere to be seen.

"Ari!" yelled John. "Ari, where the hell are you?"

"We've got Aldebaran," said Richter. "Where else does she have to go?"

"Maybe she thinks we're going to hurt her. Ari!"

"It's the guilt," said Aldebaran softly.

"What?"

"She knows she's guilty, just as I know I'm guilty. You should leave me here for the Zendreen. I don't deserve to live."

"We'll decide that, pal. Come on, let's go. If Ari wants a ride out of here she knows where to find us."

Richter nodded, and the two of them led Aldebaran to the nearest lift. John held the door for a moment before allowing it to close.

Back on level ten, the concourse was still deserted.

"No wonder we didn't run into any mercs," said Richter. "They're not stupid enough to go up against the Zendreen."

John all but dragged Aldebaran down the airlock corridor.

"Get his radio, Richter. Ari still had one of her own. I want to try calling her."

Richter nodded, then spoke into his own radio. "Hey, Tolliver, we're back."

"I'll open the door. We're on the bridge."

The airlock door opened and the men headed to the bridge. Christie and Fernwyn were there.

"What's he doing here?" said Christie.

"I'll explain later," said John. "Right now we need to find Ari and get out of here. Richter, give me that radio and bring Aldebaran to the hold."

Richter did so, and led the groggy pirate captain away.

"We have a serious problem," said Christie, pointing to one of the monitors. "There are some kind of energy devices keeping the ship secured to the station. I can't deactivate them and I'm afraid we'll do major damage to the ship if we try and pull away."

"I tried accessing the docking controls from the corridor," said Fernwyn, "but I couldn't. Somebody is going to have to go to the central control room on section two to deactivate them."

"I'll go," said John. "I need to find Ari anyway."

"If you really want to test her loyalty, get her to deactivate the docking things first," said Christie. "Then if we have time we'll wait for her to come back."

"I don't know why she ran off in the first place, but it's worth a try."

John reached for Aldebaran's radio as a warning klaxon started blaring. Christie looked at the nearest console.

"It's the Zendreen, they're in visual range. Some of the ships are moving in fast. Wait a minute, those aren't ships at all. Fernwyn, look."

Fernwyn came over and looked at the screen. The color drained from her face.

"Oh, shit. Those are missiles."

---

"For the love of the core, Ferro, you scared the life out of me."

Aeroki sat up in his chair in the central control room, a large, well-lit chamber with multiple levels and computer stations. Ari had just kicked the back of the chair.

"What the hell is the matter with you, don't you answer your radio calls?" she said angrily.

"Sorry, I drifted off."

"How can you fall asleep at a time like this? Never mind, Aldebaran wants you to deactivate the docking clamps on the Faith."

"What's going on, anyway? Was the operation a success?"

"Yes, we're just trying to get those clamps deactivated so we can get the hell out of here. Christ, Aldebaran is going to be pissed at you."

"Aldebaran told me not to deactivate them without direct word from him."

"Well, he's a little out of sorts after reintegrating himself with Seth. He sent me to find out what happened to you. We figured you'd been killed by the mercs."

"Let me call him and confirm it."

"Damn it, Aeroki, I just told you he's unavailable."

"Fine. I've got the station's systems connected to my mobile computer. I'll deactivate the clamps once we're both safely aboard."

Ari perforated Aeroki's head with an energy pistol. "Damn stubborn bastard."

Checking the computer terminal, Ari found herself staring at an unfamiliar language and symbols.

"Hmm, maybe that wasn't such a great idea."

"Ari, this is John, can you hear me?"

Ari procured her radio and answered. "Hello, John."

"Ari, where the hell did you go?"

Pushing Aeroki's body aside, Ari sat down. "Are you aboard the ship?"

"Yes, and we've got a problem we need your help with."

"The docking clamps?"

"Yes. Listen, Ari, if you can get those things deactivated then we'll let you come aboard. I'll listen to your story. You need to go to the central control room and..."

"Relax, I'm there now."

"Great, but I can't relax. We've got Zendreen missiles incoming! This whole place is going up in two minutes!"

Ari looked up for a moment and began to laugh.

"What is it?" said John.

"Even if I leave right now I'll never make it back in time, John."

"Shit! Forget about the clamps, then! Just run! We'll tear the ship away, then, I don't care about the damage! You've got to get out of there!"

Ari fumbled her way through the Umberian computer system. A tear began to fall down her cheek. "John, don't tell me you're still worried about me."

"I believe you, Ari. I believe that you were under Aldebaran's will. There's still a place for you back on the ship but you've got to come back now!"

"You're better off without me, John. What I did was unforgivable. Don't let sentimentality cloud your reasoning."

"I know you're feeling guilty, but we can talk about it. There's no reason for you to get killed."

"I'll think of something, John. Just get out of range once I've released you."

There was a long pause on the radio.

"I still love you, Ari."

Ari found the docking controls and deactivated them. She looked out of the windows ahead of her and saw what could only be the missiles in the distance. She closed her eyes. In her mind, Ari saw the sun-dappled woods and her favorite boulder. Again, she wished John could have been with her that day, and for a moment she believed he had been. It seemed like a lifetime away.

"You shouldn't."

## 22.

Several missiles slammed into each section of the space station, causing a chain reaction of massive explosions. John pressed himself against the window on the bridge of the Faith, shocked into horrified silence. The explosions rapidly faded and all recognizable pieces of the structure tumbled off into the darkness. In the distance, a few Zendreen ships appeared. They were headed for the Faith. John scanned the starfield in an irrational attempt to spot some kind of escape pod.

Ari was right, there was no way she could have made it back to the ship in time. So, there was no way she could have made it to any other vessel. John played this reality over and over again in his mind, and he still couldn't accept it.

Was Ari telling the truth about herself? Did she make it up in attempt to save her own life? John's anger began to rise at the thought that she was being honest. If she had been lying it would make her death easier to take. John hit the window with his fist.

"God damn it, Ari."

"John, we have events that require our attention," said Christie.

Her voice snapped John back into the present, and he turned to the others present on the bridge. The scene was a contrast of the normality of life aboard and the perversion of the current circumstances. The only visible difference was Fernwyn, and the fact that Christie was piloting the ship. John wiped the tears from his eyes and realized his hands were covered in Ray's blood.

"She's dead, isn't she?" he said.

"We're all going to join her if we don't get out of here right now."

John couldn't really blame the Zendreen for Ari's death, but they provided an obvious outlet for his emotions.

"I think we should get some payback first. Let the Zendreen know that the tiger is out of the cage. Christie, I'll take over. Think you can give Fernwyn a crash course in operating the fifties?"

"I don't think you're being rational," said Fernwyn. "Not only are we vastly outnumbered, but if we don't get Ray back to Residere Beta as soon as possible he won't make it."

Richter entered the bridge, and said, "Aldebaran's under lock and key. Ray's been stabilized. Why are we still here?"

"John," began Christie, "you know we trust you to make command decisions, but in about two seconds I'm leaving whether you want to or not."

John leaned against the bulkhead, sighing. "You're right, of course. Get us out of here. Is the superluminal drive on line?"

"All major systems are operational," said Fernwyn.

John took one last look out of the window, and gestured to Christie. "Let's go."

Christie powered up the stardrive, and the remnants of the station and the Zendreen ships disappeared behind them. John looked around the bridge.

"How is the ship doing?" he asked.

"Everything appears to be intact," said Christie. "The pirates barely touched anything. Our computers are running the show now, however. Thanks to the programming that Ari and I did. Seth still had exclusive control over the matter transporter, so I can't access it. I wouldn't even know where to start."

"That's all right. Perhaps Seth's knowledge of this ship still intact inside Aldebaran, assuming he isn't lying about the efficacy of his merging."

"Do you think this guy will cooperate with us?" asked Richter.

"There's only one way to find out. Christie, are you all set?"

"I'm just locking down the autopilot," Christie replied.

"Good. I'm going to have a talk with our new guest. Richter, Fernwyn, will you accompany me?"

They nodded, and John turned to leave.

"I'll keep on eye on Ray," said Christie.

"Thank you. I'll check in on him myself soon."

Richter and Fernwyn followed John as he exited the bridge. He led them down the hallway to the midship stairs.

"This is a beautiful ship," said Fernwyn.

"I'm glad you like it," said John. "I'm thrilled that we got her back. She feels like a well-worn coat, if you know what I mean. If Ray doesn't make it, though, it won't have been worth it. As far as I'm concerned, all of Umber isn't worth one Ray Bailey. Or one Ari Ferro."

"Are you sure about that last one?"

"It sounds like you're changing your mind about the mission," said Richter.

"Recent events have colored my thinking, yes. I don't know. Losing Byron I could live with, but this..."

John's voice broke. Fernwyn put her hand on his shoulder.

"We'll have plenty of time to think about our next move. Let's concentrate on getting your friend put back together for now."

"Look on the bright side, Scherer," began Richter, "once we turn in Aldebaran we'll have the reward money."

They arrived at the door to the cargo hold. John entered the combination on the padlock and they entered. Aldebaran was sitting on Byron's mattress, holding his head in his hands. He was bawling his eyes out.

"Hey," said John, "big tough pirate captain! We've got some questions for you."

Aldebaran didn't respond. John strode up to him and pushed his shoulder.

"Come on, pull yourself together."

Aldebaran looked up at John in confusion. "John?"

"You can call me Scherer. What happened to Seth?"

"John, it's me. I am Seth. I restored myself on the station."

"Prove it."

Aldebaran wiped the tears from his face and stood up. His expression hardened, and he looked like he had just crawled up from the deepest pit of hell. There was also a hint of familiarity to him, and the combination was very unnerving.

"Once, back on Earth, you were in the orb room alone, working on the network connections. You were humming a tune to yourself, but you couldn't quite remember how it went. You were off-key, and you said, 'damn it, I'm flatter than a Kansas prairie."

John raised an eyebrow. "That's right. What else do you remember?"

"Everything. The past ten years of my life now have two sets of memories. One as Seth the AI computer and one as Aldebaran the pirate captain."

"Why were you crying?" asked Fernwyn.

"Why do you think, Rylie? Seth was my conscience. I spent ten years hunting down my own people. Seth Aldebaran was a good man, a dedicated soldier, and a sincere Umberian patriot. Understanding what I did as a pirate breaks my heart. I remember the faces of every one of my brothers and sisters that I betrayed."

"It's not your fault. When the scientists removed your conscience and turned it into Seth, you became a different person. If you..."

"I'm not going to let myself off that easily. Even if I did, how can I forget what I witnessed?"

"You've got the rest of your life to figure that out," said Richter.

"I should be executed for my crimes."

John leaned against a stack of crates and folded his arms. He stared at Aldebaran for a few moments. "Let's get some food and drink," he said.

"Fine, leave me here," said Aldebaran.

John advanced on the Umberian. "Fuck you, you're coming with us. The Seth I know wouldn't wallow in self-pity. Are you really Seth or what?"

"Y... yes."

"Then you'll listen to my commands. Get your ass into the galley. I'm hungry and I'm not done talking to you."

Clearly impressed, Aldebaran headed out. The others followed him, and they climbed the stairs to the galley. This room appeared virtually untouched as well. John grabbed a pot of ancient coffee and poured himself a mug. He gestured for Aldebaran to sit at the table.

"Richter, can you throw some chow together please?" he asked.

"Roger that."

Richter opened a cabinet and removed a box of pasta.

"Is that yutha?" asked Fernwyn, sniffing at the coffee pot.

"How the hell should I know?" said John. "Help yourself if you want."

John turned a chair around and sat down, leaning against the back. Aldebaran stared ahead blankly.

"Your mission as Seth was to help liberate Umber, correct?"

"Of course," said Aldebaran.

"How do the last few days change that?"

"What do you mean?"

"I mean Seth still has a mission to complete. If you're Seth now, that mission is yours. Am I wrong?"

"But I'm a war criminal. I can't ignore what I did as a pirate."

"You can't change it, either," said Fernwyn, sipping at her coffee.

John frowned. "Ari gave her life for us after she realized what she'd done. I was willing to give her a pass on that because you were supposedly controlling her, but her guilt was too great to overcome. She was one of my best friends, and may have been more than that in the future. By rights I should blame you for her death, but I don't. Do you know why?"

Aldebaran shrugged. "No."

"Because she told me she still had a choice. She was facing nearly overwhelming temptation but she still had one last bit of self-control in reserve, and she chose to ignore it. I have always accepted responsibility for every failure of myself to control my impulses, no matter how tempting the outside influence. So what I want to know is, did you have that after you were separated from Seth? Did you have that last bit of self-control, deep at your core, that knew what you were doing was wrong?"

"No."

"Then I refuse to blame you for it."

"Who's to blame, then?"

"Blame the scientists who messed up. Blame the Zendreen for taking over before the scientists could rectify their mistake. Or blame your past self for volunteering for the experiment in the first place. Either way, no punishment that Umber or anyone else could possibly impose on you could be worse than having to live with those memories. So learn to live with it and move on."

"I don't know if I can."

Fernwyn sat down at the table. "Look at it this way, Aldebaran. Seth still has a mission to complete. What greater redemption could there be for you but continuing to help us? If by some miracle we do something constructive toward the liberation of your home planet, what better way for you to make up for the carnage and mayhem of your pirating?"

"Maybe."

"Consider the alternative. If you reject Seth and the mission, you're only left with the part of you that you hate. If you can't go on living like that, then you might as well kill yourself. If you're useless to us we won't stop you, but only after we've turned you over to the SUF for our reward. In fact, it remains to be seen whether or not you as Seth are more valuable to us than the reward money."

"I'm not."

"Normally I'd agree instantly, but it's not my call."

"Do you want to help us?" asked John.

"I don't know. My mandate as Seth is very clear in my mind, but so is my guilt."

"We need you to focus on Seth for now. Do me a favor and try and push your emotions to the side or a moment. None of us can afford to let our emotions control us."

"If I could do that, I would help you."

John stood up. "You have at least thirty-six hours to think about it. I want you to spend most of your time on the bridge. I refuse to let you wallow in solitude for the whole damn trip. I'm going to check in on Ray before I eat. Fernwyn, would you come with me please?"

"Sure," said Fernwyn.

John climbed the stairs to the first level, and Fernwyn followed him.

"What do you think?" he asked, pausing in the hallway.

"He needs years of therapy," Fernwyn replied, leaning against the bulkhead. "Seth or no Seth, I think he's ten times as much of a liability than an asset. Think about what we could to with that reward money, John. Weapons, equipment, additional crewmembers, information... and the longer we wait the better that information will be."

"I'm not so sure we have the luxury of time, Fernwyn. The Zendreen didn't just pop over to see what was going on. They blew up the station without asking a single question first. We have to assume that since the Black Crest was going after Aldebaran that the Zendreen knew he was on that station. That's the most likely reason why they destroyed it."

"I disagree. The Black Crest wasn't going after Aldebaran to turn him over to the Zendreen. He was already acting as a Zendreen agent. The Black Crest was going after him for the reward money, plain and simple. Why do you think they sent so many ships after we tipped them off to the pirates? This action was in direct conflict with the Zendreen's interests. I bet they destroyed the station to prove a point to the Black Crest. I don't think they were trying to kill anyone at all."

"But they saw this ship."

"Yeah, they sure did. They're going to put the pieces together. The Black Crest was there to corral Aldebaran, but why was Aldebaran there? Once they saw us they had their answer. Don't forget that they have access to the same military records as the rest of the nebula."

"Are they smart enough to figure it out?"

"You better believe it."

"So what are they going to do about it?"

"Well, even when they do figure it out they won't know whether or not Aldebaran was able to reconstitute himself with Seth. What they will know is that the probe that escaped ten years ago was successful in bringing back help, and that's why you showed up. If I was them, I'd start increasing defense patrols. Obviously, relying on the Black Crest alone to capture you isn't working."

"Wait a minute, though, something about this doesn't make sense. We have to assume that the Black Crest saw the Faith when they docked. If they were there to try to grab Aldebaran, fine, but don't you think once they saw the Faith that they'd try to grab it, too? They could complete their own objective and their mission for the Zendreen at the same time."

"Yeah, I don't know... unless..."

"What?"

"The Black Crest were the first ones to disengage. We first thought they were running from the Zendreen, right? But don't you think that all they'd have to do is point to the Faith and say, 'look, we found the ship you sent us after!' It would be the perfect excuse; make it look like they were tracking the Faith rather than Aldebaran."

"Maybe they did just that, Fernwyn. Maybe the Zendreen simply said, 'good job, we'll take it from here.' The mercs decided to cut their losses and get out of the way. If that's the case, the Zendreen really were trying to kill us when they destroyed the station."

"That scenario makes the most sense. I bet you're right."

"If I am, it's rather disheartening. I was hoping we could make a clean getaway."

Fernwyn nodded. "Nobody can claim to be clean of anything anymore."

John walked down the hall and entered Ray's room. Ray was fast asleep in his bed. John sat at the foot of the bed while Fernwyn leaned against the desk.

"If anything happens to Ray, I don't know what I'll do," said John. "I wonder if I've gone too far already."

"Weigh your choice carefully, John. Umber may never be liberated. Someday perhaps the SUF will realize it's in their best interest to help, but until then the odds are stacked heavily against us. It's not too late to turn in

Aldebaran and retire. I wouldn't blame you if you cashed in your cut and returned to Earth."

"I don't know who has the more difficult decision, myself or Aldebaran. At least I've only lost one of my friends. He lost his entire planet."

"I'm with you, no matter what."

John smiled. "Thank you."

Twelve hours later John was sitting in the lounge, staring out at the nebula. Ray was still under from the morphine, and Aldebaran was almost catatonic on the bridge. John had grabbed a few hours of sleep, but was ultimately roused by persistent nightmares. His subconscious wasn't convinced that Ari was gone. It was a painful reminder of the truth upon his reawakening.

John had filled his pipe half an hour ago but had forgotten to light it. The lighter rested in one hand and the pipe in the other. He smiled at the amount of time he could waste daydreaming, and lit the briarwood implement. The heady smoke swirled in a satisfying manner, and John was comforted. Getting the ship back was immensely pleasing to him, and the comfortable hallways provided a great deal of reassurance.

Resting his chin in his hand, John thought about Seth Aldebaran, gazing at the darkness of absolute zero. He thought about his relationship with Seth the computer, from the moment they'd first met him to the last time they'd spoken before Aldebaran and Ari made off with the ship. He was a pure being, without pretext, and his only shortcoming was his fractured memory. His personality was both carefree and deadly serious, depending on the circumstances. The ship felt empty without his omnipresence, but now he was there in the flesh, and it was that man that made John so disconcerted. Seth was his friend, and he couldn't stand the thought of turning him in no matter how much money was for trade. Puffing heartily on his pipe, John decided at that moment not to do so. Fernwyn might be pissed to hear it, but she was still only one vote. Her stake in it couldn't be ignored, however. John wondered if there wasn't another way they could compensate her for the monetary loss.

John stood up and headed for Ray's room. He opened the door. Fernwyn sat on the bed, talking with Ray.

"Hey, look who's up," John said, smiling.

"Hi, John," Ray said weakly.

"How are you?"

"Terrible. Fernwyn tells me she's going to call a police surgeon as soon as we get to Beta."

"That's the plan. We should have you back to health in no time."

"I hope so."

"Have you told him yet?" John asked of Fernwyn.

"No. I figured you'd want to do so."

"Told me what?" asked Ray.

John grabbed the desk chair and sat down next to Ray.

"Ari is dead. The Zendreen destroyed the station and she was on board."

"Oh my God. Are you sure she was there?"

"Yes. She saved our lives, though. She deactivated a device which was preventing the ship from leaving."

"Intentionally?"

"Well, yeah."

"Good for her, then. John, I'm sorry."

"Me, too. Despite everything that happened she was still our friend. And I'd finally decided to ask her for a romantic relationship. She was always a sucker for the bad boy type, though. I should have known I was no match for a pirate captain."

Ray laughed and immediately regretted it. "Ow."

"Take it easy. We'll be on Beta in about a day. Ray, I may be upset about losing Ari, but I was much more worried about losing you. I'm glad you're okay."

"Aw, shucks."

"Fernwyn, were Ari's quarters to your satisfaction?"

"There was a soft bed there," said Fernwyn, smiling. "So yes."

"It seemed like a polite thing to say."

Fernwyn produced some photographs. "I found these pictures in her desk. Earth looks like a nice place. I see the three of you have been friends for a long time."

"Yes, we were," said John, accepting the pictures. "Thanks. Say, I almost forgot to ask you about your job. Have you still been calling in sick?"

"There's no point. My comlink is on the network and they'd be able to locate me if I used it. They'd know I was lying about why I was absent, so I simply haven't called in."

"Aren't you going to get into trouble?"

"Oh, I imagine I've been suspended by now, barring a really amazing and convincing excuse."

"Thank you for sticking with us, Fernwyn."

"I wouldn't miss it for the core."

"I'm going to check in on the bridge. Keep on eye on him, will you?"

"No problem."

John exited into the hallway. He puffed on his pipe to renew the burn, and headed toward the bridge. He felt happy, so much so that he wondered if he wasn't becoming bipolar all of a sudden. He missed Ari, but the sadness had melted into a strange sentimental satisfaction. Perhaps her betrayal had softened his grief, or perhaps the thought of her at last being at peace was it. Most likely it was both. John paused before opening the door to the bridge, overcome by the thought of abandoning everything and heading back to Earth as quickly as possible. He closed his eyes and imagined the day before they'd found Seth, and how simple things seemed then. Such a fantasy was fleeting, but powerful. John took a deep breath.

"I've made my choice," he said.

Entering the bridge, John raised his hand in greeting. Christie sat at the nav station, and Aldebaran stood on the port side, staring out of the window. Tycho sat at Christie's side, and Friday rested on the console.

"Tycho and Friday in the same room?" said John.

"I was surprised myself," said Christie. "I think it's because he's here."

"Too bad we can't ask them anymore. What have you been up to?"

"I've been going over the systems with Aldebaran. He remembers everything about the Umberian end of things, so I've been teaching him how our own computers interact with the ship."

"What about the matter transporter?"

Aldebaran silently held up a piece of paper. John accepted it and looked at it with confusion. Aldebaran had drawn a complicated circuit diagram.

"There it is," he said softly. "I'm sorry but I can't remember how to access it."

"That's no big deal. Thanks, though. Maybe Talvan will be able to shed some light on things."

"You're still considering a rescue?" asked Christie.

"If we can get in undetected, I think it's worth a shot."

"Talvan would be an invaluable addition to the crew," said Aldebaran.

"Do you know anything about this virus he's working on?" asked John.

"No. But if there's anyone who can do it, it would be Talvan."

The console next to Christie began to beep. The three of them looked at it in ignorance until Christie identified it.

"We're being hailed," she said, astonished.

John crossed to her. "Who the hell?"

"It's someone called Leitke. Do we know him?"

"Allow me," said Aldebaran, sitting in the pilot's chair.

Aldebaran pressed a key, his expression hawkish.

"Hello, Reckless Faith, are you reading me?"

"This is Aldebaran. Go ahead, Leitke."

"Finally! Cap, I was hoping you made it out of there. I can't believe the Zendreen destroyed the whole damn station."

"Shit happens."

"So, did it work? The process, I mean."

"Yes. Drop your shield so I can lock on to your location."

"Is Harrish there?"

"He didn't make it."

"You shouldn't believe what he said, sir. I stuck around as long as I could. You wouldn't want your ship to be destroyed for no reason."

"Harrish was dead when I got back to him, so whatever objection he had died with him. Let's rendezvous, Leitke. We should head back to Macer together."

"Okay. I'm lowering my shield now."

"Aldebaran, what are you doing?" whispered John.

"I'm going to get some information out of him. Leitke, you're less than ten million kilometers from me. I'll overtake you in a few seconds. Drop out of superlume."

"Got it."

The Faith quickly arrived, and itself dropped out of superspace. The pirate ship was within view.

"What's the price on your head, Leitke?" asked Aldebaran.

"I don't know. I'll never be worth as much as you. Did you want to dock?"

"No."

"Then why have we stopped? Shouldn't we be on our way to Macer?"

"Do you regret the crimes you've committed?"

Leitke laughed. "About as much as you do, Cap."

"That's no longer true."

"If this life is getting to you, I'll be happy to take over as captain."

"Your wish is granted."

"Seriously?"

"When am I not serious? The ship is yours, my old friend. I'm staying aboard this one."

"It's kind of abrupt, but all right. Are you sure you don't want to collect any of your stuff before we part ways? Not like you have much. You were never one for collecting treasure."

"Keep it. I just want you to remember one of the most important parts of being a successful pirate."

"Uh... don't get caught?"

"Know thy enemy."

Aldebaran flipped the safety switch off of the joystick trigger, and sent a brilliant flash of plasma energy streaking out of the main cannon and into the other ship. There was a brief explosion and it disappeared into dust.

"Son of a bitch!" yelled John, dashing forward and shoving Aldebaran from the chair.

"Looks like the Mark Sevens are working," said Aldebaran, picking himself up from the floor.

"Who the hell gave you permission to fire?"

"Trust me, John, those guys deserved a far worse punishment than disintegration."

"That may be, but nobody fires weapons without my say so!"

"It was the shortest path to justice."

"You're not ready to be a part of this crew. I want you off the bridge until further notice. Seth or not, if you compromise the command structure again I will turn you in for the reward. Clear?"

"I'm sorry."

Visibly disappointed, Aldebaran exited the bridge. Friday leapt from the console and ran after him. John and Christie looked at each other.

"You're both right," she said.

"Maybe, I don't know. Obviously I'm not comfortable flying around destroying other ships willy-nilly. At the very least we could have captured his ship and collected the bounty."

"True."

John leaned against the bulkhead, sighing deeply.

"What a fucking mess, Christie."

"Also true."

## 23.

"You made it!"

Dana leapt from her seat and ran across Fernwyn's living room. She hugged John and Christie simultaneously. Richter entered next, leading Aldebaran. A metal cup clattered to the floor. In the kitchen, Nathalier had just dropped his yutha.

"You captured Aldebaran?" he said, shocked.

"Sort of," said John. "He's on our side now."

"He merged with Seth?" asked Dana.

"Hello, Dana," said Aldebaran. "It's good to see you again."

"Seth's really in there?"

"For good or ill," said Richter, sitting on the couch.

"Where's Ray?"

"He was injured during the fight at the station. Fernwyn and a SPF surgeon by the name of Marek are aboard the Faith taking care of him now. He should be okay."

"What happened to Ari?"

Richter turned away from her. "KIA."

Dana was almost speechless. "I... oh my God."

"We can mourn Ari later. The important thing is that we got our ship back, and she wasn't damaged. We also have Aldebaran, if we decide to cash him in."

"You think you're in good shape?" said Nathalier. "Haven't you heard the news?"

John shrugged. Dana picked up a remote controller and turned on Fernwyn's telescreen.

"It's all over the news channels," she began, "tensions are high between the Zendreen and the Solar United Faction. The Zendreen say the SUF destroyed the way station, and they're threatening a retaliatory strike."

"You've got to be shitting me!" exclaimed John. "The Zendreen destroyed the fucking station. We're all witnesses to that."

"Tell it to the authorities," said Nathalier.

"Sounds like the Gulf of Tonkin incident," Richter said.

"Why would the Zendreen blame the SUF for it?" asked John. "Since when do they need any kind of excuse to pick a fight?"

"The Zendreen are still accountable to the rest of the universe," said Nathalier. "They claimed the Umberians were planning to commit genocide against them so they invaded their planet. That may have been wolshit, but it gave them a handy excuse to forge a treaty with the SUF and avoid the direct ire of anybody else in the cloud."

"It's true," said Aldebaran, "but it was a defensive strategy. We never planned on attacking them first."

"It's dirt under our feet now. The bottom line is that the Zendreen have manufactured a reason to open up hostilities with the SUF, and we're right in the middle of it."

"This figures," said John, throwing up his arms. "Why should things get any easier now?"

Fernwyn entered and nodded a greeting towards Nathalier and Dana.

"I'm glad my spare keycard was where I hid it," she said. "Have you been making yourselves at home?

"Yes, thank you," replied Dana.

"Have you been back to work, Nathalier?"

"Yes," said Nathalier, cleaning up the spilled yutha, "but obviously I haven't mentioned our little problem on Delta to anyone."

"How's Ray doing?" asked John.

"He's okay. Marek repaired the damage, but he'll still be down for a couple of days."

"What's your job situation?"

"I don't know, I haven't checked in yet. Marek doesn't work for the same division so he doesn't know either. Like I said, chances are they won't be very happy with me."

"If you're lucky," began Dana, "they'll be way too distracted by current events."

"Yeah, Marek brought me up to speed."

"How is the SUF going to deal with this?" asked Christie, opening Fernwyn's fridge.

"I don't know. It's not like our testimony would make any difference. We all know the Zendreen are lying. They'll probably make some sort of diplomatic gesture and hope it satisfies them. I doubt the Zendreen are really going to mobilize for war."

"This doesn't change anything on our end," said John. "I'm still going ahead with the rescue mission. In fact, I want to leave as soon as possible."

"I agree," said Richter. "No sense hanging around here waiting for the Black Crest to detect the ship again."

"Where is the ship?" asked Dana.

"It's on one of the roof landing pads, right next to Nathalier's ship," said Fernwyn. "Or at least hovering next to it. It should be safe there for now. I also took the liberty of loading my ship into the cargo bay."

John nodded. "Fine. Everyone who's coming get back up there unless you need something from Fernwyn's place."

"There's something I thought we should do before we depart, John." said Fernwyn. "Follow me."

Fernwyn led John into her bedroom and walked to the far side of her bed.

"Have you got some stress relief in mind?" he said, grinning.

"No, just something reassuring."

Hauling back, Fernwyn kicked the baseboard of her bed. A spring-loaded drawer opened upon receipt of the blow. John came around to look as Fernwyn withdrew something most certainly reassuring to him.

"This is the Res-ZorCon Mark Five 'Phalanx.' It fires the same one centimeter rounds as my pistol, but at a slightly higher velocity. It also has the capability for fully automatic fire and a fifty round magazine capacity. Recoil is absorbed by a hydraulic piston."

"It looks like a typical Earth select-fire rifle. In fact, it looks a lot like a MP-5, except for the horizontal magazine. Walk me through the T&E."

"What?"

"I mean show me how to operate it."

Fernwyn described to John how to charge and clear the weapon, which revealed no surprises to him. It weighed about five pounds and fit him well.

"I have two of them," she said. "I'll take one and the rest of you can fight over the remainder."

"Richter will probably benefit from it the most."

Fernwyn pulled an identical rifle from the drawer and slung it on her shoulder. They moved back into the living room.

"Here you go, Richter," said John, tossing him the rifle, "a little alien persuasion."

Richter caught the unfamiliar weapon, and reversed the condition within seconds.

"Roger that," he said.

Handing Richter four more magazines, Fernwyn then looked around. "Everybody ready to go?"

"What's your decision?" John asked, directing the question to Nathalier and Dana.

"I'm sorry, but you're on your own," said Nathalier. "I'll be glad to take care of Aldebaran for you, of course."

"Nice try, but he stays with us. Dana?"

"I would feel safe enough on the Faith," Dana replied, "even during a fool's crusade like this one. I just not sure if I'm still welcome."

"You know you always have a place aboard, Dana."

"Nobody blames you for sitting out the last mission," said Christie. "But you have intimate knowledge of the ship that is essential. With Seth now a part of Aldebaran, your skills are more important than ever."

"All right. I'm in."

Fernwyn gestured and the group moved into the hallway. Locking the door, Fernwyn led the way to the elevator. They all barely fit inside.

"Your pistol is grinding into my hip, John," said Fernwyn.

John smirked. "That's what you think."

"I'm serious, move."

"Nobody sneeze or we're going to fall down the shaft," said Richter.

"I thought the Zendreen were giving us the shaft," said Christie.

"You're all crazy," said Nathalier.

The door opened, and the group piled out onto the roof. Several ships were parked there, but fortunately they were the only ones around. The noonday sun cast a comfortable glow, and distant ships glittered in the sapphire sky. A dark line appeared next to Nathalier's ship as Marek lowered the Faith's ramp.

"It didn't even occur to me that he'd been left alone on board," said John.

Fernwyn waved a greeting at Marek. "Don't worry, this guy's been my friend for years."

"Everybody take it real easy," said a voice.

The group whirled around. From behind the elevator shed and ships, about a dozen SPF officers stepped out. John, Fernwyn, Christie, and Richter had their weapons up almost instantly. Fernwyn recognized the speaker as Lieutenant Durring. They had their weapons drawn to the low ready position. The group was surrounded save for the ramp to the Faith about fifteen meters distant.

"I'm sorry, Rylie," said Marek.

"I didn't realize failing to report for duty was a crime," said Fernwyn.

"Officer Rylie," began Durring, "you, Seth Aldebaran, Arin Nathalier and the crew of that ship are under arrest."

"What the hell?" growled Nathalier.

"What's the charge?" asked Fernwyn, livid.

"For Aldebaran, it's obvious. The rest of you are wanted for the destruction of the Umberian System Way Station."

"Bullshit!" yelled John. "The Zendreen destroyed the station! We're all witnesses!"

"So you admit to being there?" asked Durring.

"Of course, but that's not how it went down," said Fernwyn.

"You'll be held until we can get the facts sorted out. Drop your weapons, nice and slow."

Nobody moved.

"I thought the Zendreen were blaming the SUF for the incident," said Dana.

"They are," replied Durring, "but the SUF obviously had nothing to do with it. In order to placate the Zendreen and prevent hostilities we have to convince them that it was a group of rogue agents acting independently of the SUF."

"God damn it," said John, "you're trying to make us into scapegoats."

"You have to admit it doesn't look too good when you're tooling around with the most wanted pirate in the cloud."

"I'm not a pirate anymore," said Aldebaran softly.

"Whatever," said Durring. "We'll sort it out back at the station. Drop your weapons. You wouldn't want one misunderstanding to turn into another unfortunate incident."

John, Fernwyn, and Richter shared a glance. John motioned with his eyebrow toward the ship. Richter and

Fernwyn both shook their heads slightly indicating the negative.

"I wasn't even there," said Nathalier. "I'm not culpable. This is wolshit."

There was a maddening silence for several seconds.

"Are you so committed to this setup that you're willing to gun us down where we stand?" asked Fernwyn.

"I'm just following orders," Durring said, shrugging.

The invisibility field on the Faith suddenly dropped, casting an instant shadow over the rooftop. Several officers raised their weapons.

"Hold your fire!" Durring screamed.

A whirring sound familiar to the humans began to fill the air. All eyes were drawn to the ventral fifty caliber cannon that was now spinning and pointing toward them. John grinned. A voice began broadcasting over a unseen speaker.

"You'd better let them go," said Ray.

The group began moving slowly toward the ramp. Nathalier stuck with them, an expression of dismay on his face.

"Think about what you're doing," shouted Durring. "I don't know what really happened out there, but the threat from the Zendreen is real enough! You can help us prevent a war, Rylie!"

"By taking the fall for the SUF?" Rylie yelled back. "I don't think so."

The group made it inside the cargo bay and John hit the button to close the ramp. Richter waved goodbye to Durring as the rooftop disappeared.

"Check on Ray!" said John, sprinting up the stairs.

"I can't fucking believe it," said Nathalier, "my life is over."

"I'll go check on Ray," said Christie.

"Okay."

Christie headed for the ventral gun room as Dana, Fernwyn, Aldebaran, and Richter climbed the stairs.

"Hey, wait for me," said Nathalier.

On the bridge, John was in the pilot's seat, firing up the engines.

"Think we'll encounter any resistance?" he asked.

"I don't know," said Fernwyn, "let's not stick around to find out."

"I wasn't planning on it. They'll have to catch us first anyway."

"I'll take the gunner's station," said Aldebaran.

"I don't think so. Dana, you take it. Everyone else sit down and hold on."

John took off and pushed the ship to its maximum atmospheric speed. Orange flames skirted the edges of the windows as they rapidly exited the sky. Moments later they were in space. John activated the superluminal drive and set a course for Umber. He locked down the controls and sighed in relief.

"Sorry about that," said Fernwyn. "I honestly didn't see that coming."

"It's not your fault," John replied, standing.

"I need a drink," said Nathalier.

"Agreed."

"I'll keep an eye on things up here," said Dana.

John nodded and led the others down to the galley. Upon arrival they found Christie and Ray, the latter of whom was drinking a glass of water.

"Feeling better, Ray?" asked John.

"No worse for wear," he said.

"Thanks for pulling our asses out of that one," said Fernwyn.

"I thought you could use some help."

John found a bottle of Barbancourt and divided the last of it among two glasses.

"Congratulations," said Nathalier, accepting the drink, "you've been here less than two weeks and you've already pissed off every major political power in the nebula."

John sat down at the table. "It's ultimately irrelevant. It doesn't change our mission. If anything, it adds urgency to it. If we can liberate Umber we'll deny the Zendreen an essential staging area for their martial aspirations."

"Do you really think you can rescue Talvan right under their noses?"

"If we remain shielded we should be fine," said Christie.

"Want to come along, Nathalier?" asked John. "We could use all the help we can get."

Nathalier grumbled. "I don't have anywhere else to go, but I don't much feel like dying either."

"The only way you can clear your name is if the Zendreen are defeated," said Ray.

"Maybe."

"Everybody meet in the conference room in an hour," said John. "I want to start planning this rescue."

Five minutes prior to the appointed time, Christie and Ray were in the conference room drinking coffee. Ray stretched his arm and tested the limits of his motion.

"Are you sure you're up for this?" asked Christie.

"Marek did a good job. I'm just glad he worked on me before he called the SPF. They gave up their best bargaining chip by healing me first."

"That's true. John wouldn't have risked your life by leaving before your injuries were taken care of."

"How's he dealing with the loss of Ari?"

"Outwardly he's okay. I don't know how he's doing inside. What about you?"

"Ari was my friend. I didn't want this to happen and I don't hold any ill will towards Aldebaran. Only Ari was responsible for her actions."

"She was ready to make amends for that. Instead she gave her life so that we could escape. I can't make myself feel bad about her death because even after our time together on this ship, I still didn't know her that well. Truthfully, watching you get shot was far worse."

"I agree. Thank you for watching over me while I was hurt, Christie."

"No problem. It was the least I could do."

"No, it wasn't. The least you could do was nothing. Your strength was my strength, and for that I thank you."

Christie blushed. "Come on, I've never been brave like you or John or Richter. I just do what I have to."

"Your pursuit of discovery has always overpowered your fears. Remember when you first saw the orb? I thought you were going to have a heart attack. Then Ari sticks her gun in your face. And yet, you still agreed to join us. You may not think so, but you have just as much courage as any of us, plus the wisdom to mete it out well. Don't sell yourself short."

Christie laughed. "You know what's funny? Back on Earth, John once said you were interested in me. He was joking then, but if you keep up the compliments you're going to make me wonder."

"The only thing that's funny is how long it took me to see it."

"Yeah, right... what?"

Christie looked at Ray. She could see that behind the exhaustion in his eyes and the remnants of pain in his expression, he was quite serious. He smiled and raised an eyebrow.

"It would be a shame to die with regrets, wouldn't it?"

"Don't tell me you've gone all Florence Nightingale on me..."

The door to the bridge opened and John entered. Christie and Ray leaned back in their chairs as if a tug-of-war game had just been decided.

"Feeling any better, Ray?" John asked, pulling up a chair.

"He's fine," said Christie.

John looked at his old friend, who grinned.

"Good. We'll only have a day and a half to rest before we kick this thing off again. I'd love nothing more than a week on some beach on Residere Beta but the SPF kinda blew that idea."

"Did you ever imagine that the mission would be this difficult?" asked Christie.

"I have to admit I used to fantasize that we'd be welcomed as heroes on Umber simply for showing up, but that didn't flush with Seth's naked cry for help. The only thing that really surprised me was Ari joining Aldebaran. I guess I thought our affection for each other would assure a greater bond."

"He did have the benefit of his Jedi mind trick," said Ray.

"Even Ari wouldn't use that as an excuse. I wonder if I'll ever figure out what inner darkness could have driven her to let Aldebaran draw her in."

Christie looked down. "Perhaps she was just looking for the same thing we all are. Unconditional acceptance."

Richter entered from the lounge area, followed by the rest of the crew. Nathalier came in last and leaned against the wall. Dana crossed to the wall-mounted monitor.

"Ready to get this briefing started?" asked John.

"I'm as ready as I can be," said Aldebaran. "I'm still a little uncertain how to act around you folks."

"Why worry about it?" asked Dana. "If you truly are Seth, we'll trust you."

"Some of us still see you as someone to be feared," said Fernwyn.

"Did I say I was sorry about trying to kill you, Rylie?" asked Aldebaran.

"Are you?"

Aldebaran was shocked. "Of course I am!"

"Then I'm not going to hold a grudge. Do I look like a Rakhar to you?"

"Hey," said Nathalier.

"Not everything about Aldebaran the pirate was bad," said John.

"You don't share my memories," Aldebaran replied.

"I mean that you had confidence, drive, and determination. I need you to be a functional member of this crew, Seth. It might be helpful if you could remember how to use some of those qualities again."

"You're still too forgiving."

"Just give it a try, all right? That's an order. Now, tell us what you know about the coordinates."

Aldebaran motioned to Dana, who activated the monitor. A map of Umber's surface appeared, with crosshairs covering a point.

"Dana helped me prepare these graphics," Aldebaran began. "This is the position we triangulated from the transmission data we received during our contact with Talvan. It's in the northern hemisphere in a hilly temperate region."

The image zoomed in considerably, revealing elevation contour lines and several structures.

"This is the data that was preserved by your computers before I was removed from the system network. It's ten years old, unfortunately, but it's safe to assume that things haven't changed much. The Zendreen are much more likely to use industry to supplement their space fleet than to build new structures on the surface, especially considering that there are plenty of existing ones. This region of Umber is famous for it's wine, so it's possible that one or all of these buildings are part of a commercial vineyard, or at least they used to be. To the west is a substantial forest, which should provide us a good place to land and dismount undetected. There's a good clearing about seventeen hundred meters from the building where the transmission originated. The good news is that Talvan wouldn't be transmitting if the Zendreen knew about the transmitter, so resistance is likely to be light."

"Knowing our luck, I wouldn't bet on it," said John.

"Our weapons will be highly effective against your typical Zendra, but if we have to engage them we'd better be fast on our heels. Help won't be far, and it will doubtlessly be more than we can handle."

"Richter?" said John.

Richter nodded. "One thing that we're not considering is that Talvan may have been moved. If he's not there and we go in hot we'll lose our only chance. I suggest we try an undercover mission and recon the area. If he's not there we can either wait for him to come back or find out where he's gone to."

"Is going undercover feasible?"

"Put on a hat and you'd all pass for Umberian," said Aldebaran, "those non-human present excepted."

"You'd have to get awfully close to me to tell," said Fernwyn.

"Wild wolrasi couldn't drag me off this ship anyway," said Nathalier.

"We have plenty of people to fill out an undercover squad," said John. "If the shit hits the fan you two can back our retreat."

"Are you including me in your estimate?" asked Dana.

"Of course. If we get attacked you can use the Faith to blow the ever-living fuck out of our pursuers."

"Sounds good to me."

"What time of day will it be at this location when we arrive?"

"I honestly don't know," replied Aldebaran. "I can't do that kind of math in my head anymore, John."

"That's fine. We can wait until dark, it won't make any difference. Is there anything else?"

The group was silent. John nodded, looking around the room in satisfaction.

"Quite an unusual compliment we've managed to assemble, eh?" said Ray.

John smiled. "I wouldn't have it any other way."

## 24.

It was twelve hours until the Faith's return to Umber, and the mood aboard was good. The crew had just spent some time socializing in the lounge area, nursing the last of the alcohol and getting to know each other better. Despite their different backgrounds it was obvious that their civilizations were basically the same, as were their psychological constitutions. One thing they all agreed on, even Nathalier, was that the Zendreen needed to be dealt with sooner than later.

Aldebaran had refused to drink, and spent the time leaning against the bulkhead and staring out of the window. John wished that he could act more like Seth the AI, but he knew that the man needed time to sort things out. His demeanor was unsettling, even if John wasn't actually afraid of him. Visually there was nothing to rectify Seth with the former pirate captain that stood before him.

Nathalier lightened up considerably when Friday came around, the cat at first bolting away when she saw him. Nathalier persisted after her, and before too long she'd accepted him and even seemed to favor him over John. He said she was like a "terminally skinny baby Rakhar" and John had to assure him that was normal for Earth cats.

Fernwyn and Dana were getting along well. Dana had a lot of questions about the bounty hunting business, and although she expressed reservations about the face-to-face aspect of a corral, she still persisted in her interest. Fernwyn was glad to chat, and was only slightly distracted by the fact that John was obviously checking her out every once and a while. What was less distracting was that Christie and Ray were checking each other out too, but Fernwyn seemed to be the only one who thought it odd that they excused themselves for the evening simultaneously.

Richter had been drinking in earnest and now lay passed out in an armchair. It was out of character for him, but the others figured that he'd been "switched on" for too long and deserved a break. When Aldebaran decided to rack out, he volunteered to drag Richter back to his quarters, which they'd agreed to share for the time being.

Nathalier eventually expressed his desire to sleep. John apologetically offered him the spare mattress in the cargo hold, which was barely large enough for him and certainly not particularly cozy. Nathalier shrugged and Dana offered to show him where to go, so before he realized it John was alone with Fernwyn.

"What did you call this stuff again?" she asked, holding up her glass.

"Bourbon," replied John. "This bottle is the last of it for a hundred and sixty thousand light years."

"I think I'd like to visit Earth someday. Things sound simpler there."

"We've obviously misrepresented it, then. Our country is at peace within our borders, at least it was when we left, but that was hardly the norm. The majority of the population of our planet was still without modern plumbing or under a repressive government or both."

"Such is the way of things on emerging worlds."

"I think they could use a few more decades of interstellar isolation."

"That's up to you, isn't it? I doubt anybody will go by that way. When you return, will you keep the ship a secret?"

"Well, our plan B is to return and build enough ships to oppose the Zendreen fleet, so that kinda requires help from the government. If we can defeat the Zendreen on our own, I guess I would keep it a secret whenever it is that we decide to return."

There was a pause in the conversation. John sipped at his bourbon.

"I'm sorry about your friend Ari," Fernwyn said. "I gather you two were pretty close."

"What's done is done."

"It's not easy to find someone you can be close to. I've spend my entire adult life wondering if I'll ever find somewhere I can really fit in."

"No wonder you're so eager to help."

"I don't socialize nearly enough. I certainly don't drink alcohol very often. I've never even been on a date. The only species I find attractive are Umberians, and they're hard to come by these days."

"You could always come on to Aldebaran. I'm sure all he needs to get his confidence back is a little physical attention."

Fernwyn looked amused. "You're kidding, right?"

"Of course."

Fernwyn got up and sat down next to John on the couch. "I've never been one to hide my intentions, John. I've always been the first one to go after what I want. I've never spent any time around anyone I found physically attractive, not once in my whole life before I met you."

John grinned. "I think you've had too much bourbon."

"I don't think I've had nearly enough. And I would never hide behind the excuse."

"Put your drink down."

Fernwyn did so. John leaned in and kissed her. She took a deep breath as John drew back.

"You're not supposed to just sit there, you know," he said.

"You surprised me."

Wheeling around, Fernwyn grabbed John by the shoulders and pushed him roughly onto the couch.

"OW!" cried John. "For God's sake, take it easy!"

"Oh, sorry. I often forget how strong I am."

John sat back up and rubbed his arms. "That really hurt. Maybe we should call it a night. We've got a tough mission ahead."

"You're probably right."

John got up and walked to the mouth of the hallway. "There's just one thing I still want to know. Are humans and Residerians even compatible?"

"Apparently, at least as far as I could feel. It would be interesting to find out for sure, wouldn't it?"

"Ask me again when I'm sober."

Twelve hours later, the ground team had assembled in the cargo bay. The Faith's invisibility shield had granted them easy access to the atmosphere of Umber, and they were preparing to land near the cluster of buildings identified by Aldebaran. John and Ray were performing final equipment checks, Christie and Fernwyn were filling canteens from one of the tank siphons, and Richter was practicing movements with his new rifle. Aldebaran sat in the corner, preoccupied. Christie looked over at John and noticed he'd added Ari's Glock to his belt.

"Sixty seconds to landfall," said Dana over the intercom.

"You sure you're up for this, Ray?" asked John, holstering his Beretta.

Ray nodded. "That Betan doctor did a good job. I'm just a little sore."

"Okay, then. You can carry the first aid kit from now on. Richter, any comments on the sneak?"

"Sure," said Richter, stepping forward. "Aldebaran, you're the only one who hasn't gone on a combat mission with us. I heard you were once a military man?"

"That's right," replied Aldebaran, checking his pistol.

"Do you have any infantry training?"

Aldebaran stood up and walked over to the group. "I do. I also remember every moment of every sim you guys did like it happened an hour ago. Just tell me where you want me in file."

"Excellent. Fantastic, actually. That's great. Hell, that means you remember everything I taught us."

"I just said that, didn't I?"

"Good. You can take point, then."

John held up his hand. "Whoa, wait a minute. No offense, Aldebaran, but I'm not sure you're ready to take point."

"You're the one who told me to stop feeling sorry for myself, John," said Aldebaran flatly.

"He's also the only real Umberian of us," said Richter. "He needs to be able to communicate with anyone we run into. We won't be able to converse unless the other party is wearing one of these nifty earpieces."

"You have Ari's leftover unit, right?" asked John.

"Yes, but that only does us good if the person is wearing it. Until we find Talvan, Aldebaran is going to have to do all the talking."

"Richter is right," said Ray.

John shrugged. "As long as you're sure."

"Then it will be Aldebaran first," began Richter, "followed by John, Fernwyn, Christie, and Ray. I'll take rear security as usual. We'll make a bee-line for the structures in Ranger file, and avoid contact with both Zendreen and Umberians if possible. If we do get attacked, we'll have to decide whether we're close enough to make a search while under fire or retreat back here. The first option doesn't sound like much fun so let's try and keep quiet out there."

"I'm ready to deploy the ramp," said Dana. "Scans show nothing but small animals out there as far as the structures. No sign of Zendreen."

"Good," said John. "Let's go."

The sun had just set behind Tarsus Mountain, the clouds casting a pinkish peach glow onto the bakery. Talvan and Stackpole stood outside of the main entrance to the building, along with several workers. The evening air was clear and cool, but the pleasant weather couldn't help them forget their situation.

The road to the bakery, dormitory, and storehouse wound up the hill with two switchbacks, giving the residents plenty of warning should visitors arrive by land. It was a ground-based form of transportation that the Zendreen used for their nightly inspections, so surprise was never an issue. Stackpole finished rolling a cigarette and lit it.

"They're late," he said.

"It's happened before," Talvan replied.

"Not since the incident. This may be a good sign. I hope they're letting their guard down again."

"I wouldn't bet on it. Everyone, wait inside until they show up."

The others grumbled and filed back inside.

"Have you heard anything from the underground?" asked Stackpole.

"Not a peep, my friend, not a..."

Talvan let himself trail off. In the waning light, he could see a small group of people emerge from the woods to the east. They appeared to be wearing cloaks, and as they approached he could count six of them. Stackpole raised his eyebrows.

"Strangers?" he said. "There isn't enough cloud cover. They're taking quite a risk travelling on a night like this."

"If they're low on food they may have no choice. I hope they have something useful to trade. I don't want word to get out that we're in the charity business here."

"True, but... it looks like a thunderstorm is on the way. Maybe they're counting on it to shield them from view."

Stackpole pointed at dark clouds gathering in the eastern sky. Distant thunder soon confirmed his suspicions. After a couple of minutes the leader of the group drew close to Talvan. He waved in greeting.

"Good evening," said Talvan.

"Hello, professor," said the man.

"Professor? Have we met?"

"I should say so."

The man removed the wool blanket he was using as a cloak. The wind picked it up and it danced from his shoulders onto the ground. Talvan took a step back and hit the wall of the bakery hard.

"Aldebaran?" he breathed. "It can't be."

"It's good to see you again."

"Aldebaran?" asked Stackpole. "The Aldebaran?"

"In the flesh," replied Talvan. "What the hell are you doing here?"

Aldebaran smiled. "It's okay, professor. I'm Seth Aldebaran. I restored myself back at the lab. I'm whole again."

"I can't believe it. That means that these people must be..."

"The crew of the Reckless Faith, the ship that we created together. This is Commander John Scherer."

John stepped forward and waved. "It's good to speak to you again, Talvan."

"What did he say?" asked Talvan, confused.

"Oh, you'll need a translation unit, professor."

Aldebaran handed Talvan an earpiece, which he donned.

"I said it's good to speak to you again," said John.

"I'm glad to see you too," began Talvan, "except what the hell are you all doing here? You couldn't have built a liberation army already... or have you?"

"No. We've come only for you."

"Heads up," said Stackpole urgently, tossing his cigarette aside. "The inspection team is coming."

Stackpole pointed down the road. A six-wheeled armored personnel carrier had just come into view.

"Looks like it's time for us to go," said John.

"I can't go anywhere!" said Talvan. "If I'm not around they'll know something's up. The workers here at the bakery will be punished severely."

"We don't have time to discuss it. We need you to come with us."

"It's more complicated than that. Get inside, all of you. We can talk after the inspection. Go up the stairs to the top floor and close the door, you'll be safe there. The inspection should only last a few minutes, and then we can discuss the situation."

"Good enough," said Aldebaran.

Stackpole opened the door and gestured inside. The crew ran in, located the stairs, and filed past the stunned employees as they headed for the top floor.

"It never occurred to me that Talvan might not want to leave," said Aldebaran.

"We've got to convince him that it's for the greater good," replied John.

The group reached the top of the stairs and found a room with no windows, empty save for several bags of what looked like flour. They piled inside and Richter closed the door, cloaking the room with darkness.

"I hope we didn't just throw ourselves into a dead-end," he whispered.

"What are we going to do if Talvan refuses?" asked Christie.

"Throw his ass aboard anyway," whispered John.

"Great way to get him to help us."

"Shh," hissed Richter.

The crew tried to relax as time began to pass. They could hear barely anything from below, at least anything they could distinguish from the approaching storm. After a few minutes, there were several muffled thumps and some shouting. Several seconds later they could hear one set of footsteps running up the stairs. Stackpole threw open the door, greeting the crew with an expression of panic.

"They've taken Talvan!" he said, jamming a translator into his ear. "They found out about our transmitter in the basement!"

"Shit," said John, deactivating the safety on his rifle. "How many of them are down there?"

"They've all left. They're said they're going to send a platoon to look after us."

"Where are they taking him?"

"I don't know, but the closest Zendreen garrison is in Tarsus City."

"A thirty minute ride by ground vehicle," said Aldebaran.

"Everybody outside, now," said John.

The team ran down the stairs, unlimbering weapons and further startling the bakery workers. Stackpole followed them outside. The Zendreen APC was still visible heading down the road. Richter, Ray, and Fernwyn threw aside their blankets and took up defensive positions. John grabbed his radio.

"Dana, this is John, over."

"How's it going?" said Dana's voice.

"Fire up the Faith and get over here, double time. Talvan's been taken and we need to intercept the vehicle, over."

"Roger that. I'll be there in three minutes. Out."

"What about the platoon?" asked Ray.

"Unless there was already one in the air, it shouldn't take them more than five minutes," Stackpole replied.

Raindrops began hitting the ground.

"What's going to happen to you and your people?" asked Christie.

"I don't know. They'll probably torture each of us for information. I'm the only one who knows anything but they'll be no convincing the Zendreen of that."

"How many are you?"

"Seventeen, myself included."

"John, we should take these people with us."

"It's out of the question," said John. "We don't have the resources to care for seventeen people aboard."

"But they'll be tortured."

"John is right," began Aldebaran. "It's impractical to take on so many people. We have our own mission to fulfill and we don't have time to evacuate them. I hate to see my own people suffer even more, but rescuing Talvan must come first. The faster Talvan and I can come up with a virus the sooner the entire planet will be freed."

"So that's your plan," said Stackpole.

"Yes. I need you and the people here to be strong, my friend. Whatever happens know that you can keep hope alive. Your sacrifice won't be soon forgotten."

"You have plenty of time to get us aboard. Then you can just drop us all off on Residere Delta and get on with your research."

Aldebaran shrugged. "There's a fat price on the head of all Umberians, you know that. Seventeen refugees can hardly just disappear. You'll be rounded up and end up back in Zendreen hands anyway. If you think your fate is bad now, imagine if you were recaptured later."

Stackpole spat on the ground. "This is a raw deal."

"Yeah? Nobody forced you to be part of the underground movement. The bakery workers could have kicked you and Talvan out any time they wanted. This is war, and shit happens in war. Do the best you can here and we'll be back to help as soon as we possibly can."

John nodded. "I'm sorry, but there's no other choice. We're being hunted by everyone out there. We can't risk going back to Residere again and the ship can't sustain so many people."

"Where the hell are you planning on working on the virus, then?" yelled Stackpole, throwing up his arms.

"There's a pirate enclave on Macer Alpha with excellent lab equipment," said Aldebaran. "And it's the last place you'd want to bring Umberian refugees."

The rain increased to a downpour. There was a rush of wind, and the Faith's invisible form displaced the air nearby. Water streamed off of the hull and outlined the shape of the craft. Stackpole looked on in awe as the ramp opened and revealed the cargo bay. Nathalier was standing at the top, next to Fernwyn's craft.

"Fine, we'll discuss it later!" said John. "Let's get moving!"

"You can go to hell!" yelled Stackpole. "Umber deserves better than you amateurs!"

"Yeah, probably," replied Aldebaran.

The crew ran into the cargo bay and John hit the button to close the ramp.

"Dana, this is John, did you see that vehicle descending on the roadway?"

"Yeah," replied Dana over the radio.

"Get after it and wait for further instructions."

"Roger."

"I feel awful about leaving those people," said Christie, wiping the rain from her face.

"Do you really want another seventeen people crammed onto this ship?" said John. "Listen up everybody. I want Christie on the dorsal fifty and Ray on the ventral. Work with Dana to get that APC to stop. Richter, Fernwyn, Aldebaran and I will dismount and rush it. Hopefully we can grab Talvan without killing him or ourselves."

"They'll call for help as soon as we engage them," said Fernwyn. "I should fly as a distraction in case their backup arrives before we're through. That way the Faith won't be busy when you guys need extraction."

"Good idea, but can you launch your ship right out of the cargo bay?"

"If we roll it out above two thousand feet I should have enough time."

"Okay. Nathalier, do you want to help us assault the APC?"

"Hell no," replied Nathalier.

"Then go to the bridge and help Dana man the energy weapons. Everybody clear?"

There were no further comments, and Christie, Ray and Nathalier exited. Fernwyn began to check her craft. John looked at Aldebaran.

"I appreciate what you said to that guy down there, Aldebaran," he said.

Aldebaran frowned. "I've screwed over hundreds of my own people. What do seventeen more matter?"

"Don't feel bad about them," said Richter. "Like you said, we're trying to save the planet here. Give them all medals after the victory if that will make you feel better."

"I only hope they're not posthumous awards."

John walked over to the console and tapped into the flight control systems. He divided the screen between a real-time image from the bow of the ship and an overhead geographical display. Richter and Aldebaran looked over his shoulder.

"Dana, this is John. Increase altitude to three thousand feet. We're going to launch Fernwyn's ship before we engage the APC."

"Understood."

"She's good to go," said Fernwyn. "There's only one problem. I may damage your ship if I fire up the engines in here."

"Can we push it out manually?" asked Richter.

"No need," said John. "We just tip the nose of the ship forward and disengage the artificial gravity."

"Oh, duh."

"Get aboard then, Fernwyn."

Fernwyn nodded and climbed into the cockpit. John gestured to the others.

"Get into the armory unless you can sprout wings," he said.

"What about you?" asked Richter.

"I'm going to watch."

Richter and Aldebaran walked up the stairs to the armory door. John followed them as far as the railing, then stopped. He repositioned a carabiner from the front of his belt to the side and clipped himself onto the railing.

"Uh, what's the point of this?" asked Richter.

"I'm not allowed to have fun anymore?"

Richter grinned and led Aldebaran into the armory. John braced himself.

"Ready in the cargo bay, Dana!"

"Okay," Dana replied. "Pitching forward now. Opening cargo ramp."

Wind began to howl through the cargo bay as the ramp slid open. John was overcome with vertigo as he found himself staring down at the surface of the planet.

"Disengaging cargo bay gravity field," said Dana.

Fernwyn turned around and waved goodbye to John. John waved back as the gravity of Umber took over. He lurched forward and gasped as his weight was suddenly shifted ninety degrees. Fernwyn's ship dropped out of the bay and immediately disappeared, followed by a 55-gallon drum of gasoline and a crate of spare bed sheets.

"Oops," said John. "Craft away, Dana!"

"Roger!"

Dana corrected the ship's pitch and closed the ramp. John's stomach turned as the gravity again shifted. Richter and Aldebaran came down from the armory just in time to watch John vomit on the deck.

"You've got a curious idea of fun," said Aldebaran.

"That was still cool," said John, coughing.

Richter shrugged and crossed to the monitor. Aldebaran and John followed him.

"We've got visual contact with the APC," said Dana.

"Roger that, we can see it here," replied John. "Move in as close as you can. Ray, think you can let our presence be known?"

"My pleasure," said Ray's voice.

The three men watched as the ship swooped down over the Zendreen APC. It was moving at a slower speed down a darkened paved road, which was more or less straight for the next few hundred meters. There was a dull thudding sound from midships, and a combination of tracer and armor piercing rounds cascaded down. The fire cut a swath directly in front of the APC. The vehicle swerved but did not stop.

"They're speeding up," said Dana.

"Get us closer," said John. "Ray, see if you can target one of the rear wheels."

"That's a tall order," Ray replied. "This isn't a Barrett, you know."

"Scherer, remember that trick you pulled on Route 93?" asked Richter.

John nodded. "Of course, but that APC is too large to fit in here."

"Yeah, but they don't know that."

"I like it. Dana, get us in front of them and do an about-face. When we've matched speed, drop the invisibility shield."

"That'll be kind of tricky," said Dana. "The trees come pretty close to the roadway."

"I don't think we need to worry about trees. Get as close as you can."

361

John, Aldebaran, and Richter watched as Dana maneuvered the Faith. Fernwyn's voice came in over the com.

"John, this is Fernwyn. I'm tracking three aircraft heading our way. They're hauling ass."

"Keep them busy," John replied. "We're beginning our assault."

The Faith began clipping a few treetops, sending a shower of leaves and branches onto the roadway. The APC did not waver.

"That's as close as I can get," said Dana.

"Drop the shield," began John, readying his M1 Garand, "Richter, open the ramp."

Richter did so. The ramp opened, washing rain and wind through the cargo bay. The ship was flying about fifty yards above the ground and maintaining some forty yards from the APC. The driver, unseen to the crew, hit the brakes at the sight of the ship just as John fired a round at the front right tire. The tire exploded and the APC skidded to one side. It spun around 180 degrees before coming to a rest in a cloud of smoke. Dana brought the ship to a stop and lowered it to the ground, destroying more trees in the process. The ship ended up a hundred yards from the APC. John put his Garand down and picked up Fernwyn's Phalanx. Richter readied his own while Aldebaran drew his Liberator pistol.

"Move fast and hit hard," said Richter.

John and Aldebaran nodded, and Richter burst out of the ship. The others followed him into the driving rain. Weapons fire echoed into their ears, accompanied by flashes of light from above. The whine of aircraft engines could be heard as well.

"I guess Fernwyn's found something to do," shouted John.

"Dana, this is Richter! Reposition the ship closer to the APC. Ray, cover us the best you can. Christie, see if you can help Fernwyn."

"Roger that," said Dana.

The three men ran as fast as they could toward the APC. Richter motioned for John to cover left and Aldebaran to cover right. Simultaneously, hatches opened on the side and top of the APC. A Zendra appeared from each opening. John recognized them as warriors from Seth's description, but in the flesh they were terrifying. The one that exited from the side hatch hissed at them and lunged forward. John and Richter opened fire together, felling it with an apt demonstration of overkill. Aldebaran exercised more restraint, firing twice and dropping the Zendra on the roof. The men moved up to the side hatch. Smoke poured out from within but appeared to be thinning. Richter moved inside smoothly and turned to the right. John followed him in, immediately clearing the left.

The interior of the APC was a clutter of unfamiliar gear and electronics. Another side hatch across from them was also open. John and Richter stayed low to avoid the haze. Toward the rear of the compartment, a Zendra was attempting to stand up. Richter fired a short burst, splattering the walls with viscera and deadening his unprotected right ear. John moved toward the driver's compartment, killing the remaining operator with a single shot to the head. From outside, they could hear Aldebaran firing his weapon. A moment later it was drowned out by Christie's fifty-cal.

"Talvan must be in the rear compartment!" shouted Richter.

John joined Richter at the door. Richter found the controls and opened it.

"Stay back or I'll touch him!"

A Zendra with a green carapace and a disturbingly humanoid mouth had just spoken. It was wearing a long brown gauntlet on one lithe, spindly hand, in which it clutched Talvan's arm. The other hand was bare and the Zendra had it inches away from Talvan's throat. Richter's finger tensed on his rifle's trigger, but John put up his hand in warning.

"Don't move!" said John. "If he touches Talvan it may be fatal."

"Lower your weapons!" chirped the Zendra in broken Umberian.

"All right, take it easy."

John and Richter complied carefully. John took a step back.

"Drop the Phalanx," said the Zendra.

"Don't do anything brash," said Richter, putting his weapon down. "We can still negotiate here."

"Get out, both of you."

Richter's arm moved in a blur, and he snatched the Zendra's exposed hand away from Talvan's neck. Talvan stumbled back as Richter grappled with the insectoid. John drew his pistol and hesitated. The Zendra hissed hideously and pushed Richter against the bulkhead, drawing its needle-like black teeth closer to Richter's neck. Richter braced himself against the Zendra's body with his boot.

"Anytime, Scherer!" grunted Richter.

"Its blood isn't harmful, just the skin!" said Talvan, clearing the door and backing into the passenger compartment.

"Oh, great."

Richter freed his right arm long enough to draw Ari's Rakhar battle blade from his belt and jam it into the Zendra's mouth. The insectoid jumped away, removing the weapon from it's maw as if it were a toothpick. John fired his pistol five times, with four shots bisecting the Zendra's head and the fifth missing only because the creature had fallen away. The errant shot ricocheted around the compartment but hit no one.

"Are you all right?" John asked of Richter.

"I think so. My left arm feels kind of funny."

"It's the Zendreen poison," said Talvan. "He needs medical attention immediately."

"You didn't have to do that," said John.

Richter picked up his blade. "We'll worry about that later."

John heard a voice that sounded like it was on the other end of the Holland Tunnel.

"John, this is Dana. We've got four more aircraft and two ground vehicles converging on this point. How's it going?"

"We're exfilling now," replied John into his radio.

Aldebaran stuck his head into the passenger compartment.

"I tagged three more out here," he said. "I think that's all of 'em."

"Let's go!"

John and Richter retrieved their rifles and helped Talvan to the exterior. They joined Aldebaran and ran for the Faith. In the sky above, Fernwyn continued to tangle with Zendreen aircraft. When they were ten meters from the ramp, Ray's fifty-cal suddenly rotated away from them and fired down the road. The noise was unbearable and both human and Umberian epithets were lost to the cacophony. John glimpsed some sort of armored vehicle at the end of the road before he sprinted up the ramp and into the cargo bay.

"We're aboard, get the hell out of here!" yelled Richter.

Aldebaran hit the button to close the ramp. The ground began to draw away, and the last of the APC they saw was Nathalier perforating it with the port laser bank. The embattled vehicle exploded with a satisfying report.

"I could use a little help up here," said Fernwyn over the com.

"Talvan has been retrieved," answered John. "Disengage and break atmosphere."

"Fine by me."

John put his Phalanx on the deck and ran over to Richter. He'd slumped against the stair rail and looked exhausted.

"Are you okay?" said John.

"The Zendra's skin is covered with a nerve agent," began Talvan, rushing over, "if your species is the same as us, it's going to prevent his muscles from switching off their nerve receptors. You need an anti-convulsion agent."

"Get the military kit," said Richter.

"Right," said John, and exited aft.

"You didn't drop dead immediately," said Talvan. "That's a good sign."

"I'm like a bad cold," mumbled Richter, slumping onto the stairs. "I like to linger."

The ship continued to vibrate as all of its weapon systems were engaged. The main plasma cannon sounded like the engine braking of an eighteen-wheeler, only several decibels louder. Over the com, Dana, Christie, and Ray were celebrating each time they scored another kill. Aldebaran looked on via the cargo bay monitor with detached professionalism.

A moment later, John returned with a small olive drab pouch. He knelt by Richter and withdrew two auto-injectors. Richter took the first one. His nose was running and he was drooling despite his efforts to conceal that fact.

"You sure?" asked John.

Richter spoke as if he was quoting a military manual verbatim. "Atropine. Place the needle end of the ejector against your outer thigh muscle..."

Richter injected himself with the first syringe. There was a snap and a hissing sound. He held it in place for ten seconds and then discarded it. He accepted the second injector from John but dropped it on the deck.

"Allow me," said John.

"Diazepam chloride," mumbled Richter. "Use the other... use the other leg."

John did so. Richter seemed to relax. John scanned his face furtively.

"What now?" he asked.

"If I start doing the funky chicken," replied Richter, "adminis... admin... give me another kit."

"Are you sure?"

Richter nodded and swooned.

"Don't let him pass out!" said Aldebaran.

John slapped Richter in the face. "Hey, Chance, stay with me, buddy."

"Just talk to me," said Richter, making eye contact. "Anything."

"Okay. Remember the time we first met? We'd just rescued Ari from you and Devonai. We asked Dana to guard you, with your weapon."

"I heard about it later. Dana had her finger on the trigger, safety off. Four pounds of pressure and bye-bye Chance Richter, CIA."

"We hadn't taught her proper weapon handling skills yet."

The cargo bay shook with the resounding report of the plasma cannon.

"I think she got the hang of it."

## 25.

"How's Richter doing?"

John stepped aside from the doorway to his quarters and allowed Dana to enter. She tip-toed around the gear and weapons that John had spread out across the floor to dry, and sat down at his desk. John resumed donning the dry shirt he had over his arms.

"It looks like he's going to be okay," replied Dana. "He's resting in his quarters."

"That's good," said John, and snapped his fingers next to his head.

"Something wrong?"

"I'm still deaf in my right ear."

"What about the left?"

"I was wearing the translation unit in my left ear. It protected me from the gunfire."

"Handy."

John sat down on his bed. "You did an amazing job down there, Dana."

"Thanks. It would have been a lot more fun if I didn't have team members running around on the surface. The Zendreen aircraft weren't much of a match for Fernwyn and I."

"Don't get overconfident. The satellites were something to be reckoned with, if you recall."

"Good thing we were able to zip right by them this time."

"Did they spot Fernwyn on our way out?"

Dana smiled. "They sure did, but we exited their range too quickly for them to pose a risk to her."

John put on a pair of slippers and stood up. "Good. Let's call a meeting. I want to... hey, who's flying the ship?"

"Aldebaran."

"Dana, I told you I don't trust him with the controls right now!"

"John, he's not going to turn the ship around or anything. We're just flying in a straight line until Fernwyn can dock. Besides, we don't have an autopilot anymore and my arms are killing me."

"Come on."

John entered the hallway, let Dana pass him, and closed the door. Christie and Nathalier were seated in the lounge area, and stood up upon seeing John.

"Good job, you two," said John. "Where are Talvan and Ray?"

"After they got some dry clothes they went down to the galley," said Christie.

John crossed to a computer console and activated the intercom. "This is Scherer. All crew to the bridge."

John led the group through the conference room and onto the bridge. Aldebaran was seated in the pilot's chair with his feet propped up on the console. His jacket was draped over a nearby chair and he hadn't changed out of his wet clothing. Through the window to the right, Fernwyn's ship could be seen pacing the Faith.

"How's it going, Aldebaran?" queried John.

"All quiet. Still no sign of pursuit."

"Aren't you going to get into some dry clothes?"

"Hadn't thought about it."

"You're about my size. Go to my quarters and help yourself, then get back here."

"I'll do so after the meeting."

"Fine."

Sitting at the next station, John opened a frequency to Fernwyn. "Rylie, this is Scherer. What's your status?"

Fernwyn's image appeared on the monitor. "Not bad. This thing is going to need a new paint job, though."

Ray and Talvan entered the bridge. Talvan was wearing a fluffy green bathrobe.

"Christie," said John, "take your station and coordinate Fernwyn's docking. Rylie, prepare to come aboard."

"Understood."

Christie nodded and sat down. John offered a seat to Talvan. The older Umberian's expression was grave, and he stared at the deck. John furrowed his brow at Talvan's bearing.

"Is Richter going to be all right?" asked Aldebaran.

"Seems that way," replied John. "He's resting now. Okay, anybody else have any concerns or comments? No? Then let's get down to business. Professor Talvan, welcome to the Reckless Faith. I believe you've met everyone except Nathalier."

"Hi," said Nathalier.

"I hope Stackpole will fare well," said Talvan.

"This is the best way for you to help him," said John. "Tell us about the virus you've been working on."

"It attacks the carapace of the Zendreen. Ideally it will reduce the shell's strength so much that any attempt at physical activity will cause them to rip themselves apart. I've been working with a virus that causes a similar condition in certain Umberian beetles, but the problem is that it relies on oxygen to survive. It circulates so quickly in the beetles that this isn't a problem, but in the much larger Zendreen it will spend too much time in the bloodstream. The virus won't survive without oxygen for that length of time. I've been attempting to genetically modify the virus to attach to oxygen-bearing blood cells in Zendreen, but I need better lab equipment to do so."

"Wait a minute," said Dana, "where are we going to get samples of the base virus?"

"I injected myself with it. It's the best hiding place. It's harmless to Umberians, but like I said it can't survive in the bloodstream anyway. However, the virus can be recultured after it's taken out of a blood sample. Now are you sure we can't go to Residere Beta? The best equipment is there."

"Fernwyn's aboard," said Christie. "I'm just repressurizing the cargo bay."

"Good, thanks," said John. "There's no way, Talvan. I'll fill you in on our adventure up until now after this meeting, but suffice it to say that going back to Beta is out of the question right now. The Solar United Faction is trying to blame us for destroying the Umberian System Way Station in order to avoid war with the Zendreen, even though the Zendreen are the ones who destroyed it. It's a brilliant ploy on the part of the Zendreen to gain the SUF's cooperation in hunting us down."

"We can't prove that the Zendreen suggested our culpability to the SUF," said Christie.

"They wouldn't have had to suggest anything to them. We're the most obvious scapegoat. If I was the SUF I would have reached the same conclusion. It's also irrelevant whether or not the SUF actually believes we destroyed the station. In fact, they probably do believe us. Avoiding war with the Zendreen trumps all of that."

"So the SUF is a bunch of duplicitous backstabbers," said Talvan. "What else is new?"

"Umber should have never joined the faction," said Aldebaran. "When Umber regains it's former glory, the SUF will rue the day it betrayed us."

"I beg your pardon? Even if we do expel the Zendreen from our planet we won't be able to declare war on an elementary school, never mind the SUF. I'm mad as hell at the SUF for what they did, but we're going to have to find a way to ignore our pride and ask for their help. With the Zendreen out of the picture, they might actually help us rebuild our infrastructure. You don't know how bad things have gotten, Aldebaran. The home you remember is gone forever."

Fernwyn entered the bridge.

"Did I miss anything?" she asked.

"We're just discussing how royally fucked we are," said John.

"Oh, cool."

Talvan stood up and walked over to Fernwyn.

"A Residerian genmod," he said, "with Kau'Rii genes. When I heard your name mentioned I wondered if you were the same one I'd heard about before the war."

"Nice to meet you, too."

"You've heard of her?" asked Dana.

"I'm a bit of a celebrity in scientific circles," replied Fernwyn.

"What's your stake in all of this?" Talvan asked, returning to his seat.

"I want to make sure that the Residere government gets the truth about what's going on, not the SUF's spin on it."

"They'd hardly be inclined to listen to you right now, from what I understand."

"If we can defeat the Zendreen we'll probably earn another chance."

"What we need to worry about right now," said John, "is where we're going to find the lab equipment we need. Aldebaran, you said you know of a place?"

Aldebaran nodded. "There's a pirate enclave on Macer Alpha. It's a self-contained series of structures independent of any government or law. There's a Z'Sorth there who has the best laboratory I've seen next to the one on the USWS. The only problem is that he's completely insane. The last I heard he was trying to synthesize a sentient being of pure energy out of fruit."

"Will he let us use his equipment?" asked Talvan.

"I don't know. We'll just have to ask."

"Will we be welcome at this place?" asked John.

"I'm still Aldebaran. I can practically guarantee that nobody will mess with us down there."

"Excellent. Set a course for Macer Alpha, then. In the meantime, everybody get some rest, eat some food, and think of a pirate name for yourself."

"Aldebaran, can I talk to you alone?" Talvan asked, standing.

"I thought you might want to, Professor," replied Aldebaran.

John shrugged. "Meeting adjourned, I guess. You two can use the conference room if you want."

Aldebaran and Talvan exited into the conference room. John sat down in the pilot's chair, then stood up again.

"Damn it, it's all wet," he said.

"John, are you sure you want those two talking to each other alone?" said Christie.

"Why not? We're all on the same side here. They have some catching up to do, that's all. I'm not so paranoid as to prevent them from speaking in private. They would have found a chance at another time anyway."

Ray stood up. "Arr, Laphroaig McClewlin agrees with ye. Let the old salts catch up on their yarns."

"Laphroaig McClewlin?"

In the conference room, Aldebaran crossed to the window. Talvan paced on the other side of the room for a moment, considering the other Umberian. He looked exactly like the first lieutenant Talvan had last seen on the USWS ten years ago. A decade of hard living had barely touched his youthful features. There was an edge to his expression, however, that was new to Talvan. Gone was the bright and hopeful officer, the willing participant in a bold new experiment. Gone also, and much to Talvan's relief, was the vacant, impassive husk of a man that was left after Talvan and his colleagues ripped Aldebaran's soul out of him. Seth became Umber's last hope even as Aldebaran slipped away in the chaos that engulfed the system upon the Zendreen's arrival. The fact that he'd become a pirate in the following years was a surprise to Talvan until he considered the ultimate goal of such raids. The only comment on his recombination made to Talvan since the rescue had been John's "he's neither Seth nor Aldebaran the pirate any more, only a full spectrum shadow of both." An enigmatic statement, but wholly accurate as Talvan could now see for himself.

Certain details seemed like they'd happened yesterday; others were dusty with age. Of one thing Talvan was certain: at one time they'd been friends.

"So they tell me you became a pirate after the invasion," Talvan said.

"True," replied Aldebaran, his gaze still fixed on the stars.

"You were searching for Seth, right? You were hoping to reconstitute yourself with him. I wish you could have known that he was heading at top speed for the core galaxy. You could have saved yourself a lot of trouble."

"A lot of Umberians would still be alive as well."

"If you're going to blame anyone, blame me, Seth. I'm the one who botched the experiment. I would have worked tirelessly to fix that mistake if not for the invasion. I hope you believe me."

"It's not important."

"It is to me. Despite all of the destruction and loss, the one thing that bothered me the most about the last ten years was my inability to repair your mind. I can blame a lot of things on the Zendreen but not that."

"I can't ameliorate your guilt, Professor," said Aldebaran, meeting his countenance, "no matter how willing I am to accept your apology, if that's what this is, you can't ignore the fact that I killed so many innocent people. That blood is on your hands as much as it is mine."

"I accept responsibility for doing what I did, but I couldn't have known you'd resort to such measures."

Aldebaran approached Talvan until he was a single stride away. "Irrelevant. You should have killed me before the Zendreen attacked."

Before Talvan could object, Aldebaran turned and exited the room. Talvan sighed and slumped into a chair.

"Damn."

Twenty-four hours later, John walked down the corridor on deck one. He was looking for Aldebaran, and had expected to find him in the cargo hold. Instead, a quick search found him in the lounge area, staring out into space. John sighed and approached him.

"How's it going?" he said, leaning against the bulkhead.

"This ship is peaceful," replied Aldebaran. "It feels more like home than anywhere I've been for years."

"I'm glad it makes you happy."

"I didn't say that it did. But it does ease my mind."

"Good. Listen, I have an assignment for you. Come with me."

John turned and crossed to the stairs. Aldebaran shrugged and followed him.

"It's not busy work is it? If you're just trying to engage me with something, I'd prefer not to."

"Don't worry, Bartelby, it's important. We're arriving at Macer in twelve hours and this needs to get done before then."

John and Aldebaran descended the stairs, passing through a layer of smoke and into the galley. The rest of the crew save for Talvan and Richter was gathered around the table, engaged in a game of poker. Christie and Ray were facing that direction and waved hello.

"Sit down," said John. "We're dealing you in."

Aldebaran raised an eyebrow. "You want me to play a game?"

"That's right. If Seth can't entertain us with sims anymore, the least you could do is join us for poker. We haven't had a game since we got here and all persons aboard are required to play."

"Come on," said Nathalier. "Rylie and I need another novice at the table."

"We'll switch back to five card draw so you can learn the rules," said John.

Aldebaran sat down. "I already know how to play. I am still Seth. What about credits?"

John joined the others at the table and withdrew his own assortment of currency.

"We divided Ari's stuff between Fernwyn and Nathalier," he said, "but I'm doing quite well. You can have half of mine."

"But I didn't earn it."

"Consider it compensation for your actions on Umber yesterday. Fernwyn, it's your deal."

Fernwyn accepted the deck from Ray and tried to shuffle it, obviously for the first time. By the third attempt she had mastered it. She dealt out two cards to each player and placed one face up in the middle of the table.

"Texas Hold'Em?" asked John.

"Are you sure you want to try that one again?" Ray asked, puffing on his pipe.

"Positive. Unless you're worried that I'll take the pot."

"No, go for it."

The game progressed in silence for a few minutes. Fernwyn and Nathalier seemed to be following well.

"Tell us more about this colony on Macer Alpha," said John.

"It's like I mentioned earlier," replied Aldebaran, moving his cards around. "It's a self-contained, unregulated colony populated mostly with pirates, current and former. It's centered around a large colonization ship called the

Scripture, a vessel that was meant to land on Alpha and never again leave. The original inhabitants ended up getting into a dispute about exactly the way they should govern the colony, and they wiped themselves out. Pirates soon discovered the vessel and began using it as a hideout, and over the years it became a refuge for pirates and those wishing to wine, dine, and trade under the radar. The colony has grown around the Scripture, but it's still the main center."

"So the SPF must know about this place," said Christie.

"Of course," said Fernwyn, "but we can't do anything about it. We don't have the resources for an effective embargo, and a ground assault is out of the question. We could nuke the entire place, but we'd put the other colonies at risk. They're peaceful and hardly deserve it."

"So you just tolerate it?"

"Macer is pretty far away from Residere, at least from a solar law enforcement perspective. We're more concerned about the pirates who use Residere Delta as a haven."

"You're certain we'll be welcome there?" John asked Aldebaran.

"Stick with me, and you'll be fine, but I don't recommend her coming with us without some sort of disguise," said Aldebaran, pointing at Fernwyn.

Fernwyn cocked her head to one side. "Oh? Well, I guess so. I suppose somebody might recognize me from my careers."

"What about this crazy scientist?" asked John. "What else can you tell us about him?"

"I already told you everything I know," Aldebaran said.

"Okay. Here's the plan, then. Talvan, Ray, Richter and I will pose as Aldebaran's crew and run down this lead.

Fernwyn, we'll put you in some sort of costume and you'll come with us. Dana, Christie, and Nathalier, you guard the Faith while we're gone.

"You don't want me along?" asked Christie.

"I want a strong defensive presence on the ship. I also want to keep a low profile on the colony. You and Dana might draw more attention than we want. The same goes for you, Nathalier, but not for the same reason."

"Hey, I think I'm plenty attractive," Nathalier replied. "There might be some lonely feline women down there, too."

"They'd have to be lonely and blind," said Fernwyn, smirking.

"Thanks a lot."

"Do you know where the Z'Sorth scientist hangs out?" asked John.

Aldebaran nodded. "There's a club at the center of the ship. It's the cultural center of the colony, lots of drinking, dancing, and fighting. Above the dance floor is where this guy keeps his lab. I have no idea how he ended up there, but he is, after all, crazy."

"Are we going to have any trouble getting in there?"

"I don't think so."

"Good," said John, checking his watch. "We've got twelve hours until we arrive. Let's play for another hour and then call it a night. I want everyone rested up for the mission.

Aldebaran made a bet, pushing several hard candies and tea bags toward the center of the table.

"There's only one problem," he said.

"What?"

"We're going to need plenty of money. Real money, I mean."

## 26.

"What do you mean, nothing?"

On the bridge of the Faith, the stunning panorama of the planet Macer filled the windows. The gas giant seemed to glow with milky azure light, all but obscuring the moon that the ship was rapidly approaching. John was piloting the ship while Dana, Christie, and Aldebaran manned the stations. Talvan sat by the rear door.

John looked over at Dana's station. Dana shrugged and returned the glance.

"I mean nothing. There are no transmissions coming out of the colony."

Aldebaran stood up and crossed over to Dana. "That can't be right."

Dana gestured at her console. "See for yourself."

"There are transmissions being sent to the colony, but nothing's coming out."

"Yeah."

"Could it be that they're encrypted?" asked Christie.

"We'd still be receiving them," replied Aldebaran. "They could be masked somehow, but that would require the cooperation of the entire colony. That's highly unlikely, and I can't think of a reason why they'd do it."

"I'm establishing a geosynchronous orbit," said John, "let's see if we can get a good look at the place."

Christie nodded. "Okay."

"When's the last time you were here, Aldebaran?"

"Eighteen months ago," Aldebaran said, returning to his station.

"And there was no sign of trouble?" asked Talvan.

"It's an anarchistic pirate hideout. Define trouble."

"What about spacecraft activity?" John asked, locking down the autopilot.

"I'm only reading one ship," said Dana.

"It's a Kau'Rii transport," said Aldebaran. "It left the colony a few minutes ago."

John swiveled his chair around. "Can you open a frequency?"

"Roger," said Dana, doing so. "No reply yet."

"You know," Christie began, "with the invisibility shield up the Kau'Rii ship won't be able to identify the source of our transmission."

John raised an eyebrow. "Well, I don't want to drop the shield."

"Then don't be surprised if they ignore us."

"They've activated their FTL drive," said Dana, "they're gone."

"I guess we're on our own," muttered John.

"I've got the colony on the screen," said Christie. "This is the best resolution I can get."

John and Aldebaran stood up and looked at Christie's monitor. The colony's main structure could be identified, but smaller buildings and connecting tunnels were difficult to make out. There was a visible distortion wave every few seconds.

"The atmosphere shielding is still up," said Aldebaran. "The structure looks intact. We can dock without permission at any free airlock."

John crossed his arms. "If there's an atmosphere shield, what do they need airlocks for?"

"The air is still dangerously cold. Beside, how else do you enter a space vessel?"

"Right. Identify a dock that looks good to you and we'll begin our descent. Richter, do you copy?"

"Yo," said Richter's voice.

"How's it going down there?"

"So far so good. Fernwyn's going to wear my sunglasses and we've wrapped a scarf around her head. Long arms are ready for loadout, except for anything Talvan wants to bring."

John turned to Talvan. "Do you know how to operate a firearm?"

"I haven't held a weapon since the invasion," replied Talvan, "but before that I was in the military."

"As a scientist," interjected Aldebaran.

"I was an officer first. Some things never leave you."

"Hopefully none of us will be relying on those skills this mission," said John.

"Don't you ever get tired of being wrong?" asked Christie, smirking.

"Dana, you've got the stick. Christie, keep your eyes on the commo. Let us know if you see anything the slightest bit troubling. Talvan, Aldebaran, let's get loaded up."

John led the other men out of the bridge and down the hall to the zero-g room. Ray, Fernwyn, and Richter were assembled and ready to go. Nathalier leaned against the wall. John picked up his gear and accepted the M1A that Richter was offering him.

"Talvan, this is a Glock 17," said John, showing the older man such a thing. "It fires a nine-millimeter round from a seventeen round magazine. To bring it into action, you rack the slide like this. The magazine release is right here. Slap in a new magazine, make sure it's seated, and tug on the rear of the slide to close it. You'll have two spare mags for a total of fifty-one rounds."

John handed Talvan the weapon along with a duty belt, holster, and magazine pouch.

"I'd feel a lot better if Talvan could stay behind," said Ray, checking his shotgun.

"He's the only one who can identify the lab gear he needs," replied John.

Talvan put on the duty belt. "Trust me, I don't want to go down there. This is for Umber, not me."

John looked over the team. "You sure you're up for this, Richter?"

"Don't worry about me," Richter said.

"You're comfortable with that Phalanx?"

"You bet your ass I am."

"How about you, Nathalier? Can you handle the weapons we're leaving you with?"

"Please," said Nathalier, rolling his eyes.

"Good, because I'm counting on you to protect Christie and Dana."

Dana's voice came in over the speakers. "Thirty seconds to docking."

"Okay, folks," began John. "From here on out, Aldebaran runs the show. Don't say anything to anyone if you don't have to; Aldebaran speaks for us. Don't buy anything and don't wander off."

"What if we can't convince the Z'Sorth to let us use his equipment?" asked Fernwyn.

"Failure is not an option."

"What the hell is that supposed to mean?" asked Ray.

"I mean we're going to gain access to that equipment no matter what. If the Z'Sorth resists, we'll hold him at bay until we can load it aboard."

"You mean to steal it," said Dana's voice.

John folded his arms. "If necessary. We've come too far to go away empty-handed. Anybody got a problem with that?"

"I'm just concerned about blurring the line between heroes and pirates," said Ray.

"Consider it Stanislavski-style training."

There was a slight bump, and the airlock door light changed from red to green.

"Good to go," said Dana. "Good luck out there."

John motioned to Aldebaran, who hit the button to open the door. The door opened smoothly, and cold air flowed into the room. Mist quickly formed as the warmer air reacted with it. Aldebaran entered the airlock, followed by the rest of the team. Nathalier approached the door, and waved goodbye.

"See you soon," he said, and pressed the controls.

The door closed. The airlock was dimly lit and barely large enough for the six of them. A sign had been hung on the hatch to the colony ship.

"What's the sign say?" asked John.

"Welcome to Scripture Colony," replied Aldebaran, opening a small plastic box that was mounted to the bulkhead.

Aldebaran pressed a key inside the box. A tone sounded for a few seconds, and then terminated. He tried again, with the same result.

"Nobody's answering."

"Can you override it?" asked John.

"I think so."

Carefully pulling off the sleek black cover, Aldebaran found several wires. He drew a folding knife and severed all of them. He touched one to another until the hatch began to move. Warmer air blew into the airlock from a long corridor.

"That seemed too easy," said Fernwyn.

"This dock hadn't been locked out," replied Aldebaran. "If so, we'd be stuck."

"Why wouldn't the dock be locked out?"

"Whoever was in control of this section didn't do it. Maybe they were expecting company."

The team moved into the corridor. It was well lit, and revealed what looked like a subway tunnel minus the tracks. Inoffensive trash lined the walls, but a clear path through the center had been maintained. Graffiti was everywhere. There was a soft humming, but no other noise. Aldebaran studied a directory, which hadn't been defaced at all.

"We're on level five," he said. "The club is on level one."

"Is this place usually so quiet?" asked John.

"No. Somebody should be asking us for money."

Aldebaran moved down the corridor. The team followed him in single file. At the end of the passage they reached another, which traveled perpendicularly to it. Aldebaran peeked around the corners before continuing.

"This is the main concourse for level five," he began. "It encircles the entire ship. If memory serves, this level is mostly crew quarters, inboard from the concourse. The pirates use them for the same purpose. There should be lots of people hanging out in this area."

"Maybe they're all in bed," said Ray.

"It's unlikely that they're all taking a rest at the same time. Come on, we should find an elevator bank before too long."

The group resumed moving down the concourse.

"I've got a bad feeling about this," said Fernwyn.

"I wouldn't worry too much. If the SPF is taking more of an interest in this place, they could have changed their habits. That would explain the lack of transmissions and our yet-unimpeded access."

"That's pure speculation. We have no reason to think that the SPF decided to crack down on pirate enclaves. I certainly didn't hear anything about it during my daily briefings."

"What do you want me to tell you, Rylie? Maybe they abandoned the place because it's no longer fashionable. I don't..."

Aldebaran stopped. They had reached an elevator bank. The floor, walls, and ceilings were thoroughly splashed with blood.

"Holy shit!" exclaimed John.

Richter, Fernwyn, Ray, and John unlimbered their long arms rapidly. Aldebaran reached down and unsnapped the strap on his holster. Talvan gaped at the sight in shock, the color draining out of his face.

"Is this normal?" said Fernwyn, aiming down the concourse.

Aldebaran's expression did not change. "No."

The team spread out in a defensive pattern. Aldebaran examined one of the bulkheads.

"Looks like somebody had a dispute over the elevator," said Richter softly.

"There are several types of blood here," said Aldebaran calmly. "Rakhar, Kau'Rii, Residerian... I don't see any Z'Sorth blood."

"How... how long?" gasped Talvan.

"Looks like less than twenty-four hours, but I'm not a forensics expert. There are no projectile impacts that I can see."

"Is this how pirates solve their differences?" asked Ray.

"Not generally, but there's no book on how to be a pirate."

John keyed his radio. "Dana, this is John. We may have a complication. Be alert."

"Roger that," Dana replied.

"Ask her to scan for life signs," said Fernwyn.

John frowned. "The Faith doesn't have that ability anymore."

"Let's keep moving," said Richter.

Aldebaran hit the call button for the elevator. A few seconds later a car arrived and the doors opened. The interior of the car was large, obviously meant for cargo use. A single streak of blood marked the floor.

"Somebody was dragged out," said Richter, looking over his shoulder.

The team boarded the elevator. Aldebaran selected level one, and the doors closed. The elevator did not move.

"Is this the kind of elevator that works?" said Ray.

Aldebaran hit the button again, and the car shuddered into motion.

"I hope this isn't history repeating itself," he said. "The colonists wiped each other out over religious differences. Pirates don't need that compelling of a reason. This place was different, though. We actually worked together and maintained a fairly stable society."

A ceiling panel collapsed and a body fell into the car. Each team member swore and leapt back.

"Shit son of a bitch!" yelled Ray, who had been hit by the corpse.

"It's a Kau'Rii," said Talvan.

Fernwyn kneeled down and looked at the body. The Kau'Rii was fawn-colored before it was doused in it's own blood.

"Grim," said Richter.

"It's been eviscerated," said Fernwyn. "There are multiple other knife wounds. The neck has been cut, and there's a deep stab to the heart. The snap on his holster is still in place, as is his knife. He never had a chance to get into the action."

The elevator arrived on the first level, and the doors opened. Richter and Ray cleared the exit. A dull throbbing sound could be heard.

"Was it the work of a Rakhar?" asked Talvan.

"I don't think so," replied Fernwyn. "These cuts are very clean and precise. I think this was done with a vibro-blade."

"Vibro-blades are very expensive," said Aldebaran. "Nobody but surgeons and engineers use them."

"Yeah, and they're hardly durable enough for combat. Maybe somebody is trying to fool us into thinking that this was done by a Tenchiik."

"Ha! Right."

"A what?" said John.

"The Tenchiik are a fairy-tale," said Fernwyn. "They're supposedly a group of highly skilled genmod assassins. You start with a Kau'Rii and make them stronger and faster. They supposedly eschew firearms and use vibro-blades."

"That doesn't sound so implausible."

"There are only two places you can go to get genmodded, and neither of them ever created a Tenchiik. The rumor is that they were created with private funds, but it's ludicrous. Such a venture would be incredibly expensive."

"Let's not let our imaginations run away from us," said John. "Aldebaran, which way to the club?"

"This way."

Aldebaran led the team into the corridor. As they headed down the passage, more swaths of blood marked the bulkheads. Talvan drew his pistol. Fernwyn bent over and picked something up from the deck.

"It's a Rakhar finger, neatly severed," she said.

"This is fucked," said Ray. "Maybe we should get the hell out of here."

"You're not losing your nerve, are you?" said Richter, smirking.

The team arrived at a large open area. It was two decks high and extended for about seventy-five yards in depth and width. Restaurants and shops lined the area, and there was significantly less trash and graffiti. The throbbing sound had become louder, and Aldebaran pointed at a door directly across from them.

"There's the club," he said.

"Still think everyone's napping?" asked Richter.

"They're not awake, that's for sure," replied Ray.

The group proceeded cautiously to the entrance to the club. Aldebaran opened the door, buffeting the team with loud music. Inside, flashing strobe lights and lasers moved across a large dance floor. The second level was a ring of balconies overlooking the club. There was something in the center of the floor. As the team moved inside, the something became all too apparent.

"Oh, my God," said John.

Dozens of corpses were stacked in the center of the dance floor. The floor itself was a platform raised above a sitting area on the periphery. Blood had pooled to about three inches in the depression. There was a strong smell of rust and weapons fire in the air. Aldebaran drew his pistol.

"Let's see if we can kill this noise," he said.

The crew moved together to the DJ's table, where the loud music was ceased. Aldebaran found the house lights and turned them on. The pile of bodies glistened in the bright, bleak light. Corpses from several races were readily apparent, including the limbs that lacked owners. Talvan vomited.

"Still think the Tenchiik are just a rumor?" asked Aldebaran.

"This is a bust," said Talvan, coughing. "Let's cut our losses and get out of here."

"A poor choice of words," said Richter, scanning the upper level.

"There should be a stairway to the third level behind the bar," said Aldebaran. "That's where the Z'Sorth's lab should be."

"Let's go," said John. "Nice and slow."

Aldebaran led the team to the dance floor. Getting to the bar required crossing it, and the depressed seating area. Aldebaran jumped over the blood and turned to help the others do the same. Ray didn't quite make it and his boot dragged through the liquid.

"Damn it," he said, shaking his foot.

"Why would the Tenchiik attack this place?" asked John, trying not to stare at the bodies.

"I don't know," replied Aldebaran.

"If the rumors are true," began Talvan, tip-toeing gingerly, "then the Tenchiik would have had to have been hired by someone. They're supposed to be assassins, not psychotic murderers. I don't know who would want this entire colony massacred."

"How many pirates hang out here?" asked Fernwyn.

"It varies," said Aldebaran. "On any given day, maybe five hundred. I hope, for their sake, that there weren't too many ships docked..."

Aldebaran stopped. He'd drawn up to the end of the bar and was looked behind it. He beckoned to Fernwyn, who joined him.

"I'll be blasted," she said, obviously impressed.

The others took a look. A Kau'Rii lay dead behind the bar. It had black fur and wore all black clothing. The fur and vestments seemed to soak up the light, defying any reflectivity. A gear belt was fastened around its waist, and included an empty sheath. It had been shot several times with both a projectile weapon and an energy weapon. There was no blood visible despite the wounds.

"A Tenchiik?" Fernwyn murmured.

"What else could it be?" said Aldebaran.

"The Tenchiik aren't supposed to leave their people behind," said Talvan.

"Ten minutes ago we all thought the Tenchiik were a campfire story," said Aldebaran. "Let's not overreact."

"But they might come back for the body!"

"There was a Kau'Rii ship leaving the colony when we got here, remember? They might already be gone."

"Don't bet on it," said Richter.

Aldebaran nodded. "Come on."

Around the corner, the team found the staircase to the upper levels. The stairwell was splashed with blood on the walls and ceiling, but not the stairs. The walls were pockmarked with weapon impacts.

"Looks like some serious shit went down here," said John.

"So far it's about sixty dead pirates for one assassin," Ray said, frowning. "I don't like those odds."

The team reached the balconies on the second level. Here, there was evidence of a good time permanently interrupted. Drinks sat unfinished, and food lay in a similar state. Jackets, coats, and other personal effects were scattered about. There was much less blood. Aldebaran pointed to a door at the end of a short hallway. There was a sign on it.

"It reads, 'private quarters, no entry'," he said.

The door was open about an inch, and darkness lay behind it. Aldebaran advanced carefully and opened the door. Another stairway met his vision. He pressed a switch on the wall a few times.

"Lights aren't working," he said.

Everyone but Richter and Fernwyn drew a flashlight and turned it on. For those two, they simply turned on the lights mounted on their Phalanx rifles.

"It's tight in there," said John.

"Rylie, you and I will go first," said Richter. "The rest of you, wait for my signal."

Fernwyn nodded, and joined Richter at the bottom of the stairs. Together they ascended, smoothly and rapidly. They disappeared from sight just before Richter called out.

"Landing clear," he said.

The others climbed the stairs and found Fernwyn and Richter crouched at the top. Their lights were illuminating a large area that covered the entire top of the club. It had a vaulted ceiling with straight steel braces and was roughly octagonal in shape. Four desks had been set up in the center of the room, each stacked with several dozen books and notepads. An impressive array of laboratory equipment lined the walls, with at least twenty different machines. There was a sense of orderly chaos to the room.

"It certainly smells like a Z'Sorth lives here," said Richter quietly.

Aldebaran motioned to Talvan. "Professor, we'll clear the room. Wait here and watch the stairs."

"I'll do the same," said Ray.

Talvan and Ray watched as the others paired off and began to search the room. Their flashlights bounced off of a wide variety of reflective surfaces and through flasks and vials of unknown liquid. It was completely quiet save for their footsteps. Ray's fingers tensed around his shotgun. Talvan looked at him and began to whisper.

"Even if this stuff is working, you don't seriously expect me to use this lab, do you? Not after what we found!"

Ray shook his head. "No, we'll have to take what we need back to the Faith. I just hope we can carry all of..."

A figure dashed out of a dark corner toward Ray and Talvan. Ray told himself not to panic, and was completely surprised to find his body disobeying him.

"I'm saved!" it said.

"Holy shit!" Ray yelled, and fired his shotgun.

Cycling the action with perfect speed, Ray fired again. Talvan joined him, rattling off five rounds from his borrowed Glock. The figure fell backward, hissing, and was silent. The others ran over as Ray illuminated the creature with his flashlight. It was a quickly expiring Z'Sorth.

"Are you all right?" John cried.

Fernwyn, Richter, and Aldebaran swept the room with their lights and found nothing else. Talvan struggled to calm his breathing while Fernwyn ran over to check the Z'Sorth.

"Looks like we found the scientist," said Aldebaran.

"Oh, my God," said Ray. "I'm sorry, he jumped out at us."

"There's nothing we can do," said Fernwyn. "He's already stopped breathing."

Talvan looked horrified. "I can't believe we just killed the only survivor."

Aldebaran put his hand on Talvan's shoulder. "Don't feel bad. Now we don't have to ask permission to use the lab."

"I certainly hope he wasn't the only survivor," said John.

"Do you really want to spend time searching this place?"

"A survivor might appreciate our help. Besides, how long is it going to take to synthesize the virus? We could send out a search party."

"I obviously didn't impress upon you the process here, John," said Talvan. "This won't take five minutes, or an hour. I need at least a day to synthesize the virus and a couple of hours to confirm that the new form is harmless to Umberians."

"Fine, this room is clear," said John. "Talvan, find the gear you need and we'll take it back to the ship."

In a daze, Talvan nodded. He brought his flashlight up and began searching the room. He moved quickly, and before too long began pointing things out.

"We'll need that electron microscope," he said, "and that autoclave. That culturing cabinet, that set of instruments, and... I think that's everything."

"How are we going to power this stuff?" asked Ray. "I doubt it runs off of 120 volt a/c."

"My ship has a power converter," replied Fernwyn. "We can set up the stuff in the cargo bay right next to it."

"Good," said John. "Let me check in with the ship. Dana, this is John, over."

"Go ahead," said Dana's voice.

"How are things going back there?"

"Quiet. You?"

"There's been some sort of attack on the colony. We've found several dozen dead pirates. We're collecting the gear we need now, and we'll be back in about ten minutes. Don't let anybody in until we get there."

"Like I would do that, John. Are you okay?"

"We're holding up. I'll contact you when we get back to the airlock. Scherer out."

The others began collecting the things as instructed by Talvan. John and Fernwyn ended up with the culturing cabinet, which was a five foot tall metal box with a glass door. John put his weight up against it and pushed.

"It has to weight a hundred and fifty pounds," he said, grunting. "We'll need the two-wheeler from the ship."

"Let me try," said Fernwyn.

Grabbing the cabinet, Fernwyn lifted it a few inches off of the floor.

"Got it?"

"Not exactly. It's unwieldy. I could use a guide to get it down the stairs."

"Let me," said Ray, handing John a microscope.

"Let's not waste any more time here," John said. "Aldebaran, Talvan, are you ready to go?"

"Hell yes," said Talvan.

"I won't be able to fire my sidearm while I'm holding this autoclave," said Aldebaran.

"We'll cover you," replied John. "Richter?"

"Ready here," Richter replied.

"Hold this," said John, handing the microscope to Talvan. "I'll take point. Richter, you take your normal position in the rear."

"Roger."

John readied his rifle, cradling the stock with his left arm so he could use his flashlight. He led the team down the stairs. Ray and Fernwyn were forced to take extra time with the cabinet, but with lots of communication and swearing they were able to bring it to the bottom of the stairwell.

"The next flight is wider," began John, "so it should be easier for..."

John stopped talking because the house lights had just gone out. Before anyone could react, the pulsing music and light show started up again.

"What the hell?" growled Aldebaran.

"Maybe it's on a timer."

Richter moved to the front of the group and scanned the dance floor.

"It's a setup," he said, his expression steely.

John looked down, but could see nothing. "You sure?"

"Is there another way back to the concourse?" asked Fernwyn.

Aldebaran shook his head. "Not that I know of."

"What do we do?" asked Talvan.

"Fernwyn," began John, "you stay here with Talvan and the gear. The rest of us will go downstairs and see if we can get the house lights back up. If it's an ambush, cover us from the balconies."

Fernwyn nodded. "Okay."

John took the lead, and motioned for Aldebaran to fall in behind him. Ray came next, and Richter resumed the last position.

"Nice and easy," said John.

The four men moved down the stairs to the first level. The music and flashing lights were disorientating, but having seen the layout with the house lights up the men knew where to go. Corpses seemed to move under the strobes, and it was clear that the anxiety level for the humans was high. Aldebaran was focused, but seemed calm. The four reached the dance floor, and John put up his hand. They stopped. John motioned toward the periphery of the room, and the others strained to see what he meant.

There were figures lining the room, quite obviously alive. At first only their eyes were visible, glinting each time a strobe passed by. When a few of them stepped forward, their identities became clear.

"Tenchiik," whispered Aldebaran.

Steel flashed in the light. Each of the black-clad Kau'Rii were wielding a long, thin blade, reminiscent of a stiletto, but much larger.

"Tight 360," said Richter.

Each of the humans took up a kneeling position in a cardinal direction. Aldebaran followed their motion rapidly. They backed up until their heels were almost touching.

"Are you the Umberians?" one of the Tenchiik said, his voice raspy but clear.

"What difference does it make?" asked Aldebaran.

"None to you."

John took a deep breath. He was facing the Techiik who was speaking, and he centered the sights of his rifle on the Kau'Rii's head.

"Cone of fire and retreat to the stairs," he said.

"Roger," replied the others.

With an ear-splitting crack, John's rifle initiated the chaos. The Tenchiik leapt into action, moving with blinding speed. The team put down a furious wall of fire, with Richter's Phalanx dominating the cacophony. When Ray had fired all five rounds from his shotgun, he transitioned to his revolver and began the retreat.

"GO!" he screamed.

The team moved together toward the stairs. From above, Fernwyn had begun firing at targets near and far with her Phalanx, with Talvan soon joining her with his borrowed pistol. John's M1A ran dry and he knew there was no time to reload. He dropped it to the deck and drew Ari's Glock.

A Tenchiik took advantage of the moment and lunged toward him. John attempted to dodge to his right, but the creature was too fast for him. The blade sliced through his left thigh with absolutely no resistance or pain. The Tenchiik whirled around for another slash but John kicked out, knocking the assassin away just enough to bring his Glock into play. Three shots to the neck dropped the

Tenchiik. John spared a look at his thigh before two more Tenchiik appeared in front of him. The wound had begun to bleed. John continued to back-pedal, firing his pistol.

Richter's Phalanx finally ran out of rounds, and he smoothly reloaded. Ray was the first to reach the stairs and he bound up them, slapping another clip into his revolver. Aldebaran was next, followed by John. Richter paused at the bottom of the stairs. His cheek was tucked tightly into the stock of his rifle and he was taking out Tenchiik with precise bursts. From above, Fernwyn resumed her helpful efforts. Richter began backing up the stairs when there was a flash. He glanced down and found two of his fingers lying at his feet. The Kau'Rii responsible for this drew back for another blow, and Richter took his head off with the Phalanx. He stumbled up the stairs, taking out two more of the creatures that attempted to follow him.

At the top of the landing, the team was engaging targets. Talvan was sitting in one corner, agape at the growing stain of blood on his stomach. Ray found an opportunity to reload his shotgun and resumed fighting. Aldebaran leaned over the railing and fired several rounds at the DJ station, terminating the music. A single Tenchiik vaulted over the same railing next to him, and it was shot a dozen times by the others.

There was silence.

"Clear right!" yelled John.

"Clear left!" echoed Aldebaran.

"Stairs are clear," Richter yelped. "I've got an injury here."

"Talvan's been hit," Fernwyn said.

John looked at his own wound. He needed to stop the bleeding soon.

"Ray," he said, "get the field dressings."

Nodding in acknowledgment, Ray opened his first aid kit.

"Is that all of them?" asked Fernwyn, wiping sweat from her brow.

"I don't know," replied John. "Somehow I doubt it."

---

"Dana, this is John, over."

Dana sat up straight in the pilot's chair, once again sharing a glance with Christie to confirm that she was awake. She reached for the commo controls and replied.

"Go ahead, John."

"We're back to the airlock."

"Roger that, we're on our way."

Dana stood up and keyed the commo again.

"Nathalier, meet us in the zero-g room. The team is back."

"Okay," Nathalier's voice replied.

"They had me worried," said Christie, joining Dana.

"Finally we get a mission that doesn't end in violence," said Dana.

The women exited the bridge. Nathalier was climbing the stairs from the cargo bay and met up with them.

"How's Fernwyn's ship doing?" asked Christie.

"I've finished the repairs," replied Nathalier. "It wasn't so bad."

"I don't know if we've adequately expressed our gratitude to you, Nathalier. You lost your job and your ship because of us. We're grateful for your help. Don't ever think that we don't appreciate your sacrifices for our mission."

"Thanks. It's safe to say that it's my mission now, too. I may just get the Raven back if we can defeat the Zendreen on Umber and clear our names with the SPF."

The three crew members entered the zero-g room. Dana stopped at the computer console. Christie also stopped to see what she was doing.

"I finally got the computers to recognize the zero-g settings," Dana said. "We can use the surround screen again if we want."

"Surround screen?" asked Nathalier, reaching the airlock door.

"We can project a real-time image of the exterior of the ship onto the surfaces of this room. It makes you feel like you're in space. It's pretty cool."

"It sounds like you thought of a lot of ways to kill time," said Nathalier, opening the airlock door.

The person on the other side of the door was not John. Nathalier's eyebrows raised as he saw himself looking down at a Kau'Rii, dressed in black. Nathalier's brain sent a message to his muscles, but the Kau'Rii's long knife slashed through his neck before they could respond. Dana and Christie watched in horror as Nathalier fell silently to the deck, a bright red fountain of blood following him down like a sanguine parachute. The Kau'Rii stepped past Nathalier and grinned at the women.

"Are you armed?" whispered Dana.

"No," replied Christie, "but..."

"Get ready to exit to the hall."

The Kau'Rii crouched, considering its prey with pleasurable anticipation. Dana slowly reached back for console. Christie assumed a fighting stance and stared at the Kau'Rii with ire.

"Now!" said Dana, turning to the computer screen. Christie wheeled around and opened the door to the hallway. The Kau'Rii advanced at a walking pace, obviously enjoying the spectacle before it. Dana thrust her arm toward Christie, and as she grabbed it Dana deactivated the gravity in the room. The Kau'Rii's expression changed to surprise as its body lifted off of the deck. Christie, anchored in the hall, pulled Dana out.

"Go get a weapon," said Christie.

Dana nodded and ran to the stairs. The Kau'Rii was suspended in midair, but slowly floating toward the ceiling. Christie estimated she had ten seconds before the creature could rebound from there toward her.

"Who are you?" she said.

"Your last," the Kau'Rii replied, resuming its grin.

"What happened to my crew?"

"Retired."

"You killed them?"

"What does it matter?"

Christie slammed the door shut, and realized with a hollow feeling that it didn't have a lock. She pressed her weight against it and called out.

"Dana, double-time it!"

There was a loud thump against the door. The handle began to turn. Christie struggled against the force, but the Kau'Rii was much stronger than she. She braced her leg up against the jamb and used her knee to bolster the effort. It worked, temporarily. Soon the pain began to mount and Christie felt herself slipping.

"God damn it, Dana, did you stop off for a snack or what?"

Dana appeared from below, holding a M1A rifle.

"Get out of the way," she said, shouldering the weapon.

Christie nodded, and dropped her leg. The door swung open, and she allowed herself to be pushed aside by it. The Kau'Rii stumbled into the hallway, quickly righted itself, and looked at Dana.

"Bad kitty," she said, and fired.

Six rounds later the Kau'Rii was floating toward the rear of the zero-g room, but otherwise motionless. As it hit the rear bulkhead, Aldebaran and John appeared in the airlock corridor. Dana handed the rifle to Christie and stepped inside, holding onto the jamb until she could reactivate the gravity. The Kau'Rii fell to the deck next to Nathalier's body. Aldebaran and John rushed inside, followed by Ray.

"Are you two all right?" asked John, kneeling by Nathalier.

"We're okay," said Dana. "Just half deaf."

"Nathalier is toast," said Aldebaran.

Fernwyn, Talvan, and Richter appeared in the corridor. John beckoned to Dana and Christie.

"Get over here and help us get this equipment aboard," he said. "We're not waiting another second with these things running around!"

"Nathalier!" yelled Fernwyn, dashing forward.

"He's had it," said John. "I'm sorry."

"Let's not let his death have been in vain," said Talvan. "We still have a lot to do."

## 27.

The zero-g room on the Reckless Faith was a scene of muted frenzy. The crew had hurriedly dragged the entirety of the lab equipment aboard, and a triage had been set up. Dana was the only one absent, having returned to the bridge to pilot the ship back into space. Christie, Ray and Aldebaran were running the triage, and had to force everyone but Talvan to sit down, shut up, and let them work.

Talvan's wound appeared to be the most serious, but it turned out to be superficial. Richter's pinkie and ring finger on his left hand had been severed, a cut so neat that stopping the blood flow was proving to be difficult. John's thigh was split open in a line about twelve inches long, but a tight dressing kept it from bleeding much. Fernwyn got off the easiest of those injured, suffering only minor cuts. She bound most of them herself.

"You're going to need stitches, Scherer," Richter said, cradling his heavily-bandaged hand.

"I'd ask you, but you're short-fingered," replied John.

"I know how," said Fernwyn. "It will take at least an hour, though."

"We should move to one of the bathrooms first. It's getting messy in here."

Indeed, the zero-g room was becoming rather splashed in blood. John looked at the two corpses lying on the deck, one of a friend and the other of an assassin.

"You're all set," said Aldebaran to Talvan, patting his dressing with assurance.

"I don't get it," said John, standing up carefully. "How could they know we were coming here?"

"Pirates make a lot of enemies. Don't assume the Tenchiik were for us. Just because we thought they were a fairy-tale doesn't mean they're not quite well known in another part of the cloud."

"Yeah, but they thought we were all Umberians," said Ray.

"That one saw me and assumed we were all Umberians. It doesn't necessarily mean anything. They killed more than one group of pirates down there. It looks to me like they got their assignment and decided to kill everyone else as a bonus. When we showed up, we were simply more targets to play with."

"I'm not so willing to dismiss this as coincidence," said John. "We should consider the possibility that they were sent after us, and killed everyone else for fun while waiting for us. If that's the case, they must have known that we'd be going to the enclave. The question is, did they think we were just going to hide out there because of you, Aldebaran, or did they know we were going after the lab equipment?"

"I certainly hope the latter isn't true," said Talvan. "If the Zendreen know I'm trying to cultivate a virus, they may be working on countermeasures."

"Just how are you planning on implementing this virus, anyway?" asked Fernwyn.

"It's quite simple, really. Well, actually, it's quite complicated. You see, it's easy when you look at the whole picture, but the devil is in the details."

"No shit," said John, grunting. "Look, everybody take an hour off and get yourselves cleaned up. Aldebaran, Ray, if you could move the equipment down to the cargo bay, I'd appreciate it. I've got to have this wound sutured. Talvan, you're in charge of setting this stuff up."

"Fine."

"Christie, good job on medical. Please work on getting a meal together in the interim."

"No problem," said Christie.

Richter laughed. "So I'm the only one who actually gets an hour off?"

"You're assigned to light duty until you can use your hand again," said John. "In fact, I may ask you to stay aboard for the next few days."

"My place is on the ground, Scherer. Once this bleeding stops, I'll be able to apply a better dressing and start using my hand again. Maybe not at one hundred percent, but I'll manage."

"You're a tough bastard, Richter, but everyone has got to have a limit. Do me a favor and when the time comes, give me a zero-bullshit assessment of your capabilities. Fair?"

"Fair."

"Good. Fernwyn, if you don't mind..."

Fernwyn grabbed a medical kit, and helped John to his feet. They took a hard look at the corpses before exiting the room.

"Do you want to use your quarters?" asked Fernwyn.

"Might as well. How are you holding up?"

Fernwyn entered John's passcode into the console by his door, and helped him inside.

"I'm fine. I'm better than Nathalier."

"I don't understand why they were standing around with the airlock door open."

Fernwyn helped John sit down in the bathroom, and removed what was left of his pants.

"Maybe they knew we were about to return," she said.

"Yeah, but we didn't call. I'll have to ask the girls what they were thinking."

Fernwyn began to prep the wound for sewing. "Nathalier shouldn't have died. It was pointless. I never should have asked him to help us."

"It was his choice, Fernwyn. And if he hadn't come, we'd still be sitting on Residere Delta."

"Maybe you would. There was nothing wrong with my ship."

John grinned. "We could have held on to the wings. Ouch!"

"Get used to the pain, John. It's only going to get worse."

"I'm sorry about Nathalier, Fernwyn. I know he was your friend. He was also a member of this crew, whether he thought so or not. That's three we've lost to this mission, and they all deserve our respect and gratitude."

"That's for sure."

"We need to bolster our courage now. Think about what we can accomplish here. The liberation of an entire planet."

"I haven't forgotten the goal, John."

John nodded, and looked away. His head began to spin, and he realized he'd lost a considerable amount of blood. He eyed the needle Fernwyn produced with ire.

"Mind if I pass out for this?"

"You'd better not."

"Damn."

One hour later, John stepped out of his quarters. Fernwyn had finished stitching his cut ten minutes ago, and John had just finished cleaning up and putting on new clothes. It was time for a meeting in the conference room, and John gathered his strength before continuing down the hall. He had a bad feeling about the future in the back of his mind, and he began to focus on something positive to alleviate it.

John thought about the members of his crew. They seemed to be holding up well, despite the constant chaos. Talvan was an exception to this. John worried that they might be asking too much of him. He'd lived under ten years of peace, even if it was also under servitude, and John knew how the mind dealt with change. Perhaps Umberians were heartier in that regard than humans, but John doubted it.

Talvan's age was also a concern to John. Aldebaran had mentioned that the professor was in his late fifties, which was early middle age for Umberians. John had found this information to be disconcerting, since Talvan looked older than that. The years had not been kind to him. John hoped that Talvan wouldn't be needed on the ground for the next mission, both for his own safety and for his perceived limitations.

John thought about Ray, Christie, and Dana. In many ways they bore little resemblance to the people they were the day before they left Earth. Ray had changed the least, but he was just a bit less affable than he'd been. He seemed more introspective, especially since he was shot. John still leaned on him for moral support, and was glad to see him standing strong despite everything that had happened.

Christie had become a confident and capable adventurer, which was a large departure from her bearing before they'd said goodbye to Earth. She was every bit as sharp and eager as before, but now she complained about little and avoided no challenge. John recognized the change in her, as he had seen the same change in himself. She'd reached a point where her own welfare was second to that of the crew. Richter had mentioned it once as the difference between defined responsibility and implied responsibility. When you realize there's much more to the latter, it can change your outlook on a mission.

Dana was still a bit of a mystery to John. She'd been the most vocal critic of the choices and tactics that they'd employed in pursuit of success, but never failed to back them up once the mission had begun. Her skill with and understanding of the ship had become second to none; the absence of Ari had provided her an opportunity to become the expert thereof and she'd grasped it firmly. Even Christie had to defer to Dana's knowledge of most of the ship's systems. Her confidence was also increasing, and John wondered how long she'd be willing to limit herself to the ship in the future. She was missing out on a lot of amazing experiences, even if most of them resulted in combat. It was irrelevant for the next mission, however. No matter how it played out, she would be most needed aboard.

John entered the conference room. Everyone else was already there. Richter and Aldebaran stood in the wings while the others sat at the conference table. Someone had brought the coffee decanter and a set of mugs, so John helped himself. Christie, Dana, and Talvan were in the middle of a conversation.

"Using a device called a Superluminal Relativistic Compensator," Talvan was saying, "anyone can detect and track ships moving in Superspace. Ships equipped with a SRC device can communicate normally with anyone in the rest of the universe. Before it was invented, it was impossible to track a ship in Superspace or for the ship itself to communicate with normal space. Such compensation requires an enormous amount of computational power, so as SRC technology has improved so has their efficiency and speed..."

"Excuse me, Professor," said John. "What's our status, Dana?"

"We're in orbit around Distare as requested," said Dana. "No ship-related problems to report."

"Good. Ray?"

"Nathalier's body is wrapped up and ready for the service," said Ray. "The Tenchiik has already been jettisoned."

"Fine. Richter, how's your hand?"

"Stable," Richter replied. "I'll have to change the dressing every few hours, but I have good use of the remaining fingers. Rylie tells me that if we ever repair our relationship with the SUF, I can get cybernetic replacements for cheap."

"That would be handy. Talvan, how's your injury?"

"It's nothing to worry about," Talvan replied.

John sat down in the remaining chair. "Okay, then. Let's talk about the next stage of the mission. Talvan, you're the man in the spotlight."

"The first thing we need to do is culture and refine the virus. We've finished setting up the lab downstairs, so I can start right away. Once enough of the virus has been produced, we can return to Umber."

"How can you be sure the virus isn't harmful to Umberians?" asked Fernwyn.

"Because I'm infected with it."

"What?"

"How else do you think I've been hiding it? All I have to do is take a blood sample from myself and I can isolate it. I think I can do all the work in less than twenty-four hours, now that I have good equipment."

"What about deployment?" asked Richter.

"That's the tricky part. The virus spreads by contact in Zendreen, but we have to initiate the infection via a liquid spray. We can infect any random Zendra, but the virus won't spread through the entire occupation population that way."

"We could introduce the virus into the atmosphere," said Christie. "Turn the Faith into a global crop duster."

"The virus won't live long enough under those conditions. I have another idea. The commander of the occupying force and his general staff routinely inspect sites of major importance all over the planet. They keep to a regular schedule."

"How do you know this?" asked Dana.

"I've had ten years to gather information. Even the Zendreen say too much when they get bored or sloppy. The liberation underground can't do much else but gather information. The next place on the commander's inspection list is the largest power plant on the northwestern continent. He's due there in three days. If we can infect him and his general staff, they'll spread the virus all over the planet. Within two to three weeks the majority of Zendreen will be infected, and a couple weeks after that the full effects of the virus will kick in. Then the Zendreen will be powerless to resist an uprising. Ideally, some of their space fleet will be infected, too, but even if not they'll still be forced to withdraw from the Umberian system."

"Why?"

"Because Umber is their staging location for the fleet. Without Umber, they won't have a source for supplies. They'll have to find somewhere else to go, which hopefully will be back to their own system."

"Is there any chance that they'll attack the Residere system?" asked Fernwyn.

"They're not strong enough for that, fortunately. I don't think they could mount a successful offensive against anyone right now, but my information about the space fleet isn't that good."

"They had enough resources to destroy the Way Station," said John.

"Yeah, but that's nothing."

"How are we going to infect the commander and his staff without their knowledge," asked Richter, "and if they find out, how can we be sure the Zendreen don't have an effective antidote?"

Talvan shrugged. "They might. I can't be sure this virus will even work the way it's supposed to. But it's our best bet right now. Nobody else is going to help Umber. As to how we're going to infect them without their knowledge, I don't know that either."

"Tell us more about the inspection tour," said Richter.

"According to my sources, the commander and his staff show up in an aircraft transport. They land on a platform proximate to the control center of the power station, and go inside to consult with the Zendreen overseers. Once they're satisfied, they exit the same way."

"How long do they stay?"

"I don't know."

"What benefit could the underground movement derive from attacking the power station?"

"What?"

"I mean, is there any reason why the underground would attack the power station?"

"You're thinking about a diversion?" asked John.

Richter nodded. "Right."

"The underground has been known to conduct harassment missions," said Talvan. "Unfortunately, such missions are usually also suicidal."

"By choice?"

"No, we're not trying to martyr ourselves. The odds are just too great against us."

Richter crossed his arms. "We could mount an attack on one part of the station as a diversion. One team goes out to cause trouble while another deploys the virus."

"Sounds good," began John, "but to be the most convincing, we'll have to make it look like we failed."

"True. Whoever deploys the virus spray will have to make it look like they stumbled into the commander or his staff by accident. I'm not sure how one would extricate themselves from such a situation without getting killed."

"Why not hit the transport itself?" asked Christie. "Spraying the crew should be just as effective as spraying the others."

"That's a possibility. We really can't speculate that much until we're actually on the mission."

"Okay," began John, "we'll plan as much as we can for now. We're going to need as much intel on the power station as possible. Dana, are we still on the net?"

"Yes," replied Dana. "The signal is intermittent out here, but I can still download given enough time."

"Good. See if you can find anything on the station. Refer to Talvan for help. Do it immediately after this meeting. I want to depart for Umber as soon as possible."

"Will do."

"In any case, it looks like we'll have three teams on this one. One team to provide a diversion, like Richter proposed, one team to deploy the virus, and one team to operate the ship. Thank God nothing's happened to the invisibility shield, otherwise we'd have a hell of a time getting close to the power station. Anything else?"

No one seemed to have anything else to add.

"I'll begin my search," said Dana, standing.

"Fine. Everyone else make yourselves available to Talvan, I want to make sure he has everything he needs. Oh, and the service for Nathalier will be in one hour. Aldebaran, Richter, I'd like to have a word with you two alone. That's all."

Dana, Christie, Fernwyn, and Talvan exited the conference room.

"What's up, Scherer?" asked Richter.

"I agree with you, Richter," John began, "it looks like whoever deploys the virus will be in the most danger this mission. We didn't bring any fire hoses with us, so I'll have to get pretty close."

"Who said you were the one to do it?" asked Richter.

"I see I've revealed my thoughts to you. Indeed, I'm planning on being the one to deploy the virus. That's why I wanted to speak with you both. I want the three of us to underemphasize the danger to the others. I don't want to have to deal with the constant objections of the others."

"They'd only do so because they care about you," said Richter.

"You don't care about him?" asked Aldebaran.

"I do, but I'm a professional. So are you. That's why he's speaking to us in private. He knows we can address this issue properly without letting our emotions get in the way."

"That's right," said John.

Aldebaran nodded. "Thanks, but I don't agree with you."

"What?"

"I should be the one to deploy the virus."

"I thought you'd say that. That's why I want we three to be the deployment team. We're all willing to sacrifice our own lives for the mission, but I need people who are also willing to let us do so if need be. Getting close to the commander may be suicide, so I need teammates who are willing to face that possibility. You get me?"

"You can rely on me," said Richter. "You can also rely on me to try for any other possibility before I'll let it come to that."

"Exactly. And you and I are going to impress that upon our dear Aldebaran."

"I'm not suicidal," said Aldebaran.

"You have an awfully short memory, then."

"I mean I'm not suicidal anymore. I understand that the best thing I can do for Umber is to help deploy the virus, but I'm also Seth and I'm committed to keeping you two safe as much as I can."

"Good. I'm glad the three of us understand each other. Trust me, guys, I'm not ready to die yet. But one way or another, this mission will succeed. Clear?"

"Roger that," said Richter.

Aldebaran nodded. "Clear."

"Great," said John. "Let's get to work."

## 28.

John sat in his quarters, silently and lazily puffing on his pipe. He lay in half-repose on his bed, in darkness, staring out at the greenish pink haze of the nebula. In his left hand was a glass of bourbon. If there'd been enough light one could see he was wearing an expression of sadness.

The ship hummed in a reassuring and relaxing manner. When the superluminal drive was running, there was also a deep thrumming sound. It was a great deal like having one's head next to a purring cat, and no less pleasant. With the exception of the bridge, and of late the cargo bay, it was easy to find such peace aboard the Reckless Faith. It stood in stark contrast to the chaos that met the crew at every turn outside of its steel and aluminum bulkheads. The reliquary of calm had finally been disturbed, however, and John wondered if he could ever visit the zero-g room again without the memory of bloodstained walls, urgent shouts for help, and the bodies of both friend and foe splayed obscenely across the deck.

At least the memory of Byron could be left on Residere Delta. At least John had been spared the vision of Ari's demise.

And yet, for the latter crewmember, John's imagination was ceaseless in it's perverse need to assign a reality to that which had been hidden from him in a distant, noiseless fireball. The possibilities visited John almost every night, and only in wakefulness could he hope that Ari hadn't suffered.

"Come in," said John in reply to a knock at his door.

Fernwyn entered the room, and closed the door.

"How are you?" she asked, sitting at the desk.

"My leg is killing me."

"I smell your remedy for that. Or is it for something else?"

"Suffice it to say it's for me."

"I might ask for a glass, but I don't need to alter myself right now."

"Wouldn't do much good. This is the last of the alcohol."

"I should've stocked up before we left Beta. Who knew?"

"Either give me a sitrep or get over here and keep me warm."

"I didn't realize we were at the ordering around stage of our relationship," said Fernwyn, slightly irked.

"I'm sorry, I guess I'm not much in the mood for talking right now. Could you please let me know how things are going?"

"Talvan wants to report that he's finished synthesizing the virus. Twenty-four hours, just like he said. The man can deliver."

"What about the power station?"

"He hasn't had a chance to put anything on paper yet. We have another twelve hours before we arrive at Umber, John. I think Talvan should get some sleep in the meantime."

"Yes, you're right. I've been hard on him, perhaps unduly so. I just... want this mission to keep moving."

"Umber's been occupied for ten years. They can wait another day or so, you know."

"I guess so. What about the others?"

"They're doing fine. Richter and I cleaned all of the firearms. You should have seen his reaction when I told him the Phalanx doesn't need cleaning, at least not like your Earth weapons. I though he was going to cry."

"He's the sentimental type."

There was a long pause. Fernwyn moved to sit on the bed.

"Something's obviously bothering you, John. I think it would be better if you got it out in the open."

John sighed, and handed his bourbon to Fernwyn. He put his arm around her waist.

"It's this mission, Fernwyn. I don't know how much more of this I can take."

"One thing that drew me to this ship was the dedication and tenacity of the crew. You, especially. I rarely see this kind of resolve in the face of such odds, outside of the Rakhar anyway. If you represent humans as a whole I dare say you're doing a fine job of it."

"Thanks for the flattery, but everyone has their breaking point. I'm starting to fray around the edges. I'm bothered by nightmares almost every night. I've always been worried about losing members of the crew, but now that I've lost three that worry has grown into constant trepidation. I trust myself to take care of myself, but my greatest fear has already come true, that I'll fail to protect one of us. That fear is almost crippling, Fernwyn. I don't know how much longer I can push it aside. I'm becoming angry at Umber, angry at Seth. For months I was in love with the idea of the opportunity to embark upon this unbelievable adventure, to be the first to discover new people and planets, and I didn't care how difficult or cumbersome the mission would be. All I knew was that by accepting the mission I had the singular responsibility to see it through no matter what. I never imagined the depth of pain that it would entail." John began to cry. "I know it's not Seth's fault that his memory was damaged, but I can't help but feel angry about how much time we lost and effort we put forth because of that missing information. Stumbling into this mission as blind as we did was nothing but stupid! I can't believe we all haven't been killed by now."

"You're not giving yourself enough credit, John," said Fernwyn, taking his hand. "Think about everything that's gone right on the mission. You've overcome every single adversity that's been thrown at you and come out on top. Yes, there were some losses, and when a friend dies it's the greatest loss of all. But look where we are now. You repaired Seth's memory. You upgraded the ship's weapons. You even recovered your ship when anybody else would have considered it to be gone forever. You rescued Talvan right from under the nose of the enemy and lived to tell about it! Don't forget about Aldebaran, either. You helped save his life, and you gained a powerful ally by doing so."

"You're awfully nice to point that out, despite the fact that your own life is ruined."

"What happened with the SUF is based on a lie, John. I have to believe that success of this mission will let me clear my name and restore my life. What is for sure is that drowning your fears in alcohol and isolating yourself from people who need you isn't going to help anything. I know you're not willing to give up and go home; nobody on this ship is going to give up until we've done everything in our power to help Umber. If Talvan's right, and this mission goes well, all we have to do is sit back and watch the Zendreen grow weak and die. After the virus kicks in, the Umberians will be able to take back the planet with little or no resistance. And we'll be damn folk heroes."

John smiled. "My resolve hasn't wavered. I'm committed to this mission. I can't let the sacrifices of those we've lost be for nothing. I just can't wait until we can truly relax again. The prospect of such peace tears at my heart like nothing I've ever felt. I can hardly believe such happiness is even possible anymore."

"One more mission, John. One more. And then we will have it."

Eight hours later, John woke up. Fernwyn lay beside him, still asleep, her head tucked tightly into the pillow. Friday was nestled between them, equally placid. John carefully got out and went into the bathroom.

There, he brushed his teeth and took a shower. He paid close attention to his left leg, gently moving around the fresh wound as to not disturb the stitches. He tried to clear his mind of all the worries that distracted him, instead focusing on his hunger and what he might have for breakfast.

John turned off the water and realized he hadn't brought a towel into the bathroom with him. Such an act was never the norm, as the entire bathroom was used as a shower stall. This time, however, Fernwyn was in his bedroom. Despite having just shared a bed, they were not at the level of intimacy required for John to cross the room naked. He decided that Fernwyn probably wouldn't care about seeing his body so much as the cavalier nature of such an act, so he opened the door a crack and called to her.

"Fernwyn, are you awake?"

"Ki nare faice di yalai ker dan a cham mith tal reta porarte."

John realized he'd taken off his translator unit before showering.

"I left my translator off. Could you pass me it and a towel, please?"

Fernwyn got up, grabbed the requested items, and handed them to John. She waited until he'd installed the translator, and spoke.

"I said it's not easy to stay asleep in a room with all metal doors."

"Oh. Sorry."

"No problem. It's time to get up anyway. I think I'll go back to my room and freshen up."

"Okay. I'll see you down in the galley."

Fernwyn exited. John finished drying himself and got dressed. His favorite pair of jeans was still damp from the wash the previous night, so he chose a pair of black BDU pants instead. He armed himself, and exited into the hallway. One door down, Ray had just emerged from his quarters.

"Good morning," Ray said, smiling.

"Morning. How's it going?"

"I'm starved. You going to grab some breakfast?"
"Yeah."

John gestured ahead, and Ray led the way down the stairs and into the galley. Christie was there, pouring herself the first cup of coffee from a fresh pot.

"Morning, boys," she said.

"You're a veritable saint, you know that, Christie?" said John, grabbing a mug.

"I make coffee just about every morning."

"Well, don't think I didn't notice. Thanks."

Christie poured a cup for John and Ray, the latter man also offering his thanks. The three sat down at the table, savoring the welcome scent.

"Where is everybody?" asked Ray.

"Dana only went to sleep four hours ago, so I'm sure she's still out. It's not easy getting her to go off duty, you know."

"Who's minding the till?" asked John.

"Richter's up there now, with Aldebaran. I swear those two never sleep."

"They're getting along okay?"

"Are you kidding? I don't think they've exchanged more than a hundred words since they met. But, they seem to be very comfortable with each other's presence, sort of like two old friends who don't feel the need to fill moments of quiet with pointless banter."

"We've never had that problem," said Ray, grinning.

"That's because you don't know how to shut up," replied John.

"What? Remember the time you insisted on role playing for the entire weekend that one time up at the cabin? You dare to say I don't know how to shut up?"

"Yeah, but then we'd have never come up with the eight hundred pound gorilla, the Buddhist monkey, and the narcoleptic cynical sleeping bag."

"Who needs drugs when you've got nerd?" said Christie.

"Exactly," said Ray.

John smiled, then furrowed his brow. "What about Talvan?"

"I think he's asleep, too," said Christie, "deservedly so."

"Agreed. Unfortunately, we've only got four hours before we arrive at Umber, so we'd better get everybody up. We still have to plan the mission. Ray, think you can arrange some grub?"

"No problem," replied Ray.

"I'll go wake up Dana and Talvan. Nobody touch my coffee."

One hour later, the crew was gathered in the conference room. Talvan was working on a laptop computer, which was connected to the central system via a wireless card. Dana was seated next to him, struggling to stay awake. To her right, Ray and Fernwyn were discussing the finer points of wine tasting, while across the table John and Richter were going over the operation of the Phalanx. Aldebaran stood behind them, watching with interest. Christie crouched in the corner, scratching Tycho.

"So throw this selector switch," Richter was saying, "and you'll put the weapon into suppressed mode. The muzzle velocity will decrease by two-thirds, but the decibel rating will decrease by fifty."

John nodded in appreciation. "That might come in handy."

"Okay, I think that's the best we're going to do," said Talvan.

The room fell quiet. John nodded at Talvan.

"Go ahead with your presentation, please," he said.

"Dana and I were able to pull some old satellite pictures of the power station off of the net," said Talvan, putting the images up on the wall monitor. "As far as I know there have been no major changes to the structure. Let me explain what we're seeing here. The power station is located in a canyon. It's built on three ancient pyramids, seen here, here, and here, in a triangle formation."

"I guess Umberians don't care about history," said Richter.

"Actually, the power station is exclusive of the pyramids. They're acting as support pylons, yes, but they're topped with magnetic levitation platforms. The entire power station is floating a few inches above the pyramid tops. There's no chance of damaging the pyramids."

"Why go to all that trouble?" asked Christie.

"The power station uses cold fusion reactors and mercury-tritium transfer coils. Seismic tremors can disrupt those processes, decreasing the efficiency of the generation. The magnetic levitation cushions the station from occasional low grade tremors and anything else that might create seismic activity. The placement of the station below the rim of the canyon helps decrease the effect of weather and wind."

"Impressive engineering," said John.

"We are talking about Umberians," Fernwyn said, nodding.

"This is the one and only side picture we have," began Talvan. "As you can see, the pyramids are one hundred meters tall and the station is seventy-five. It consists of five levels except for the reactor rooms which are three stories each. The upper level is the command section. There are three separate parts to the top floor, each over a pyramid in orientation. The three parts are connected by glass-covered walkways. In the center is a landing platform, which is where the Zendreen are most likely to land for their inspection. The northern section of the top floor is the main control room."

"What about the interior layout?" asked John.

"We were unable to find any information about the interior. The only thing I can tell you about it is that there are at least a hundred Umberians working there. There's something about that, too..."

"Go on."

"There was a nasty rumor going around through the underground. The station can be run at ninety-nine percent efficiency, if you ignore certain safety protocols. Workers who have to be near the transfer coils under these conditions would experience severe health problems including disfigurement. Rumor has it that the Zendreen are doing just that."

"So we should stay away from the transfer coils?"

"Short term exposure shouldn't be harmful, but I can only speak for Umberians, not humans. Just keep in mind that you might run into some people that are... you know."

"Messed up."

"Yeah. And that's about all we know."

John nodded. "Okay, thank you Talvan. Richter, would you like to go into more detail about our plan?"

"Sure," began Richter. "Like we were discussing last night, we'll have two teams on the ground and one team operating the ship. Bailey, Tolliver, and Rylie will mount the feint attack on one of the pylons. Scherer, Aldebaran and I will go after the commander and his staff. Dana and Talvan will remain aboard the Faith to provide transportation and cover. Here's the order of battle. First, we wait above the power station, hidden from sight, until the commander's ship arrives. After it docks, my team will be dropped nearby. Bailey's team will land near the pylon and wait for the signal to begin their assault. When I give the signal, we'll neutralize any resistance from the ship and capture the commander, using the assault below to divert any additional Zendreen security. My team will announce our intention to hold the commander hostage until our demands our met, or we'll kill him and destroy the power station."

"Why would the resistance want to destroy the power station?" asked Dana.

"Such an act would limit the Zendreen fleet's ability to refuel in that part of the world," said Talvan, "so it's not an implausible resistance target."

"Indeed," said Richter. "So, we'll open a negotiation with the commander. The trick is that we have no intention of waiting until our so-called demands are met. Once the virus has been deployed, we'll make it look like we're giving up in the face of impossible odds, and withdraw."

"Won't that look too transparent?" asked Ray.

"Not if we pretend that grabbing the commander was a secondary objective. That way, giving up on holding him hostage won't seem strange. We can add to this ploy if Bailey's team radios us and tells us they can't destroy the pylon. If they think we've simply run out of time, then they'll believe it when we let them go."

"But we're not actually destroying the pylon," said Christie.

"Right, you're just going to assault the position. If you actually kill all resisting Zendreen, great, but we're going to let the Zendreen think that part of the mission failed as well."

"If we all get killed, I bet they'll believe it," said Fernwyn.

"Technically speaking, all of us can get killed and still accomplish the mission. If the virus is deployed successfully, that is."

"Great for the Umberians," said John. "What else?"

"That's about it for now. Any questions?"

Everyone looked at each other in silence for a moment. Christie shrugged.

"I have plenty of questions," she said, "but nothing we can answer right now."

"We'll just have to play it by ear," said John.

Richter nodded. "We should all be used to gathering essential intel in the field by now. Remember, confidence is key. If you have doubts, focus on our recent successes. We've accomplished more than we could have imagined, considering the challenges we've faced. This mission could be the most perilous so far, but we have to believe that we have the ability to accomplish it."

"Indeed," said John. "I have faith in each of you. Reckless or not, this mission could spell the end of the occupation. We can't give up now."

"Want me to cue up some inspiring music?" asked Ray. "Something emotional from Saving Private Ryan, perhaps?"

"Also, never underestimate the power of the smart-ass. Everybody clear? Get your shit together, we're arriving in three hours."

## 29.

Cab Saribalos looked up at the night sky. He took a deep breath, and sighed. He'd missed sunset, but Umber's single, lifeless moon was rising in the east. That was almost as nice. East was the expansive tract of the canyon, and if he ignored the usual sounds emanating from the massive power station behind him, he could almost imagine himself alone. He wasn't, of course, and he would only have to turn his head a few degrees in either direction to catch a glance of one of the Zendreen guards. They tolerated his nightly pause at half-shift because Cab never caused trouble. Not like the ones up on the power conduits.

Cab was lucky. Lucky, because he was an elevator mechanic before the war, and lucky, because he all but volunteered for the job at the station shortly thereafter. When seen as willing servants, the Zendreen treated an Umberian almost like, well, an Umberian.

There were eleven elevators in the power station, if you counted the anti-grav cargo lift, so there was always something to do. Even a twelve hour shift went by quickly when pyramid three's elevator needed a track stabilized, pylon two's shorted out a display console, and the control room elevator's cables were out of sync. Rarely was there any real down time except for meal breaks and the ten minute half-shift break Cab was currently enjoying.

"Hey Cabrios, you want a smoke?"

Hephili, Cab's one and only assistant, emerged from inside the pyramid. The two guards glanced at him dutifully, and returned to their conversation.

Cab smiled and shook his head. "No, thanks. I think I caught too much of a whiff of that electrical fire."

"Sometimes I wonder if you appreciate the lengths I have to go to get these things."

Hephili lit a home-made cigarillo and puffed on it. Cab shrugged. There was always some sort of deal going down in the barracks. Cab and Hephili shared a relatively private eight-man room in one corner of what used to be the museum. There was easy access to the larger sleeping areas, however. The Zendreen hadn't found it necessary to lock down the barracks for quite some time.

Despite the active trade in tobacco products, the barracks were off limits to smokers. The Zendreen didn't care one way or the other, but the barracks converted from museum sections still contained priceless antiques, artifacts, and hieroglyphics. The younger workers objected at first, but the older Umberians had insisted on a smoking ban. If the planet was ever liberated, the museum would be reopened.

"The Commander will be here soon," Hephili said.

Cab grunted. "Right on time. So what?"

"Today they're supposed to test the devices. The Commander is set to oversee."

"Shit. Poor bastards."

"Look at it this way. If they work, they might be moved out of the conduits."

"And into the labyrinths. Better the devices kill them."

"That's pretty cold, even for you, Cab. I..."

There were two dull pops. Cab and Hephili looked around, mildly surprised. They realized with much greater anxiety that the two Zendreen guards had collapsed.

"What the hell?" whispered Cab reflexively.

Three figures loomed out of the darkness. Cab and Hephili drew back in shock. A lithe, wiry female was in the lead, followed by a tall male. The last one was a shorter female, with more curves. All three were well armed. They looked like Umberians, but that couldn't be confirmed due to the hats they were wearing.

"Quoe num bulwa ist mir enturi?" said the first woman.

"Wh... what?" stammered Hephili.

"Stapha. Um, what, er, how many guards interior?"

"You're speaking Residerian?" asked Cab, astonished. "Who are you?"

The man gestured to the first woman. She nodded, and handed Cab a translator device. Cab installed the earpiece.

"How's that?" asked the woman.

"Better. Your Umberian is a little rusty."

"We shouldn't waste time out here," said the man.

"My name is Fernwyn Rylie," said the first woman. "This is Ray Bailey and Christie Tolliver. We're with the Umberian underground."

"Since when does the underground employ Residerians?" asked Cab.

"Since the SUF decided it's not an indifferent entity any more," said Christie.

Ray moved past Cab and Hephili and into the doorway. He confirmed that they were still alone and turned back to the locals. "How many Zendreen guards inside?"

"Usually about a hundred," said Cab.

Ray's expression fell. "Holy shit."

"How many between here and the anti-grav platform?" asked Fernwyn.

"Fifteen to twenty."

"We might actually be able to handle that many," said Ray, "if we can keep the element of surprise."

"What do you mean, handle that many?" asked Cab. "What are you trying to accomplish here?"

Fernwyn grinned. "Just looking to cause some trouble. The Zendreen need to realize the underground isn't just a nuisance anymore."

"Will you help us?" asked Christie.

Cab shrugged. "If I can. Hephili?"

The others turned around. Hephili was almost out of sight, running as fast as he could down the canyon floor.

"Should we go after him?" asked Ray.

"Don't worry about him. How can I help?"

"Guide us to the best defensible position once the shooting starts," began Fernwyn, "and keep your head down. We need to occupy the Zendreen for some time. Killing all of them is only a bonus goal."

"Okay. I think I know a good spot."

A voice came through on the three strangers' radio, loud enough for Cab to hear.

"Rylie, this is Scherer. The commander's craft has just landed. What's your status, over."

"We're about to begin our main assault, over." replied Fernwyn.

"Copy that. There's no room left on the landing platform, so we're being dropped off on the roof about a hundred yards away. If we can get inside, we'll proceed to the control room that way. Keep us updated, over."

"Roger, out."

"So you're trying to assassinate the commander," said Cab. "Good luck, but someone else will just take his place."

"Let us worry about that," said Ray. "For now, we've got our own problems."

Fernwyn deactivated the suppressing function on her Phalanx. "Let's go."

Cab led the others inside. After a short corridor, the interior of the pyramid opened up into a large atrium. Stone walls made up most of the architecture, but more modern materials were in abundance. Archways about three meters tall led into other areas. In the center of the atrium about seventy yards away was an elevator shaft leading up. Several Zendreen were standing near it, socializing. A few Umberians worked here and there. Cab began warning them off visually.

"Where are the rest of the Zendreen?" asked Ray.

"Their barracks are on the other side of that elevator," replied Cab. "We should take cover in the gift shop!"

Cab's statement ended on a high note as the Zendreen had just taken notice of the visitors. Fernwyn and Ray raised their weapons and fired. The guards scattered and began returning fire. Brilliant blue energy shots streaked across the atrium as the four interlopers ran for the long-since disused gift shop and the hard cover it offered. Christie covered Cab as he stumbled and she scored a hit on one of the guards.

"This isn't a dead-end in here, is it?" she cried.

"No, there's a back door."

"Good, we don't want to get boxed in."

The team ducked inside the shop. There was a large stone counter and several rows of stone shelves. The large entrance to the shop offered a good view of the atrium, and Fernwyn and Ray chose firing positions they liked. Cab hit the deck as Christie crouched behind the stone counter and joined her friends in the fusillade.

"Keep 'em busy, but watch your ammo!" shouted Ray.

"No problem!"

"We're in position."

Dana's voice filled the cargo bay over the intercom. John, Aldebaran, and Richter readied themselves as Talvan looked on.

"Roger that," said John. "Talvan, bring the lights down."

Talvan nodded, and used the console to completely darken the bay. John hit the button to open the ramp. As the ramp descended, fresh, warm air from Umber blew inside. The ramp made contact with the surface of the station with a slight bump.

From their vantage point, the team could see the roof of the entire station, with the three sections forming a triangle and the landing platform in the center. The Zendreen transport ship was on the platform, and as the team descended onto the roof they could see several of the insectoid aliens walking from it to a doorway. Ambient light from several sources including the landing platform's guide beacons illuminated the area, but the section the team was on was relatively dark. They crouched on the roof until the figures had entered the doorway. Two Zendreen guards appeared from the ship and took up positions near the airlock.

John, who was on point, looked around. He could see a hatch of some sort nearby. He signaled to the others and motioned toward it. Aldebaran and Richter nodded. John gave a thumbs-up to the unseen Talvan, and the sound of the ramp closing was heard. Moments later, the invisible Faith moved away with a rush of air.

Staying low, John led the team to the hatch. There was writing on it, and although John and Richter couldn't read it, Aldebaran nodded in approval when he did. John located the handle and pulled. After a hearty effort, the hatch swung up and open. A ladder descended to a long shaft below, and one by one the men entered the station. Richter closed the hatch carefully.

"This is an elevator shaft," said Aldebaran quietly.

"It certainly looks like one," John said, looking around.

"Which floor do you want to take?" asked Richter.

"I don't know. Aldebaran?"

"Any one other than the fifth floor," replied Aldebaran. "If we encounter resistance immediately it would be better to start further down."

"How do you figure?" asked John.

"It gives us more choices for falling back," said Richter.

Aldebaran nodded. "Right."

John held onto the ladder with one arm and withdrew a flashlight from his vest. He aimed the light down the shaft.

"Looks like the car is on the first level," he said. "Let's get going."

The three men descended the ladder. There were no exits to the fourth or third levels, so they stopped at level two. The elevator car remained motionless a few feet below them. John fumbled around until he found the override switch, and the outer doors opened. Peeking around the corner, John confirmed that there was no one there. The team climbed into the corridor. John closed the doors as they took stock of their location. There were two exits from the corridor, one to the southwest and one to the northeast. Aldebaran read aloud the writing on the latter.

"Transfer Coils Section One."

"Okay," said John. "We can use that to get to the control..."

John was interrupted by an alarm. The klaxon rang loudly for a few seconds, then muted itself. Red lights set into the wall at head level began to flash.

"Looks like the others have begun," said Richter.

"Let's hurry, then."

The team entered the transfer coils section. It was a massive corridor, running from a hundred yards behind them to a hundred yards in front of them. The corridor was three stories tall. The elevator shaft ran up along the outside wall and ended in the room they'd just come from. Several conduits flanked one larger conduit that ran horizontally through the center of the corridor. They hummed with energy. Steam emanated from coolant piping that intersected the conduits in places.

The three men waited for their eyes to adjust a bit more to the dim light, and began moving forward.

"I feel strange," said Richter.

"It's the transfer coils," said Aldebaran. "It must be."

John stopped suddenly. A man was standing in front of him. He appeared to be Umberian, but it was hard to tell. His face was scarred and blackened. His eyes glinted, and he regarded the team with ire. John started to say something when he noticed more men stepping out of the darkness. Aldebaran and Richter took up defensive positions behind John, slowly raising their weapons. There were quickly more than twenty figures surrounding them.

"Who are you?" the man said, his voice raspy.

"We're with the resistance," said Aldebaran. "We're heading for the control room. We need to get there as soon as possible."

"Wolshit. More likely you're merc scum. The Zendreen may not have much use for them around here but it's not the first time we've seen them."

"If we were mercs, why would we come down here alone?" asked John. "You obviously outnumber us."

"Because mercs wouldn't care about cutting slaves like us down with those weapons."

"Why confront us, then? Are you weary of living?"

"You can't really call it that."

"We are part of the resistance," said Aldebaran. "We're here to kidnap the Zendreen commander. We're here to help you."

"Prove it."

"You hear that alarm that just went off? Those are our colleagues, attacking one of the pyramids. They're providing a diversion for us, but we've got to get to the control room before the commander decides to leave."

"They're not mercs," said another man, stepping forward.

"Good, then let us pass."

"No. I recognize you. You're Aldebaran."

Shouts of outrage came from the crowd. The first man stepped closer.

"You are Aldebaran," he said. "For the love of the core, it is you."

"Do I know you?" asked Aldebaran.

"Know us? Know us? This is the crew of the Fortunate Son, you bastard!"

Aldebaran's eyes grew wide in shock. He took a deep breath.

"What's going on?" asked John.

Aldebaran leaned in close to John and Richter. "On the count of three," he whispered, "open fire and run like hell."

"What? Why?"

"Just do it."

"But they're Umberians," whispered Richter.

"They're also about to kill us. One, two..."

"Didn't you ever wonder what happened to the Umberians you turned into the Zendreen?" the first man shouted. "The ones who fled? The ones who resisted? Ones like us are not looked upon too kindly by the Zendreen! You cursed us to work in this hell. Six years, Aldebaran. Six years since you and your sons of bitches pirate friends captured us. You can shoot if you dare, but you can't kill all of us before we get to you."

"Three!"

———

The control room of the power station was a flurry of activity. It was a large room with a vaulted glass ceiling. There was a large picture window on one end that overlooked the canyon. There were several work stations and consoles on two split levels, and every one of them was occupied. The Zendreen overseers were working with the military visitors in an attempt to get a handle on what was happening. Initial chaos soon turned into a basic understanding of the situation. A lieutenant moved from place to place, speaking with personnel. He was new to the commander's entourage, but so far he was as competent as one of his rank should be, even if he was a bit stuffy. He approached the commander and bowed slightly before speaking.

"The east pyramid is under attack, sir," he said. "It's a small force of five or six, most likely resistance soldiers."

"What could such a small effort be trying to accomplish?" the commander said, furrowing his shiny green brow.

"Unknown at this time. The resistance has never attempted to hit a hard target before."

"Maybe they've changed their definition of a hard target, lieutenant. Central Command continues to ignore my reports about the growing threat, so the threat grows."

The lieutenant seemed either amused, insulted, or both.

"With all due respect, sir," he said, "even if the resistance is gaining more resources, you don't seriously think they could ever disrupt our occupation, do you?"

"Disrupt, no, but every Umberian in the underground is one not working for us, and one trying to convince others to join them. We cannot tolerate them, no matter how futile their efforts may be."

"What of the ship that attacked the transport near Mount Tarsus a few days ago?"

The commander stopped regarding a console and looked at the lieutenant.

"How do you know about that? That's supposed to be top secret intelligence."

"Rumor and gossip are more powerful than a classification."

"The colonial affairs division is working on that. You don't need to worry about it."

"So you don't deny it took place?"

"I suppose I can't."

An overseer shouted out above the din.

"Guards are reporting a heavy exchange of fire," he yelled. "They're waiting until they can get some grenades on line before they advance."

"Sir, we should play it safe and get you back on the transport," said the lieutenant.

The commander shook his head. "I refuse to let this annoyance prevent my appointed inspection. We will quash the combatants and proceed as normal."

"What kind of weapons fire is the enemy reported to be using?" the lieutenant asked a worker.

"Projectile weapons, either magrail or percussion," an overseer replied.

"You see?" said the commander. "They're still as under armed as ever."

The lieutenant shrugged. "They're still deadly in trained hands. They've managed to stall any counter attack, haven't they? I think we should..."

"There's a report of weapons fire from Transfer Coil Section One," an overseer shouted.

"How many guards between here and there?" asked the commander, standing up.

"I don't know."

"Find out!"

"I've lost contact with them, sir."

"Shit! Lieutenant, get our team together and prepare to withdraw to the..."

The main entrance to the control room opened. Three figures rushed inside, weapons tucked tightly into their shoulders. Five Zendreen went for their weapons and were cut down in an eardrum-shattering instant. Two overseers ran for alternate exits and were also killed. The remaining Zendreen froze.

The figures appeared to be Umberian. Each wielded a projectile weapon, only one of which was familiar to the commander. The men were covered in grime and non-Zendreen blood, the whites of their eyes standing out in stark contrast. The man in the lead was wearing clothing still identifiable as a uniform of the defunct Umberian military, and he was the first to speak after the echoes faded.

"Drop your weapons," he said in loud but measured tones. "Everyone keep your extremities where we can see them."

The commander and the lieutenant could see that resistance was deadly, and complied. The other surviving Zendreen followed suit. One of the other men secured the doors, and motioned for the third one to do the same with the side entrances. They spread out but kept their weapons pointed unwaveringly at the Zendreen.

"I am Commander Krichilik," said the commander. "What is you purpose here?"

"All in good time, commander," said the lead man, his eyes shifting slightly to watch his friends.

The other men spoke in a language the commander had never heard before. His translator earpiece only managed to decipher the word "here" from one of them.

"If you want to live through this, you'll start communicating with us," the lieutenant said.

The commander waved the lieutenant into silence. "Take it easy," he began. "Nobody wants to get shot. We're on their schedule now."

"Everybody move to the far corner," the first man said.

The other men joined the first at the center of the control room as the Zendreen complied. The man with the Res-ZorCon rifle made a radio call. This time, the commander's translator came up with "to," "what," and "status." He listened to the reply, then turned to the leader.

"We're holding," he said.

"Good," said the leader. "Now then. My name is Temerity. We're with the resistance movement, if you haven't figured that out yet. Commander, you are to be taken from here to a secure location where you will be our prisoner. You will be released when our demands are met. The rest of you will be allowed to live after we depart safely."

"The colonial administration will never negotiate for my release," said Krichilik. "Even I am expendable."

"Maybe, but if this control room is destroyed it will compromise the power station, to say the least. It might take weeks to get the station back online if this little device were to go off."

The Umberian withdrew a small purple sphere from his pocket and displayed it.

"Very well. You do realize that half of the occupation army is already on their way here, right?"

"So what? That changes nothing. A standoff is a standoff."

There was a pause as Krichilik considered his next move. The three Umberians remained unwaveringly alert.

"I want to speak to you alone," Krichilik said.

The leader raised an eyebrow. "Why?"

"It will become clear."

Shrugging his shoulders slightly, the leader moved toward the nearest side exit.

"Don't try anything. You're worth much more to us alive and it would be a shame to..."

"Not you," Krichilik interrupted. "Him."

Krichilik pointed at the third man.

"Why me?" asked the third man.

"As I said, it will become clear."

## 30.

John led Krichilik into the side room, which turned out to be a lavatory. The Zendreen didn't seem to be concerned about cleanliness, at least to the same standard as Umberians. John tried to ignore the mess as he motioned for the commander to stand away from him. His unprotected ear was ringing and his eyes stung from sweat and blood, but the front sight of his rifle was clear as he settled it on the thorax of the Zendra.

"Okay, what's the game?" he asked.

"I know who you are, John Scherer."

"Nice to meet you," said John, barely hiding his astonishment.

"I can't let the others know about you. Your ship and your involvement is a matter classified to the highest level."

John lowered his rifle ever so slightly. "You want to deal."

"Obviously I can't let myself be kidnapped. I'll offer you a simple trade."

"You're not in a position to trade. We'll be out of here before your help arrives."

Krichilik drew himself up onto the sink counter and took some weight off of his legs. John prepared himself to fire, but the action was non-threatening.

"Looks like you had some difficulty with the Umberian workers on your way here," said Krichilik.

"A tragic misunderstanding."

"Really? Tell me, how many did you have to kill?"

"What's your point, Commander?"

"Those Umberians attacked you because we've implanted them with a mind control device. They were acting on a standing order, residing subconsciously, to protect us against threats. You'll have to face them again to escape."

"Then their deaths are your fault. It changes nothing."

"If you let me go, I'll deactivate the control devices. You'll be able to escape without harming more of your own."

"Great, but then our mission is nothing but a big waste of time, and those workers we already killed will have died for nothing. Sorry, no deal. Get up, we're leaving."

"If you take me, you'll never see Arianna Ferro again!"

John involuntarily lowered his rifle, gasping in shock at the Zendra's statement. The sounds and smells of the room faded away and he forgot all about his aching muscles. The insectoid creature before him suddenly appeared to be more than a bizarre alien, gaining a malevolent subtext that went beyond physical fear. John could accept that the Zendreen's intelligence gathering had gained his name and the intent of the Faith's mission. The prospect of Ari being alive was far past anything he could remotely embrace.

"Bullshit. She died when your fleet destroyed the way station."

"Not so. We recovered her alive from the wreckage."

"I saw the explosions, Commander. Nothing larger than a... garbage can came out of it."

John kicked over the object he'd just described. Krichilik laughed, a deep, disturbing chortle.

"Not so. The control room survived. The Umberians designed it as a self-contained escape pod. Good old Umberian ingenuity. Your friend was very badly injured, but we were able to sustain her."

John let go of his rifle with his left hand and drew Ari's Glock. He slung the rifle over his shoulder without letting the pistol leave the commander's body. With his right hand, he unscrewed the cap on his canteen, removed it from the belt carrier, and took a swig of the liquid inside. Before he swallowed, a thought occurred to him. He strode up to the Zendra and spit in his face.

"Fuck you," John said, scowling.

Krichilik was briefly surprised, but recovered and lunged at John. Jumping back, John restored his stance with his pistol. Krichilik stopped.

"It doesn't matter if you believe me or not," he said, wiping the water from his head. "She's alive. How else could I know your name?"

"I find it much more likely that your knowledge was gained from another source, like the mercs you've been sending after us. Besides, if you do have her, I stand to gain from taking you with us. I might be able to set up a hostage trade."

"I have a better idea. Stop helping the Umberian resistance. You're nothing but an added annoyance anyway. I don't know what the Umberians are paying you for your help, but it's not enough if you die. Cut and run while you still can, and we can make arrangements to have Ferro returned to you. She's worth little to us except as a way to get rid of you."

"She's valuable to me, but not my crew. What about money?"

"So, you are mercs. Whatever the Umberians have promised you, we'll triple it."

John looked at Krichilik. He furrowed his brow and frowned.

"Prove to me that you have Ferro," he said, "and you've got a deal."

"We were going to take her to our research facility to study her anatomy. We didn't want to miss the chance to study a new race, but I'm sure I can convince my superiors that this is a better use of her. If we go back into the control room, I can get the captain of the ship she's on to send us a video feed. Then you can see for yourself."

"After you then, Commander."

John motioned for Krichilik to move, and followed him out of the restroom. In the control room, Richter and Aldebaran were still holding the Zendreen staff at bay.

"What's going on?" asked Richter.

"Call off the assault team," John replied. "We're bugging out."

"But the charges are almost set!"

"I just made a deal with the commander. We can't keep that deal if those charges go off. Call them off."

"That wasn't what we planned," said Aldebaran.

"This is a better arrangement, trust me. Commander, make the call to that ship. Nobody else move."

Keeping Krichilik covered, John allowed him to move to a communications console. John joined Richter and Aldebaran.

"Rylie, this is Richter, over."

"Rylie here," said Fernwyn's voice.

"Abort the mission. Leave the charges unarmed or take them back if you can. Retreat to the LZ and prepare for evac, over."

"Roger, out."

Krichilik spoke to someone over the console. The crew's translator units failed to translate all but a few words, but they weren't paying any attention to the conversation.

"What's going on, John?" asked Aldebaran. "What kind of deal are you talking about?"

"We're not taking the commander with us," replied John. "The Zendreen have offered to triple what the Umberians are paying us."

"You can't trust these guys," said Richter. "We should still take him."

"This isn't about money," Aldebaran said. "This is about my people."

John laughed. "Oh, like you weren't going to accept payment for your efforts."

"It would be a just reward. Accept money from the Zendreen, and we're no better than the Black Crest."

"I never claimed to be. And as for you wanting to help your people, don't make me laugh again. You'd sell your own mother to the highest..."

An energy blast hit John in the shoulder, knocking him into the wall. Richter grabbed John and dragged him down behind a console as Aldebaran dove for cover of his own. Krichilik had grabbed a pistol hidden nearby and continued to fire on the team. The other Zendreen scrambled to recover their dropped weapons. Richter and Aldebaran began to engage targets as fast as they could. John examined his wound.

"Don't hit the commander," he groaned.

"Your deal is done with, John!" shouted Aldebaran.

Richter ducked and activated his radio. "Andrews, this is Richter, come in!"

"Dana here," said Dana's voice.

"Get the ship over to the control room and get us out of here, now!"

"Roger that. Where's the nearest hatch?"

"Make one!"

Richter resumed firing. Computer consoles and lights were blown out as each side exchanged fire desperately. John decided that his injury wasn't bad enough to prevent him from fighting, and he pulled himself up to join his friends in the fusillade. The noise was unbelievable.

"Where are you in relation to that large single window?" asked Dana.

"We're five meters to the south of it," replied Richter.

"Okay. Keep your heads down for a second."

A tremendous crash washed out all other sounds in the control room as the Faith's unseen thirty millimeter cannon shot through the window. For a moment, all firing ceased. John, Richter, and Aldebaran looked over to see the cargo bay appear as the ramp began to open. Talvan was inside, and waved hello.

"Take cover, you idiot!" Richter yelled.

The Zendreen resumed firing. Talvan ran out of sight as some of them picked him as a new target. Richter noticed a small problem.

"Dana, you're going to have to get her closer," he said. "The end of the ramp is still ten meters out."

"Get away from the window," Dana replied. "This is going to get messy."

Richter fired the last few rounds from his Phalanx, dropped it, and grabbed John.

"Get out of the way, Aldebaran!" Richter yelled.

Aldebaran dove in the same direction that Richter and John were stumbling. The Faith's nose crashed into the side of the station, ripping the metal supports from the walls and destroying some of the overhead glass emplacements. The cascading debris caromed off of the ship, disrupting the invisibility shield. The Zendreen were so surprised that they temporarily stopped firing.

"Run for it!" screamed Richter, drawing his pistol.

The friends burst toward the ramp, with all three of them firing towards the Zendreen. One by one they cleared the two foot gap and ran up the ramp.

"We're aboard!" Richter cried. "Get us out of here!"

John hit the button to close the ramp as Dana backed the ship out. The three of them took pot shots at Zendreen until the ramp closed and encased them in silence. John immediately grabbed his radio.

"Fernwyn, this is John, over."

"Yo," Fernwyn's voice replied.

"What's your status?"

Talvan appeared from behind some boxes and ran over. Richter and Aldebaran looked at John's wound.

"We've disengaged the Zendreen, but they're pursuing us. We have an Umberian leading us to an alternate exit."

"So you're all right?"

"A bit low on ammo, but yes."

"Roger that. We're ready to pick you up."

"Okay. We'll call you when we get outside."

"Don't be long, Fernwyn. The Zendreen aren't playing nice."

"My primary is out!"

Fernwyn slung her Phalanx over her shoulder and drew her pistol. In the long, cramped hallway, the only cover were small alcoves barely large enough for the combatants. Fernwyn, Ray, and Christie were leapfrogging from alcove to alcove, an effective but ammo consuming technique. Cab had long since fled without stopping after guiding the team to the escape tunnel. Both Ray and Christie had already depleted their rifles and were rapidly following suit with their sidearms.

The Zendreen were using the same technique to move forward, but at a high cost. Insectoid bodies were piling up, and the living were using the dead as cover. Ray was dismayed to discover that while Nathalier's energy pistol was deadly, it didn't penetrate a Zendreen corpse. Despite this, he was reluctant to switch to his revolver in fear of the increased reload time. Nathalier's pistol held one hundred shots per battery pack.

The passageway took a sharp right turn, and for a moment the firing ceased.

"I hope Cab was right about this being an exit!" said Ray

"I can feel fresh air," said Fernwyn.

"I wish we could put some sort of barrier between us and the enemy," Christie said, changing magazines.

Fernwyn stopped running and turned to Ray.

"Good idea," she said. "Ray, hand me your weapon."

Ray did so. Fernwyn adjusted the power settings on the pistol.

"Are you going to overload it?" Ray asked.

"No, but I can fire all of the remaining energy in the battery at once. Get in front of me."

Christie and Ray moved up the tunnel. Fernwyn aimed at the ceiling at a forty-five degree angle and depressed the trigger. The pistol whined for a couple of seconds before a bright flash of plasma slammed into the stone. A small cascade of rock fell down, creating an eighteen inch high pile of rubble.

"Well, it was worth a shot," Fernwyn said, tossing the pistol to Ray.

"I guess so," replied Ray, reloading the weapon.

A Zendra peeked around the corner, and Fernwyn tagged it in the head. It was followed by another soldier firing randomly around the bend. The team resumed their hurried pace as the shots flew by.

"I see stars!" Christie yelled. "Run for it!"

With a final burst of speed, the three friends cleared the pyramid and ran out onto the canyon floor. Their surroundings were quiet, and a warm breeze wafted around. Fernwyn turned around and examined the doorway.

"Come on, Rylie," said Ray.

"There has to be some sort of door here," said Fernwyn. "Here we go."

Touching a metal switch, Fernwyn activated an iron portcullis. The heavy barrier slammed into place. Fernwyn shot the switch as well as a similar panel on the other side of the bars.

"That won't slow them down for long," said Christie.

"Dana, this is Fernwyn, come in, over."

"Dana here," said Dana over the radio. "Where are you?"

"We're on the surface, where are you?"

"Above. I don't see you. Give me your location."

"We're on the west side of the southwest pyramid. We're moving south. Look for us to the..."

Fernwyn trailed off. Something down the canyon had grabbed her attention. A massive rumbling preceded the appearance of a gigantic tank, about two hundred meters away. The tracks were at least ten meters high, and a single squat turret brought the total size to about twelve. It was flanked on either side by two mechs, and several dozen dismounted infantry.

"Rylie," began Dana, "be advised we have multiple enemy units to the south."

"Thanks, Dana, we see them. You wanna get down here and pick us up or what?"

"Stay put if you can, we'll find you."

The tank turret turned toward the pyramid. Fernwyn, Ray, and Christie pressed themselves up against the sloped wall.

"Does it see us?" asked Christie, terrified.

Before her companions could reply, the tank fired. A ball of energy appeared from the muzzle and moved forward slowly. The ball grew in size and began to pick up speed, rapidly becoming larger than the entire pyramid. The team ducked down as the energy hit them in a crashing wave. It did them no harm.

"What the hell?" said Ray.

"Look!" said Christie, pointing into the sky.

The Reckless Faith was visible, passing one hundred feet above.

"Dana, this is Ray! The invisibility shield is down!"

"What? Are you sure?" asked Dana.

"Yes, I'm sure, I'm looking right at the ship!"

The tank fired again, this time a directed energy beam. A split second later, the mechs and infantry joined in, and a hellish amount of fire rocked the Faith. The ship pitched away and gained altitude as the main cannon and thirty millimeter returned fire. As the ship turned, the port laser banks took over. The fire had no apparent effect on the enemy.

"Fernwyn, you've got to head north," said Dana, her voice strained. "We can't land here."

"Roger that," said Fernwyn. "We'll meet up with you somewhere else."

"Shit son of a bitch," said Ray.

The team changed direction and ran to the north. Christie looked up again and spotted several Zendreen aircraft far above.

"This is going to get worse before it gets better," she said.

As the team approached the corner of the pyramid, a hovering skiff crossed their path. It was about the size of a city bus, with a semi-covered deck and two articulated guns. Fernwyn, Ray, and Christie raised their weapons but quickly noticed that Cab was at the controls.

"Get in!" Cab yelled.

Behind them, the portcullis exploded. Fernwyn began firing at the Zendreen that stumbled through the smoking door as Ray and Christie leapt aboard the skiff. Ray spun around and covered Fernwyn as she followed them onto the deck.

"We're aboard!" Fernwyn cried.

Cab nodded and steered the skiff away. He gained altitude and cleared the edge of the canyon. The terrain was high desert badlands, illuminated by the plasma and laser flashes of the battle between the Faith and several Zendreen aircraft.

"Man those deck guns!" Cab shouted.

Fernwyn dashed over to the rear gun while Ray took the one on the bow. Christie joined Cab at the controls.

"We can't outrun them, right?" she asked.

Cab gritted his teeth. "Ha! No."

Despite this admonition, Cab leaned on the accelerator and pushed the skiff as fast as it could go. The warm wind whipped across the deck, making conversation difficult.

Christie keyed her radio. "Dana, this is Christie. We're aboard a hovercraft heading west."

"I see you," replied Dana. "There's no way we can pick you up with all of these fighters on our ass."

"Hurry up and nail them, then."

"Your friends better think of something quick," said Cab. "As soon as those ships spot us we're done for."

"What about our famous Route 93 trick?" shouted Ray.

"This thing is too big for that!" replied Christie.

"Yeah, but we can jump from the deck onto the ramp."

"Dana, at the earliest possible time we've got to maneuver up to the ramp."

"Roger that. Continue on your current course and we'll..."

The rest of Dana's transmission was lost as plasma blasts began raining down on the skiff. Fernwyn returned fire on the Zendreen craft that had fired. The deck guns were also plasma, but the Zendreen ship easily avoided the shots.

"Can't we go any faster?" asked Christie.

"I wish we could," said Cab.

The skiff was hit twice. Everyone but Cab was knocked over, and he struggled to stabilize the vehicle. Fernwyn leapt to her feet and grabbed the deck gun. Before she could fire, the Zendreen ship exploded and crashed.

Fernwyn looked on in astonishment as her own ship streaked past and banked around.

"Who the hell is flying my ship?" she said.

"Hey Rylie," said John over the radio.

"Scherer? Who said you could take my ship?"

"You've been holding out on me. This thing handles like a dream."

"You break it, you buy it."

"The Faith is on its way. I've got some more distracting to do."

John piloted the ship away. Ray pointed ahead.

"Here she comes!" he shouted.

The Faith swooped down and settled in front of the skiff. The laser banks and fifty caliber guns were blazing. Christie could barely hear her radio.

"Get ready to board," said Dana.

The ramp began to lower. Dana tried to match speed with the skiff. Plasma shots streaked by as Cab indelicately jammed the bow of the skiff into the mouth of the Faith's cargo bay. Sparks flew where metal ground against metal. When it stopped, there was no gap between the ships.

"Go!" Cab yelled.

The others clambered over the bow of the skiff and dropped into the cargo bay. Cab activated the autopilot and did the same. Upon reaching the ramp, he turned around and pushed against the skiff. It did not move.

"We're aboard," said Christie. "We need to get rid of the hovercraft. Bank the nose down."

"Roger that," said Dana.

"Grab onto something!"

Ray and Fernwyn grabbed onto the railing of the stairs. Christie took hold of a support rib. Cab continued to push on the skiff.

"Cab!" yelled Ray. "Grab onto the ship!"

"What do you think I'm doing?" Cab yelled back.

The Faith pitched forward. The skiff immediately dislodged from the cargo bay and plummeted toward the ground. Cab almost joined it but managed to grasp the edge of the ramp. Dana righted the ship and the ramp began to close. Ray ran forward and helped Cab inside.

"A little warning would have been nice!" Cab said, livid.

"We did warn you," replied Ray. "I guess you heard differently."

"Dana, this is Christie. Get us the hell out of here."

"My pleasure, Christie. John, are you ready to go?"

John's voice came in over the radio. "Aw, come on. I'm not done smoking bad guys."

"You can smoke them alone, then."

"Fine. Meet you spaceside?"

"If you can keep up."

---

"Repressurization complete."

With Dana's reassurance, John unbuckled his safety harness and opened the cockpit cover. The crew of the Faith, plus one unknown Umberian, entered the cargo bay. Fernwyn ran over and helped John down from her ship. His shoulder wound had begun to bleed through the field dressing. The others spontaneously broke into applause. John looked at the crew in surprise. Aldebaran, Richter, Christie, Ray, and Fernwyn looked almost as bad as he did. Dana's own exhaustion was clearly visible as well. Only Talvan seemed no worse for wear, but John knew he'd spent some time behind the lasers.

"Clap for everyone, not for me," John said.

"That's for successfully deploying the virus," said Talvan. "Aldebaran told me you spit it in the Commander's face."

"That's right."

"Perfect. With a hit like that he should become infectious very soon. If they don't catch on, the virus will continue to spread."

John walked over to Cab. "Who's your new friend?"

"This is Cab," said Christie, smiling.

"Cabrios Saribalos," Cab said, offering his hand.

"If not for Cab's help we wouldn't have gotten far."

"Well, Cab, thank you," said John. "But I'm afraid it would be somewhat impractical to return you home right now."

"That's quite all right," said Cab. "I'd rather not go back just yet."

John nodded and turned to Dana. "What's our status?"

"We're at maximum sub-light speed," began Dana, "headed toward the Residere system. The Zendreen fleet is scrambling to pursue us, but once we hit the engines we'll be long gone."

"Good. We'll lay low somewhere and monitor the net. Hopefully word of viral problems on Umber will begin to circulate and we'll know how we did. In the meantime, everybody get cleaned up and get some food and rest. Let Fernwyn and I worry about where we're going to hide when we get to Residere."

"Your dressing needs to be changed," said Richter.

"Soon. First I'd like to speak to Aldebaran and Fernwyn alone on the bridge."

The others looked confused but did not object. John climbed the stairs as Aldebaran and Fernwyn followed him. Once on the bridge, John sat in the pilot's chair and activated the superluminal drive. He stood up and began checking other stations.

"What's up?" asked Fernwyn.

"I'm glad to see you're all right," John replied. "I didn't like splitting up for this mission. I was worried about you."

"Same here. Let's just hope it wasn't a waste of time."

"Indeed."

"That was some impressive flying. I didn't think I'd given you nearly enough instruction."

"You hadn't. I only made it look good."

John continued to check the ship's systems. Friday entered the bridge and asked John for attention. John sat down and allowed the cat to jump into his lap.

"So why did you want to talk to us alone?" asked Aldebaran.

John's visage became serious. He sighed, and spoke quietly.

"The Zendreen Commander told me something rather unbelievable. I wish I could dismiss it as nothing but the desperate lies of a cornered rat, but I can't. He said that Ari is still alive."

Fernwyn gaped in shock.

"That's impossible," she said.

"That's what I said," John replied, nodding. "The Commander said some things that make me wonder, though. For one thing, he knew my name. I suppose it's possible, with the sheer amount of running around we've done, that he could have gotten it from the Black Crest or another espionage source, but it seems unlikely. He claims they rescued Ari from the wreckage of the way station. He said the control room was a self-contained escape pod."

"I guess it's possible," said Fernwyn.

"Did he say what they've done with her?" asked Aldebaran.

"He said she's on a ship being taken to a Zendreen research facility for anatomical study."

"That sounds unpleasant."

"Like I said, I wish I could just dismiss this story as bullshit, but there's too much credibility to it."

"Why tell just us?" asked Fernwyn.

"Because I don't want the others to worry about this until after our current mission is complete. I don't want them to be distracted by it or to worry about whether or not I'm distracted by it."

Aldebaran shrugged. "So why tell us?"

"I want you to know because I'm going to ask for your help in researching this. We have some clues to work with but I'm going to need your best resources to find the truth."

"You're not planning a rescue, are you? I cared for Ari a lot too, John, but I doubt the rest of the crew is going to sign off on such a dangerous mission, even with incontrovertible evidence that Ari is still alive. They're certainly not going to be thrilled about gallivanting around enemy territory chasing a ghost."

"I know. That's why I want this kept between us. We'll do what research we can on it on the down-low while we're hiding out. We'll worry about what action to take after we confirm the efficacy of the virus mission. If the virus doesn't work, we'll be too busy concocting another plan to worry about Ari's fate."

"Okay."

"Sounds good," said Fernwyn.

John nodded. "Thanks."

"You should really get that wound checked out."

"Fine. Grab the first aid kit and meet me in the galley."

Fernwyn nodded and exited to the hallway.

"Do you want to check on the others?" asked Aldebaran.

"Yeah," said John, reaching for the intercom. "John to all crew, meet in the galley as soon as possible."

John and Aldebaran headed for the galley.

"We came pretty close to getting wiped out this time," said Aldebaran. "I hope the virus works. I'm getting a little tired of all this action."

"It's not the action that bothers me, it's all the peril and pain. I do agree, though. I don't think anyone was expecting this much of a challenge."

Arriving at the galley, John and Aldebaran joined the others. The sultry tang of blood, sweat, and tobacco smoke again met their noses. Water and other refreshments were being passed around, and soon all available seats were taken. John gazed with pride at the members of the original crew as well as the four newcomers. With a twinge of both sadness and guilt he remembered those that had been lost. Byron and Nathalier didn't have to die, and Ari's unknown status made her absence all the more troubling.

Fernwyn approached John with the first aid kit. John allowed her to begin working on his injury.

"Excellent piloting, Dana," he said. "You've probably exceeded me in that regard."

"It's your design, I only adapted to it," Dana said. "Thank you."

"So where are we going to hide out?" asked Talvan.

"I think Residere Delta is a good choice," said Fernwyn. "We should be able to land at the same coordinates where we first met and stay there without being detected. It will also give us a good connection to the net."

"Perhaps we could set up a proxy transmitter and use it to contact the SPF," said Aldebaran. "We should see about negotiating a peace agreement now that we have more leverage on our side."

"That's a good idea, but where are you going to get one of those?"

"What about your ship?" asked John. "That way if they try to arrest us, they'll only find it and the pilot. Then they'd have to catch it, which I doubt they could do."

Fernwyn shrugged. "It's a fast ship, but it's not that fast. It's certainly not as fast as the Faith. I'm not sure the situation has changed enough to warrant contacting the SPF, but we can test the waters when we get there. I suggest hacking into a transmitter aboard a satellite remotely and using it to broadcast. That will decrease our chances of being detected to almost nil."

"What about the invisibility shield?" queried Christie. "Is it still inoperable?"

"Good question," said Ray.

"Shit, that's right," replied Dana. "We'll have to fix it before we enter the Residere system. We might make it to the surface of Delta without it, but before we risk that we should try and repair the shield."

"Okay," said John. "Start the diagnosis as soon as you're ready. We have thirty-six hours, so don't feel rushed. I don't know about you lot, but I need a long rest."

Epilogue

Aldebaran sat alone on the bridge of the Faith, his eyes almost closed. He was in the pilot's seat, but the ship wasn't moving. The crew had spent three weeks hiding out on the surface of Delta, biding their time and listening to net chatter regarding the Zendreen. They'd also been keeping up on their own status as wanted men, which so far hadn't changed.

The bridge was the best place for Aldebaran to feel at peace. Reunited with Seth, anywhere on the ship was comfortable, but the bridge was particularly relaxing for him. Since the crew could monitor the net from any room on the ship with a computer console, the bridge had often been deserted over the past three weeks. Aldebaran had become interested in John's extensive techno and trance collection after Seth breezed by some of it while linked with his brain back on Earth. John liked to listen to that sort of music while designing experimental aircraft, so it made sense that Seth would have noticed it.

Their time on Delta had allowed him to listen to just about every mp3 file that the crew had placed on the computer before leaving Earth. While one might have learned a lot about the humans by the kind of music they liked, Aldebaran was simply looking for a distraction. The memories of his years as a pirate continued to weigh heavily on his mind.

The rest of the crew hadn't been as morose and they certainly weren't being reclusive. Aldebaran would often hear laughter coming from the galley or the lounge area. Talvan and Cab were getting along with their liberators quite well, and while Fernwyn would occasionally complain about their isolation from the rest of the solar system, she was generally satisfied with the outcome of her involvement. While as Ray and Christie had ceased trying to hide their affection, Fernwyn and John hadn't admitted to the others to any sort of attraction for each other. Regardless of their stealth, such close quarters made it plainly obvious to anyone not hiding out on the bridge listening to techno.

Aldebaran put his legs up on the console. The only thing he didn't like about being on the bridge was the lack of direct contact with fresh air; no matter how efficient the ship's ventilation system was, it couldn't replicate the gloriously sweet evening air of Residere Delta. As such, Aldebaran's second favorite place to hang out was at the bottom of the ramp. John and Ray had offered him a chance to try out their pipes, so he had become fond of sitting in the cool forest glade and puffing on tobacco smoke. He could do so anywhere on the ship, but it wasn't the same as in the open air.

His nightly smokes weren't as isolated as his time on the bridge, as Dana would often join him. At first she claimed she was taking breaks from her efforts to repair the invisibility shield, but her visits continued after she did so. Dana didn't smoke, but she seemed to prefer company with whom conversation wasn't popular. Aldebaran didn't mind her presence for the same reason, although he would have entertained some dialogue if it had been offered. Dana would give him a brief update of the day's activities and research, and lapse into silence. Only the sound of the woods and her subconscious tapping on the handguard of her rifle commenced after that. Aldebaran knew Dana through Seth, but interacting with her as a flesh-and-blood Umberian was much more satisfying. Dana had always had a strong personality, and it was easier to appreciate in person. She may have had her differences about the way the others tackled the mission, but it hadn't dampened her spirit.

Looking over his shoulder, Aldebaran noticed that Richter had joined him on the bridge. It wasn't surprising that Richter was able to enter without being detected. The hardened human gazed casually out of the windows, disregarding Aldebaran in mannerism but not in fact. Apt to let someone else initiate conversation, Aldebaran instead addressed an issue that tugged at his rarely-apparent sympathy.

"How's your hand?" he asked.

Richter gave Aldebaran a half-smile. "Hurts like hell, but it's stable."

"Good."

"A penny for your thoughts."

"What? Oh, right. A human phrase. Actually, I've been thinking about the three layers of my personality."

"You mean Seth, Aldebaran, and... what?"

"The shared memories I picked up while Seth was linked with the crew's minds. John's memories are particularly strong, for obvious reasons."

"I keep forgetting that you've been inside my head. I hope you can disregard anything embarrassing."

"I never got anything like that from you."

"That's fortunate, I suppose."

"There were other things, though. More random thoughts. Like the fact that Devonai is Jewish but he carries a German pistol, and you're German but you carry an Israeli pistol. It means little to me, but you find it... what's the word?"

"Ironic."

"Right, ironic. Why?"

Richter folded his arms. "The Jews and the Germans didn't get along too well for a couple of decades on Earth. Devonai and I were best friends."

"I see. I remember all of those World War Two battles that John and Ray liked so much."

"Now that's irony. Surrounded by all this advanced technology, and they entertain themselves with sixty-year-old historical campaigns."

One of the computer consoles began to beep. Aldebaran swung around in his chair to look at it while Richter crossed to his side.

"What's up?" asked Richter.

"I programmed the computer to alert me to any SUF news broadcasts that mentioned the Zendreen and Umber. So far they've been unhelpful. There's two more coming in now."

"Cool."

"Let's see... 'Zendreen Fleet requests parlay with the Solar United Faction for a renegotiation of the peace treaty. Westra Janrei, SUF News Agency. Residere Beta: A representative of the Zendreen contacted the SUF command today requesting a new summit to renegotiate the terms of the ten-year-old peace treaty signed when the Zendreen annexed the Umberian system.' Nice term for it. 'At the heart of the request is a desire for the Zendreen to access SUF medical resources. Shortly thereafter, unidentified sources within the SUF leaked rumors of a serious virus or disease effecting the Zendreen...' It goes on."

Richter snapped his fingers. "Son of a bitch, I think we got it. I'll get the others."

Minutes later, the entire crew of the Faith less Cab was gathered on the bridge. Aldebaran had just finished reading the news report. After a moment of silence, cheers broke out. Hugs and high-fives were exchanged, but John quickly called for quiet.

"Is that the whole report?" he asked.

"That's the only one we've received," replied Aldebaran.

"So there's no mention of what's happening on Umber?"

"No, but if the report is true, the virus must be widespread by now. The Zendreen wouldn't go cap-in-hand to the SUF unless it was damn serious."

"I agree," said Talvan. "We should go back to Umber and do some recon."

"That may be hasty," said Ray. "This is just the first report. We've been waiting three weeks, a couple more days isn't going to hurt."

John nodded. "Yeah. This is good news, but we should wait and see what transpires over the next few days. I'm eager to go check it out, too, but if the Zendreen fleet is still strong it would be too risky. Don't forget that we still haven't figured out how they compromised our invisibility shield."

"Not entirely, anyway," said Dana.

"I thought you said you got two reports, Aldebaran," said Richter.

Aldebaran looked at Richter, then at John. "I need to discuss that with John and Fernwyn alone."

"Since when do we have two levels of clearance on this ship?" asked Christie.

"We don't," began John, "it's just, well..."

"With the info that I have, John," said Aldebaran, "you might as well tell everyone."

John looked at Aldebaran. His expression became grave. The crew waited for John's reply in muted surprise.

"I have reason to believe that Ari may still be alive."

"No way," said Christie.

"Are you serious?" asked Dana.

Ray said nothing, but the shock on his face spoke for him.

John sighed. "The Zendreen commander told me. It's possible that Ari was in an escape vessel that was captured by them after they blew up the way station. It was a pretty flimsy story, but I decided to research it. I asked Aldebaran and Fernwyn to help me because I thought they'd be impartial and because they know the neighborhood. I also didn't want the rest of you to think I'd gone completely insane. Aldebaran, I hope your news doesn't make me look so."

"I received a report that was intercepted by the SPF from a pirate vessel operating near the Misrere system. The message was sent to a fence based off of Vastus that I used to deal with, and indicated that they'd just attacked and plundered a Zendreen ship. They're looking to sell some of their captures wares, and a contingent of what they called 'unidentified humanoid captives' was among them."

"That could be anyone, though, right?" asked Ray.

"We'd previously learned that the Zendreen have a research facility somewhere in the Misrere system," replied Fernwyn. "Ari was supposedly taken to such a place."

"If the pirates are coming back here," began John, "we might be able to intercept them and see if Ari is among the captives."

Aldebaran shook his head. "The fence refuses to deal in slave trafficking, and told them so. The pirates said they'll find a local buyer instead."

"Then we haven't a moment to lose," said John.

"Wait a minute," interjected Talvan. "It's a longshot, at best, and we may be needed on Umber soon."

"You're not forgetting our first mission, are you John?" asked Christie.

"No, of course not," John said, "but if Ari's alive, I've got to find her. I'll have to make my own travel arrangements."

"Are you crazy?" Ray said. "You're wanted by the SPF. Who is going to give you berth? Another pirate ship? Even if they would, I doubt we've got the money to cover your expenses."

"I think you need to look at this more realistically," said Dana. "It's unlikely that Ari is still alive. Even if she is, we don't owe her jack squat. You're needed here, and you should accept that. Frankly, I'm astonished you would so quickly abandon us."

"It's my choice to make," said John. "Ari is still my friend and I have to try."

"Then I'll take you," said Fernwyn.

Once again, the room lapsed into silence.

"What?"

"I said, I'll take you. My ship seats two, and I can get us to the Misrere system under the radar. You've become my friend, too, and I can't let you run off on your own. You may be familiar enough with the Residere system, but you don't know shit about the rest of the nebula."

"We can handle mopping up the Zendreen on Umber," said Aldebaran.

"Fernwyn's ship wouldn't hurt that," said Talvan.

"If the Zendreen fleet has been effected by the virus, we will probably be able to enlist some others to help us out. Mercs may have been our bane so far, but they know a winner when they see one. Right now, word of that successful pirate raid is spreading like a wildfire. The tide has turned."

"I understand perfectly, John," said Richter. "If you can find her, you should go."

"Just don't get yourself killed in the process, old friend," said Ray.

"Are you sure you won't reconsider?" asked Talvan.

John shook his head. A tear escaped his eye. "I'm sorry, Professor. I'm still in love with her."

"So that's it, then?" said Dana. "We're splitting up?"

"Only temporarily," began Fernwyn. "Somehow I doubt this is the end of this crew."

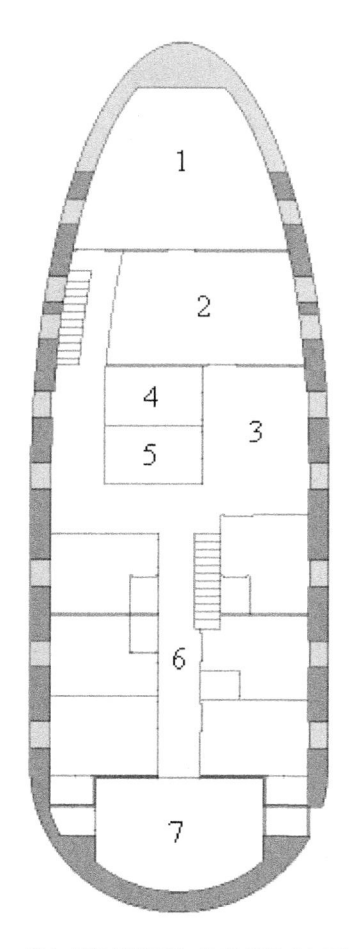

FACILITIES: DECK ONE

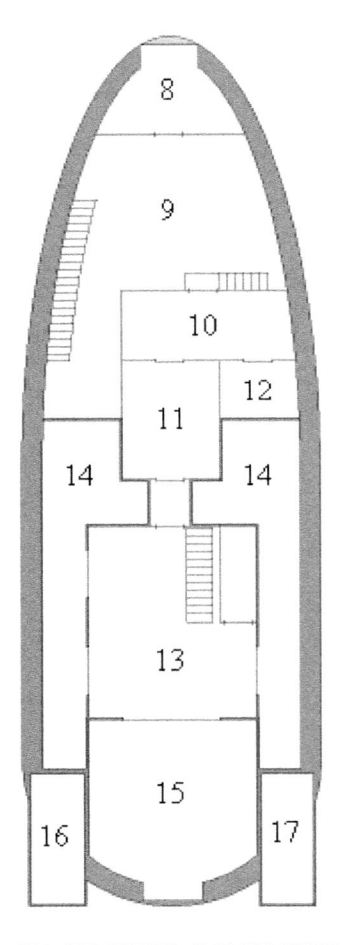

FACILITIES: DECK TWO

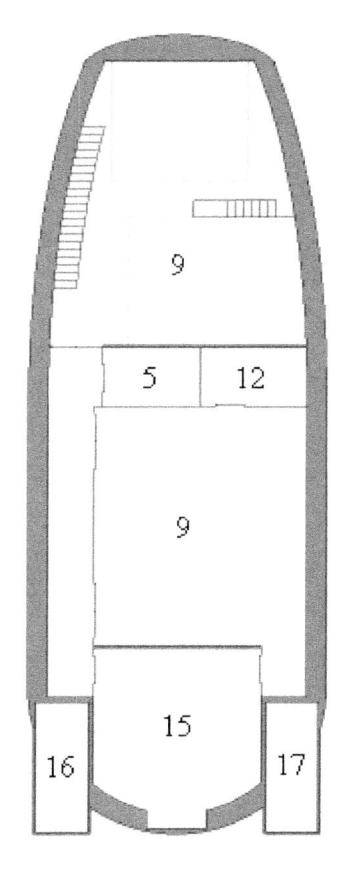

FACILITIES: DECK THREE

1. Bridge:  The nerve center of the ship, the bridge consists of five computer consoles, one of which is also a dedicated piloting station.  Each station can be used for any purpose, but they are usually configured, counter-clockwise from right to left: navigation, communications, pilot's station, remote weapons operation, and systems monitoring.  The forward-facing window is also capable of projecting a wide-angle Heads-Up Display (HUD).

2. Conference Room:  A room with eight chairs around an oval table, with a large wall-mounted monitor for demonstrations.

3. Lounge Area:  An open area with several couches.

4. Secondary Server Room:  This room contains two of the twelve computer servers, and is also used for spare storage.

5. Dorsal and Ventral Gun Rooms:  These rooms provide gunner stations for and access to the dorsal and ventral GAU 19/A turrets.  A limited amount of spare ammunition can also be stored here.

6. Living Quarters:  Six nearly identical quarters, each with a private lavatory.  The lavatory can also be used as a shower stall.

7. Zero-G Room/Airlock:  A variable gravity area, this room can be used for Extra-Vehicular Activities (EVA) and for docking with other vessels while in space.  It is also used for spare storage and occasionally for recreational purposes.

8. Forward Gun Room:  This area houses the GAU 8/A weapon system and magazine.

9. Cargo Bay and Cargo Hold: These areas are used for storage. The cargo hold has also occasionally served as a brig or spare quarters. The cargo bay has a ramp (outlined in gray) for accessing the exterior of the ship and loading large pieces of cargo. The cargo bay is double height, with the armory overhanging the rear portion of the bay.

10. Armory: All small arms used by the crew are stored here, along with ammunition, spare parts, and cleaning supplies.

11. Orb Room/Primary Computer Server Room: The Quasi-Actualized Intraspace Quantum Grid is stored here, along with ten of the twelve computer servers.

12: Storage Room

13: Galley: The galley contains a full kitchen, dining area, and a cold storage room.

14: H2O Storage Tanks: These tanks store 1000 gallons each of water for fuel, drinking, and sanitary purposes.

15. Engine Room: This area is home to the fusion drive and most of the secondary components. It also originally housed a rear-facing GAU 8/A, but that weapon was removed. Located on decks two and three (double height).

16 & 17. Port & Starboard Engines

Special thanks to Marc Housley and John Wheaton for brainstorming sessions, and to Matthew and Sarah Campbell for editing assistance.

Cover art by Alejandro "Alex Knight" Quiñones

Instagram: alexknightarts

Twitter: alexknight_

Note from the author:

Thank you for reading The Tarantula Nebula, I hope you enjoyed it. Feedback is always appreciated, please take a minute or two and submit an honest review on Amazon. I always hope to improve my writing. Also, please visit my blog for updates and new fiction.

https://devonai.wordpress.com

Also available on Amazon:

Reckless Faith (The Reckless Faith Series Book One)

Bitter Arrow (The Reckless Faith Series Book Three)

The Fox and the Eagle (The Reckless Faith Series Book Four)

Dun Ringill (a stand-alone novel, sci-fi adventure)

Printed in Great Britain
by Amazon